She held ... ...
and I forge...

Someone had used a knife to carve a word ... ... he knuckles on both: GREEDY and SLUT.

"Bloody hell," I said. She thought magic had done this, this brutal, malicious thing. "When did this happen?"

"I cannot tell you." She stared at the marks. "The curse did this to me while I slept. I never woke, not once."

I gently took her hand and examined the wound. It appeared at first glance to be written in dark-red ink, but when I brushed a fingertip over the letters I felt the cut marks in her skin. "How did you explain the stains on your linens, milady?"

"There were none. That's why it has to be magic." She watched my face. "That, and I suffer no discomfort. I can't even feel them."

Ladies were taught never to show pain, but not to feel it? "Were the other incidents like this?"

Her head moved in a tight nod. "The same two words every time, on the inside of my arms, the back of my neck, and . . ."

"And?"

She glanced over her shoulder and lowered her voice to a whisper. "On my knees."

Whoever had done this hadn't used a spell—more like a very thin, sharp boning knife.

LYNN VIEHL

DISENCHANTED & CO.

Pocket Books

New York   London   Toronto   Sydney   New Delhi

Pocket Books
A Division of Simon & Schuster, Inc.
1230 Avenue of the Americas
New York, NY 10020

This book is a work of fiction. Any references to historical events, real people, or real places are used fictitiously. Other names, characters, places, and events are products of the author's imagination, and any resemblance to actual events or places or persons, living or dead, is entirely coincidental.

First Pocket Books paperback edition February 2014

POCKET and colophon are registered trademarks of Simon & Schuster, Inc.

For information about special discounts for bulk purchases, please contact Simon & Schuster Special Sales at 1-866-506-1949 or business@simonandschuster.com.

The Simon & Schuster Speakers Bureau can bring authors to your live event. For more information or to book an event, contact the Simon & Schuster Speakers Bureau at 1-866-248-3049 or visit our website at www.simonspeakers.com.

Cover illustration by Gordon Crabb

Manufactured in the United States of America

10 9 8 7 6 5 4 3 2 1

ISBN 978-1-4767-2235-1
ISBN 978-1-4767-4726-2 (ebook)

*In memory of Constable William Matthew Jefferson,
a devoted husband, loving father, wonderful
grandfather, and a very good cop.
I think you would have liked this one, Grandpa.*

CONTENTS

∽

DISENCHANTED & CO.

PART 1

❧

HER LADYSHIP'S CURSE

CHAPTER ONE

"I know his first wife put a curse on me," Lady Walsh said. The lace edging her silk gloves fluttered as she folded her hands and placed them in a ladylike spot on her lap. "It's the only explanation."

A yawn tugged at my jaw; I swallowed it along with a mouthful of tea. "If you want an exormage, Lady Walsh, there's a small horde of them on the first floor."

Her soft brown eyes shimmered. "Over the last month I've had fifteen of them to the house. The curse rendered them powerless. They couldn't even determine the nature of it."

"That's probably because there is no such thing as a curse," I said as kindly as I could. I heard a familiar scratching sound at the door and collected some coppers from my drawer. "Excuse me for a moment, milady. I have a delivery."

I closed the inner door to my office before I went to the entry and yanked it open. "Back for another go, then, Gert?"

"Satan's whore. I will not rest until I have sent you back to the hell that spawned you." The old woman produced a long gnarled twig and shook it at my face. "Wither and burn, wither and burn."

I folded my arms and waited several seconds, but

neither I nor anything else burst into flames. "Apparently not today, love."

"I am made powerless." Gert lowered her stick and glared at me. "The Evil One protects you."

"Aye, and you'd think he'd give me a doorman." She looked thinner and hungrier than usual. "Go have some tea. You'll feel better." I offered her the coppers, which she snatched from my palm.

"Abbadon's pit of eternal fire awaits you," Gert promised. "You cannot escape it."

"I won't try, I promise." I watched her hobble off and then eyed the incantation she'd scribbled on the door's glass. No doubt it was meant to send me directly to some highly unpleasant level of hell, I thought as I took out my handkerchief and wiped it off. Gert always came with a backup plan for my doom.

I returned to my office, where Lady Walsh sat staring at the door. "Sorry about that."

She regarded me with appalled fascination. "You truly don't believe in magic."

"I truly don't." I smiled. "I also have an appointment to get to downtown. Do you want me to call for your coach, or do you need a private carri?"

"Wait. Please. I can show you proof." The corkscrew curls framing her face bobbled as she began stripping off her gloves. "You can't imagine how difficult it's been, trying to hide this from my husband. When I woke this morning and saw them, I nearly screamed."

I tried logic. "I presume your husband's first wife died before he married you?" When she nodded, I asked, "How is it that would she even know about you, much less cast a curse on you from the grave?"

"I can't say how these spells work, Miss Kittredge, but obviously her spirit has refused to leave the house." She fiddled with a fold of her skirt. "I think seeing how happy I make Nolan has caused her to become jealous and vengeful."

I was going to be late for my fictitious appointment, it seemed. "I'm sure an unexpected rash can seem like something malicious and supernatural in origin, especially for a woman as beautiful as you, but—"

She held out her soft, pale hands, and I forgot to breathe. Someone had used a knife to carve a word below the knuckles on each: GREEDY and SLUT.

My own hands trembled before I clenched them into fists. "Bloody hell." She thought magic had done this, this brutal, malicious thing. "When did this happen?"

"I cannot tell you. After my husband left me last night, I slept alone with the doors and windows bolted from the inside." She stared at the marks. "The curse did this to me while I slept. I never woke, not once."

I gently took the hand marked SLUT and examined the wound. It appeared at first glance to be written in dark-red ink, but when I brushed a fingertip over the letters I felt the cut marks in her skin. "How did you explain the stains on your linens, milady?"

"There were none. Nothing on my gown, either. That's why it has to be magic." She watched my face. "That, and I suffer no discomfort. I can't even feel them."

Ladies were taught never to show pain, but not to feel it? "Were the other incidents like this?"

Her head moved in a tight nod. "The same two words

every time, on the insides of my arms, the back of my neck, and . . ."

"And?"

She glanced over her shoulder and lowered her voice to a whisper. "On my knees."

Whoever had done this hadn't used a spell—more like a very thin, sharp boning knife. I knew of some salves that numbed the skin; that would explain why she didn't feel the cuts. Or if someone had slipped some drugs into her wine at dinner, and gained access to her bedchamber through a hidden door or crawlspace . . . "Does your husband have any children from his first marriage?"

"Three. His son and two daughters. We are all quite good friends." She hesitated before she added, "No, that's not exactly true. They want their father to be happy. They tolerate me because I do that, I make him happy." Suddenly she clutched at my hands. "I know your reputation, Miss Kittredge. There is no one in the city that can dispel magic as you do. I'm afraid to go to sleep. I keep thinking one morning I'll look in the mirror and she'll have cut them into my face—"

She collapsed against me and burst into tears.

I supported her by the elbows and made some comforting noises. This was why I seldom took on female clients; their silly notions and endless waterworks made it difficult to ferret out the truth. But someone had been secretly assaulting Lady Walsh, and no woman should have to endure that—in or out of her own bed.

I helped her back over to the client's chair and silently passed her my handkerchief before I took her teacup over to the cart to refresh it and give her a little time to mop up and compose herself. My tea was nothing special—whatever was on sale that week at the grocer's—but I added a dash of soother to the brew before I brought it back to her.

"You haven't told your husband about these attacks." I didn't have to make it a question.

"I can't trouble dear Nolan with this." She put her gloves back on before she sipped from her cup. "He's so loving and attentive, it would destroy him." She gave me an owl-eyed look of mute, helpless appeal.

She was an old rich man's young trophy wife, likely the most fetching daughter of a posh who had fallen on hard times. Marrying Nolan Walsh would have resulted in some restoration of her family's fortunes and likewise assured Lady Walsh of a lifetime of comfortable financial security. She'd personally slice herself up before she endangered that.

I knew I was probably going to regret this. I didn't like working for the rich or titled, and I had other, very good reasons to avoid the Hill. But someone had gone to vicious lengths to torment her, and it was obvious from the repeated attacks that they had no intention of stopping.

"How will you bring me into your household?"

She brightened immediately. "I thought I would have you as a cousin—a very distant one, of course—who has only just discovered our family connection." Her smile turned self-conscious. "I'm afraid that genealogy is one of my little self-indulgences."

"Well, it isn't one of mine, so you'd better be the one to make the discovery." Now, when to call. I checked my brooch watch and thought about the rest of my day. "Dinner is too intimate for a new acquaintance; it'll have to be tea. I'll also need an excuse to visit your bedchamber."

She nodded quickly. "I keep some family portints on my vanity. I can remark on your resemblance to my great-aunt Hortense and invite you up to see them."

"*Our* great-aunt Hortense." I sighed. "Lady Walsh, you should know that in the past I've been hired by other families on the Hill. Some of your servants might recognize me. If anyone asks, it's best that we not lie about how I earn my living."

"I'm sure that Nolan will think it's charming that you, ah, work for yourself." She glanced at the gold letters spelling out *Disenchanted & Co.* on the frosted glass of my office door. "He's very progressive that way about women, you know. He even believes we should have the vote, bless him."

But he would never employ any women at his bank, I guessed, or trust them to manage their own funds. "Good on your husband." I held out my hand. "I'll see you at four."

Lady Walsh clasped my hand tightly. "Thank you so much, Miss Kittredge. Oh, dear, what is your given name? With our connection I should call you by that."

"I'm known as Kit." Only one person left in the world still called me Charmian, but one day he'd walk in front of my carri and I'd put an end to that. "And you?"

"I'm Diana, and forever in your debt, Kit." She gave my hand a final fervent squeeze and went to the door. A man dressed in cream-and-scarlet livery standing outside opened it for her and closed it before he followed her out of sight.

Odd that I hadn't seen him when I'd confronted Gert. Most footmen waited with the coach; only the wealthiest of women used them as body servants.

"Or your dear, loving Nolan doesn't quite trust you to leave the house alone," I murmured under my breath as I picked up my keylace and knotted it around my wrist. "I wonder why."

After I locked up the office, I took the stairs down to the underground level, better known to me and the other tenants of the Davies Building as the Dungeon.

The sole occupant of the understair had once been a royal machinist, one of the finest who had ever served H.M., or so the Honorable Reginald P. Docket would have everyone believe. We never asked why he had given up his choice position to immigrate; no one left England for the Provincial Union of Victoriana unless they had made a horrible marriage or committed an unpardonable offense against the Crown. Since Docket remained a bachelor, and his constructs sometimes didn't perform according to spec, I imagined it to be the latter.

"Who's that?" A sweaty face smeared with grease popped up from behind a cabinet filled with cogs and gears. "Kit? Oh, fabulous. You're just in time for the latest bash."

"Am I?" I glanced around me to see if anything appeared ready to clout me, fall on me, or explode. Most everything did. "I can come back later, if you like."

Docket waved a wrench. "Nonsense. This is just the sort of thing you females love."

I studied the cabinet he'd been fiddling with, which seemed to be sprouting mechanical arms with hooks on the end. "It's a tenner printing press?"

"No. Take off your jacket and I'll show you."

"It's almost new," I warned him as I shrugged out of it. "I'm very fond of it."

"Precisely why you need my HangItAll." He adjusted one of the dials on the side of the cabinet and stepped away as its internal works began to grind and whistle. "Hold it out. Go on, it won't bite you."

With a great many misgivings, I held out my jacket. One of the mechanical arms stretched out, folding over on itself to form an elongated triangle with its hook at the top. It inserted one corner of the triangle into a sleeve as it pulled my jacket out of my hand and then tilted up as it inserted the opposite corner. The arm retracted my jacket into the cabinet, catching a rod inside with the hook and neatly hanging it.

"You see?" Docket beamed. "You'll never have to wait for a maid to answer your bell again."

"That's good, because I don't have any maids or bells," I reminded him as I peered into the cabinet. "You've got this working off your boiler, then?"

"I started out with hydraulics, but the joints leaked oil onto the garms. Bloody mess it was." He caressed the side of the cabinet with his hand. "What do you think? I'll wager someday one of these will be in every man's front hall, and every female's boudoir."

"Possibly the wash house." I reached in and removed my jacket from the interior, which caused him to yelp. Then I held it up so he could see the condensate drip from the sodden hem. "If you change the name to WashItAll."

"Bloody hell, that wasn't supposed to happen." As he watched me wring out the sopping-wet material, he scratched at his chin whiskers. "WashItAll's not bad. Would it sell, do you think?"

"I suppose, if you came up with a way to dry them as well." I glanced down at the puddle forming around the base of the cabinet. "And install a catch basin."

"Capital idea." Never one to brood, Docket closed off the boiler feed valve and wiped his hands on a dirty rag. "So what can I do for you today, love?"

"I need some dippers and an echo." I briefly described Lady Walsh's situation, leaving out the names and personal details, and added, "The echo will have to be very small. Something I can hide in a satchel or under my skirts."

"I've just the thing." He disappeared into his mechanized warren, and after some loud banging and scraping emerged with an envelope and a small mallet. He led me over to the nearest worktable, shoved aside some blueprints, and set them out.

"Best tuck the dippers somewhere they can't be spotted," he said, carefully counting out from the envelope five thin, folded strips of paper. "Dip or dab them with a drop of wine, trace of powder, or whatever you think is tainted. If all's not as it should be, they'll show color."

I removed and unfolded one strip and sniffed it. The chemical odor wasn't so strong that it would be detected coming from my person. "Blue for drugs, black for poison?"

"Aye."

I took out my da's pocket watch and tucked them in the back of the case. I could get at them easily by pretending to check the time. I glanced at the little mallet beside the envelope "I can't go about hammering on the walls, Doc."

"Don't have to." He gestured for me to follow him over to one of the dungeon's support walls. He placed the flat end of the mallet head against the wall, and flipped up the cap on the other end, revealing a magnifying lens. "Press in the bottom of the handle, like so."

He demonstrated, and through the lens I saw a wide, solid green bar appear. The bar glowed faintly, as if it were hot.

"That's a strut on the other side of the wall. Move it along careful-like"—he slid the mallet slowly across the wall until the green bar disappeared and the lens filled with rough green pebbles—"and there, you see? That's the fill between the struts. The foundation walls down here don't have any hidey-holes, but if there's one in your manor house, it will show black on the lens. Then you've only to find the seams and pop it open."

I took the mallet from him and studied it. "What makes it glow like that?"

He grinned, showing all the gaps in his teeth. "If I told you that, I'd have to marry you."

Not because he loved me, I imagined, but to keep me from bearing witness. Once a woman gave her hand in marriage, she became her husband's legal property. Property could not testify against its owner—something I imagined would prove useful if the Crown ever questioned the origins, and the exact rights claim, to any particularly clever mech.

Now it was time to dicker over price, which Docket and I usually took out in barter. "What do you want for them?"

"Two weeks' laundering and five hot suppers hand-delivered," he said promptly.

"One week laundering and two hot suppers by bucket," I countered. As he started to bluster, I added, "And a grand pudding."

He gave me a suspicious look. "What sort? Not plum. Too hot for that."

"Summer pudding," I said, and moved in for the kill. "Fresh-picked raspberry."

"Raspberry." Docket's expression turned dreamy for a moment before he eyed me. "You'll get all of the stains out of me coveralls?"

"An act of New Parliament couldn't do that, mate."

"Aye, well, I'd just dirty them up again anyway." He wiped a filthy hand over the front of his bib. "Make it three dinners by bucket, and I'll shake on it."

"Done." I kissed his bald, shiny pate. "In lieu of the shake."

Embarrassed pleasure made his face rosy. "If only I were thirty years younger."

Chapter Two

Lady Walsh's request did make a trip downtown a necessity, but the day was so fine I decided to take the trolley. A few old ladies in the back seats frowned my way as I stood with the men at the front of the car, reminding me that I was still in my skirts. If I'd dressed in my native costume of bucks they wouldn't have given me a second glance.

The men, mostly young clerks and old gophers who couldn't afford to keep their own carri, collectively ignored me. A woman who didn't assume her proper place in public effectively rendered herself invisible to the tonners and anyone who emulated them, which were most of the respectable citizens of Rumsen. Rina called it wishful blindness.

As we passed through one of the older quarters, a funeral procession halted the trolley, and as the black-shrouded carts and carris passed, I saw a shimmering form drifting after them. The ghost of the deceased, I guessed. I often caught glimpses of such specters following the newly dead or hovering about a fresh grave. When I tried to go near them, they faded from sight.

I knew from experience that they weren't creatures of magic. While mages insisted the proper spell or ritual could bring back the spirits of the dead, I'd found enough noise-making contraptions hidden in séance chambers to explain such convenient "visitations." I had no explanation for what I sometimes saw, but I suspected they might be a trace of the spirit left behind by those who passed on. Like the scent of a lady's perfume that lingered in a room for a time after her departure, or the outlines of a face in an old, sun-faded portint.

Mum would have insisted they were fantasies of the imagination, nothing more. I often wondered how she'd explain away the chill they left behind in the air once they vanished.

At Pike Street I got off and walked to an alley between a boardinghouse and a dressmaker's shop.

The alley was famous for one thing: it was the lowest point in the city. It also had flooded every year during the storm season until one Mrs. Carina Eagle had purchased the boardinghouse and hired a road crew to dig trenches on either side for drainage pipes. As for the boarding-house, where no one ever boarded for longer than a night, it still bore the sign *Mrs. Holcomb's Rooms to Let*, but everyone knew it as the Eagle's Nest.

I stopped in front of a bruiser in a pilled tweed coat who had one shoulder propped against the corner. He was reading over a short sheet without much interest and rubbing a flat, milky-white stone between his broad thumb and the stump of his first finger.

I waited politely until he finished reading and looked up at me. "Morning, Wrecker."

"Miss Kit." He touched the brim of his cap. "She's not up yet. Late night, she had, what with all of 'em sailors what come into port yesterday."

Wrecker had been sent over to Toriana on work-release from Sydney a few years back after serving ten years in the quarries for kneecapping the wrong chap. He'd finished out his debt to the Crown and now lived as a freedman. Had Rina not hired him, he might have kept at the work he knew best. Luckily protecting her and her gels required Wreck to commit far fewer felonies.

"No worries, I'll bring her a cup."

Knowing my long-standing relationship with his mistress, he nodded and let me pass.

At the other end of the alley was the back of the boardinghouse, a red door, and a bright brass bell. After I tugged on the pull, a narrow eye-slot appeared in the door.

"Miss Kittredge to see Mrs. Eagle."

The door opened, and a fellow almost as huge as Wrecker inspected me. He was new, which meant his predecessor was either dead or in prison. "Selling or buying?" The way he ogled my body from the neck down made it clear he hoped I was selling.

"Neither," I said firmly. "I'm a friend."

He pouted a little. "Her's still abed."

"So I've been told." I went past him and made my way to the kitchen, where Mrs. Eagle's cook stood cracking eggs into a large mixpot with one hand and flipping rashers with the other.

"Morning, Almira." I asked, nipping a piece of bacon from a platter and dodging a swat from her spatula. "Have you sent up her tea?"

"Why would I? She left word that she's not to be disturbed before noon." Almira nodded toward the kettle. "If I were you, I'd drop in a pinch of willowbark."

I winced. "Rough trade last night?"

"Mariners in for their first shore leave since the Skirmish." She pulled a whisk from her apron pocket and began beating the eggs. "Randy boys, the lot of them."

I made up a tray and took it to the back stairs, where I carried it up one flight to the mistress's chambers. Walking into Mrs. Eagle's private sanctuary was like crossing the threshold of a dark church: a cool rush of shadows and incense-scented air. I made my way to the cart carefully, and after depositing the tray, I lit the wall lamp and turned to the bed.

"For the love of Jesu," a muffled voice said from beneath a mound of golden silk puffs. "Piss off."

I poured and carried a cup of tea over to the mound. "You know this is why your mother wanted you to be a nun."

"Too hard on the knees." A small head of tousled blond hair appeared, and a slender hand took the cup from me. "What do you want, and sweet Mary, don't say anything that involves my bum in motion, or I'll thump you."

"As ever-tempted as I am by your charms"—I sat down on the edge of the mound—"I came for a gown."

She waved a hand toward her armoire of indecently beautiful negligees as she guzzled the tea. "Take whatever you want and be gone with you."

"Not that sort of gown."

She pushed a handful of hair out of her eyes to give me an irate squint. "You said you were through working the Hill."

"Special exception, just this one time," I promised.

"Someone's taken the cut direct to a new and nasty level."

She yawned. "How nasty?"

"Slicing hateful words into her skin while she sleeps." I touched a whisker burn on her cheek. "Does that sound like anyone you've thrown out lately?"

"Chastity had a biter last month. Horrid man. I had Wrecker relieve him of his front teeth before showing him out." She sat up and held out her cup. "More."

I poured her tea and waited as my friend gradually roused. Without her jewels and cosmetics, Carina Eagle looked too young to be let out on her own. She had been, once upon a time, long before she had become the queen of backstreet brothels.

We'd found each other, Rina and I, drawn together as fellow outcasts in a society that wanted nothing to do with either of us. I'd had it a bit easier, coming to Rumsen as a penniless, nameless waif who'd had as much chance at being respectable as a hemp picker had of residing on the Hill.

Rina's family had been merchant class, indecently successful, and had employed their hard-earned riches in hopes of marrying her off to better. The hard-fisted gambler they'd snagged had strung them along while gaming away her bride price. When the bleeding sod had wagered Rina's maiden night in a card game, and lost, she'd been forced to pay the debt. The morning after, the vicious bastard had refused to marry her, claiming publicly that she was bespoiled goods, which conveniently canceled his financial and social obligations to her family. Rina had been ruined, of course, and turned out onto the streets.

I'd met Rina shortly after that, when she'd still been green enough to let herself be cornered. Stopping the brute I found beating her half to death in a back alley had required only a brick to the back of the head; the real task had been convincing her to come home with me so I could fix her up. She'd stayed with me for a few days, but as soon as she was mostly healed she left and went back on the stroll.

Since then I'd tried to persuade her to give up the business, but the money had always been too good, and the trade too steady. Because Rina was young, beautiful, and posh enough to attract a better sort, she'd quickly built a list of generous regulars. They'd funded the purchase of her house of ill repute, which in turn provided shelter and protection for the lost gels my friend regularly plucked from the streets. For those too young to know what they were about, Rina even found decent employment. Her success had made her notorious, but Rina took great pleasure in being the most scandalous female in Rumsen—and still banked more money in one month than I did in a year.

My friend finally emerged from her bed and tottered to the lamps to light a few more. The old, threadbare flannel gown she wore made me stifle a chuckle—it bore no resemblance to the lacy, gauzy negligees she wore when entertaining her clients.

"All right." Rina fell into an armchair and propped her brow against her hand. "Tell me who it is."

"Nolan Walsh's wife."

"Lady Diana." She exhaled heavily. "You've picked yourself a right one there. She'd be the eldest spawn of one of the Landau brothers."

I thought through all the scandals I knew that involved Landaus. "The one who gambled, or the one who drank?"

"The investor. Lost everything in mine speculation." She winced. "William or Wilson or something like that. In any case, he tugged the old school tie, sold her off. Pretty little thing, but no spine at all. You know she cried at the wedding?"

Rina faithfully attended every society wedding open to the public, always arriving heavily veiled and dressed in widow's weeds. She claimed it was to drum up trade, as virginal brides always sent their newly wed husbands looking for satisfaction elsewhere, but I knew better. Rina had a passion for watching ceremonies and rituals, the grander the better. In a strange way, they seemed to comfort her.

"Would Walsh have a hand in this?" Men who secretly abused their wives disgusted me, but there was always a possibility that the banker had acquired a taste for hurting women or perhaps had his sights set on a third wife.

"Doubtful. He shows her off too much. He'd never rip up a brand-new waistcoat and then wear it after." Rina smothered a yawn. "My money's on the son."

"Jealous?"

"Diseased. Sent home from Oxford after a bad case of the drips." She said it with a strumpet's satisfied relish. "Married five years now, but no children."

I sat back. Since he only otherwise had two daughters . . . "Oh. So that's why he married her."

"And why he took her so young," Rina agreed.

"Walsh has a good twenty, thirty more years on this earth. Plenty of time to do the deed and then some. But why are you taking this job, Kit? You know how it will end."

"She thinks she's been cursed," I said softly.

Rina *hmph*ed. "If anyone's under an evil spell, it's you." She stood and stretched. "When do you call on her?"

"Today, for tea. I'm a newfound, poor cousin." I thought for a minute. "I need something in sprigged muslin, genteel-cut but no sashing. Lace. A very *little* lace."

Already thinking, Rina nodded. "Yellowed or shabby?"

"Yellowed. I'm a working lass."

I followed her into the adjoining room, which was filled with freestanding racks of gowns. Rina had once made a vow never to wear the same gown more than twice, and after making a mutually satisfactory arrangement with her neighbor the spinster dressmaker, she had managed to keep it.

"I did a garden party play a few years ago," she said as she sorted through one rack. "Old gent, wanted all of us dressed like debs. Had each of us sit on his lap so he could fondle us while we fed him biscuits and called him Daddums."

I hid my revulsion. "I can't wear white."

"No one can, love." She winked as she extracted one gown, held it up to me, and then exchanged it for another. "If you don't soon start carrying a shade when you go out, you'll be as dark as a shaman." She switched the gown for a third, and nodded. "This will do for tea."

I glanced down. "It's pink."

"And?"

"I despise pink."

"It's baby's blush, and it makes you look like a proper lass. Turn round." When I did, she held the yoke of the bodice to my shoulders. "If I snip out the pads, it should fit." She tugged at the chain around my neck. "Can't wear this."

"I'll tuck it under." I only took off my pendant when I bathed, and even then I kept it within reach. I'd promised my mum I always would.

"Slippers." She bent to retrieve a pair from a box beneath the gowns and handed them to me.

"They're too big." And even pinker than the gown.

"Stuff the toes with paper. Satchel." She found and placed a fringed drawstring reticule on top of the slippers. "Crinoline."

"No," I said flatly.

"Kit."

"They itch and they make me sweat," I told her. "I'd rather go naked."

She glared at me. "Then it will have to be three petticoats." When I opened my mouth she tapped my cheek sharply. "This is not open for discussion, you silly twit. You're going to the Hill. You know the butler will be counting them before he lets you through the door. Showing up underdressed is as smart as standing in the marketplace and shouting you've become an agent for the Crown."

"I'd hang myself first." She was right. "I hate being female."

"Well, until you sprout a beard and a cock, there you are." She patted my shoulder. "Come on, while you're here I might as well feed you."

I left the hateful pink gown and accoutrements in Rina's bedchamber as she dressed, and then followed her down to the kitchen, where Almira had two steaming plates of eggs, bacon, and fry bread waiting for us.

"Someone's worked a charm on poor Liv," the cook told Rina. "She says she can't feel her bum."

Rina sat down and dug into her food. "That's because she sits on it too much."

"I smacked her bare with a switch meself to test it. Drew blood, but she didn't even flinch." Almira glanced at me. "Maybe someone could make herself useful while she's dawdling here?"

"My eggs will get cold," I complained.

She whisked my plate out from under my fork. "I'll keep them on the stove."

I turned to Rina, who shrugged. "All right, where's poor Liv?"

"Purple door, third floor." The cook beamed at me. "You're a good lass, Kit."

"I'm a deprived lass. I'm a starving lass." I tromped back up the stairs to the third floor, found Liv's purple door, and knocked on it. "Liv? It's Kit, Mrs. Eagle's friend from uptown. Let me in."

I heard breathing, and then two strangled words: "I can't."

I propped a hand against the door frame. "Why not?"

More breathing, and choking. "Can't . . . move."

23

I tried the knob, which jammed at first and then opened. Inside I found Liv, wide-eyed and naked on the floorboards. I knelt beside her. "What's all this, then?"

"Magic," she gasped, as if she were having trouble taking in air. "Killing me."

I looked her over, reached down, and slapped her face. "Come on. Snap out of it, there's a good gel."

She shook her head wildly, and then her eyes bulged as she gulped in a huge breath.

"Oh, sweet Jesu." She panted as if she'd been running for miles. "I couldn't breathe, I couldn't . . ." She stared at the hand she had lifted to her face and then at me. "How did you do that?"

"I walloped you." I helped her up from the floor and wrapped her in a robe. "Sit before you fall back down." When she did, I looked around her room. Aside from the usual female fripperies, I noticed nothing out of the ordinary. "What have you been using?"

"Nothing. I swear. Mistress doesn't allow it." Liv huddled in her robe. "Thank God you came, miss. I thought for sure I was going to die."

I knelt down beside her bed, lifted the skirt, and looked under it. A small brown box lay among the drifts of dust, and when I pulled it out, Liv saw it and uttered a shriek.

"It's just a box." I tugged open the string and poured the contents into my hand, which turned out to be six polished green stones. "A box of rocks."

"No," Liv whispered. "Someone put them there. Someone bespelled them to kill me. Take them away." Her voice rose to a screech. *"Take them."*

"They're rocks, Liv, not magic." As she shouted more

nonsense at me, I went to the window and tossed them out. "There. They're gone. Stop screaming."

Liv staggered to her feet and collapsed against me to give me a trembling hug. "Thank you," she sobbed. "You saved me life."

What was it about me that attracted so many tearful females? "I didn't do anything." I set her at arm's length. "You should go see the physick today, though. You might have picked a bad spider bite or something."

She wrenched away and hurried over to her dresser. "I have to leave the city. Right away, before they try again."

"Stop by the physick's first," I suggested, before I let myself out and returned downstairs.

Rina had finished her breakfast and drank some juice as she watched me eat mine. "Well?"

I swallowed a mouthful of bread. "Hysteria, or maybe a spider bite. I found a box of green rocks under her bed. She's fine." I glanced at Rina. "She's also packing her bags. Sorry."

"Probably staged it. The lazy tart never could turn more than two johnnies a night." Rina didn't seem dismayed. "So much for her numb bum. Thanks, Kit."

"My pleasure." I noticed Almira staring at me. "She'll be all right. I only gave her a little slap."

"Green stones are said to be spellbinders," the cook said. "That's rotten magic, Miss Kit."

I exchanged an amused look with Rina. "Is there any other kind?"

CHAPTER THREE

I left the Eagle's Nest with Wrecker in one of Rina's carris. She insisted on giving me a ride to my flat as repayment for disenchanting poor Liv, but the truth was she despised the city trolleys—"damn cattle carts" according to her—as well as my fondness for riding them.

"Wrecker can ferry you up the Hill at four," she advised me. "Have him wait for you, too. Walsh's so high-necked he won't bridle a half-dead nag for a poor cousin, not even if you offered to ride it to the glueworks for him."

As I waited in the alley for Wrecker to come round, I spotted a gleam of dark green on the cobblestones and picked up one of the rocks I'd tossed out Liv's window. Idly I tossed it in my hand and then dropped it in my pocket as Wrecker wheeled the carri around the corner.

Carris came into being out of necessity after the horse plagues of '66 emptied most of the coach houses in the city. I still remembered the first ones bouncing along the streets, causing women to cower and scream, and men to chase after them. From a distance they had looked a bit like burning, runaway carts, at least until the smoke cleared enough for one to see the grinning fool tonner sitting behind the great wheel.

In the twenty years since the first carri rolled off the assembly line, much had been done to improve the horseless coaches. The first big, wooden-spoke wheels had been replaced by wider, iron-rimmed rounders coated with a thick pad of gray-brown rubber. The mechs in the Chester factories had also whittled down the carri's boxy sideboards and clad them in thin, black-painted plates of copper. When the paint wore, it flaked in rows, which exposed red-gold streaks that young turks seemed to like. They would sometimes scrape off long strips to speed the process so they could boast of driving a "streaky."

Only the oldest carris still had one flat bench seat in the back and two box perches in the front; these days everyone changed them out for the custom horsehide seats. None of the newer carris used coal burners anymore; the latest were fitted with keroseel steam tanks that didn't belch black smoke or have to be refilled as often.

Wrecker pushed on the brake and reached out to give me a hand up. "Fancy a ride through the park, Miss Kit?"

He liked driving through Center Park, both to show off his mistress's carri and to worry his way through the noontime parade of tonners on horseback. So did I, but there was no time for a joyride. "I've a job to get to, sorry. Another time, Wrecker."

He nodded and glanced at my lap to see I was belted in before he let off the handbrake.

Before the gold rush days had brought every scrabbler and digger from the eastern provinces to the west coast, Rumsen had belonged to the Fleers, who had crossed the plains rather than give in to Church and state. When I was a kid, some bone hunters had dug up the foundation of the only prayerhouse the Fleers had managed to build before the army caught up with them; from the number of scorched skeletons they'd uncovered, it appeared to have burned to the ground with most of the Fleers inside.

The governor had issued the usual statement about what a tragedy it was to learn that the fugitives had accidentally torched themselves in their illegal place of worship, mainly to remind us all that for Torians it still was Church or nothing, and if any of us were to break the faith laws, the same sort of accident could happen again.

I'd once visited the site of the old prayerhouse, over which a merchants' exchange now stood. I didn't see any ghosts floating around the building, but when I'd looked up at the second floor, every window I saw slowly turned white with frost.

All trace of the Fleers had been wiped away by the Occupancy, which had established Rumsen as a troop station and trading post, although it really was more of a dumping ground for the misfits and malcontents in the service. The Crown began sending over the deserters, upstarts, and failures from the ranks; if they survived the trek through native lands, they remained in Rumsen on permanent assignment.

In those days, the only females to be had as bedservants were native, and common practice was to capture and defile them before they could be recovered by their kin. Some of the old, crude cabins the surly troops had built for themselves and their squawks (named for the way they'd screech when stolen from their tribes) still stood on the fringe of the city. Rina's people could trace their line back to a randy captain and a squawk who had borne him six children before finally cutting his throat one night while he slept.

I lived in one of the oldest sections of the town, in a small goldstone nestled among the slaterows and clopboard mercantiles. My flathouse had once been a granary, and on hot days the walls, which had once housed tons of seed wheat, still gave off a scent like that of bread baking.

Wrecker conveyed me straight to my door and even shut off the engine to jump out, come round, and hand me down like a fine lady. "Be back at half past, then?"

"That'll do." I pressed a couple of coins into his hamsize hand. "There's a decent pie shop two blocks south. Tell the counterlass that I sent you, and she'll fix you up with a special."

I let myself in through the front door, locking it behind me. Although there were seven flats in my building, I was presently the only tenant. Over the years I'd quietly bought up the leases for the other flats, and then offered for the building. At first the former owner, a hatchet-faced pork trader named Billings, had flatly refused to sell to me. "Females can't manage property," he'd informed me. "You'd do better to bank your funds and find yourself a nice young man, miss."

My money was as good as any man's, which made me think about taking him to property court, but then bad luck solved the problem for me. Five of the pork trader's buildings had been unexpectedly inspected and condemned as firetraps and promptly demolished. He'd come back to me, desperate for coin, and with a little dickering I bought the building for half my original offer.

I knew it was foolish to keep the other flats empty,

but I liked living alone. When I had a little money, I did some renovating here and there. Eventually I hoped to convert the whole place from a flathouse into a single-family home.

For convenience's sake I lived in the first-floor flat, which was also the largest, the other floors each being split between two units. This also gave me direct access to the kitchen, pantry, and bathing room.

I hung up the borrowed dress before I went in to stoke the stove and put on the kettle. I rarely cooked; it was easier to pick up something quick at the pie shop or one of the corner wichcarts. I retrieved a leftover tart from the piesafe, made my tea, and carried both into the bathing room.

I could hear my mother in the back of my head, gently scolding me: *Ladies don't eat in the bath, Charmian. They bathe.*

I set down my mug and plate and went to my tub. It was an old claw-footer, made from thick clearstone gone white on the inside from years of use. I cranked the pump for a minute before I opened the tap and tested the flow with my fingers; there was no hot water left from last night. I needed to replace the old coal boiler outside with an in-house furnace, but then walls would have to be torn out to convert the pipes, work for which no decent piper would barter. I was saving up for it, though, and in the meantime made do with what I could coax out of the old blackpot.

Wrecker arrived at my door promptly at three thirty and peered at my face as he helped me up into the carri. "You all right, Miss Kit?"

"No hot water for my bath." I pinched my cheeks to bring some color to them and recalled the ugly words sliced into the back of Diana Walsh's hands. "Wrecker, do you believe in curses?"

He pushed out his lower lip. "Don't disbelieve. All manner of things in this world, Miss Kit. Man's gotta keep an open mind."

I shivered a little and blamed it on the ice-cold bath I'd been obliged to take. "To the Hill, please, Wreck."

He nodded and started off toward the main thoroughfare.

The Hill, also known to the lesser citizens of Rumsen as Poshtown or the Vineyard, constituted the newest part of the city. The land it occupied had once been sacred to a local native tribe, long since exterminated by the first settlers, who had then plowed and cultivated the slopes into enormous vineyards. The dense, fertile black soil had produced some of the sweetest dark wines in the province, but not for very long. When the Crown had decided to prohibit drink, the army had been obliged to round up the winemakers and distillers and smash their vats and cookeries. To protect the city, the vineyard had been subjected to a controlled burn, and the ashes plowed back into the ground.

Only clover and sweet grass had flourished on the Hill until that time when it—and most of Rumsen—was bought up by a beloved bastard son of an English duke. He had the slopes cleared again so that he could build a towering mansion from which he could overlook his new domain.

The bastard son had died without issue, but rather

31

than add the property to his entitled estate, the old duke had sold it off piecemeal to other wealthy families in the queensland, who in turn built homes there for their undesirable relations. Over time the blues had intermarried with the merchant class to create the first ton. The result was the Hill: some four hundred mansions covering every square inch of the old vineyard, and housing Toriana's only claim to aristocracy.

No doubt guilt over stranding their castoff kin on the other side of the world from the queensland had loosened many purse strings; some of the finest manors ever built on Torian soil marched up the Hill. Gildstone and bronze cast work glittered in the bright midday sun, while the genteel pastel colors of the paintwork gave off a subtle glow, thanks to the ground sparkglass that had been added to the different tints.

Many of the men who built the Hill soon after begun coughing up blood. All of them died lingering, painful deaths. The city's more superstitious dolts had claimed old native magic had death-cursed the workmen, but more scientifically, it had been inhaling the sparkglass that took them out. Once breathed in, the tiny, deadly grains began eating into their noses, throats, and chests and caused them to waste away slowly from internal bleeding. The Hill was beautiful, but the price it extracted had been too costly. There wasn't a builder in Rumsen who hadn't sent a dozen men or better to early graves from glasslung.

Walsh's Folly, a modest-size palace occupying a respectable two acres, had been styled with the later fashion of turrets and crowswalks, with dozens of balconies from which the inhabitants could gaze upon the sea, the city, the pastureland to the south, and the forests to the north.

It was also pink and sported wardlings over every threshold, so I hated it at first sight.

Wrecker handed me down, promised to return in two hours, and took off before the butler could get a good look at him through the peeper. I gathered my borrowed skirt and made my way up the right steps of the two-sided stair—built so that ladies and gents could ascend separately to prevent any unintentional vulgar glimpse by male eye of female ankle—and took the correct place before the door so that I could be viewed from within. One did not knock on doors or ring bells on the Hill.

After a moderately insulting five minutes, the door slowly opened inward, and an iron-haired scarecrow in immaculate blacks glared down at me without a word.

"Miss Kittredge to see Lady Walsh." I offered him a name card and waited with a blank smile as he read every letter on it four times over. He then looked around me as if trying to find something. "I have no maid with me," I said helpfully.

"Come in," he said in a dour, disapproving tone, and barely waited until I was over the threshold before closing the door. "This way."

I followed the towering old winge through the lovely foyer and past several open doors, through which I saw beautiful rooms filled with enough antiques to stock several shops. Along the walls were portraits in oil of every Walsh who had ever drawn breath, I presumed, noting the succession of weak chins and receding hairlines.

Walsh came from a family of bankers, judging by the bleakness of their dress and the cut of their waistcoats. Men who handled money for a living were the most conservative of dressers and never enslaved themselves to the whims of fashion; they wanted to project an aura of unwavering knowledge and sober experience, not flightiness and impulsivity.

The butler halted in front of two double doors, knocking once before opening them and standing on the threshold. "A Miss Kittredge," he said in the same tone he'd use to announce that a stray dog, one that might possibly be rabid, had been found on the premises.

"Dear Cousin Kit," Lady Walsh said, rising and crossing the room to take my hands in hers. "You're as lovely as I imagined."

"You're too kind, Lady Diana." I bobbed a curtsey to mollify the butler. I thought of all the glasslung that painting this monstrosity must have inflicted and added with a touch of irony, "Your home is quite breathtaking."

"It is a lovely sanctuary from the worries of the world." She squeezed my hands before releasing them. "Now come and let me introduce you to the family."

The family present in the receiving room consisted of two men and one lady. The eldest, a weak-chinned, nearly bald man of fifty in a heavy dark-blue suit, was the master of the house, Nolan Walsh. A thin, mousy-looking woman dressed in an exquisitely fitted lavender half-mourning gown was introduced as Miranda Walsh, Nolan's younger daughter. A leaner version of Nolan stood by the mantel fiddling with a timepiece; he was the only son and doubtful heir, Nolan Jr., called Montrose.

"My wife tells me you and she are connected through the Landaus," Nolan said after introductions had been made. "It must be a happy thing for you to meet your distant cousin."

The way he emphasized *distant* made me brighten my smile. "A great and humbling happiness, milord."

Lady Walsh rang for tea, which she served with the elegance of long practice. I refused her offer of cakes and pretended to take a sip now and then while I let my tea grow stone-cold. We spoke of the fine weather, the agreeable effect it was having on the city's gardens, and whether it promised a milder winter than last season.

As we began to run out of polite topics, Montrose shambled near and bent over oddly, until I realized he was peering at my face.

"I can't see anything of Diana in you," he said in a voice that sounded female and querulous. "Are you the get of the gambler or the drinker?"

"Monty, what a thing to ask." Lady Walsh uttered an embarrassed titter. "Cousin Kit is the daughter of the third son of my great-aunt Hortense Landau." To me she said, "You do bear a striking resemblance to her, my dear."

That was my cue. "Thank you for saying so, cousin. I never had the pleasure of meeting my father's mother."

"Well, why not?" Montrose rasped. "The old bat lived until she was ninety-seven, didn't she, Di?"

"She and my father were estranged for quite some time." I noted the faint yellow tint to the whites of his muddy brown eyes, and the network of fine red lines webbing the skin around his nostrils. Even if I'd missed them, I couldn't escape his breath, which reeked of gin. The drips might have rendered Junior barren, but it was the blue ruin that was going to kill him.

Montrose showed me his overbite. "What did your old man do, marry a squawk?"

Diana became a beautiful statue, Miranda sucked in a shocked breath and tried to cover it with her bony hand, and Nolan Sr. cleared his throat.

"Why, no, sir," I said as pleasantly as I could. "That would have been against the law."

"You're as dark as one." His gaze wandered over my black hair before settling on my eyes. "Who were your mother's people?"

That proved a bit too much, even for the old man, who snapped, "That will suffice, Montrose."

"It's all right, milord." I smiled at his jackass of a son. "My mother's people were Welshires and Norders. Working class, I believe."

As I expected, admitting that one-half of my family had been common laborers explained my coloring, invalidated any suspicion that I might be trying to better my situation, and satisfied Montrose's desire to take me down to the bottom peg.

I needed to get away from these people before I decked someone. "My father always regretted the rift his marriage caused between him and the family. He had no portraits of them, but he often told me how much I reminded him of his mother." I sighed. "I only wish I could have made her acquaintance before she passed away."

"In my rooms I have a portint of Great-aunt

Hortense when she was about your age," Diana said, rising from the settee. "Would you care to see it, Kit?"

I managed a surprised smile. "Why, yes, I would very much, thank you, cousin."

Diana glanced at her stepson before addressing her husband. "If you will excuse us, my dear."

He nodded, clearly relieved. He must have assumed Diana was taking me off to give him the time and privacy to lecture his son over his wayward lip. I could just imagine how Father Walsh would scold: *Gentlemen do not speak of such scum in polite company, my lad.*

As soon as we were out of earshot, the lady touched my arm. "I'm so sorry, Kit. Monty usually doesn't drink so much before dinner. Now, shall we—"

"Think nothing of it, cousin." Aware that there were still servants around who could overhear us, I touched a finger to my lips to silence her, and then said clearly, "I am so anxious to see the portint of your great-aunt, my grandmother. Do you really believe I bear a resemblance to her?"

As Diana assured me at length of how much I did, she led me upstairs and through a maze of halls to her personal chambers, which included two sitting rooms, a dressing room, a bath, and an enormous bedchamber. A young, plump female sat working carefully to mend the torn hem of a gown hanging from a dress form. As soon as she saw us, she darted her needle and stood.

"Milady." A well-trained lass, the chambermaid didn't spare me a single glance. "Do you need something?"

"No, Betsy. This is my cousin, Miss Kittredge." She

waited until the maid dropped a curtsey my way before she added, "Actually, you know, there is something I want. Would you please run down to the apothecary and fetch me a pain powder?"

"At once, milady." The maid departed.

"I never have the headache, except now and then in the morning," Diana confided as she led me into her bedchamber. "But it's the only task I could think of that will take her some time to accomplish."

"That will help." I closed the doors before I opened my satchel and took out the echo. "Do you know how long Montrose was away on his tour after school?"

Her brows arched. "I think Nolan told me once that he spent three years traveling. Why?"

"Just curious." I went to the wall nearest her bed.

Diana went to the window to look down at the city. "My stepdaughters are both kind in their own fashion, but Montrose . . ." She shook her head. "I don't understand what compels him to be so provocative. Or vulgar."

I did, and after a moment of silent debate decided to tell her. "Montrose never made a tour, milady. He likely spent those three years in hospital, taking the cure."

"The cure?" She turned to me. "Whatever for?"

"The drips."

She swayed and then abruptly sat down on her bed. "I didn't know Montrose was already married, so I thought my father meant to offer me to him. I was so astonished when Nolan admitted his regard for me." Her hand touched her ashen cheek. "My God." She gazed up. "Montrose's wife—he must have given it to her."

"Doubtful, milady. After the first year the rot moves into the brain, where it harms no one but the unfortunate one infected." I popped the cap on the echo and checked the lens. "It is likely the reason behind these attacks. Young Walsh can never inherit, of course."

"Now I understand why Nolan is always so attentive to . . . his husbandly duties." A giggle escaped her. "I'm to provide him with a new heir."

"I'm so sorry." And I was.

She blotted her eyes with a lace handkerchief. "How could you know this? Have you been one of Montrose's . . . particular companions?"

"I have friends in the city who acquire such information. One of them shared it with me." I went around the bed and began working on the next wall.

She ran her hand over the embroidered coverlet beneath her. "He'll keep coming to me every night, won't he? Until I increase."

"There is another way," I told her. "Take a younger lover. One who has the same coloring as Lord Walsh. Someone you can trust to keep his mouth shut."

"I could never betray Nolan." But after that instant of shock, she grew silent and thoughtful.

While Lady Walsh sorted through her mental list of suitable, fertile young lovers, I finished my sweep of the room. The only recesses in the walls were spaces between the support posts, too narrow to serve as hidey-holes. I checked the two windows, the locks on which had not been tampered with, and then the door bolts, which were likewise secure. Whoever was coming into the lady's room at night was not using a hidey-hole or a secret passage. There wasn't even enough room in her armoire for someone to hide behind the gowns.

Solving poor Liv's problem had been a great deal easier, I thought, and then whirled around to look at the lady's bed. It was made of old, carefully tended terebinth, posted and canopied, and so massive it probably would have required a small army to shift it.

The frame of it sat some two and a half feet off the floor.

I knelt down and bent over sideways to look under the frame. The hardwood floor beneath it was lightly covered in dust, except for a long, wide rectangle in the center. I crawled under, stopping short of the rectangle, and extended the echo over it. I had to crane my head a bit to see into the lens, but it showed a two-by-three-foot section under the floor that was completely black.

Plenty of room for someone with a knife to hide and wait.

CHAPTER FOUR

I couldn't bring a candle under the bed without setting fire to the mattress, so I was obliged to blindly feel for the seams. Something thin and rough brushed my fingertips, and I grasped a bit of cord. When I tugged it, a section of the floor slats lifted up.

Inside the hidey-hole was a short ladder that led down into the darkness. On the top rung lay something folded and white. I reached for it, removed the handkerchief, and brought it to my face, turning away quickly as soon as I identified the scent.

It still smelled of the ether it had been soaked with.

I never have the headache, except now and then in the morning.

I replaced the handkerchief, scooted back, lowered the panel back into place, and inched back out from under the bed.

"Heavens, Kit." Diana helped me to my feet and brushed her hands over my sleeves. "You're covered with dust."

"Aye." I helped her. "There's a passageway in the floor concealed beneath your bed. Someone's been coming through it, and they've been using ether to keep you asleep while they cut you."

"I don't believe it."

I gestured toward the edge of the frame. "See for yourself. Be careful when you tug on the cord; don't snap it."

Diana crawled under the bed, gave a muffled cry, and pushed herself back out. "We have to call the police," she said as she stumbled to her feet. "At once."

"If Montrose is responsible for this, that would be very unwise." I put a restraining hand on her shoulder. "Lord Walsh has to discover what is being done to you. When you come to bed tonight, first go under there and dislodge the panel, just enough for it to be easily noticed. As soon as your husband comes to you, drop your wedding ring and kick it under the bed. Then ask him to retrieve it."

"What?" She gave me a wild look. "Why would I arrange such a farce? Someone is trying to kill me."

"Someone is trying to badly frighten you." When she began to protest, I cut her off with, "If they wanted you dead, milady, they'd have slit your throat the first night."

Her face a mask of alabaster now, she pressed a hand to her neck. "Why would they do this? What purpose would it serve?"

"I can't say, milady. But once your husband discovers the passage under your bed, I expect he'll get to the bottom of it." That might not be the result, however, and I couldn't abandon her to a husband who might be part of this scheme. "If Lord Walsh retrieves the ring and says nothing about the panel, then he is the one responsible. I can help you get away from him." When Diana gave me a surprised look, I explained, "We'll make him believe you've left to visit your family." I heard one of the outer doors opening and quickly stowed the echo before brushing the last of the dust from Lady Walsh's gown. "You must act as if nothing has happened, or the game will be over."

"Is that what this is to you? A game?" Before I could answer, she drew herself up and composed her expression. "Forgive me, Miss Kittredge. You have been most helpful, but your services are no longer required."

Which was the lady's way of telling me to piss off. "Think nothing of it, Lady Diana."

She retrieved a small silk purse from her bedside table and dropped it in my hands. "Your continued discretion is also appreciated."

From the weight I knew I was being paid three times the agreed-on fee. "I'll keep my mouth shut, milady. You needn't worry."

She assumed with perfection the exquisitely bored look of a tonner. "Why ever would I do that?"

The chambermaid stood waiting in the front sitting room, a glass of water and a twist of paper on a small silver tray.

"Betsy, Miss Kittredge is leaving," the lady told her. "Would you please show her the way out?"

Betsy looked relieved. "Yes, milady."

After running a gauntlet of frowning maids and glowering footmen, I was shown out through the side entrance reserved for tradesmen and visiting servants.

"Thank you," I said to the door Betsy closed firmly in my face before walking down the short stairs to the street. Wrecker was nowhere to be seen, and I couldn't wait for him on the street without attracting attention from a nobber—one of the private security guards who patrolled the streets of the Hill to safeguard the residents from unwelcome intruders. Nobbers liked to crack heads first and ask questions later. I started making my way down the narrow walk.

Before I could reach the thoroughfare and hail a cab, a large, gleaming coach drawn by four magnificent grays cut me off. I would have gone around it but for the silver fist-and-pike crest on the door.

Of course it would be him.

Shadows shrouded the inside of the coach and the man who said, "Get in."

The driver and the footman didn't move from their positions; I wasn't worth the trouble. So I unlatched the door and boosted myself up inside.

The interior was, like the coach and the horses and the servant's livery, a dismal gray. I perched on the rear-facing bench, taking the time to arrange my skirts and satchel before I looked out the window. Watching the scenery couldn't erase the delicious spicy scent teasing my nose or calm the nerves humming beneath every inch of my skin, but he didn't have to know that.

"Trolling on the Hill now, are we?" I asked. "What's the matter, didn't your last spell for the governor provide the promised amount of dazzle?"

No answer came, not that I expected one from Dredmore.

No, Lucien Dredmore, the former Lord Travallian, mentalist, deathmage, and current acknowledged Grand Master of the Dark Arts in the whole of Toriana, simply popped a matchit with his thumbnail and lit a thin black cigar clamped between his strong white teeth. The flame briefly illuminated his craggy features but failed to find a reflection in his black eyes. Then he shook out the matchit and blew out a thin stream of smoke.

I might have loved the smell of him, but I hated his cigars. I coughed and banged my fist against the panel under the driver's ass. "Getting out," I called.

The coach didn't even slow.

Lucien puffed a few more times before he examined the glowing tip of his smoke. "What were you doing at Walsh's, Charmian?"

"Dusting the furniture. Haven't you heard? All the maids on the Hill have gone on strike." Inside I braced myself before I looked directly at his cruelly handsome face. "Why, is Walsh someone you haven't yet fleeced?"

"Nolan Walsh is a member of a very powerful financial consortium," he said. "He does the fleecing."

"Oh, so he's your *friend*." I sat back. "I think it's fabulous that you still have one."

"Nolan wouldn't hire the likes of you," he said, as if I weren't there. "It would have been the daughter. Or the new wife."

"I don't discuss my business with thieves and liars," I told him sweetly. "But I'd happily tell them all about it before I'd confide in scum like you."

Accustomed as he was to my insults, Dredmore didn't even bat an eyelash. "There's a dark, dire force moving through the city, Charmian. You'd be smart to stay clear of it."

"A dark, *dire* force." I laughed. "That's good, Lucien, that's very good. I will say one thing for you, your showmanship never disappoints." I sensed I was running out of time and gave the panel another thump. "Stop this rubbish cart now, or I'll scream murder."

He regarded me through the cloud of smoke between us. "You'd rather tromp all the way back to that hovel of yours than accept my assistance? Why get in, then?"

"The last time I didn't," I reminded him. "You had one of your hooligans grab me and toss me in." Lucien had gagged me that time and put his hands on me as well, something I still wanted to stab him in the heart for.

He leaned forward. "Come to supper tonight."

"No." Short, unadorned, straight to the point: that was the only way to refuse Dredmore. That and the visible brandishment of one or more sharp weapons. I knew I shouldn't have left my daggers at home.

"I felt something today," he told me. "A disturbance in the netherside. Old magic."

The netherside, realm of all things mystical. Supposedly it was parked up against reality, just out of sight to ordinary folk, though mages claimed they could sense it.

"Likely a spot of indigestion."

"Hardly." He stared at my lips. "It tasted of you."

Now I was going to be sick, hopefully all over his spotless trousers and gleaming boots. "There is no such thing as the netherside or magic."

"Then why do you rabbit about disenchanting things?" he countered.

"I investigate real crimes, I expose the frauds dressing them up as magic, and I stop good, hardworking people from wasting what little they have on charlatans who do nothing." I waited a beat. "Like you."

"I will find out what you were doing at Walsh's." He

sat back. "Then you and I will have a very long discussion about the consequences for young females who are too headstrong and foolish to stay in their proper place."

I curled my upper lip. "Where's that for me, then? In your bed?"

"Such a tedious lack of imagination." He pitched his cigar out the window before he pulled down the shades. "I have you where I want you now."

I laughed. "You can't do anything in here but annoy me."

"Can't I?" Dredmore dragged me off the seat and onto his thighs, where he clamped me against his chest. "No, don't struggle, Charmian. You made the challenge." He wrapped the chain of my pendant around his fist until it became a noose around my neck. "I am only rising to the occasion."

I felt a bulge of blunt hardness against my thigh and went still, ducking my head to hide my fear. "You're pathetic."

"What happened to annoying?" His lips glanced over my cheekbone. "Lift your chin."

I stared at the vee of his waistcoat. "Go to the devil."

He released the chain, took hold of my hair, and gave it a sharp tug, and I jerked up my chin. I made myself stone as he put his mouth over mine, and I kept my teeth clamped together to prevent his tongue any access.

Like all the others, this would not count as my first kiss, I thought as he worked his lips against mine. Another mauling, most definitely, but I wasn't kissing him. I'd never kiss him. I would never, ever give in to such brute tactics—

And then I was kissing him, my mouth open to his,

my tongue curling round the silky glide of his. Dimly I felt him let go of my hair and gather me closer, his fingers at my bodice and then my breast, cupping and squeezing. He ceased that only to reach down, and then I felt my skirts sliding up over my calves and then my knees—

"No." I wrenched my face to one side, first to drag in breath and then to hold it. My body wanted to do terrible things, and my mind wanted worse, and I could not relent to either. Not here, and not with him.

"What did that feel like, Charmian?" He caught a tendril of hair hanging in my eyes and smoothed it back. "Annoyance, or something deeper? And would you like to feel it all night?"

I would have smashed my brow into his, but all it wanted to do was rest against his shoulder as my shaking hand pushed my skirts back down. "You have to stop doing this to me."

"Why?"

I straightened and looked into his black, soulless eyes as I let how I felt show on my face.

"So we remain at impasse. Very well." Carefully he lifted me and placed me back on the opposite seat. Before I could shift back into the corner, he reached out and clamped a black-gloved hand over my wrist. "You will come to me, Charmian. Perhaps not now, but soon. The portents are never wrong."

He did have the deepest, most commanding voice of any man I'd known. Sometimes I woke up in the middle of the night, covered in sweat, hearing the last echo of it humming in my ears as I remembered other times he'd touched and kissed me. If anyone could ever bespell me, it would be Lucien Dredmore.

Over my dead body.

He dodged my fist and thrust me back, calling out, "Here, Connell."

The coach came to a swift stop.

I glanced out and saw that I was back in town. "Thank you for the ride, Dredmore. Very decent of you."

"Charmian." He watched me climb out.

From there I walked a few blocks to the local fishncrisp to pick up two hot meals for me and Docket. The encounter with Dredmore had killed what appetite I had, so I ordered a pot of bisque and some crackers for myself and a big platter of fried coddles and shoelace-thin crispies for the mech. Since the owner still owed me a massive debt for dispelling all of his fish shops, I'd agreed to take meals in barter.

"Right you are, miss," the counter boy said as he loaded the meal containers into two round packing cylinders marked with his shop's brand. "Where to drop?"

I had to go home to freshen up, but I intended to spend a few hours at the office, so I gave him my building and drop numbers. He tagged them on the side of the cylinders in grease pencil, and I lingered long enough to watch him load the meal buckets into the tube.

The shops that sent hot food by bucket around the city were scrupulously honest—their business depended on it—but sometimes too many buckets in the tubes created a backup at the sorting stations, and if so I'd just stop for the meals later on my way to the office myself (and Docket would have his hand delivery). This time, however, the cylinders shot off directly.

When I left I passed a number of magic shops and tellers, most just opening for night business. While I generally ignored them for the nonsense hope peddlers that they were, Dredmore's warning and Lady Diana's strange wounds caused me to glance in a few windows.

Mages, tellers, and other practitioners of the dark arts were a clannish bunch and rarely socialized outside their ranks—Dredmore being one of the few, annoying exceptions, though he had once been titled, which evidently made him less repulsive to the tonners. They invariably lived where they worked, in small cramped lofts above their shops, which offered any and every sort of magic one could desire, from seeings to seekings to special charms.

The latest addition to their industry were warders: specialty mages who charmed wardlings forged of silver that were supposed to cast protective charms over people and homes and even whole buildings to protect them from the netherside and—what else?—ward off harmful or evil spells. One could hardly find a window or threshold in the city that hadn't been adorned with a wardling.

What was interesting to me was just how many wardlings I saw in the windows and over the doors of the magic shops. Pretty as the inscribed silver disks were, they were as useless as oversize coins. Still, warders had been growing very influential of late, which baffled me to no end. I'd never thought that the other charlatans in their trade would ever believe that manner of foolishness.

I approached an old native shaman, who crouched in

front of a neighborhood stable. He'd drawn a circle in the dirt around a white rat that had been tied to a large stone. I looked away as the old man used his blade to nick the rodent's neck; I knew he'd use the blood to paint some strange design over the threshold of the stable. One of the local's mounts must have died suddenly; the superstitious natives wouldn't touch another horse in the same stable until the rat-blood ritual was performed. I had no love for rats, but seeing any creature bled for something so meaningless revolted me.

I didn't realize I'd stopped in front of a richly decorated window until the middle-aged female proprietor unlocked the shop door, stepped out, and spoke to me. "See your future, miss?"

"I'm not a believer," I said absently, and nodded toward her window, where she had displayed a row of inscribed silver disks hanging from neck chains. "Are you lot selling wardlings as baubles now?"

Her expression turned shuttered. "Pr'aps you'd best move on, miss. 'Twill be dark soon." She turned and went back into the shop.

Tellers were the least offensive of mages, so I followed her in. "Hang on," I called after her. "I changed my mind. I do want a seeing."

"Sorry, can't. I'm about to close." She scampered behind a long counter covered with hundreds of lit candles, vials of colored stones, and large blueglass spirit snuffballs. "There's another teller four doors down. She'll see for you. She sees for anyone."

I'd never patronized a teller before, but I vaguely remembered one of Rina's gels comparing them to strumpets in that they demanded payment before service was rendered.

She wanted the money first, then. "How much is it?" I asked as I reached into my satchel for some coin.

"As I said, I'm done in for the day, miss."

"You only just opened your door," I reminded her. "Why won't you see for me?" Something occurred to me. "Do you know a witch named Gert?"

She flicked her eyes over me, as if she were afraid to look at me too long. "No. And I never seen the likes of you." She made a funny gesture and whispered, "Hope never to see again."

"Spells are nonsense," I informed her, in the event she was about to cast one. "Might as well save your breath."

She gave me a frightened look and the next thing she said came out in a hill country accent. "Ev doan nowhat to ye, elshy. Lave oof m'now."

Something buzzed in my ears. "*What* did you call me?"

She didn't utter another word but spun and ran back into a storeroom, slamming the door and locking it behind her.

I dropped my coin tuck back in my reticule and resisted the urge to give it a swing and smash a few candleglasses. That was when I noticed the dozens of smoke wisps rising around me, and how dark it had become inside the shop.

Something had blown out the teller's candles. All of them.

～

At home I ran a bath, but while I was undressing something snapped and slithered down between my breasts. I didn't realize it was my pendant until I pulled it out of my bodice and stared at the broken links.

"Damn me." The chain was older than me, and thanks to my tussle with Dredmore in the carriage it had finally snapped. I left the pendant on my vanity and went to the little cashsafe I kept behind a painting of New Yorkshire. I had another chain I'd taken in lieu of payment from a silversmith with a fireplace he thought haunted but that I'd found occupied by a nesting owl.

"I wouldn't do that if I were you."

I whirled around to see a strange old man standing in my bedchamber. "Who are you?" I yanked up my bodice to cover my chest and glanced at the door and the windows, all of which were still closed. "How did you get in here?"

He held up hands that looked too long and narrow for his short, thin frame. "I'm not going to hurt you, lass. In fact, if you'll give a moment to explain, I may be of some considerable assistance to you."

"Stuff that." I grabbed a prodder from the hearth and brandished it. Wrecker had once shown me the best spots to cripple a man and I remembered all of them. "Get out of here or I'll cosh in your skull."

He shrugged. "Go ahead."

"I'm not jesting with you, old man." Was he a burglar or a rapist? "I don't know what you want, but I've nothing worth nicking."

"You've everything I gave you, Charm, as well as a few things I didn't." He began wandering around the room, touching things that were not his. "Don't the maids ever dust in here?"

"I don't have maids. What the devil are you doing? Don't touch that." I went after him as he peered at my pendant. When I tried to grab him, my hand passed straight through him, as if he wasn't even there. My fingers came away stiff with cold, as if I'd held my hand to a block of ice.

"Bloody hell." He was a ghost, and he was talking to me. "Who are you?"

"I'm free, love. After twenty years of waiting and watching." He drew back from my vanity. "Though I imagine your da is spinning like a top in his grave. He never did like me, you know. And your mother . . ." He gave a shudder that made his form shimmer.

He was a ghost *and* a loon. "Why are you haunting me?" I demanded. "I don't know you. I didn't kill you."

"That, my gel, is a very long story." He eyed the window. "I'd leave you in peace, but it's still daylight. My sort can only go about freely after dark."

"Well, you are not staying here all day," I told him.

"I'm not inclined to. You've a green stone in your left pocket," he told me. "Give it to me."

Here was a chance to find out more about the real nature of ghosts versus the nonsense the magic trade always spouted about them. I took out the pebble and tossed it to him. Instead of passing through him as my hand had, it landed in his open palm. He closed his fingers over it and frowned.

"Nasty bit of spell put on this." He made a fist, relaxed it, and bits of green gravel fell to the floor. "Whoever gave this to you wants you dead, Charm."

"It's not mine." The magical nickname made me glower. "And I'm called Kit."

His white hair ruffled as he shook his head. "Your name is Charmian Constance. Your mother called you that after your grandmother."

"You have the wrong Charmian," I told him through my teeth.

"Your father's name was Christopher Kittredge, wasn't it? Your mother would have taken his name. She could never use mine." His expression turned thoughtful. "I'm not certain she even knew it."

My jaw dropped. "You were married to my mother?"

"No, I was her father. I'm your grandfather, Charm." He sketched a bow. "Harry White, at your service."

Talking to this mirage was giving me a headache. "Go haunt someone else, Harry White."

"The daylight problem, as I mentioned, prevents my departure." He started toward me. "Then there's the fact that you're in grave danger. Dark forces are gathering."

It was almost exactly what Dredmore had said. "What dark forces?"

He gestured at the vanity. "You'll need to wear that at all times, my dear."

Is that what he was after? My pendant? I went over and picked it up. "I do already," I said, turning around to face him. "Now what—"

I discovered I was talking to myself, as it seemed that Harry White had done the same as every ghost I'd ever encountered: vanished without a word.

Chapter Five

Being the only female tenant in my office building had some advantages, like the use of a lavatory I had to share only with the occasional female client (rare) and my own chutes for rubbish, post, and meal drops (none of the other tenants wanted the contents of their tubes mixed in with a woman's). The only significant drawback to being the sole woman on the premises was my lack of staff; I had to deal with anyone and everyone who came to call—even some of the other tenants who wandered past my door.

Tonight it was Horace Eduwin Gremley the Fourth, a clerk from the second-floor title office. Horace the Second, a semirespectable land broker, had arranged the job for his grandson when Horace the Third had deserted his wife and son for the lure of gold. I knew the lad's father had been swept off and drowned while unwisely panning during an early thaw, so I tried to be tolerant.

"Miss Kittredge"—the lad's grandfather had beaten some manners into the fourth bearer of his esteemed name, and he folded himself over in a generous bow—"I'd hoped to run into you before I left for home."

"Mr. Gremley." I gave him a tiny bob and held on to my key rather than unlock the door. "How may I be of assistance?"

His eyes skipped up and down the length of my gown. "Oh, it's nothing so important. Simply a small matter I wished to discuss with you."

We'd have to discuss it out in the hall, because the last thing I would ever do on this earth would be to closet myself alone in a room with Fourth. "Do go on."

His beady eyes darted to the knob. "It is something of a delicate nature."

Blast it, he was going to ask me out again. I glanced around him. "I don't think anyone on the other floors will hear."

"My mother bids me attend the opening of the opera." His Adam's apple bobbed. "I would be greatly honored if you would consent to be my escort."

"How kind of you to think of me." I pretended to consider it. "When is this opening?"

"Thursday next."

I produced my usual disappointed face. "I'm so sorry, but I have a previous engagement that night." As I had had the twenty-six other times when he had asked for my companionship.

"Did I say Thursday?" he said, his eyes gleaming with triumph. "Oh, dear. I meant Friday."

The little snot was actually trying to out-lie me. "Alas, Mr. Gremley, my engagement is out of the city, and of some duration. I daresay I will be gone until Sunday next."

"I see." Under the yoke of his ill-fitting jacket, his bony shoulders sagged. "Mother was adamant about my obtaining a proper escort this year. If I do not, she threatens to match me with one of the Plumsens."

Despite my annoyance I felt a pang of sympathy for

him. "The Plumsens are a very respectable family." And their da had passed to each of his daughters a perfect replica of his uptilted nozzer, giving them all the look of well-fed infant swine.

"I should be glad to have any escort, I know," Fourth said on a heartfelt sigh. "But the Plumsen daughters are nothing to you, Miss Kittredge."

"You're too kind, Mr. Gremley." Perhaps I could solve my problem with Fourth in a different manner. "I wonder, sir, have you ever been introduced to Mr. Skolnik from the first floor?"

"Skolnik the importer?" When I nodded, he looked confused. "We are nodding acquaintances, yes."

That was all he needed. "Did you know then that Mr. Skolnik has an unmarried daughter who has recently come over to live with him? Maritza, I believe her name is."

"She's not English or Torian."

"No, and I believe that she doesn't speak much English, either, but I've had the pleasure of meeting her and she's quite lovely." I described her in genteel terms, and then added, "I imagine if you persuaded Mr. Skolnik to introduce you to Maritza, she would be delighted to accept an invitation to the opera."

Fourth seemed taken aback by my suggestion. "But if she speaks so little English, how would Mama or I converse with her?"

I smiled. "With such a companion, Mr. Gremley, you need not converse at all."

I could almost hear the seldom-used gears in Fourth's head start to turn. "Mama would not be able to grill . . . I mean, inquire as to her family connections."

"Which are, of course, quite respectable." In her own country, anyway. "I have been engaged by Mr. Skolnik several times, and he is a pleasant, amiable gentleman. You might mention that I am greatly in favor of your introduction."

Fourth's grin tried to reach from one jug-handle ear to the other. "You have done me a great service, Miss Kittredge." He bowed again. "I am forever in your debt."

I bobbed. "A pleasure as always, Mr. Gremley." I still waited until he dashed to the stair before entering my office.

I checked the tubes, removed my still-hot bisque from the bucket before sending the container back through, and picked through some advertisements as I nibbled on a cracker. No invitations for tea, supper, or parties, which saved me an hour of penning polite refusals. Then I found a thin gray envelope sealed with silver wax that bore the impression of a spike-wielding fist.

I should have tossed it into the fire as I had all the others, but Dredmore's remarks still had me unsettled. I sat down behind my desk and used my letter dagger to slice off the seal.

The envelope contained a single sheet of thin silver vellum folded in thirds. The paper exuded a faint scent of smoke and burnt herbs; the black ink he'd used to pen the thick, slashing letters gleamed with a ghostly sheen. With it he'd written:

Charmian,

> *You are meddling in matters beyond your scope. I will see to Walsh, and you will refrain from call-*

*ing on his wife again. Whatever sums she promised
you are not worth your life.*

Dredmore

*P.S. Now you may burn this and eat your supper
before your bisque grows too cold.*

He always knew what I was doing or eating, and I
had no idea how he managed that. He wanted me to
believe it was magic, of course.

"Cheeky sod." I crumpled the stationery in my fist and
threw the ball of it into the hearth, where it blazed up in
a fountain of silvery sparks before shrinking to a snail of
ash. "I'll call on Lady Walsh three times a day if I please."

Thoughts of Dredmore did not entirely preoccupy my
supper hour. Rather it was the name the teller had called
me in her twangy, wrong-voweled accent: *elshy.*

I jumped as someone knocked on the office door.
"Madam Kittredge," a mellow, male voice called. "This is
NSY. Open up if you please."

I didn't please, but the Yard could break down any
door if they so chose, so I went out to let him in. Through
the panel I saw one man, fair-haired and average-sized,
dressed in a plainclothesman's long trench and low-brim.
Behind him hovered the darker shape of a beater in dark
blue, holding his trunch as if ready to smash in the glass.

I opened the door. "Yes?" I wasn't going to offer my
assistance, not to the cops.

The inspector doffed his hat, revealing the tough,
wind-weathered features and sun-faded blue eyes of a
former navyman. "Forgive the intrusion, madam—"

"It's miss," I corrected him, frowning a little. I didn't know any mariners, but his features still looked awfully familiar. "And you are?"

He inclined his head. "Inspector Thomas Doyle, Rumsen Main Station."

Now there was a name I knew; one that made me smile. "Any relation to the Middleway Doyles?"

"My grandfather Arthur." He frowned. "Hang on. Kittredge, Kittredge . . ." His expression cleared. "You're Rachel's little Charmian."

"I am, just a bit bigger." I made the last connection, although the inspector looked much different than he had at the age of five, when he'd lost to me at croke. "And you'd be Arthur's Tommy?"

He nodded and peered over my shoulder, making me realize that I was making the grandson of one of my mother's oldest friends stand out in the hall. I stepped back. "Do come in."

Doyle had a quiet word with his beater, who nodded and positioned himself beside the door. Then he came in and followed me through the front sitting room to my office, where he refused to sit or have a cup of tea.

"I appreciate it, but I've come to speak to Mr. Kittredge," he told me. "If he's stepped out, I can wait for him."

"You'll need a teller, then." I wanted to dunk my throbbing head in my tea mug but settled for sipping from it as I went behind the desk and sat down. "My father died with my mother some years ago."

He grimaced. "My condolences. I meant the Mr. Kittredge who owns this business."

"That would be me." I didn't chuckle at his reaction, but it was close. "Don't look so shocked, Inspector. Women may never have the vote, but these days we are permitted to work. And you used to call me Kit."

"So I did." He looked around again, this time as if expecting the walls to collapse on him. "How, exactly, does a woman obtain an investigator's license?"

"The usual way." I wasn't going to incriminate myself or the officials I'd bribed, or admit that for the first four years I'd been in business I'd been obliged to conduct my work without a proper license. "I'm about to have my dinner. Fancy some bisque?"

A few minutes later we were sipping mugs in front of my fire. Doyle's tough face softened as he spoke of his parents and regaled me with some of the amusing adventures they'd had at their farm. As he did, I smiled and nodded while sorting through my memories until I recalled the last time I'd seen Tommy: a birthday tea we'd both attended when I was seven years old. Mum had dropped me off with Tom, promising to return for us both in a few hours.

When he reached a lull in his own conversation, I asked, "Do you remember the time we went to Deidre's garden tea?"

Doyle nodded. "You didn't like the mage."

"He smelled of gin and had dandruff in his eyebrows." I took his empty mug and mine over to my little washbasin. "Do you remember what happened with the old sot?"

"Deidre asked him to conjure her a blue rabbit."

He came over to watch me wash the crockery. "But he couldn't."

"Were you supposed to bring a rabbit?" my seven-year-old self asked the smelly old man as he kept drawing bigger circles in the air with his stick.

Big tears welled up in Deidre's eyes, and she shrieked for her mother, who rushed over. "What's the matter, darling?" As soon as the birthday gel told her, the mother turned to the old man. "Go on, then. Give her a rabbit."

He straightened. "I've tried, madam, many times. It will not manifest."

She propped her fists on her hips. "For the ten shillings I'm paying you, it had better manifest, and right this instant."

"There must be rowan or witchbane planted nearby." The old man glanced around at the neat flower beds. "I fear I am powerless here."

"You dodgy charlatan. If I wanted to be gypped, I'd have hired a Rom." She pointed to the gate. "Piss off."

"But ye've not paid me—" The old man stopped and yelped as the birthday gel bit his hand. "Bloody little savage!"

He swung his stick at her head, but I grabbed it before he could hit her.

"You're a bad man," I said, and broke the stick in two. "Go away."

His eyes showed whites all the way around as he pointed a trembling finger at me. "It's her," he croaked. "She's done it, she has."

"Kit?"

I looked up at Doyle's concerned face and realized for the first time just how much I liked it. "Sorry." The last thing I needed was to go sweet on a cop. "Before Deidre's mum threw out the old tosser, he called me something. Something nasty. Do you remember what it was?"

"I must have missed that part of the tea." He smiled a little. "Why do you care what a drunken old bully said?"

"Because someone called me the same thing today."

The inspector wasn't looking me in the eye anymore.

"'Elshy,'" I said. "And I still don't know what it means. Do you?"

He shook his head.

Like all cops, Tommy Doyle knew how to lie. Most defenders of the truth usually did. I decided not to press the issue—for now. "So why have you come to call on Disenchanted & Company, Inspector?"

"I'm assigned to the Hill," he said. "We received a report of a disturbance at Walsh's Folly yesterday."

"How terrible." I meant his assignment, not the disturbance.

"A young woman imposed herself on one of the wealthier families." He leaned against my wall. "Apparently she claimed some sort of connection and had to be ordered off the premises."

"What cheek." The butler had reported me, I guessed. Nolan had no cause, and Diana wouldn't risk it. "I do hope you find her."

"The lass in question called herself Kittredge." His mouth stretched and curled. "Do you have a sister I don't know about?"

"As far as I know, I'm the only female Kittredge in the city." I peered down at the random notes I had scrawled on my blotter. "How odd. I called on Lady Diana Walsh yesterday, at her invitation. I had tea with her and her delightful family before I departed, and that is all. Perhaps there's been some terrible misunderstanding."

"Lady Walsh will verify your visit?" After my nod he demanded, "Did you go there to extort money from the lady?"

"Not at all." What had that creaky old winge reported, that I was a blackmailer? "I make my money honestly, Inspector. Ask anyone." I thought of Gert. "Except old witches. They're not too fond of me."

"You called on a family of means with whom you have no connection. You are unmarried, and you went alone. You know how that looks." His blue eyes searched my face. "Who hired you, and why?"

"I am not employed by the Walshes or anyone on the Hill," I said truthfully. "As for the ton's rules of behavior, they do not include women who work for their living." Now it was my turn to attack. "I didn't think the Yard gave credence to servants' gossip. So how does it work, Inspector? Do you run about chasing down every tittle-tattle you hear, or only the really juicy ones?"

Two flags of color rosied the jut of his cheekbones, giving him an unexpectedly boyish look. "Why don't you tell me the real reason you called on the lady?"

"If you don't believe what I've told you, ask her," I suggested, feeling a little pang in my heart. He'd been a lovely boy, and he was a fetching man, but he was only a few steps above a beater. "I'm sure they'd pass her a note from you, as long as it's got a Yard seal and has sprayed for nits. Not like you're a nobber, right?"

Doyle shook his head. "You shame your mother with that mouth, Kit."

"And you've covered the Doyle name with glory?" I leaned forward. "What would my dear old uncle Arthur, rest his spirit, think of his grandson, Tommy the copper?"

I'd hope that would provoke him enough to send him on his way. Instead, he grinned. "Grandda would have loved seeing me earn my shield, you brat, and you know it."

His grandfather had come from royal blood, the highest of high posh, the truest of the blue, but the old gent had been inordinately fond of Toriana's vast working classes, especially those who protected the innocent.

"Aye . . . you're right. He'd have been proud of you, Tommy." So was I, and in that moment I wished we were two other people. As we were, we'd never have a chance.

He gave me a speculative look. "Why did you leave Middleway for Rumsen? You've no people here, Kit."

"No one there, either." I wasn't going to tell him how horrible it had been, living in the house where my parents had died, sick with grief, unable to think. How the vultures had barely waited until Mum and Da were in the pyre before coming for me. "As you see, I'm doing all right."

"Very well." He retrieved his longcoat. "After your mother was sent from the queensland to Toriana, my grandfather made her his ward. She enjoyed his unwavering affection, his protection . . . and confided in him her most guarded secrets."

Old Arthur must have let something slip; he would never have told anyone, not even his own blood. "You needn't hint, Doyle. I know my mother was a nameless bastard."

"Is that all you know?" Before I could reply, he said, "You've worked on the Hill in the past, so you know what you're tempting. Walsh will do whatever he must to protect his wife's reputation. But first, he'll go excavating."

I shrugged. "Let him."

"Walsh belongs to the Tillers," he continued, referring to the grandest of not-so-secret secret societies for men in Rumsen. "He won't just dig, Kit. If he can't find what he wants, he'll plant it." He took out a card, wrote something on the back, and handed it to me. "Directions to Mum and Da's place. I know they'd love you to call."

"How kind of you to say." I took it, and after a small hesitation gave him one of my own. "Should you ever find yourself in need of my professional services, my rates are quite reasonable."

"I think ten years policing have disenchanted me nicely." But he pocketed the card. "You'll stay off the Hill, then?"

"I have no plans to return," I said honestly.

He touched his brim. "Then good day, Miss Kittredge."

"Inspector." I bobbed with the same courtesy.

CHAPTER SIX

The gurgling sound of my BrewsMaid roused me from the last minutes of my uncomfortable night sleeping on the office settee. I might have rolled over and tried for another restless hour or two, if not for the tasks that awaited me.

Tom Doyle could have done a lot more than simply ask questions on behalf of Nolan Walsh. Last night he could have hauled me in for questioning, or even tossed me in a cell to be held under suspicion. I appreciated his restraint; I also heeded his warning about Lady Diana's husband.

Too many odd things had been happening too fast. I'd met the ghost of a grandfather I'd never known existed. Doyle had been sent to question me and then had hinted he knew more about my mother than I did. Even Dredmore had made a point to warn me off Walsh while nattering on about his dark and dire forces, whatever that meant.

I'd never investigated myself or my family, but it seemed a prudent time to remedy that. I'd start by going down to the City Archives, where I could search the Hall of Records.

Before I left the office, I retreated into my private lavatory, where I kept several changes of clothes. In going into the realm of men I had two options: donning my gray switch, some face paint, and my blacks to project the appearance of a widow lady, which would be costly, or stripping myself down to the skin and donning my bucks. Since Walsh might be having me watched, and I never cared to hand out bribes unless they were absolutely necessary, I decided to go native.

Erasing every aspect of my gender didn't take much time. I sprayed my face, arms, hands, ankles, and feet with bronzen, which darkened my tanned skin to a copper brown. Making my brow fringe stand on end and stay that way required the careful application of axle grease mixed with a bit of flour. I could do nothing about the color of my eyes, but enough native women had been captured and released along with their too-dark children during the settlement that tribal people with light eyes were not uncommon now.

Finally I stuffed my crotch with a stocking-covered sausage, a trick Rina had picked up from her clients and had passed along to me. "If you're ever wondering if the bulge your beau sports is real," she had advised, "introduce him to a hungry dog."

My garments were fashioned out of scraped hides sewn together with leather lacings and decorated modestly with native beadwork. Out of respect for the real natives, I didn't wear any feathers in my hair or on my person; those were reserved for braves who had bloodied themselves in war. They were also sported by the only natives I truly despised, the shamans, who claimed to have the sight.

Native magic was every bit as phony as the kind

performed by Rumsen's resident magefolk, but far more dangerous. The city practitioners faked their spells out of greed, in order to swindle their victims; the shamans used their false conjuring to control their entire tribe, to whom magic was like a religion.

The only drawback to going native was the lack of transport; I couldn't take the trolley or hail a cab, and natives were not permitted to own carris or coaches. Instead I hired a pleasant mare from a public stable and rode on horseback to City Hall. There I had to ride past a native stablehand, but he must not have looked too closely at me, for he made only the terse, sidewise jerk of the head that served as a wordless greeting among the tribes.

Natives lived outside Rumsen on the lands permanently deeded to them by the Crown after the last treaty had been struck, and they did not permit their women to leave its boundaries. However, after failing to become the farmers the Crown had desired them to be, the tribesmen had gradually drifted back to Rumsen to seek work in the city. They were generally employed to look after horses or livestock, as they preferred animals to people, or worked in tanneries or potteries. I'd seen a few light-skinned braves serving as drivers and footmen to young bachelor masters, as they were ferocious fighters and made the best bodyguards. Given the distressing history between the races, few families trusted them around their females, and so natives were never brought on as household staff, even among the working class.

The one prime convenience the treaty had brought for the natives was equal rights as voting citizens. New

Parliament had argued for years against it, but a change in attitude toward the preservation of indigenous peoples throughout the Empire had resulted in the males of the tribes being made full citizens. Posing as a native male I had the right to access any of the government's archives whenever I pleased—something not even the wealthiest of white women could do without paying a prodigious number of bribes.

As it was a weekday, I expected the City Archives Building to be jammed—and it was. But most of the citizens came to purchase permits and licenses or pay their taxes, which created long lines outside Provincial Planning and H.M.'s Revenue & Customs. By comparison the small, cramped office of the Hall of Records was nearly empty, with only a sour-faced legal clerk and two vicars waiting in line. The collars ignored me, a poor heathen who in their view was already doomed to burn in hell everlasting. After one desultory glance I also ceased to exist for the legal clerk, who could not expect to solicit business from a citizen whose interests could only be represented in court by a tribal conciliator.

After fifteen minutes of standing and waiting—something a woman would never have been expected to do—I faced the records secretary. He was one of the thousand ubiquitous young clerks in the city, overly groomed and hopelessly attired, but he greeted me courteously enough and asked via universal hand gestures if I required an interpreter.

"I speak and read the English," I said in my deepest guttural native accent.

"Thank the Son," the secretary said baldly. "Takes

forever to hand-speak things with you lot, especially with the documents. What do you want?"

"I seek record of grandfather, soldierman, work class," I told him. "Father wish give name papers for young sister to husband's tribe."

Some of the natives believed having blood ties to important white families, particularly if they were friendly, elevated the status of a female and could result in her husband's family offering a higher bride price. Since the government collected a hefty percentage of bride prices from the tribe, they encouraged the practice.

"Do you know how to operate the sorter, then?" When I nodded, the secretary gestured toward one of the empty booths to the left of the counter.

I placed a pound note through the window slot. "How long I can use?" Generally there was a limit of one hour, but the clerks tended to give natives more time for translation purposes.

"Unless we've a rush come in, you can use it as long as you like," he said as he placed the note in his cash drawer. "If you need assistance, tap the bell."

I entered the glass-sided booth, which smelled of dust, paper, and men's sweat, and sat down on the hard-backed chair in front of the wide records sorter panel.

Three large levers were marked with the *B*, *M*, and *D* representing the three major record rondellas (Birth, Marriage, and Death). To the right of each were twenty-six smaller levers marked with every letter of the alphabet, along with two extra with *I* and *D* that sorted out incomplete or damaged records. Another row of seven levers further separated the records by province of origin, and at the bottom of the panel was a long row of even smaller annum levers with faded labels indicating years in five-decade increments.

I pulled the *B* lever and watched through the glass window of the booth as the sorter's arm descended from the ceiling, then I flipped down the *W*, another for Tull province, and the annum lever for the fifty-year span before my mother's birth date.

With its internal cogs adjusted by the levers, the arm stretched out, plucking the first sheaf of glassined documents from the archive shelves. It dropped them into a flat-sided chute, which carried them one by one to my window, where I used the stop knob to hold and glance at each one before allowing it to be whisked by the chute back to its shelf.

Surnames beginning with *W* in Tull province were common, so there were a great many records to skim through before I reached the *Wh*'s, and all the birth records of Tullan citizens of the time period named White. There were seventy-two, and not one of them named Harold, Harrison, or Harcourt.

Which was impossible, because my grandfather could not have immigrated to Toriana without registering some sort of document of origin.

I searched the records for the annum of my mother's birth and found none registered for her, either. I then went to the annum of my own birth, which I had never seen, and found the record of my delivery at Middy Women's Hospital, which noted my parents' names. Mum had been listed not as White but as Doyle. Using the new surname, I found among the birth records a writ of adoption, which named Rachel White as a foundling taken in by the Doyle family at age sixteen.

Tommy's grandfather must have gone to a great deal of trouble and expense to formally adopt my mother, but why? Had my grandfather been some sort of criminal, living underground or under a false identity?

I went back to the annum of my mother's birth and this time pulled all the incomplete records. I found one single handwritten note filed by the midwife who had attended the birth of a female child, delivered to a Harry White, Esq., and wife. My grandmother was not named but was listed as having passed in childbirth. I found no corresponding death certificate for her.

The paper trail ended there. My grandfather had come into existence on the night of my mother's birth, had evidently lived for sixteen years after without ever registering his identity, and had vanished after Arthur Doyle had adopted her.

I made note of the number stamped on the glassine seal before sending the last of the documents back to the archives, then stepped out of the booth. The other patrons had left, and I saw the secretary was finishing up his lunch at his desk. He came over to the window as soon as he saw me.

"Find what you needed?" he asked.

"No," I admitted, only just remembering to alter my voice. "If man has no papers here, where else they could be?"

"All citizens of Toriana are required by law to register birth, marriage, and death certificates." He sighed. "Unless the man was a criminal, or protected by the

Crown. Then his papers would be held by the Ministry of Prisons for the length of his sentence, or kept under seal."

I doubted even someone as high in society as Arthur Doyle could have adopted Rachel if her father had been a convict. "Where these seal papers?"

"All protected documents are kept in the secured archives belowground," he told me. "But you can't access them without a writ from the governor's office, and they won't issue those to a native. Sorry, old man."

I knew what I needed then, so I gruffly thanked him and left.

One of the strangest jobs I'd ever undertaken had been for one of the city's moles, who had contracted me by tube to investigate a sudden infestation of rats in a posh hotel, for which he was being blamed. He in turn claimed to me that the hotel had been placed under a dark enchantment by a rival establishment hoping to drive them out of business.

I'd never realized how vast and intricate the labyrinth of tubes, drainageways, and mech rooms beneath the city was until I searched them for the source of the rodents. I'd discovered the hotel's new rubbish tubes had actually been the culprit, for the builders had used substandard materials that had allowed the rats infesting the city's landfill to gnaw through a joint and come up into the hotel's kitchens. The old tunneler had been too poor to pay me, but thinking I might someday need to use his warren, I'd accepted a favor to be claimed as settlement.

Gaining access to the underground from the surface was not easy; the storm drains were protected by mesh to keep out debris, and the busy downtown traffic ruled out using one of the hatch drops spaced along the middle of the streets. Fortunately my investigation had also taught me where the less traditional access points in the city were, and I went to the nearest bathhouse where I was known.

My native disguise didn't fool the proprietor, a genial woman named Delia, for longer than an eyeblink.

"Eh, Miss Kit, is that you under all that bronze? So it is." She chuckled as she handed me a cowled cloak. "Mind you keep your head down in there. Don't want the ladies thinking I've sold them out to the savages."

She led me back through the communal baths to the private rooms used by ladies who enjoyed a rub before or after their wash. The young men who attended them worked stripped to the waist and had been trained to use their hands to deliver various degrees of pleasure. Rina always claimed the bathboys were doing a great deal more than that behind the locked doors, but I thought not. If a woman wished to be penetrated and run the risk of catching a babe, she went to her husband, or a lover who resembled her husband. If she wished to be stroked and petted and made to feel beautiful in her skin, she came here for a rub.

Delia let me into her tube room and the stairs leading down to the small sorting station beneath it. "Tell Clancy while you're down there that I don't want no holdup on the linens in those tubes today. Missus Trevors and her ducklings are coming in at three."

"All nine of them?" I pulled on my gloves and gogs. "Better let the boys have an early supper, Del."

man's shirt, trousers, and skullcap. "These first. I'll collect the waders. Use the basin to wash that muck from yer face; they'll never believe I've taken on a native 'prentice."

He left me there to change and returned just as I was scrubbing the bronzen off my face. After helping me step in and fasten the waders, he smeared his dirty hands over my cheeks, chin, and brow, and handed me a heavy tool pouch. He then shouldered two air tanks onto his bent back.

"Let me take one of those," I said.

"Master all the ways carries the tank. Ye just keep yer head down and let me do the yammering," he advised as I followed him out of the station. "'Em boys up there aren't as thick as I'd like."

We crossed through several tunnels until we reached a staircase and climbed up into the back of an enormous room packed with shelves of boxes. Before he approached the two guards sitting at the front, Hedger used a wrench to loosen a joint on a water pipe, just enough to create a steady drip.

"Here's the leak, Jimmy," he said in a loud tone, and then called out, "Tunnel service."

One of the guards strolled back. "Hang on, old man, you can't go barging in here."

"Sure and I'll leave now." Hedger nodded toward the leaking pipe. "But ye boys best put on yer waders and fetch some pails."

The guard surveyed the pipe. "How bad is it?"

"Might not burst right away," Hedger said. "Could go tomorrow, the day after. But it's a main line, lad. When she goes, she'll go a-gusher."

"Well, then what are you pissing about for?" The big man gestured toward the pipe. "Get on with it."

"Can't use me torches with ye lot in here," Hedger said patiently. "Gas'll leave ye senseless." He hefted the tanks he carried. "Only brought enough air and nozzes for me and the lad."

"Flame my ass. Oy, Jerry," the guard called to his partner. "Tunneler's got to torch a sprung pipe. Fancy an early tea?"

The other guard grumbled but left with his partner, leaving us alone in the vault room. Hedger immediately began setting up his torches.

"You needn't do that," I said. "Just tighten the joint again."

"I've got to burn a bit of it; they'll be sniffing the air and checking the pipe when they get back." He thrust a tank at me. "Keep the noz on while ye're looking, or the gas will knock ye on yer little bum."

Even with the cumbersome air tank on, being allowed to roam freely through the city's protected archives was a bit like being a hungry child turned loose in an unattended sweets shop.

I gave in to the temptation briefly and glanced inside one long box at random; the first sheaf of glassines inside held the birth records of three royal bastards, the testimony of a minister who had uncovered a massive swindling scheme to defraud and embarrass the Crown, and an old, slashed waistcoat marked as belonging to the governor's deceased valet, whose blood staining it had dried to an ugly dark maroon.

Something twinkled at me from the bottom corner of

the box, and when I took it out, I saw it was a tiny silver disk, marked with the queen's rose and edged with runes.

I dropped the wardling, shoved the box back in place, and took a deep breath through the noz. Whatever I found here would be dangerous to know, the sort of information I always avoided. But even if I were suffering from some form of hopefully temporary madness, I had to know who my grandfather was. Otherwise I'd spend the rest of my days wondering until I truly went mad.

I took a few moments and checked the sides of the long boxes, noting how they were sorted by date and surname and following the sequence back to the annum of my mother's birth. There I searched through the glassines one by one until at last I found a thin envelope marked Doyle-Weiss. Until she married, Mum had used the name Doyle. But who was this Weiss?

"Lad. Lad."

A rough hand shook my shoulder, startling me back to the present. I turned my head to Hedger, who had taken off his noz to speak. I did the same and smelled a trace of the sickening-sweet scent of gas. "What?"

"They're coming back," he whispered. "Shake yer ass, gel." He stalked back to the pipe.

I regarded the pile of glassines I'd taken from the box, which I now had no time to read. Destroying them would serve no purpose; six copies of them were stored in the protected archives of the other provinces, and the Crown would have the originals safely secured in the Royal vaults. But I had to know what they contained.

With a trembling hand I removed from the box all the glassines pertaining to my grandfather and mother and stuffed them inside my shirt before I trudged back to rejoin the old tunneler.

"Good enough, then." Hedger tapped the pipe with the side of his fist. "Did you see any seepage under the shelves, lad?"

I heard the guards unlocking the gates to the vault room behind me and managed a strangled "No, marster."

"Good on ye." Hedger tramped through the aisle of shelving, had a word with the guards about opening the outside air slats to ventilate the last of the gas from the room, and then brought one back to see the unnecessary work he'd done.

"You're sure this'll hold?" the guard asked.

"Aye, it's as strong a patch as any I've done, and none of them ever have cracked."

The guard yawned. "Get on with you, then."

As I stepped toward the hatch, the glassine in my shirt crackled, and something grabbed my collar and turned me around.

"What you got on you, boy?" the guard demanded.

"Naught but lunch, Cap'n," Hedger said, taking out a glassine bundle from his pocket and holding it up. "Wet down here. The old glassies we scram make fine wraps, keep our sandwiches dry."

If the guard demanded I show him my nonexistent sandwich, Hedger and I were going to the gaol. The whimper that broke from my lips was quite genuine.

"'Sall right, boy," the guard said, releasing my collar and giving my shoulder a rough shove. "I'd eat dirt before I'd touch scram." He turned to Hedger. "You be sure to secure that hatch, old rat."

Hedger nodded eagerly and hustled me out of the vault. Once he'd closed the hatch and spun the hub to lock it, he leaned against it and pressed a blacking-streaked fist against his heart as he murmured a prayer.

If I'd been Church, I'd have done the same. "Sorry."

"So am I." He dragged me down the tunnel until we were well away from the vault. "What were ye thinking, Kit? Ye're no thief. Were ye trying to get us shot?"

I was too shaken to lie. "The papers are about my family. There's a man who's looking into my past, and I can't let him find them."

He held out his hand. "Give 'em over."

"Hedger—"

"There's naught about ye that could rattle me bars," he snapped. "But I'll see what ye just near stretched me neck over."

I pulled out the glassines and handed them to him and watched as he sorted through them. In the midst of the pile he went still.

"Ye're Harry's Charm." He looked at me, his face gone leech white under the layer of dirt. "Why did ye never say so, gel?"

"Because I don't quite know who I am, Hedger." I tried to smile. "Did you know my grandfather?"

"Served with him, I did." His voice grew distant as he stared at nothing in particular. "Until he went up to the North Country. Then he disappeared for years, until . . ."

He didn't say anything else, and my skin prickled with unease. "Mr. Hedgeworth?"

His face darkened abruptly. "This settles things

between us." He seized my arm. "Ye're to go now, and ye're not to come back down here, do ye understand? Never again."

"Why not?"

"The debt is settled," was all he would say.

He allowed me just enough time to change back into my bucks before he marched me back to the bathhouse, where he gave me a hard push toward the stairs.

I couldn't leave without knowing. "Who was my grandfather, Mr. Hedgeworth?" I asked. "What did he do?"

His face twisted. "Get on with ye now." He turned away.

"Please," I called after him. "I have to know."

Hedger glanced back at me. "Harry saved me life. And I've cursed him every day since. Now get out."

I rode home, shoved the papers I'd stolen in my cashsafe, washed the rest of the bronzen from my body, and spent another hour soaking in the tub. I kept seeing the hatred in Hedger's eyes. Whatever Harry had done, it had made the old scrammer loathe him.

I climbed out of the tepid water to dry off and dress. It had never been my habit to avoid the truth. Weiss sounded too much like White; the name had to belong to Harry or his family. It was time to find out.

A few minutes later, I finished reading the last of the glassines I'd stolen. Harry's name, as I assumed, had been Weiss, not White. He'd been born a Hungarian.

He'd also been an agent for the Crown.

Dread iced the blood in my veins, but anger soon thawed it out and set it to boil. Harry, the nice old gent, had been a traitor. An informer. One of Her Majesty's rats. For a moment the elegant words on the royal documents proving I was the granddaughter of a filthy sodding turncoat blurred. I blinked, and they instantly rewrote themselves.

Working as a royal spy had obviously been quite lucrative for my grandfather, who had probably used his earnings to change his identity, marry, and acquire Torian citizenship. That my mother had been the daughter and I the granddaughter of a Hungarian—an enemy of the Crown—hardly registered anymore. I was bound by blood to a member of H.M.'s secret service.

After the failure of the Great Uprising, Toriana may have remained part of the Empire, and grown accustomed to the occupation and institution of Crown law, but we'd never fostered any love for it. Now and then some young hothead commoners would stage a small revolt, embarrass their parents, and spend a few years in the gaol, but they always got out quieter and wiser—or they were kept behind bars where they could make no mischief.

I knew precisely what this connection meant for me. If it became common knowledge that my grandfather had been a spy, I'd be completely and irrevocably ruined. No one would give me the time of day, much less trade with me. Unless redcoats were stationed to protect it, my home would be ransacked and burnt to the ground.

We Torians were still Empire, oh, yes, but we had never forgotten the fate of the first colonists. When the revolution had been crushed, all the survivors who refused to take an oath of loyalty to the Crown had been marched out of Valley Forge into the snows and made to dig their own graves before they'd been shot and shoved into them. Upon hearing of their comrades' fate, every man left in camp who had taken the oath of service had then killed himself, either by pistol or blade. Forty-seven men had famously marched in formation into the icy waters of the Potomac—refusing to stop even when the redcoats had begun firing on them—and had promptly drowned.

Since then every agent of the Crown who had made himself known as such on Torian soil had vanished shortly thereafter. The remains of a few would occasionally be found floating in whatever river or lake they'd been drowned in. The Crown had never been able to prove their agents had been murdered, but after several more years of the same they'd instructed the traitors to hide their work and operate under the guise of ordinary citizens.

As my grandfather had apparently done.

I'd always known my mother to be a bastard and guessed her to have been the get of some undesirable, or her people would have come forward after my parents' death to protect me. Not a single relation had. Finally I knew why.

As a schoolgel I'd made my oath to the Crown and renewed it every five years as was required by law, just as every Torian child did. I'd never especially liked or disliked being H.M.'s subject; I'd never really thought about it. It was what it was, an unchanging part of life in my country. Wondering what Toriana would have been like if we'd won the Great Uprising was nothing but a waste of time. We'd lost. After Washington's surrender at Broken Forge, the Empire would have been within its rights to jail or kill us all. No doubt our ancestors had been grateful to be allowed to continue on as occupied colonies and permitted the means to explore, settle, and develop our country into the provinces of today.

But I was born Torian, not English, and that also meant something. The Union Jack never graced my eaves; in the back of my dresser I still had a small, handmade patch with the stars and stripes the Rebels had carried. I'd sewn it myself as a gel, with a child's resentment of atrocities she'd never experienced firsthand, when everything had seemed so black and white. While I never indulged in redcoat baiting, putting out forty-seven flowers on Remembrance Day, or any of the other subtle ways Torians thumbed their noses at the Crown, I'd never been a bootlicker. I didn't think we'd ever see Independence, at least not in my lifetime, but I still dreamed of it. Most Torians did. All that had changed now that I knew the truth about my grandfather.

Harry the Hungarian. Harry the traitor.

If Nolan Walsh had enough influence to gain access to these records, and he knew my mother's history and where to look, he could ruin my life forever.

But then, anyone else who read them could as well.

I spent an endless night tossing and turning before I finally gave up on sleep and rose to dress. My dire mood dragged at me, reminding me of those first terrible days when I'd come to Rumsen, when I'd slept for an hour here and there on park benches and walked the streets in a hopeless fog. If I hadn't stopped an old gent from walking into the path of an oncoming cart, I might have been found one cold morning, starved and frozen in the gutter.

That one good deed had changed everything: the old man had insisted his thoughts had been paralyzed by evil magic, magic he believed I'd dispelled with my touch. I'd not argued with him or the fifty pounds he'd gratefully pressed in my hands. I'd asked for directions to a respectable boardinghouse.

That first fifty pounds had gone to feeding and sheltering me while I looked for work. After several more encounters similar to the one with the old man in the street, word spread about my alleged ability to dispel magic.

At first it had felt like thievery, taking money for doing nothing, but the people who had come to me were more desperate than I. I dealt with my guilt by looking for the real source of their woes, and I discovered I had a natural talent for detecting. Combining the two allowed me to provide service without feeling as if I'd become just another magic swindler, like Dredmore.

As I dragged myself from my flat the next morning, I couldn't help thinking I'd have been happier to learn that Harry had been a practicing mage, or even a fete teller.

I stopped at a corner teacart I frequented and bought a cup of Irish red and a sticky bun. As the tealass tipped her never-empty pot to fill the mug I'd brought with me, she nattered on in a friendly fashion about the comings and goings she'd seen.

"Three poshers near bought me out yesterday," she said as she added a dollop of milk-thinned cream to my mug. "Tried to pay me with brown. Lucky for me, one of his mates had proper coin."

"Probably straight off the ship," I said.

"I've seen brown notes before, course, but . . ." The gel leaned over and lowered her voice. "Strange-marked they were, miss. Red-inked all over, and a slice in the middle over the H.M.'s poor face."

I frowned. "Did they speak English?"

"Only the one with the coin said anything," she said, "and then to say 'Grassy.'"

Grazie, the Talian word for "thank you." "If they come back and try to give you any trouble," I said, "best blow for the beater."

"Had it ready in me other hand the whole time," she assured me, raising her left hand to show me the tin whistle dangling from her wristlace. "You want a 'fresher, Miss? You're looking beat today."

"Restless night." I offered her a wan smile before I surrendered my spot to a new customer and moved on.

I made myself eat the bun, which helped loosen the knot in my belly a notch and made me feel a little better. I'd worked hard and made a new life for myself here in Rumsen, and the prospect of losing it terrified me. The unfairness stung, too. If the truth about Harry ever came out, I'd be judged over something that had happened before I'd been born.

The anger boiled up inside me again. The blood in my veins might be tainted by my mother's unfortunate birth and my grandfather's foreign blood and domestic betray-als, but I didn't deserve to have my situation stolen from me for a second time. No matter what sort of traitorous bastard my grandfather had been, he'd done nothing for me, nor had I profited from his spywork. Everything I owned in this world I'd worked for and earned by myself.

I tossed the last crust of my bun in a rubbish bin outside the Davies Building and emptied the lukewarm dregs of my tea in the gutter. Harry White or Weiss or whoever he'd been be damned; I wasn't going to cower in fear or give up and run. He was a ghost; perhaps no more than an echo of a life that was over now. Whatever evil Harry had done in the past had nothing to do with me. Rumsen was my home, and I was Torian. I'd earned the right to live and do business here.

"Excuse me, miss."

I jumped a little and turned to see a heavily cloaked figure standing behind me. A hat and heavy veil disguised her face, but I recognized the reddened, callused hands.

"The nearest apothecary is one block over," I told Lady Walsh's chambermaid. "But his pain powders are mostly chalk dust."

Betsy looked around before she stepped closer. "Milady asks that you attend her, miss."

"Indeed. You can tell your lady she can—" I stopped myself, knowing any insult I offered would be passed along verbatim. "Find another distant cousin."

"You don't understand, miss." Betsy followed me into the building. "My mistress is in terrible danger."

I paused at the foot of the stairs. "Then go to Rumsen Main Station and ask for Inspector Tom Doyle. He works the Hill." I glanced back at her. "I don't anymore."

Betsy didn't give up easily. She trailed after me up the stairs and down the hall, assuring me that her mistress had been most insistent that I come to her aid and that no one else would do. It gave me a healthy amount of pleasure to close my office door in her face, but I didn't bolt it, so as soon as I moved away from it, she came in after me.

"Are you deaf?" I inquired as I took off my wrap and hung it on the coat stand. "Or simply daft?"

Rather than beg me to reconsider, Betsy went on the attack. "This is your doing, miss. All of it. If milady hadn't brought you up to the house, none of this would have happened."

"Oh, of course not." I folded my arms. "So what's happened?"

Betsy sniffed. "I'm sure I can't say. You'll have to hear it from milady."

"Have her write me a letter. I'll read it when I get time." Maybe sometime around Christmas, when I was feeling a bit more generous.

The maid followed me into my office and planted herself in front of my desk, where she tried to stare me down. I collected my morning post from the tube and began sorting through it.

Betsy broke first. "If you don't come to see her and do something, miss, she'll be ruined."

"I told you, I don't work the Hill anymore," I said flatly. "Now run along, or I'll call for the beater."

She didn't budge. "You'll want payment in advance, I suppose." She took out a pitifully small purse out of her reticule and dropped it in front of me.

I picked up the purse, which had been fashioned from a piece of felted wool, now shiny at the seams from long use.

From the weight of it, it contained a paltry few pounds in small coin. I glanced up at her. "This is *your* money."

"I've been putting a bit aside for a place of me own someday." She lifted her chin. "It should be enough, but if it isn't, I can get a little more from me beau."

I held on to the purse and sat back in my chair. "Now why would you hand over your life savings to me?"

Betsy looked ready to burst. "I'm not daft," she snapped. "Milady is a decent, fair mistress. She never shouts or hits, or gives the maid staff more work than we can do. She sees to it that we have enough to eat, proper clothes, time to go to Church and to visit our families. We sleep safe in our beds. We would do anything for her." She gave me a defiant look. "Even pay the likes of you."

I got up and came round the desk to shove the purse into her hands. "I'm not taking your money, Betsy." Before she could protest, I added, "I'll see your lady one more time, for free, but not on the Hill."

"She don't want you to come round the house," the chambermaid told me with some satisfaction. "She'll see you at her dressmaker's, the Silken Dream, today at one o'clock sharp."

"I'll be there." I let her get as far as the threshold before I added, "You may think the world of your mistress, Betsy, but being treated fairly is your due. Your right."

"Is it now?" She gave me a contemptuous look. "And here I thought you said you worked the Hill."

CHAPTER EIGHT

If Rina had seen me steeling myself to stroll into the Silken Dream that afternoon, she'd have laughed herself into a cramp. There were few things I despised or avoided as much as dressmakers, and now I had to enter the establishment of one Madam Desiree Duluc, the grandest of the gowners, the incomparable Arachne who dressed the wives, daughters, sisters, and mothers of the most important men in Rumsen.

I'd never been inside the shop during business hours, not that I could ever afford to shop there. Nothing I owned, not even the very fine burnout silk shawl Rina had given me for my last birthday, could equal in quality the simplest pair of gloves under Madam Duluc's roof. Nor did I care to put on the airs or dress of a fashionable lady; even if I had the coin to buy such creations and wear them, I'd have betrayed myself the moment I spoke in my Middy accent or removed the gloves from my unpampered hands.

No one came to the front room to toss me out on the street; I was left to stand between two semicircles of gown forms draped with the latest fashions. From the number of pure-white frills and bows and draped sashes adorning Madam's goods, the latest fashion for ladies appeared to be swishing about in as much frippery as possible, like marriage cakes with legs.

A thin, sharp-nosed woman in a dove-gray gown minced her way across the front room to join me. "Good afternoon, miss," she said in a low, soft tone. "How may we serve you?"

Not the reception I'd been expecting. "I'm looking for Lady Walsh. She asked me to meet her here."

"May I ask your name?"

"Kittredge." I found a card in my reticule and handed it to her.

"Lady Walsh has not yet arrived for her fitting, Miss Kittredge." The seamstress tucked my card under her cuff and gestured toward the back rooms. "Would you care to wait?"

I had nothing better to do, so I nodded and followed her back into a small, elegant private room already set up with a tea cart and a waiting maid.

"Sarah will serve you today, Miss Kittredge," the seamstress said. "I will return when Lady Walsh has arrived." She curtseyed deeply and withdrew.

Sarah and I exchanged a look. "Is she always that nice?" I asked on impulse.

The gel nodded. "All Madam's ladies are." She grinned. "The tea is first-brewed, miss, and the crumpets come straight out of the oven."

I gave the gleaming cart, something I could never afford even if I tripled my rates, a wistful look. "Of course they do."

I let Sarah serve me tea and would have slipped her a crumpet for herself if another lady had not stepped in. This one was dressed in an emerald satin ball gown and had her silver-streaked red hair bundled untidily atop her head. At least twenty glass-headed pins pierced the edge of her bodice, and from her sash dangled a marked length of measuring tape. The esteemed proprietor herself.

"So this is what one might make from the flour sacks," Madam Duluc said in a frightfully snooty French accent as she stared at my skirts. "*Bonjour, mademoiselle.* I fear you have made a tragic mistake to come here. Are there even three pounds in your reticule?"

"Two and six," I told her, rattling my coins. "Had three when I left the house this morning, but I bought a sticky bun for my breakfast."

"Then you will please not touch anything." Madam Duluc glanced at her assistant. "I will deal with this one, Sarah. Go and assist Madam Nancy."

After the maid bobbed and left, Madam Duluc came to stand over me. "So? Did you enjoy my tea?"

"It's lovely." I smiled. "In fact, I may start coming here instead of the bakery. The crumpets practically floated into my mouth."

"They're croissants, not crumpets, you greedy goose," she said, this time in the broad, musical accent of the Rumsen working class as she abandoned her pretense and dropped down on the settee beside me. "Now, what brings you here? Lady Walsh's maid, is it? What does the gel think, my gowns are bespelled to prevent her mistress from conceiving? Does she suspect I've cast the evil eye over the lady's corset strings?" Her expression brightened. "*Can* you cast an evil eye on corset strings?"

"No, no, and of course not." I poured her a cup and handed it to her. "I've personal business with the lady herself, Bridge."

"What? Personal?" She frowned at me. "I thought you quit working the Hill, you silly cow. Never say this is about that bloody great mage wanting to bed you. Isn't he the reason you quit?"

"It's not about Dredmore, and I did quit. I have quit. I will quit. After this." I wiped my fingers on a napkin before I touched a fold of her ball gown. "Grand fine stuff. Green's your color."

"Oh, shut up." She slapped my hand away. "We've been so busy with the mayor's ball next week, I ran out of forms. This is going to be worn by the mayor's wife. Then I have to create something even costlier for his mistress to wear when she makes an appearance with the poor sod she's cuckolding." She knocked back half her tea before borrowing my napkin to wipe her lips. "My Nancy would have genteelly tossed you out the door if I hadn't spotted you from the workroom." She eyed my gown again. "God blind me. Don't you have anything decent to wear?"

"Decent by my standards, yes." I smiled. "How are Charles and the children?"

"Charlie's getting fat, the kids are sprouting like beans, and you are terribly missed." She nudged me with her elbow. "Why don't you come round the castle more often, Kit? It's been months."

"Madam Duluc must keep up appearances," I reminded her. "I'll drop in before Christmas, I promise."

Charles Duluc, peerless textile importer and youngest son of an immensely wealthy, extremely titled French family, had come over to Toriana to look after his father's business interests and buy up more land to add to the family coffers. He was scheduled to return to France after a month, and four days before his ship was set to sail, he'd gone for a walk in the park. There he'd sat down on a bench next to two gels taking a break from work to sit in the sunshine and gossip while they ate their sack lunches.

The lass from the loomworks had offered Charles half of her sandwich, which he'd accepted with astonished pleasure, and they'd begun talking. Three hours later the Honorable Charles Duluc and Bridget Mary Sullivan had been married by special license.

It had been the stuff of every working gel's fantasies. Charles had bought the loomworks where his new bride had worked twelve hours every day since her tenth birthday, and had transferred the title and property over to her family as her bride price. Old Sully, Bridget's da, had taken over the managing and running of it while his daughter and new son-in-law had gone to the mountains for their honeymoon. By the time they'd returned, Old Sully had fired the rest of the mill managers, had cut the workers' hours in half and doubled their pay. Within two months the loomworks had increased quality and production so much that Old Sully had begun looking at expanding.

There had been some tense moments when the widowed Madam Duluc and her daughters sailed over from France to meet Charles's commoner Torian bride (even the French themselves admitted to being terrible snobs). Charles's love for Bridget, however, had been absolute and unshakable. Since his father's death had given him full control over the family fortunes, the ladies of the family had had to accept the marriage. (The fact that Charles and Bridget intended to remain in Toriana also weighed heavily in their favor.)

Charles hadn't wanted his wife to work another moment in her life, but after giving him two sons and a daughter, Bridget had grown bored with the life of a titled lady and asked her husband if she might open a shop of her own. Weaving since childhood had given Bridget an extensive understanding of fine cloth, and growing up in the shadow of the Hill had taught her that gowning the wives of the rich was the most lucrative way to use that knowledge.

I knew all this because I'd been the other lass sitting on the bench that day, and I'd gone with them to the magistrate to stand witness to their marriage. Charles and Bridget were the reason I didn't trifle with men: if I couldn't have what they'd found in each other, I'd go without.

Bridget filled me in on how the children were getting on with their tutors and how Charles had taken an undignified dunking at the beach trying to rescue their youngest's new bonnet when the wind had snatched it away. I listened and laughed, but my thoughts kept straying to Lady Diana.

"That's what he got for not tying her ribbons before setting off from the house, I told him," Bridget said, and then she abruptly changed the subject. "Now, what's this business with you and the Walshes? Come on, out with it. You look like you did when you were renting that closet at the boardinghouse."

"My good intentions got the better of me," I admitted. "This time I might have to pay dearly for them."

"Oh, Kit." Bridget's smile faded. "If you need Charlie to step in, you've only to say—"

"No, Bridge. This is something not even Charles could make vanish." Next to Rina, Bridget was my oldest mate, and I wanted to confide in her, but something held me back. I didn't have that many friends that I could risk losing one. Bridget would keep my secrets, but she'd never abandoned her working-class ideals. Knowing I was the granddaughter of an agent to the Crown would forever change her opinion of me. "I'll conclude my business with the lady, and then hopefully it'll be done with."

Bridget glanced up at a soft knock on the door. "Do come in," she said in her beautifully fake French accent.

Sarah stepped in and bobbed. "If you please, Madam, Lady Walsh has arrived."

"Show her to the Rose Room, if you would, Sarah." When the gel left, Bridget turned to me. "I can start her fitting while you talk with her. They always treat me like I'm invisible when they're standing in their drawers."

I shook my head. "She won't talk if you're there."

Her eyes narrowed. "Do you know what you're taking on with this one, Kit?"

"Absolutely." After today I intended to steer clear of all the Walshes.

"Well, then I'll let you get on with it." Bridget stood and brushed some crumbs from the emerald satin. "Rose Room's at the end of the hall on the left. Take as long as you like, but Kit"—she caught my arm as I went past her, and tugged me close for a careful hug so neither of us would be stuck by the pinned bodice—"whatever this personal business is between you and the lady, finish it now. You don't want the Hill coming down on your heels or your head. That deathmage, either."

I walked down to the Rose Room, where Betsy stood on guard outside the door. She ignored me entirely, so I did the same and stepped inside, where I found Lady Walsh pacing back and forth, her gait rapid and jerky.

"Milady," I said, closing the door but not moving too far from it. "You asked to meet with me?"

She came to an abrupt halt, moved toward me, and stopped again to take a deep breath. I could almost hear her governess talking inside her head: *A lady does not rush. A lady does not lunge. A lady does not throttle.*

"Miss Kittredge, your advice to me has resulted in the unhappiest of situations." She spoke as if she couldn't unclench her teeth. "I followed your suggestion to entice my husband to discover the panel under my bed."

"You dropped your ring, and he found it."

She nodded tightly. "When Nolan discovered the panel, he became quite furious. In truth, I have never seen my husband so angry."

She had called me here to tell me that it had worked? "I'm sure he'll see to your protection, Lady Walsh."

"Indeed he will not." Her stiff expression began to waver. "He accused me of being disloyal to him."

"Disloyal?" I echoed. "For getting cut up in your sleep by some intruder? Has he gone off, then?"

"Nolan believes I am responsible for the passage," she snapped. "That I am using it to commit adultery. He even accused me of drugging him each night to prevent him from discovering my infidelity." She straightened her spine and looked down her nose. "Because I took your advice, he is now threatening to divorce me."

"But when you showed him the cuts on your hands,

didn't he . . ." As she shook her head, I groaned. "For the love of Jesu, milady, you have to show him your wounds."

"I can't."

I wanted to shake her until her pearly teeth rattled. "They're the only proof you've got of what's being done to you."

"There is no more proof." She stripped off her gloves and thrust both hands at me.

Lady Diana didn't have a mark on her. The ugly words had vanished, as if they'd never been cut into her skin. I took hold of her hands, checking them to see if she'd somehow disguised them with face paint, but all I felt was smooth skin. She didn't even have scars. "This is not possible."

"But it is, as you see." She sniffed. "Now do you believe it's a curse, Miss Kittredge?"

"No." I held on to one hand as she tried to pull away. "Be still." I took my magnifying glass out of my reticule and held it just above the skin. Examining one hand turned up nothing, but on the other I discovered a tiny fragment of dark red clinging to one of the fine hairs of her skin. When I gently nudged the fragment with my fingernail, she made a pained sound. When I plucked it off, the hair came with it.

"What are you doing?" Lady Diana demanded.

I carefully transferred the fragment to a bit of paper and folded it up. "Collecting evidence." I pointed to one of the padded benches. "I have to go and consult with someone on this. If you want to know the truth, you'll wait here for me."

෴

Bridget generously provided me with her carri, which I drove back to my office building. I left it parked at the curb and dashed down to the Dungeon, making my way through clouds of steam as I shouted for Docket.

"Hold on to your hatpins, gel." The old man emerged from the steam, wearing but a towel wrapped around his skinny hips. "Come back later, Kit. I'm having a soak."

I glanced at the contraption behind him, which resembled a giant teakettle. "A soak, or a boil?"

"That's just the collection chamber." He pointed to some hastily rigged pipes hanging over it. "Steam comes down from there, and the gap between me and the pipes cools it enough to make it tolerable. It's a heathen practice. I'm calling it the Waterless Bathe." He grimaced. "Haven't worked out what to do about soap, though."

I shook my head. "Get some clothes on, mate. I need you to look at something under the scope."

Once he was decent, Doc brought me over to one of his workbenches fitted with a large vertical tube standing in an adjusted bracket. "Let's have it." When I gave him the folded paper containing the fragment I'd removed from Lady Diana's hand, he opened it and gently placed it under the tube.

As he looked through the gogs he'd fitted to the magnifying tube, I explained where I'd found the fragment, and what had been done to Lady Diana. "She claimed the cuts didn't hurt, and she never found any blood on her nightdresses or linens."

Doc grunted. "I'll wager all the wounds vanished within a day of her finding them as well."

"How did you know?"

"She wasn't cut, love." He moved away from the scope, searched through some jars on a nearby shelf, and then handed me a jar of thick, dark-red liquid. "Wound paste. They made it out of animal blood mixed with a strong resin. My guess is someone used this to paint the words on her and scored the lines as they dried to make them appear like real cuts. You need a solvent to remove it or it acts like a new scab. If she tried to pull it off herself, she'd bleed."

I'd never heard of such a thing. "Who uses this stuff?"

"Anyone with the know-how, I suppose," he admitted. "It's an old soldier's trick. Cowards resort to it to prevent being sent into battle."

"And you?"

"Sometimes I need an extra week or two to pull together the rent." He ducked his head. "Me showing the landlord a wound that's temporarily laid me up usually does the trick."

And here all this time I'd been bartering with him. "Can I borrow this?" When he nodded, I took the jar and gave his shoulder a squeeze. "The next time you need help with the rent, mate, you come to me."

By the time I got back to Bridget's, Lady Diana had worked herself into a frazzle.

"Where have you been?" she snapped as soon as she saw me. "How could you leave like that? Nolan expected me home an hour ago. He'll be furious."

"Hang Nolan," I said, and held up the jar of wound paste. "This is what was used on you."

I repeated everything Doc had told me, and with

every word Lady Diana's face grew pinker. Once I'd detailed how the paste simulated wounds, I told her the rest of what I'd worked out.

"Your assailant assumed you would hide the wounds from your family and deliberately placed them on portions of your body that could be easily covered. By removing them the next night, he could make you think you were under the influence of a malignant spell. Or perhaps . . ." I wasn't sure I wanted to complete my other thought.

"Tell me," she urged.

I chose my words carefully. "Perhaps to tamper with your wits."

"No one could be that evil." She pulled on her gloves. "I am a devoted wife and stepmother. I treat our servants well. I have never inflicted harm on another person in my life. Why would anyone take such horrible vengeance against me? I've done nothing."

I thought of the words that had been written on her skin. "You and your family profited by your marriage to Lord Walsh, which was arranged so that he might obtain another heir. To someone in your household, that makes you a greedy slut."

Her head snapped up. "You will not speak those words to me," she said through white lips.

Oh, *now* she was putting on airs. "Would you rather your husband say them in open court?"

"He will not, if you would come to dinner on Friday and tell my husband how you discovered the panel."

I stepped back. "You'd do better to take the wound paste with you, milady. That will explain—"

"Nolan will think only that I used it on myself. You, on the other hand, can attest to my true motives, and how you were the one to discover the panel under the bed." Tears sparkled in her eyes. "You are my only hope now."

She really had no idea of how much trouble she was in. "I'm a commoner, milady. As such he'll believe I was paid by you to lie to him."

"Have you no one to vouch for your personal integrity?" Before I could answer, her expression brightened. "You are acquainted with Lucien Dredmore, are you not? He has much influence."

I could imagine what Dredmore would demand in return for such a favor. My body and spirit on a silver platter, at the very least. "The gentleman and I are not the best of friends."

"If Nolan is granted a divorce on grounds of adultery, do you know what will happen to me?" Her voice was rising to a shriek. "To my family?"

"How would I, milady? I'm just a gel who works for her living," I reminded her. "One your butler reported to the police as a blackmailer."

"Mother of mercy." She closed her eyes and then pulled out her skirts.

Watching her drop to her knees turned my stomach. "Lady Walsh, please, don't do that."

"If this is what I am reduced to, so be it." She bowed her head. "I humbly beg you to take pity on me, Miss Kittredge. I beseech you to come to speak to my husband and save me from the ruin of my life."

As I looked down at her, I thought of the day I'd left

107

Middleway. I'd never begged anything from the men who had stolen my life. I'd known what they would have done to me if I had.

I took Lady Diana by the arms and pulled her up from her knees. "Betsy."

The chambermaid darted inside. "Yes, miss?"

"Take your lady home." I looked into hopeless eyes and managed a smile. "I have much to do if I am to dine with her and Lord Walsh on Friday."

Lady Walsh threw her arms around me and held me like a beloved sister. "You are the kindest creature in all of Rumsen."

The kindest, or the daftest. "He's likely having you watched, so I'll go out the back. Have Betsy sleep in your chamber until Friday, and then we'll sort all this out at dinner."

Betsy cloaked her lady before whisking her away, while I went to the workroom to bid my friend farewell.

"Lady Walsh will be unable to have her fitting today," I told Bridget, who was undressing behind a screen. "What does one wear to dinner on the Hill?"

"Nothing in your wardrobe." She handed the emerald ballgown off to Nance and pulled on a simpler dress styled to resemble the gray uniforms her ladies wore, but made of pure silver silk. (Charles had vowed she would never wear anything else.) "Or what you'd find in the collection of a professional lady's, if that's what you're thinking."

"Can one rent a dress for two and six?" I wondered out loud.

"From the rag pile at the tin shop, perhaps." Bridget muttered something rude as she came out from behind the screen. "Louise, has Lady Richmond settled her account with us?"

"No, Madam," a gel hemming purple taffeta skirts said through a mouthful of pins. "She offered a bracelet in trade, but it proved to be paste."

Bridget gave me a critical look. "Set aside the blue evening for mademoiselle. She will be back on Friday in time for us to dress her for her dinner with Lord and Lady Walsh." Before I could protest, she tapped my cheek. "It's a gift."

"My birthday isn't until January, Madam."

"Christmas, then." She gave me a steely look, leaned close, and whispered, "Or I can sew your stubborn ass into that emerald satin, if you like."

I gave in gracefully. "Madam is most generous. Now, can someone direct me to the back door?"

Bridget personally escorted me to the trade entrance, but she didn't lecture me along the way. She only stopped me at the door. "Charlie's mother told me that she'd had a mage enchant all his suits to ward off women before he left France. She was afraid of him picking up something nasty from a strumpet."

I sighed. "You can't make suits female-proof."

"Can't you? He never looked at another woman, that whole trip, until he sat down next to us in the park. No, truly, I asked him. Said he never felt a spot of interest." She took my hand. "I know how you feel about magic, Kit, but there is something about you. I don't know what, but I feel it. Everyone does. If you hadn't been with me that day . . ." She shook her head. "Don't let the Walshes take advantage. You're too good for them." She kissed my cheek. "Now be off with you. I'll see you here Friday noon, not a minute later."

As I left the Silken Dream, I thought of Dredmore, and how I might convince him to accompany me to the Walshes. I'd definitely have to lie. Or perhaps hire some muscle to kidnap and drug him.

Suddenly, something flew past my face and burst against a nearby stack of crates. I smothered a shriek as I flattened myself against the brick wall and looked from one end of the alley to the other. "What the bloody hell?"

Two men appeared, both wearing hooded capes, shirts, and trousers of dark red. They marched toward me in unison, one hefting a sparkling glass globe filled with swirling darkness.

My heart wanted to depart my chest, and my knees shook, but I had no time for hysteria. The all-red garments identified the pair to me as a particularly illegal class of magic-wielding scum; they were unlicensed hired killers, known as snuffmages.

I ducked as one threw the second globe at me, covering my head with my arms as I was showered with glass and filth. What they were throwing had to be snuffballs, another magical farce. The globes, I'd heard, were filled with some sort of black dust bespelled to kill anything it touched.

Naturally I was still breathing, and once I shook off the debris, I found the courage to smile at them. "I think your balls are on the blink today, boys," I said breathlessly. "Got anything else?"

Both men drew long, sharp-edged daggers with rune-carved blades.

"That might work." I turned, hoisted up my skirts, and ran.

I almost made it to the end of the alley before a clawing hand latched onto my collar. He tried to haul my back against him so he could cut my throat, but I dropped out from under his encircling arm and rammed the top of my head into his groin. That doubled him over in time to protect me from most of the slash of the second one's blade.

I rolled onto my hands, tucked my head under, and flipped over, which freed my legs from my skirts. One of my slippers went flying as I drove the heel of my foot into the second assassin's elbow, knocking the blade from his grasp. Then the first one recovered enough to hurl himself on top of me and we both collapsed.

He was too heavy to dislodge, and I was facedown against the paving stones, probably the worst position to defend myself. His hand clamped across my mouth before I could let out a scream, and he used it to pull my head back and expose my throat.

I knew then I was done for, so I closed my eyes and waited for it. Instead of feeling the blade at my neck, I heard a nasty, bone-crunching thump, and the crushing weight slid off me to one side. I crawled out from under his limp arm and leg and staggered to my feet to watch a third man in a black hooded cloak striding out of the alley.

A strong arm came round me as Tom Doyle caught my fist. "It's all right, Kit. I've got you."

So he did.

∽

Inspector Doyle left his beater with the body of the snuffmage whose skull had been bashed in while he took me to his carri and got me out of there.

"That was nice of you," I said when I'd caught my breath.

"I'm a nice chap, most days." He draped his jacket around me. "I'll take you to the women's hospital."

"No, I've only bruises and scratches." I pushed my arms into his sleeves and tried not to shake. "A ride home is all I need."

"We'll go to the station first, clean you up," he said, and started the engine.

I was too rattled by what had happened to argue, so I kept my head down on the way to Rumsen Main and ignored the stares as Doyle took me in past the desk sergeant and several dozen citizens in trouble or complaining of it. The whispers that erupted in our wake made me glance down. My skirts were stained and torn, my bodice soaked with filth. I smelled as good as I looked.

"Almost there," Doyle said, guiding me through rows of desks where property clerks and secretaries ogled me like I was a naked strumpet.

I noted the stark black lettering on the door glass of the office he ushered me into. "*Chief* Inspector Doyle, is it? Very impressive." I watched him draw the curtains so that no one in the station could look in. "Working the Hill's done great things for you."

"Pity I can't say the same about the dispelling busi-ness for you." He led me over to an old leather-covered armchair and sat me down before retrieving a care kit from his desk and a ewer of water from the adjoining lavatory. "Let's have a look, then."

I shrugged out of the jacket and held out the rent, bloodstained sleeve on my right arm.

He scowled. "Why didn't you tell me you were cut?"

"It's just a scratch. One of them caught me with the tip of a blade as I went down." I tore the remnants of the sleeve away from the wound and inspected it. "See? It's not too deep."

He dampened a cloth in the ewer and gently cleaned the cut. "What were you doing on that side of town, Kit?"

"I needed a dress for a dinner engagement." I winced as he took a pair of tweezers from the kit and plucked a bit of gravel from the wound. "Why were you out following me?"

He met my gaze. "How do you know I was?"

"Men generally stay out of the high fashion district." I saw him take out a small brown bottle marked with a marigold label. "No, Tommy, not calendula," I begged. "It'll sting like blazes."

"It's the only thing to keep it from infecting and help it heal," he told me as he soaked another cloth with the tincture. "So stop whining." He ignored my hiss and began cleaning the gash. "I wasn't following you. I was following Lady Walsh."

"Really—" I let out the breath I'd been holding. "What for?"

He set aside the cloth and took out a roll of bandaging cotton. "That's none of your business." He straightened my arm before he began winding the bandage over the cut. "Why would someone send two snuffmages after you?"

"They weren't especially attached to their money?" I grimaced as he pulled the bandage tight. "Are you cleaning me up or torturing me?"

"I'm questioning your involvement in a violent public altercation." When I didn't respond, he added, "A man died in that alley, Kit. It's my job to find out why."

My shoulders sagged. "I don't know who they were, other than snuffmages," I said honestly. "They were waiting outside the dressmaker's for me. They heaved a couple of their ridiculous snuffballs my way, and when that didn't work, they came after me with their blades." I would not mention the man in the black cloak. "That's everything I know."

"Rumsen snuffmages like to use bloodbane in those silly snuffballs," he informed me. "It's enchanted to kill anything it touches."

"They were filled with black powder." I picked up a fold of my skirt spattered with the stuff, smeared it on my fingers, and held it up in front of him. "Look, I'm not dying. Praise heaven."

"You turned it into that."

I chuckled. "Sure I did. Right after I pulled a hare out of my hat."

"Magic has no effect on you," Doyle continued smoothly. "My grandfather remarked on it several times before we left Middy." He tied off the bandage and gave me a hard look. "Said your mother had the same gift."

"How lucky for me." Panic surged through me as I

checked my battered brooch watch, which fell from a tear in my bodice into my hand. "Oh, look at the time. How dreadfully late it is. I must be off."

"You're not leaving," he said, standing.

"I've answered your questions, Tommy. I'm in desperate need of a bath and new clothes, and I don't think you have either tucked away in your kit." I tried to stand, felt my knees wobble, and sat back down. "Damn me."

"You'll feel better after you have a rest." He nodded toward the wide couch on one side of the office. "It's more comfortable than it looks."

I couldn't imagine sleeping in a police station, even one supervised by my handsome savior. "So is my bed."

"I'm sending our staff warder over to your flat to have a look." He held up a hand to stop my protest. "The snuffmage who got away has his reputation to mend. He's likely already set a trap."

"But you said that magic doesn't work on me," I reminded him.

"On you directly, no," he agreed. "But he can get to your boiler, your ceilings, or your walls. They like to make it look like a tragic accident."

"Father and Son, Tommy, that's all magic ever is—" I stopped myself. "You can't enter my flat without my permission."

"You're still under suspicion of extortion, and you're a woman." He leaned down. "Which we both know means I can fair burn the place to the ground if I wish."

He smelled of wool and soap, and I wanted to bury my face against his broad chest. "You wouldn't do that to me."

His stern expression thawed to something gentler. "Kit, you've no idea what I might do."

The door to his office opened, and a sweet-faced elderly woman wearing a feminine version of a beater's uniform and carrying a cup and saucer came in.

"Hot and sweet, my dear," she said, as she put the cup in my hands. She frowned at the bandage on my arm. "Shouldn't she be in hospital, Tommy?"

He made a disgusted sound.

"Wouldn't let him take you, dear? Can't say as I blame you." She began tidying up around us. "Dreadful places, they are. Whenever I go to visit one of the lads, it sucks all the energy out of me."

"The stench doesn't help, either." I spotted the embroidered symbols on the lapel of her dark-blue jacket. "You're a mage?"

"Staff warder," she corrected, beaming. "Mrs. Mary Harris, at your service."

I turned to Doyle. "You send sweet old ladies into potential crime scenes?"

"She has more arrests than any three men in the station," he told me. "And trust me, you wouldn't want to go up against our Mary in some dark alley. Last time someone did, we needed three whitecarts."

"Stop that, Tommy, you'll frighten the lass," the warder scolded. To me she said, "I've had some scuffles with snuffmages, and they're not a pretty bunch. What can you tell me about them?"

"They didn't kill me," I said.

She chuckled. "I meant, what did you notice about them?"

"There were two, a bruiser and a dink," I said. "Dressed head to toe in dark red. They threw snuffballs filled with dirt at me, and then went for their daggers. Neither said a single word."

"They don't put dirt in snuffballs." Mrs. Harris thought for a moment. "Sounds like rogue partners—ex–guild members who hire out their services to very bad men," she tacked on when she caught Tommy's frown. "They work in pairs to ensure the killing's done. The one who escaped, was he the dink?" At my nod she sighed. "It's the little ones you always have to mind; they develop their spellcraft a bit more to make up for their lack of stature and muscle. The local guild master's a head shorter than me." She glanced at Doyle. "Speaking of the little pest, he's waiting for a word with you, Tom. Expect he wants to protect the guild by disavowing this lot."

Tom took my keys from my reticule and handed them to the warder as he gave her my address. "She'll need a full sweep, Mary. Do take Caldwell and Nelams with you."

"Nicholson as well, I think. Lovely to meet you, dear." Mary left before I could reply.

"You know where I live?" I demanded.

"I know where you live, and that you bought the entire building for a pittance," he said. "I also know you live there alone, that you are very good friends with madams Eagle and Duluc, and that you've banked a modest sum, some of which you use now and then for home improvements."

I coughed. "You have been busy."

"Your business has also made you a fair number of

enemies among the magic community." He cocked his head. "Would you like to know what they say about you?"

"I'm a demoness sent from hell to plague them," I said dutifully. "An evil harpy who feeds on magic. Satan's strumpet, Beelzebub's bawd, Houdini's whore . . ." I stopped and sighed. "The names change occasionally, but the whining never ends."

"One of them might have sent those snuffmages after you," Doyle said. "Or perhaps it was someone from the Hill."

"Magical assassination. You'd think they'd save a few quid and simply have me run down in the street." I sipped the tea, which was horribly sweet but settled my stomach. "There's no need to go to all this fuss. I'll be fine."

"You're an unprotected woman operating a dangerous business, tramping about the Hill and offending the tonners right and left, and now someone's tried to snuff you." He folded his arms. "It's not anyone's definition of fine, Kit."

I tried to stare him down, but it was impossible. "I hate being female."

"I rather like that you are." He astounded me by bending down and pressing a quick kiss to my dirty brow. "Now be a good gel and have a nap."

Chapter Nine

Inspector Tom Doyle hadn't charged me with murder (a great relief) but had treated me like a wayward younger sister (a great pity)—and he didn't trust me. I discovered that as soon as I tried the door and found it locked. Bars covered his window from the inside, and they were padlocked.

I wasn't going anywhere until the canny sod released me, so I trudged over to his leather couch. The stiff-looking cushions felt like clouds under my weight, and I curled up on one end, propping my hurt arm against my side.

I'd made enemies of any number of charlatans, but they'd never attacked me. The few I'd confronted had muttered uncomplimentary things about my virtue and my supposed allegiance with the forces of darkness, but for the most part I'd scared them off. Gert was the only persistent one, but she couldn't afford a half sack of bruised fruit, never mind snuffmages. I'd always thought my disbelief in their nonsense had frightened most of the magic peddlers; this because they depended so heavily on faith in their abilities to pull off their tricks. That and I'd exposed too many of them too easily.

Magic has no effect on you.

It had no effect on me because it had no effect,

period. It was all daft words and colored rocks, harmless powders, useless runes, and worthless . . . something. Despite the fact that I never napped, I was suddenly so tired I couldn't even open my mouth to yawn. My eyes closed on their own, my body went lax, and then I was out like a wick in high wind, drifting into a memory of the last man I wished to think of.

I'd met Dredmore at the home of a merchant named Wiggins, one of Rina's regulars. She'd brought me to the nice old gent's to look at a collection of bacco boxes, which Wiggins claimed had been bespelled. I'd just begun my examination when Dredmore had swept in.

I'd taken in the swirling greatcoat, mirror-polished boots, and impossibly intricate weave of his cravat before I resisted the urge to bob and looked directly into his dark eyes. I expected to see the languid contempt of a tonner, but he showed no emotion at all. I might have been gazing into silverblacked mirrors. The experience should have left me cold, but I made the mistake of looking at his mouth, which had been fashioned for all manner of intimate sin. My mouth went dry, and when I met his gaze a second time, I saw something fierce and hungry looking back.

Mr. Wiggins's voice shook as he performed the quickest of introductions. "Such an honor to have you here, milord," he added. "I'll leave you to get acquainted with Miss Kittredge and Mrs. Eagle, then." He scurried out of the room.

"Ladies." Dredmore made it sound like an insult. "I am here on behalf of Mr. Wiggins's business partner." He looked down his nose at me. "Doubtless you have little real experience in dispelling enchantments, Miss Kittredge, but you and your friend may remain and observe."

Normally I didn't mind being patronized by a member of the ton. They were raised from birth to believe anyone without money or connections was beneath their notice. He likely assumed I'd feel flattered to be personally addressed by him, theatrical arrogant ponce that he was.

But something about the man put my teeth on edge, and I reacted accordingly.

"How generous of you." I set down the box I was holding so I wouldn't chuck it at his head. "As it happens, milord, I have a vast amount of experience in exposing charlatans who convince the ignorant to believe in enchantments. Perhaps you should leave."

He stiffened. "Are you calling me a fraud?"

"Dear me." I feigned dismay. "Did that shoe fit?"

"We should go, Kit," I heard Rina say.

She sounded nervous, and since no man ever made her that, I eyed the intruder again. "Why? We were here first."

"I am a deathmage, Miss Kittredge," he informed me, his voice all midnight and silk. "Those who cross me do not live to regret it."

All manner of mages swindled the cits of Rumsen—heartmages hawking love potions and marriage spells, birthmages who chanted over new mothers and infants, even painmages who pretended to cure headaches, sore backs, and the like—but none trifled in the business of death. I'd heard only a handful had ever been licensed to practice the blackest of the dark arts, and then only under very specific circumstances.

"Oh, so you're billing yourself as a thoughtful, magical killer." I ignored the strangled sound Rina made as I nodded agreeably. "Thriving market for death curses these days, what with the economy waffling about and so many pockets to let. Do you scare old tonners to the grave exclusively, or are you chasing after whitecarts as well?"

"*Kit,*" Rina almost shrieked.

"You have said quite enough, madam." Dredmore took a step toward me and held up a stone. "You will be silent and do exactly as I say."

Now Rina looked ready to murder. "You leave her alone."

I eyed the blue pebble he held in his hand, clutched the front of my throat, and made a strangled sound. As the first glimmer of triumph appeared on his face, I dropped my hand and laughed. "Oh, dear, that didn't work out very well, did it? Bad luck. Want to give it another go?"

"Jesu, Kit." Rina dropped into a chair and covered her eyes.

"You're still speaking." Dredmore peered down at me as if I'd grown a second head. "What manner of protection do you carry?"

"A brain, you dolt." I went back to the bacco boxes. "I don't believe in magic, charms, curses, or any other supernatural power, which is why you can't scare me into holding my tongue. So leave off."

"He might cut it out, though," Rina muttered, before grimacing at Dredmore. "Not a suggestion, milord."

"Quiet now, both of you." I turned over one of the boxes, produced my magnifying lens, and closely examined the felt. "Interesting. Mr. Wiggins said these boxes are solid silver and as old as he is, which should make them all at least a hundred years old. Yet this felt appears to be quite new."

Dredmore came to stand beside me. "I sense no spell at work here."

"Oh, brilliant." Carefully I peeled back one corner of the felt, revealing the metal base. Although the top and inside of the box were dull silver with a very convincing patina, the base was a bright, rosy color. "As I expected. Made of copper."

Rina joined us. "It's a fake, then?"

"Yes, and not a very good one." I went to the door and called for Mr. Wiggins. When he came in, I brought the box to him. "Is this one of the boxes that popped in and out of your collection?"

He nodded. "It belonged to Lord Cornwall, and I always display it next to Sir Walter Raleigh's. It disappeared that night and reappeared in the afternoon on Friday." His eyes bulged as I turned it over to show him the copper bottom. "Good heavens. That's not my box."

"No, it isn't. It's a replica of the one that was stolen from your collection." I set it down. "A counterfeiter would need about two days to make a mold from the original, cast the copper, and silverplate it." I rubbed my finger against one blackened whorl on the lid and showed the streaked tip to Wiggins. "Boot polish, not tarnish. They use it to dull the new plating, make it look old."

Wiggins looked at the rest of his boxes. "But that means . . . more than half of my boxes . . ."

"Have been stolen and replaced with fakes." I took out my kerchief and wiped the polish from my finger. "Who dusts your collection, Mr. Wiggins?"

"I believe that would be Bertha."

He turned and shouted the name, and a few moments later a plump maid strolled in.

"Bertha, someone has been stealing my bacco boxes and replacing them with counterfeits."

"Someone like you," Rina guessed.

The maid paled. "Please, sir, I didn't want to. It's me husband. He gambles, you see, and he lost his position, and he said you have so much, and we so little . . ." Her voice trailed off as she removed a cloth-wrapped bundle from her apron and held it out. "I can put this one back. I won't do it again, I swear."

"You'd spend twenty years at hard labor, all for a worthless sod." Rina shook her head as she opened her reticule.

Wiggins looked down at the large handful of coin Rina gave him. "What's this for?"

"Pawnshops," she said. "To avoid suspicion she'll have sold them to several, so have her take you round to each one. Tell them the boxes are stolen goods, mention the Yard, and they should sell them back to you for whatever pittance they gave her."

"Thank you, miss," Bertha gushed. "I promise, I'll never steal again, no matter what—"

"And once you've gotten your things back," Rina said to Wiggins, "send this stupid, thieving cow to me. I'll take her round to see some of the gels that have gone to prison for their men. Maybe that'll make her more honest in the future."

Dredmore came up behind me. "That was exceedingly clever of you, Miss Kittredge."

"Not as impressive as your waving a wand about and muttering incantations, I'll wager." I felt the hand he'd dropped on my shoulder. "Is this another attempt at a spell? If it's to make my skin crawl, I think this time it's actually working."

His hand tightened. "You want to come away with me now."

"I want a bathe." I walked away from him, ignored the way my shoulder tingled, and collected Rina.

We'd been enemies ever since that first meeting, and nothing would ever change that. But while Dredmore could be vastly annoying, he'd never been able to do anything to harm me or my business.

The memory faded to a shadow as a shape hovered over me, large and dark and at first indistinct. I made out a black cloak, and under the cloak, a man—the man from the alley, the one who had saved my life, I realized. His eyes glowed like two stars in an empty midnight, cool and distant, but his hands felt warm and soothing on my face.

"Did they touch you?" a deep, utterly furious voice demanded.

"Of course they touched me," I whispered against his palm. "They squashed me. They cut me."

"Did they violate you?" the voice insisted.

"No, of course not." I frowned. "They only tried to kill

me. With 'magic' balls, if you can believe it. The dolts."

My body floated off the cushions onto something harder and less cozy. This fantasy was becoming damnably uncomfortable.

"You live because magic cannot harm you," he murmured. "I can reach you only through your dreams." His arm supported my shoulders and my knees. I felt his groin against my hip, and his thighs beneath my buttocks. He traced the edges of my bandage and pressed my cheek against his chest, which filled me with a sense of drowsy well-being.

"That's nice." I snuggled. "Stay with me . . ."

His soft voice chilled. "What have you taken, Charmian?"

"Nothing. I drank some tea. It was awfully sweet. Like the old lady who brought it." I breathed in the scent of burnt herbs and the sea and found the rest of my voice. "Do put me down, Dredmore."

"You've been drugged."

That made more sense of what was happening to me. "By you." I batted him with a useless hand.

"Not by me." He caught my fingers and brought them to his lips. "I don't have to employ drugs. If I'd wanted you, I'd have carried you out of that alley. Now, where are you?"

"I'm here with you, idiot." I wanted to scratch his eyes out, but I couldn't feel my fingernails. "Why can't you leave me alone?"

"I have asked myself the same question each day for five years," he assured me. "The problem is, I don't wish to know the answer."

"Oh." Somehow that made me feel a little better, and I relaxed against him. "Thank you for saving my life."

"You're welcome."

"But you're a very bad man. You do know that."

"Charmian." Lips touched the end of my nose. "You have no idea."

"You're not to kiss me when I'm drugged and help-less." I glared at him. "I don't want your kisses. I don't want you. I don't even like you."

"You don't have to like it, my sweet," he said, and this time kissed my mouth. "You have only to stop fighting me. Allow me to release you."

I frowned. "I'm not under arrest. I'm drugged. I'm dreaming. Why haven't you put me down?"

"This." He wrapped a hand around my neck. "This is the dream, the drug. The prison you've lived in your entire life. It's time you rid yourself of it." His starlit eyes glittered down at me. "I will free you, my gel, very soon, and then you will be mine."

His fingers bit into my neck, so tight that I couldn't speak or breathe. I latched on to his wrist and pulled, but I had no strength. Then a blue light blinded me, and he swore and hurled me away.

I woke up as I hit hard wood face-first. I yelped and then pushed myself up onto my elbows. I was on the floor beside Doyle's couch. My head wobbled as I looked around me, but the office was empty.

"Bloody hell." My belly heaved, and I crawled over to a rubbish can just in time.

"Steady, Kit." Rina knelt beside me and supported

my head with kid-gloved hands. "Go on, I've got you."

The heaves continued until I couldn't bring anything else up, and then a little longer as my belly refused to be convinced it was empty.

Once the final spasm passed, Rina wiped my mouth with one corner of her black fichu. "There now, that's better." She helped me up and held me steady. "Where's the bloody lav?"

"Through there," I heard Doyle say.

I let Rina tend to me, rinsing out my mouth with the water she held to my lips and blowing into the handkerchief she placed over my nose.

"Let's have a look now." She tipped my head back and peered into my eyes, and swore softly. "Bugger me, you've been dosed."

I saw Doyle in the doorway at the same time I became aware of my painfully heavy bladder. "Loo."

Rina turned to the inspector. "Out." She pushed the door closed after him and helped me with my skirts.

I hissed as my bare bottom touched the cold porcelain. "What are you doing here?"

"I went round your place this morning, saw the copper wardlings, and came here," she said. "Who rolled you?"

"Two snuffmages waiting outside Bridget's." I finished and put my clothes to rights. "Why did you go to the flat? You know I'm never there after seven."

"No, you were here, and all night, too." She grabbed my chin and looked into my eyes again. "The swine in charge said when they couldn't rouse you, they brought in a physick. Sweet Mary, look at your eyes."

All I remembered was the dream of being strangled by Dredmore. "A little nap never hurt anyone."

"A little?" Her brows rose. "Love, you've been out cold for the last eighteen hours."

Rina ushered me back into the office, where Doyle was waiting for us. "I'm taking her."

"Not yet." He took out a notebook. "I need some answers from her."

"I really like him," I confided to Rina. "Too bad he's the law."

"Shut up, Kit." To Doyle, Rina said, "Has she been charged with an offense? No? You lot too busy dosing her with ruddy joy, then?"

"Tommy?" I tried to wave a hand and nearly smacked myself in the eye. "He wouldn't do that. He likes me too much."

"Shut up, Kit." Doyle snapped his notebook closed and regarded Rina. "I did nothing of the sort to her. What kind of man do you think I am?"

"Like all the others in the world. Stupid. Did you really think it would make her talk?" She tightened her arm around me. "The poor gel's never had it, you dolt. Much as you dosed her, I'm surprised she woke up at all."

"We don't drug suspects," Doyle said between clenched teeth. "She ran afoul of some snuffmages; maybe they added more than killing powder to bespell her."

"Bespelled my ass." Rina thrust me toward him. "Look at her eyes. You know what poppy dust does to the whites. Go on, look. Red as roses, they are." She brought a fold of my skirt up to her nose and sniffed it. "Nothing but charcoal."

Doyle looked and muttered words unbecoming an officer of the Yard. "Someone must have slipped it to her another way."

"In here?" Rina made a rude sound. "How?"

"In my tea," I offered dully. "Tasted funny."

"The guild master." The inspector swore softly.

"Sodding bastards tried to get at her again, right under your noses. Come on, love, we're leaving." Rina steered me toward the door.

He stepped in front of it. "You'll need protection."

"Wreck," Rina called out.

The door opened inward, hitting Doyle in the back and shoving him aside. He spun around, fist curled, and then took a step back.

Wrecker stepped in and turned toward the inspector, his face bland. "Take care of this one, milady?"

"Not just yet, Wreck." To Doyle, Rina said, "Here's my protection." She patted the broad wall of Wrecker's chest. "Got anything bigger than this, cop?" When Doyle remained silent, she said, "Didn't think so."

My throat burned and I thought my head might tumble off my shoulders a few times on the way out of the station, but by the time Rina and Wrecker helped me into the carri and we were on our way, my thoughts cleared.

"Don't take me home," I told my friend. "I need to go in to work."

"With you nattering on and your eyes like that?" Rina hooted. "They'll toss your ass out in the street and cancel your office lease. No, love, we're going to the Lily."

"I don't have time for a bath."

"That's tragic." Rina sniffed. "So is the way you smell."

I didn't have the strength to bicker, so I leaned back against the neck rest and closed my eyes.

If the guild master had drugged my tea, it may have been to render me helpless against a second attack—and he would have needed at least one man on the inside. I knew Doyle couldn't have been involved; he wouldn't have saved my life to attack me in a police station. If for any reason Dredmore wanted me dead, he could have stood by in the alley and watched the snuffmage cut my throat. I was less sure of Mary Harris, but I couldn't imagine why a nice old lady who believed she protected people with her idiot spells would get mixed up with hired killers.

Drugging me helpless was too similar to what had been done to Diana Walsh. It stank of the same combination of cunning and cowardice.

As the last of the joy's effects faded, I began to feel wretched. I wanted to go home and barricade myself in my flat. But even there I wouldn't be safe, not from someone who could doctor my tea in a police station, or assault me in my sleep.

Dredmore.

Physicks believed that dreams were the mind's suppressed desires and fears. Across the pond, there were new types of phsyicks who even studied dreams in hopes of connecting them to body ailments. I'd never thought much about it—I hardly ever remembered my dreams— but Lucien Dredmore kissing and then trying to choke me to death in my mind could be nothing more than a garden-variety nightmare.

Besides, why would he try to kill me in my dreams when he'd saved me in the alley?

When we reached the Lily, I was able to climb down out of the carri without assistance. Rina still took my arm as if she was afraid I'd run away.

"Two for the works," she told the gel at the desk inside, who gave me a single scandalized glance before accepting Rina's payment.

"Will you be having a massage today, madam?" the desklass asked.

"No, and we don't need maids; we'll see to ourselves." Rina took the key the gel handed her and glanced back at Wrecker. "Go back to the house and ask Almira to give you a complete change for Miss Kit. Tell her something light and warm."

"Right away, milady." Wrecker touched his cap and took off.

"You can't throw away my skirts," I told Rina as she walked me back to the private bathing room. "I need them."

"As what? Cleaning rags? 'Sall they're good for now." She unlocked the door and gave me a little push. "Come on, the stink of you is about to make me puke."

"I need the skirts"—I paused as Rina pulled my bodice out of my waister and over my head—"to test the powder on them from the snuffmages' balls"—I turned so she could unknot the mangle of my fasteners—"and see if it contains poppy dust."

"I've already checked it; it's charcoal, nothing more." She pulled out a fold on my skirt and bent over to examine the stain. "No one would toss this much red joy at you, Kit. It'd cost the earth. The coppers were the ones that dosed you."

"They've no motive," I reminded her as I tried to unlace the front of my chemise. My fingers felt thick and I fumbled until she pushed my hands aside. "Doyle thinks I'm in on some extortion scheme. You don't try to kill someone you think is nicking coin from the tonners."

"In case you've forgotten, my gel, Doyle works for the Hill," she snapped. "If they told him to dress you like a performing ape, put you on a leash, and take you for a walk, he'd be trotting you round Central Square right now."

"No." I set my jaw. "Not Tommy. He's not like that."

"For bleeding Christ's sake, Kit, he's little more than a nobber in fancy dress. Get over him." She helped me out of my drawers and pointed to the slats. "Use the hot," she said as she began undressing, "or you'll never work that dried muck out of your hair."

I stood naked on the spaced slats and reached up for the red shower pull. The water that gushed over me was almost too hot to bear, but I stood under the wide stream and let it soak me thoroughly. Once my hair was plastered to my skull, I reached for a handful of scented soap mash and began working it into my snarled, filthy locks.

Rina came over with a handled sponge but set it aside to peek under the bandage on my arm. "Shit. That sod have the decency to clean this?"

I felt like yanking on the blue pull. "He's not a sod, and yes, he did, quite nicely."

"Nicely my ass." She dipped the end of the sponge

into the bowl on the soap stand, coating it well before going to work on my back. "No such thing as a *nice* copper."

"You've met all of them at Rumsen Main, I suppose." I picked up another handle and went to work on my front.

Once I was properly soaped up, I tugged on the purple pull and lifted my face into the warm stream. I might have stood there for a year, it felt so good, but once I'd washed all the soap away, I released the pull and wiped my hands up my face and over my head.

"Get in and soak," Rina told me before she went to another slat stand to wash herself.

I climbed down the short steps into the pool, letting my cooled skin grow accustomed to the heat before I slipped down and let the water close over my head briefly. Once I'd soaked enough, I straightened and went to sit on one of the submerged benches, where Rina joined me.

"You'll come stay with me until they nail the bastards after you," she decided as she reclined back against the tile rest. "You can have poor Liv's rooms."

"Can't," I told her. "I have to go back to Walsh's on Friday for dinner."

"What? Dinner at Walsh's?" She sat up and stared at me. "You fancy a trip to the loonhouse? I can save us all a lot of grief and have Wrecker take you there directly."

"They wouldn't have me." I splashed her a little. "I promised the lady I'd save her marriage. She's in a bad way, Rina, and some of it's my doing."

"Oh, and she's seen to it that you're covered in diamonds, has she?" she demanded. "Kit, someone just tried to kill you. Twice. If you're lucky and lay low, maybe they won't try a third time and succeed."

"I'll be careful." I turned to her. "You can help me."

She smacked the side of my head. "There. Did that help?"

"No." I rubbed the sore spot. "You know enough dusters to find out if someone's been buying red."

"Someone like?"

Mentioning the dream would only get me smacked again. "I think it could have been Dredmore."

"Lucien Dredmore's mixed up in this?" She groaned as she fell back. "Of course he is. I suppose you accidentally ran afoul of him. How many times does this make it? Forty? Fifty?"

"He nabbed me on the Hill after I had tea at Walsh's," I admitted. "He warned me off them."

"Lovely." She made a contemptuous sound. "I'll send him some posies to express my gratitude."

"Dredmore knows something about Nolan Walsh and his financial business," I said thoughtfully. "And he never dirties his hands with paltry scams. Has to be something much bigger to tempt him."

"That black-eyed beast wants only one thing," Rina snapped. "You. And he'll tell you whatever he likes if it means having you."

I sank down. "I won't let him."

"He's never made a real effort, you daft twit." Rina turned on me. "Come on, Kit. You know the man's got more funds than three governors. His servants are nothing more than a gang of kneecappers and necktwisters.

If he decides to pluck you off the street like a bun from a corner cart and take you to that tomb of his on the cliffs, who's to stop him? Who's to care?"

"Bridget. Docket." I gave her a hopeful look. "You."

"Oh, yes. A loomgel, a nutty mech, and a pissed strumpet." She rolled her eyes. "Why am I worried? You're safe as houses."

"The honorable wife of Lord Duluc, the cleverest of disgraced mechs, and Queen of the Night," I corrected her softly. "My dearest mates in all the world, who would never let Dredmore take me from them."

"I love you like my own sister, you know." Rina took hold of my hair and used it to wriggle my head. "I'd march down to the garden gates of hell for you, if that's what it takes. But, Kit, it's Dredmore after you now. Even the devil himself would have enough sense to step out of the way."

"He won't have me," I insisted. "Nothing bad is going to happen. I promise."

"I'll know for certain." Rina climbed out of the pool and went to ring the bell. When one of the bathhouse maids appeared, she said, "Send for my man."

"Why are we leaving?" I asked when she returned. "We just got here."

"Out with you." She tossed a towel at me. "We're going to see the Eye."

I slogged up the steps. "Whose eye?"

"Besides yours, the only honest one in the city," she said, her expression grim. "We're going to see my teller."

Chapter Ten

I argued with Rina from the bathhouse to the front steps of a quiet, sober-looking redstone in the heart of the bookmakers' district.

"How long have you been letting this charlatan take your coin?" I said as she rang the bell. "And why didn't you ever tell me you were buying portents?"

"I don't pay the Eye in coin. We have an evening together now and then to settle our accounts." She turned as a houseman answered the bell. "Madam Eagle and a friend to see the master."

We were shown into a dark hall lit only by candles and made to wait there as the houseman went to the back of the house. I noted the marks marching along the wainscot railing. They weren't runes, but something like them. "For pity's sake, Rina. I thought you were smarter than this."

"The Eye is very dear to me," she said, wagging a finger under my nose. "If you care to remain in *my* good graces, then you'll hold your tongue and let him do his work."

"Work." I felt like spitting. "Swindling you out of sex for nothing."

"Do shut up, love." Rina smiled as a small man in an oddly cut white robe emerged. The lack of light made it impossible to make out his features. "Master Harvison."

"Madam Eagle." He bowed low before turning to me. "Madam's friend." He did not bow to me but glanced at Rina. "She is not a believer."

"Neither was I when I first came to you, Harvi." Rina put a hand on my shoulder. "But my dear friend is in desperate need of your wisdom." When I opened my mouth to disagree, she stomped on my foot. "I would consider it a personal favor if you would see for her."

"Please," Harvison said, gesturing down the hall. "Join me for tea."

We followed him into a shabby but comfortable little den. I'd never seen such furnishings, all made of gleaming lacquered woods and delicate little cushions. A table that sat too low to the ground had a brazier set in its center and a tray with tiny cups. A bowl of dark herbs and some twisted brown roots waited to be used, probably to poison someone.

He lived among the best bookmakers in the city, but I didn't see one book. There were plenty of scrolls, however, each tied with twines of various colors and stacked on end in big porcelain pots. Magic spells were usually written on much smaller rolls, but perhaps his handwriting required more paper for his nonsense.

"Please, be seated." Harvison went around the room lighting oil lamps, until they shed enough light for me to clearly see his face. One dark eye gleamed, sharp and bright, but where the other should have been was only a smooth stretch of skin.

I leaned toward Rina. "He's only got one eye," I whispered.

"No, young miss. I have two," Harvison answered for her. "The other lies beneath the flesh you see. So it has been since I first drew breath."

I watched him fill two cups with his brew, but when he reached for a third I spoke up. "None for me, thank you. I'm a little off tea right now."

"You're insulting my friend," Rina hissed.

"She is being only cautious," Harvison said. "Something experience teaches us, but fear strips away." He gave me his full attention. "You have been crossed by magic many times."

"Not so I've noticed," I told him. I made out the peculiar shape of his eye, but it wasn't the droop I was accustomed to seeing. "Where are you from, teller?"

He bowed again. "Here. My father bought my mother from Hokkaidō before the Imperial Family instituted the blockade."

Now the odd-looking runes in his hall made sense. "You're half Nihon."

"And half Torian," Rina put in.

I'd deal with her later. "Every Nihon, pureblood or not, was deported after the blockade. The Crown has denied them residency ever since. So how did you manage to stay in Rumsen, Mr. Harvison?"

"My mother was property, not wife," he said simply. "My father claimed me as the same, until he discovered he could sire no children with his wife."

Keeping slaves had been banned before my birth. "Did he have you declared his heir?" When he nodded, I relaxed a little. "So you're a freedman."

"I have never been anything else." He gestured to the

cushion on the floor opposite his own. "Now I will see for you, madam's friend."

I thought of the teller who had tried to chase me out of her shop, and climbed down awkwardly to sit on the cushion. "What do you want? Hair? Fingernails? Spit? Blood?"

"Your hands, please." He stretched out his own, palms up.

I'd never touched a slave, declared or not, and Nihon universally despised Torians. I might not get my hands back.

I will free you, my gel, very soon, Dredmore said behind my eyes, *and then you will be mine.*

I clapped my hands over Harvison's. The moment I touched him, he went stiff and still. I watched his face, but I didn't see him twitch or take a breath.

Slowly he withdrew his hands. "I am blinded."

"I didn't touch his good eye," I assured Rina. "I swear."

"What I mean to say is that I cannot see for you, young miss," Harvison said faintly. "You are like the ward, and the warded." He stared at my neck. "You wear a talisman."

"A necklace, with a pendant," I corrected. "Most women wear them."

"May I see it?"

My first impulse was to say no, but then I thought of what Harry had said about my pendant. "All right." I reached back for the clasp.

Harvison remained silent for a long time as he studied my pendant. Only when Rina cleared her throat did he seem to remember we were in the room. "Forgive me, dear ladies. This is something of a puzzle." He regarded me. "This was given to you, was it not? When you were very young."

I nodded. "It was a gift from my mother."

"The stone is powerful. Or perhaps I should say, it contains power." He placed the pendant gently on the table, and I noticed his hand shook as he drew it back. "You must wear it at all times, or you will be in grave danger."

"Danger she's got aplenty. Lucien Dredmore's after her," Rina said tightly. "Can't you see how that right bastard will try to take her?"

"He cannot." Harvison gave me a sad smile. "If the *onmyouji* is to possess her, she must give herself freely."

"Right, then, that'll never happen." I stood. "Thank you for not pretending to see something. Rina, we should go."

My friend ignored me. "She's been cursed. Is that what you're saying?"

Harvison made a helpless gesture. "She is beyond me, dear one. I believe she is beyond all who see."

"Then see for me." Rina dropped down and put her hands in his. "See if I lose her to that conniving devil."

Harvison nodded toward me. "She must leave the room."

"Oh, *she* will be glad to." I stalked out, brushed past his houseman and through the front entry. I was more angry with myself than Rina for allowing her to involve me in this rubbish. She did it out of love; I knew better.

Wrecker eyed me from the carri. "Had enough of One Eye, then, Miss Kit?"

"That I have. Be a sport and turn your head." As soon as he did, I waved down a horse-drawn cab. "I'm going home. Rina will be furious, but tell her I said to tough it."

"Just be careful, miss," Wrecker suggested. "Her won't like knowing something bad's happened to you."

I nodded and let the driver help me into the cab. Once I was shut in, I wrapped my hand around my pendant, holding it so tight it cut into my palm. What Harvison had said about it containing power was nonsense, of course . . . but I kept remembering how his hand shook. Before I could think better of it, I reached back and thumbed the clasp, releasing it so I could pull the chain from my neck. I thrust the pendant into my reticule and dropped it on the bench beside me.

Harry White appeared on the rear-facing seat. "Took you long enough. What were you waiting for, lass? Her Majesty's Diamond Jube?"

I curled my hands into fists. "My mother wore only two pieces of jewelry when she was alive," I told him. "One was her wedding ring. What was the other?"

"A gold chain round her left ankle," he replied at once. "On the chain hung a silver ring set with seven stones in the shape of a star. Three rubies, three sapphires, and a black diamond."

No one knew about my mother's anklet but my father and me. "You gave it to her."

"Technically, no. When she came to the morgue to identify me, she took the ring from my body." He showed me his left hand, and the pale circle left around the base of his fourth finger. "Your father had the ankle chain made."

"So she could hide it under her skirts," I guessed.

He nodded. "Anyone who saw it would have treated her very badly."

"Because you were a spy."

"No, my dear," he said. "Because the star was my mark. Because I was Houdini."

I stared at the specter. "*You're* Houdini."

"I was."

"Harry Houdini the escape artist," I said. "The man no manacle, lock, or prison could hold. The greatest mage who ever lived. The supreme master of all the arts, shadow and light."

He inclined his head.

I thumped the carri's side panel three times with my fist and called out, "Stopping here."

The cab came to a halt, and the driver jumped down and opened the door. "Can't stop here, miss. 'Tis yet near a mile."

I reached for my reticule. "I'm tired of riding with a lying jackass."

"What did you call me?" the driver demanded.

"Not you," I said, gesturing at Harry. "Him."

"Perhaps I should have mentioned before," my grandfather put in, "that no one but you can see or hear me."

"What?" I turned on him. "So now you're only haunting *me*?"

"Something like that," he agreed.

I regarded the driver. "You see the man sitting in the seat across from me, don't you?"

He ducked his head in. "I don't see no man, miss."

"He's right there. Right in front of your nose."

The driver pushed his cap back to scratch his pate. "I don't drive them what been bespelled, miss. Naught but trouble they are."

"Apologize and tell him to drive on before he shouts for a beater," Harry suggested.

"I'm so very sorry," I said to the driver. "I had a bit of a bump earlier, and now I'm seeing things that aren't there." I rested my head against the cushions. "If you would be so kind as to drive on, I'd be eternally grateful."

"As you will, miss." He shut the door and scrambled up top.

"You're a terrible liar," Harry said. "You get that from your grandmother, you know."

I closed my eyes. "According to the documents I found in the city's protected archives, I have no grand-mother."

"On the contrary, you're named after my Charmian." He crossed over and sat beside me. "How did you get into the archives?"

"I turned into a specter and walked right past the guards; got that one from you." I looked at him. This close he seemed as solid and real as a living, breathing man. "Why are you haunting me, Harry?"

"I'm your guardian." He waited until I stopped laugh-ing before he added, "Well, I would have been if your father hadn't meddled in things he didn't understand. Nevertheless, I am most definitely not your enemy."

"What do you want from me?"

"It's the other way round, dear gel. You have only to call on me, and I will rush to your side." He pulled down the window shade. "Unless it's daylight outside, or course."

I didn't understand his aversion to sunlight. "But if you can't go outside during the day, then where do you go?"

He gave me an inscrutable smile. "Beyond this realm."

"So you spend all your days in the netherside, is that it?" I should have known he'd lie to me. "Do you perform there as the Great Houdini for all the other spirits, or do you just lie about doing nothing?"

"I don't care for where I go." He sniffed. "I would stay here if I could."

"That's it, then." I picked up my reticule. "I've had more than enough nonsense for one night, Harry."

"My birth name was Ehrich Weiss," he said quickly, "and I was not an agent for the Crown."

I loosened the ribbons and reached inside. "Your papers say differently." As soon as my fingers touched my pendant, Harry promptly vanished.

Perhaps this was what Harvison meant; perhaps my pendant contained the power to chase off bloody stupid men who annoyed me beyond all measure.

"I need a few more of you," I told the pendant, before I refastened its chain around my neck.

Once the driver reached my flat, he brought the cab to a stop, but he didn't climb down to help me out. He also drove off before I could pay him, and the last thing I heard before he turned the corner were the protective curses he was chanting.

∽

At noon on Friday I took a cab to the Silken Dream, where Bridget came to whisk me back to her private workroom and dress me herself.

"You look awful." Bridget, dressed in a lavender gown that should have clashed with her red hair and somehow didn't, looked marvelous. "Burning the candle in the middle as well as at both ends, are you?"

"Be nice to me," I said. "Last time I was here, someone tried to cut my throat in your alley."

"So the beaters told me." She encircled my waist with a measuring lace. "Two snuffmages, and you without a scratch. Why am I not surprised?"

"I'll have you know they gave me a very nasty cut." I held up my arm. "The chief inspector personally bandaged it."

"Rina said he did quite a bit more." She propped her hands on her hips. "Was the bandaging before or after he let someone try to poison you with joy?"

"He didn't know they'd try again at the Yard, or he would have stopped them. He's a friend." I wound my good arm through hers. "Just like you."

"I can't toss you in the gaol," she chided. "Much as I want to these days . . ."

Bridget not only dressed me in the heavenly blue gown intended for the empty-pursed Lady Richmond, she had Sarah brush out the rat's nest on my head and arranged it into a crown of shining, interlaced coils. I only protested when Bridget brought a jeweler's case into the dressing room.

"You can't bedeck me in baubles," I told her. "Walsh believes I'm poor."

"You *are* poor," Bridget said flatly. "But you're going to dine with one of the finest families on the Hill, so it will be assumed that you have enough connections to borrow something decent. Which you do. Now shut up." She took out a small waterfall of liquid silver strands and draped them around my neck. "These are spun quicksilver. Don't fuss with them or they'll tangle."

"I won't breathe." The slippery weight of the cool silver made me shiver, then I winced as she snapped two heavy clips on my earlobes. "I don't like earbaubs."

"One does not call perfectly matched snow pearls 'earbaubs,'" she corrected, coming around to inspect my face. "Yes, that will do. Now a wristlet."

Instead of more pearls or quicksilver she wound a snake made of small sapphires around my wrist. Its eyes had been fashioned from tiny clear globes, each containing an even tinier red glowworm.

I held my arm away. "This is too much. I'll only smash it."

"It's warded, and you'll wear it for me." She cupped my face between my hands. "Or I'll tell Charlie everything, and he'll have his men whisk you onto a yacht bound for Bali before you can sneeze."

"You wouldn't." Of course she would, and Charles would do anything to make her happy, even if it meant shipping my ass round the world ten times. "I can deal with the Walshes one more time."

"You'd better," she warned, "because after tonight, Rina won't let you go within a mile of the Hill." She kissed my cheek. "Nor will I."

Once Bridget had sprayed me with a little of the

outrageously dear French perfume she wore, she sent me off to the Hill in her own coach. I'd ridden in the crystal-sided coach once before, when she and Charlie had sent me home from their castle in it, but this time it felt different. Since real wealth was forever out of my reach, I'd never considered what it felt like to be treated like royalty on a regular basis. It was a bit like strolling about in a dream where nothing could touch or harm you.

My dream evaporated when I passed Dredmore's coach coming from Walsh's Folly. A terrible panic seized me at the thought of seeing him again, until I forced myself to breathe and relax. It had been a dream, nothing more, and he couldn't assault me in front of the family.

A footman in tails and gloves leapt off the back of the coach and helped me down. He glanced at the house and murmured something in French about waiting for me.

Delightful as the ride had been, it had to end, so I smiled at him. "I'll be fine, thank you."

This time the butler was waiting outside the door for me. He watched Bridget's coach depart and then gave me a somewhat creak-kneed, respectfully low bow.

"Mistress Kittredge, you are very welcome."

It had to hurt the old winge to say that, so I merely nodded and let him usher me along like the fine lady I wasn't.

The family had assembled this time in a larger reception room adjacent to the formal dining hall. The butler announced me at the door before discreetly withdrawing.

Lady Diana pounced on me, clamping her hands on mine. "It is so good of you to come," she said, her voice as tight as her eyes were reddened and puffy from weep-ing. She turned to the side and beamed at her husband. "Darling, you remember Miss Kittredge."

Nolan Sr. ignored me and glared at his wife. "I thought I'd made myself clear about visitors, Diana."

"I asked Miss Kittredge to dine with us before we had that conversation, my dear," she said. "She has been most helpful to me."

"As what?" Montrose said. "Your procurer of men?"

"Forgive my brother, Miss Kittredge." An older woman sitting beside Miranda rose. She had a narrow face and frizzled hair but kind eyes. "Stepmama?"

"Yes, ah, Miss Kittredge, this is Lady Laurana Walsh, my elder stepdaughter."

Laurana didn't curtsey but held out her hand, which I shook reflexively. "I'm the spinster who does good works," she explained. "When last you called I was working with the wretched foundlings at the school my mother founded in Scoursie. We try to teach them to read and write, even if it's simply their names. Keeps them from being claimed by farm overseers as runaway pickers."

Miranda uttered a squeak of dismay. "Laury, please."

"Lady Laurana's efforts on the behalf of the poor are highly admirable." A sixth figure emerged from the shadows by the fireplace. "Good evening, Charmian."

"Dredmore." I turned to Lady Diana so I wouldn't have to look at him for longer than a blink. "I hope you were able to rest undisturbed the last few nights," I said in a lower voice.

"I was, to some extent." She looked as if she wanted to say more, and then a footman stepped in from the dining hall and announced that dinner was served. "I hope you enjoy pheasant, Miss Kittredge." She went from me to Nolan, and when the Walsh siblings followed them into the other room, I was left alone with Dredmore.

"You look like a winter sylph," he said as he came to take my arm. As soon as he did, he bent down. "I told you to stay away from here."

"And yet, here I am," I replied, starting forward to follow the others.

He pulled me back round to face him, but he didn't look at me. He watched the dining hall and talked over my head. "Make an excuse during the meal to leave, and go."

I raised my brows. "Any suggestions?"

"A migraine. Your monthlies. A sudden eruption of boils on your ass," he grated. "I don't care, just get the hell out of here."

"Go suck a tube," I suggested gently before leading him in to dine.

CHAPTER ELEVEN

A dining table of glossy cherrywood parted the hall, ready to serve fifty comfortably, but fortunately the servants had set three facing three on either side of the master's chair, or we would have had to shout our remarks to each other.

Lady Diana sat at her husband's right, Laurana at his left, with Montrose and Miranda seated by their sister and me between Dredmore and Diana. The candlelit centerpiece, a small, frothy volcano of porcelain and gold flowers, cast a warm glow over the exquisitely set table.

As the footmen placed small urns with some sort of pinkish-gray shellfish on ice, I counted the utensils. Accustomed to three, I had to now manage twelve, and Lady Diana was politely waiting for me to start. I glanced at Dredmore, who was no help, and then Lord Walsh, who employed the smallest two-pronged fork to stab one of the shellfish. Leashing in a sigh of relief, I did the same and gingerly tasted what turned out to be half-cooked clams.

"Where do you reside, Miss Kittredge?" Laurana asked before she sampled her cocktail.

"I keep a flat on Estarlin," I said. "Near the fruit market, if you know it."

"I shop there several times a week," she said, grimacing as she set down her fork and gestured for the footman to take away the little urn. "They always have the best apples and nuts in Rumsen."

"My sister delights in playing the servant," Montrose drawled. "I fully expect to come round some day and find her scrubbing out the loos."

Miranda choked and buried her face in her napkin as she tried to control her blush as well as her coughing.

"Do you play kitchen maid, Cousin Kit?" Montrose continued. "I should dearly like to watch you turn a spit or two."

"My cooking is dreadful, sir," I admitted freely. "You'd do better by bucket."

He laughed, too long and too loud, until his father snapped something low and harsh at him. Montrose didn't show an ounce of remorse. "She's got a quick tongue, Dad, why not let her employ it for our amusement?"

I felt something touch the top of my thigh and looked down as Dredmore spread his hand over it and dug his fingers in. I slipped a knife from the collection by my plate into my hand, taking care to let only him see it. Before I could stab him, however, he took his hand away.

To avoid eating the rest of the clams, I engaged Lady Diana in another meaningless discussion of the weather, turning now and then to include Dredmore in the conversation. The second course, a steaming shallow bowl of green turtle soup, proved slightly more edible, although I picked out the blanched fernheads floating on the top and pushed them out of sight on the plate under my bowl. Baby fernheads were said to be delicious, but if picked too late in the season they could be poisonous.

Dredmore reached for his wine and murmured to me, "They're too young to make you ill."

"I know," I muttered back. "I have you for that."

"You and Lord Dredmore are acquainted, I understand," Nolan said.

As soon as I realized he was speaking to me, I set down my spoon. "Yes, milord. We've met several times in the course of our business."

Miranda had gotten over her coughing attack, for I heard her ask, "Have you no family to look after your concerns, Miss Kittredge?"

"Di's family hasn't two coins to rub together," Montrose said, handing his empty wineglass to the footman and holding his hand aloft until it was refilled. "What of your mother's people, cousin? Isn't there some broad-backed farmer among them who would take you to bed?"

Following the family's example and ignoring the little skink grew harder by the moment. "My mother was an orphan," I answered Miranda. "She passed away while I was still in school."

The footmen presented the third course, a golden fillet of flounder trimmed and garnished to look as if it were ready to jump off the platter and wriggle its way back to the sea. No one else seemed especially impressed by the presentation but me. Nolan dissected his fillet with stiff displeasure; the Walsh sisters picked daintily at the delicate flesh with their forks, and Montrose simply drank. Lady Diana made a brave show of appetite but I never saw her actually eat more than a single sliver or quarter spoon of any dish served.

I'd seen too many forms of mold in the tunnels

under the city to have any desire for the fourth course, an assortment of mushrooms poached in sherry. The fifth course actually made me angry, as the men were served braised slices of tomatoes swimming in pinked cream, while the Walsh ladies and I were instead served creamed beets cut out to resemble tomatoes. I despised beets, but objecting would have been rude, so I just pushed them around with the right fork.

"Miss Kittredge seems unhappy with her lady's dish," Montrose observed aloud. "Doubtless the working class allow their females to consume vast quantities of lord-apples."

I tilted my head to look at him. "I'm sorry, I don't understand what you mean."

"It's believed that tomatoes invigorate the male humors," Laurana said, her expression as serene as her words were shocking. "They are never served to ladies in good society."

"Lest they drive you to uncontrollable lust, Miss Kittredge," Montrose tacked on sweetly.

That remark finally undid Miranda, whose fork clattered on the table. "Father, I'm not feeling at all well. May I be excused?" At his nod she slipped out of her chair and hurried out of the hall.

"My younger sister is a widow," Montrose told me. "She dislikes being reminded that she is no longer free to indulge in nightly congress. Ouch, damn you, Laury."

"You need to eat more and drink less, Monty." Laurana, who had rapped his hand with the handle of her fork, took his nearly empty goblet and handed it to her footman. "No more wine for you tonight."

Her brother scowled as he jerked to his feet. "To the devil with all of you." He stomped out of the hall.

Nolan said nothing but watched the footman clear Montrose's setting. I glanced down at my beets and saw my plate half-filled with tomatoes. I turned my head to see Dredmore calmly eating my beets.

"Clear for Miss Kittredge," Lady Diana, who must have seen the switch, said quickly to her footman.

The cook, a stout little man in immaculate chef's whites, brought in the sixth and main course, a fully dressed pheasant with feathers intact, perched on a lifelike branch made of bread. Glowing dark-red roses, sculpted from what appeared to be jellied cranberries, clustered around the bird, along with sprigs of dark chocolate twigs with candied violets. The bird's long brown-and-black-striped tail feathers rose at a steep angle and shifted along with the cook's movements, making it seem as if the pheasant were about to launch itself from the platter and take flight.

After receiving a nod from Nolan, the cook carried the bird to a side carving table and skillfully removed the feathered sham from the carcass before beginning to carve it to pieces.

The scent should have made my mouth water, for I dearly loved roasted fowl of any variety, but what was left of my appetite deserted me. Seeing the exotic bird dressed to appear as it had been in life made me feel like a murderer instead of a dinner guest. Fortunately I was served only a small slice, which I forced down and complimented as best I could.

I ate a few buttered peas from the seventh, mixed

vegetable course and drained my water glass to ease my tight throat while Diana told a long and relatively dull anecdote about the new fashion of wearing flounce-brimmed hats. Then the eighth course arrived, an aromatic potato-herb tartlet flavored by slivers of black truffle and topped with a layer of toasted bleu Cheshire.

The pheasant had likely been the most expensive dish I would ever eat in my life, but the tartlet was surely humble pie.

I'd only tasted bleu Cheshire once, when my father had spent an inordinate amount of coin to purchase a small wedge of it for my mother, whose secret vice was exotic cheese.

"I don't know whether to eat it," Mum had teased, "or have it encased in glass and carted over to the art museum."

In the end Mum had insisted we each have a bite of the precious stuff, and I'd fallen in love, probably because I'd known I'd never taste it again. Now and then when I had a few extra coins I'd buy a little half round of Danish blue, but it was nothing by comparison.

It would have been criminal to send it back to the kitchen untouched, I told myself as I began eating it. The first taste almost brought a moan from my throat, and sent tears to sting my eyes. I rested my hands against the table, mainly to keep from shoving the tartlet by the handfuls into my mouth.

Dredmore's fingers brushed over mine, sending a jolt of pleasure up my arm and into my chest. As he reached for his goblet, he murmured, "Don't weep."

"Drop dead," I whispered back, furious with him and myself for lowering my guard.

The final, cold courses were frozen puree of cress and maple-almond iced cream, both of which I ate in hopes of cooling off. Like the other ladies I abstained from drinking the coffee offered at the end of the meal and commented as favorably as I could on the cook's menu.

Nolan didn't excuse himself or Dredmore to his study for the gentlemen's after-dinner ritual of bourbon and cigars but stood and spoke to his remaining child. "You must be very tired, my dear."

"I'm fine, Father." Laurana gave him and Diana a sharp look. "However, I do have some letters to write. Miss Kittredge, I hope someday to bump shoulders with you at the fruit market. Dredmore, Stepmama." She nodded to the others before departing.

"We'll go to my study now," Nolan said, taking his wife's arm in a decidedly unaffectionate grip.

Dredmore had a hand on me before I could dodge him, and he used it to guide me out of the hall behind the Walshes. "You should have left when you could, Charmian. This will not be pleasant."

"I knew that the moment I saw you by the fire." I drew my arm from his, but he only put his hand at the small of my back. "Stop touching me."

"No." When I would have walked ahead, he hooked his fingers in my waister and tugged me back beside him. "Listen to me, you stubborn wench. Whatever accusations Walsh makes, say nothing. I will do the talking."

"The day I need you to speak for me," I said, "I'll cut out *your* tongue."

As soon as we were gathered in the study, Nolan closed the doors and went to stand with his back to the painting of an Elizabethan Walsh whose weak chin had been disguised by his black goatee and wide white ruff. Both Lord Walshes regarded me with expressions of haughty disgust, but the one who was still breathing had a decidedly ugly gleam in his eyes.

"Miss Kittredge, while I'm sure your behavior goes unnoticed among the commoners, I find your involvement in our private family matters entirely intolerable," Nolan announced. "Whatever promises of remuneration my wife has given you, I will not abide your interference for another moment."

My lack of breeding had nothing on his rudeness. "I came to speak on your lady wife's behalf, milord," I said stiffly. "That is the only reason I came."

"I have no interest in anything you might say to me," Nolan snapped before he regarded Dredmore. "Lucien, I will have the truth of the matter. Tonight."

Before my nemesis could employ his trickery to make matters worse, I said, "You will hear what I have to say, Lord Walsh. Your wife hired me to dispel a curse she believed had been put on her. I am the one who first discovered the panel under her bed, along with evidence that someone in this household has been assaulting her person. It is possible that both of you are being drugged each night as well."

Nolan whirled on his wife. "How much did you pay her to lie for you this time? Fifty pounds? A hundred?"

"I have been paid nothing," I told his back. "Your wife is the victim here, sir, not the transgressor."

"The victim." He strode over to me. "My wife is nothing but a lying, cheating whore who smuggles her lover into the house under my very nose."

"Why would she bring this imaginary lover to the house, when it would be far more prudent to meet him in town on one of her shopping excursions?" I pointed out. "She could have a dozen lovers in town, and you'd never know it."

Diana uttered a distressed sound.

"Wherever she conducts her affairs, my wife hasn't the wits to conceal them," Nolan assured me.

"I have seen the evidence with my own eyes, milord, and it is inarguable. Your wife is being tormented." I went to Diana and put my arm around her. "Someone in this house has been stealing into her bedchamber, painting terrible words on her body, and then removing them a day later. When she came to me, she truly believed the words were being cut into her skin."

Dredmore stepped between us. "That is enough, Charmian."

"Who in this household would do such nonsense?" Walsh bellowed over Dredmore's shoulder, his face mottling dark red. "No one, I say. No one but this whore, my wife."

"It will be someone who has theatrical or military experience," I said tightly. "Probably military, as it's a soldier's trick. The assailant wishes you to believe that your wife is greedy and promiscuous. Someone who wants to drive her out of her wits with terror and give you just cause to divorce her." As Diana sagged with my words, I led her over to an armchair. "I'd say it's working, wouldn't you?"

Dredmore stared at me. "What do you mean, soldier's trick?"

"They've been using wound paste on her," I told him. "When it dries it looks like the real thing, and if you try to remove it, it tears the skin, like a fresh scab."

"I'll not listen to another moment of this!" Nolan said, sweeping his arm toward the mage. "Do your work now, Dredmore."

"I can do nothing with Miss Kittredge present," Dredmore replied. "She must be removed from the house."

Diana suddenly revived and latched on to my arm. "You can't leave, Kit. Not before you make him understand what's been done to me. Please, I beg you."

"We've arrived at a stalemate, milords," I told the men. I pried Diana's fingers away and went to Lord Walsh. "Dredmore will not perform for you in front of me because he knows I will expose him for the fraud he is. Your lady wife desires me to stay and prove her innocence."

The red patches on Lord Walsh's face turned purple. "You *dare* challenge my authority, in my own house?"

"My only wish is to investigate the matter further, milord," I pushed on. "Allow me to speak with your servants; one of them has surely witnessed something to lead us to the—"

I didn't expect him to backhand me, but once I was on the floor, my face throbbing, I saw Walsh draw back his boot and suddenly understood Diana's bruises and why Dredmore had wanted me to go. I brought up my arms to protect my face and waited for the next blow, which never came.

"Allow me, my lord."

The kick never landed; instead two strong arms snatched me from the floor and carried me away. By the time I dropped my hands from my face, Dredmore had me through the front entry and halfway to his coach.

"No." I twisted and nearly freed myself before he shifted me up and over his shoulder. "I can't leave her like this. He'll kill her." I pounded my fists against his back. "Put me down."

"He won't risk beating her now, not when she can use her injuries against him in court. You, however, will not get off so lightly." Dredmore tossed me in the coach and slammed the door, securing it from the outside. When I tried to dart out the other door, I found it locked. The windows were too small for me to crawl through, so I sat and watched as Dredmore walked back to speak with Nolan Walsh, who had come out of the house after us.

Walsh blustered while Dredmore soothed, and while I couldn't hear what they said, it was obvious it was about me. Then Walsh did a curious thing; he gestured for the butler, who handed Dredmore a large satchel. Dredmore nodded before he returned to the coach and handed off the satchel to his driver before climbing in with me.

"My turn, is it?" I lunged at him only to be pinned against his body. I maneuvered my arms between us and pushed at his chest. "I can still scream."

"I can still have you gagged." He ducked my fist and jerked me closer to pin my arms between us. "And bound, if you like."

Being an inch from his face brought on all sorts of

ugly feelings and ideas, but he grabbed my hair and held me in place.

"If you wish to bite me, Charmian," he said softly, "there are far better spots than my face."

"So you like it rough." I changed tactics and moved a breath closer. "How will it be, Lucien? You tied naked between the posts, me in leathers, snapping a little whip? Is that what it takes to brick your chimney?"

Instead of being offended, the cold bastard smiled at me. "You've been spending too much time among strumpets, my sweet." He wrenched me around so that my back was pressed to his front. "Sit still, or I will show you *exactly* what I like."

I sat still. Not because he ordered me to, but to give myself time to think. From what I saw through the coach window, it was obvious that he was taking me out of the city. We left behind the dark streets and alleyways, rode through the pasturelands, and started up the cliff roads. Since Dredmore owned most of the coastal property beyond Rumsen, that meant our destination was his lair.

Castle Travallian, or so it had been before Dredmore had been disowned.

I'd seen it once when I'd gone atop one of the taller buildings downtown and looked over toward the sea. From there the manor had looked like little more than a pile of rubble. It came into view as the coach left the road and started up a long, winding path between two rows of black iron gaslamp poles. The cessation of jolting made me look down at the smooth pavers of obsidian rock, cut and fitted together so perfectly, I barely made out the seams.

"I had the stone shipped in from the islands," he said. "The masons called it the road to hell."

Was it to be mine? "I suppose Torian granite wasn't dark or dramatic enough for you."

"The islanders worship a fire god who they believe dwells in their volcano," he said instead of answering. "Every year before planting season they take a young virgin up to the edge of the crater and toss her in. Her sacrifice pleases the god, who then provides a bountiful harvest."

"For burning a gel to death." I tried to sit up. "How delightful. How do they celebrate the harvest? By setting little babies on fire?"

"They feast on the fruits of their labors." He tugged me back, tucking my head against his neck. "It's not as grim as it sounds. According to legend, courageous virgins are given eternal life as the god's handmaidens."

"There's a bloody fabulous reward for you." I felt him touching my hair and snapped my head away. "Trapped to serve forever the bastard who killed them. Where do I sign up for the next sacrifice?"

"Perhaps they love their god so much that they don't mind," he suggested.

"I wish you'd . . . stop . . ." My voice died and my neck cricked as the coach came to a stop.

The cliffside manor was not a heap of rubble but a magnificent edifice that seemed to be growing out of the very ground. This effect came from the cliff stones, which had originally been an enormous pile of black and white granite boulders hewn and squared at the topmost peaks to form the great house's foundation. Other, identical stones had been quarried and brought to build atop them, creating a manor that soared some five stories above the cliff's edge.

Dredmore's driver opened the door, blocking it when I tried to scramble out.

"I have her, Connell."

Somehow Dredmore managed to hoist me under his arm as he maneuvered me out of the coach, and he carried me like that across the drive.

"I'm not a sack of turnips. Put me down." I struggled to get my head up to see where he was taking me. *"Dredmore."*

He flipped me over so that he held me like a new husband about to cross the threshold with his bride. "Welcome to Morehaven, Charmian."

Chapter Twelve

Dredmore carried me into his lair as if it were my new home, and for a moment I wondered if it would be. As solitary and standoffish as Dredmore was, he wouldn't have brought me here for a nightcap or a friendly chat. No, I had the feeling I was headed straight for some underground torture chamber or filthy cage.

Dredmore had no enemies, it was said, because he disposed of them before they could become known as such. As a licensed deathmage, he had the Crown's blessing to kill whomever he deemed needed to die, but I'd always thought the threat a better deterrent. Why would anyone cross a man who could legally murder you?

Other than me, naturally.

"What are you doing?" I asked as he carried me over to a dimly lit staircase and began ascending. "The dungeon is downstairs."

"I have no dungeon." He turned and went up another flight before stepping into a hall. "I have guest rooms."

I tried not to gawk at the magnificent paintings we passed, but the place was like a bloody national museum. "You are obliged to kidnap people in order to have gues— My God, is that an original Raphael?"

"I do what I must, and yes, it is."

I glanced over the railing to see Connell carrying

the satchel into one of the rooms downstairs. "What did Walsh put in the bag? Some leftover pheasant? Can I have some? I'm feeling peckish."

"Of course you are." He stopped in front of a door, and a valet opened it from the inside.

"Help me," I told the manservant in my best terrified, helpless tone. "I've been brought here against my will."

"That will be all for tonight, Winslow," Dredmore said as he carried me into the chamber.

"Yes, milord." The valet bowed and left.

I listened for the latch of the lock but heard nothing.

"He doesn't seem too worried about me," I said as Dredmore halted in front of a roaring fire. "Have you trained your servants to ignore your captives? How do you go about that, by making threats on their lives, or dropping a few more coins in their monthly wage packets?"

Dredmore held on to me. "I'm going to put you down now, Charmian, so that we may talk. Don't run."

I sighed. "Really, Lucien, you must stop reading so many romantic novels. I'm very happy that you abducted me. I've wanted to see the inside of this place for ages. You should really allow the tour companies to put you on their rounds. They'd pay you heaps to let a few nosy old ladies shuffle through here every week."

"Morehaven is not a curiosity shop." He lowered one arm and set me down on my feet. "Don't run."

I held on to him until I found my balance, and smiled up at him. "Why would I run from you?"

"You hate me," he said. "You want me dead. If I walked in front of your carri, you'd run me down in the street."

"Is that what you think?"

"It's what you've said you'd do," he reminded me, "along with shoving a spell scroll down my throat, using a rusted blade to relieve me of my manhood, setting my coach alight with me locked in it, and oh, yes, my personal favorite, hiring a thug to toss me over my own cliffs."

"Lucien, Lucien." I kept beaming as I stroked my hand up his arm and curled it around his neck. "Have you no understanding of women?"

"Evidently not."

"Let me show you exactly what I've always dreamed of doing to you." I pulled his head down toward mine, and as soon as his eyelids drooped and his mouth parted, I clutched his neck and rammed my knee into his groin.

Dredmore shifted to deflect my blow with his hip, which I had expected, and tried to shove me to the floor, which I had not. I curled over under his weight, spun on my heel, and got out from under it at the last possible moment. He landed on the floor; I ran.

Connell, who was standing guard at the end of the hall, ran toward me and tried to seize me, but I dropped to my knees and slid between his legs, leaping up on the other side to hurl myself at the banister. I hoisted up my skirts, put a leg over, and took a long, perilous slide down to the next landing, where I jumped off and took the steps to the first floor two at a time.

I saw the front entry and knew I was going to make it. I was going to best Lucien Dredmore, and I was never going to let him forget it, either.

A figure stepped out of the shadows to block my path to the door, and I gaped at Dredmore's face.

I whipped my head back to glance at the stairs. He hadn't followed me down; I was sure of it. "How did you do that?"

He smiled a little. "Guess."

The only thing that could have gotten him downstairs so instantly was magic. What if he could do all that they said he could? Cast spells, exorcise spirits . . . kill with a touch . . .

I whirled, hauled up my skirts, and ran in the opposite direction. I didn't hear Dredmore shout or footsteps behind me and looked frantically for the chute or tube he had used to get to the first floor ahead of me. I found nothing, not even a bucket-waiter. All the windows and doors I stopped at to try wouldn't open.

I made it to the kitchen and hurried toward the first weapon I saw, a thin-bladed boning knife left sitting on a cutting block. Did I want to stab Dredmore in the heart? Many times. But could I actually do that? As I reached for the blade, my hand trembled, and I stared at it, suddenly and completely terrified out of my wits.

Not yet, something whispered inside my head. *Hang on.*

"Are you finished?" Dredmore asked me from where he stood, just inside the kitchen. "Or would you like to scamper around the house a bit more?"

I drew my hand back from the knife, and glanced at a cook's stool sitting by the banked hearth. Every door in the kitchen was locked, but the one leading out to the garden had a long panel of glass in the center.

I grabbed the blade, turned, and threw it at a spot

on the wall beside Dredmore, who instinctively ducked. That gave me enough time to get to the stool, pick it up, and hurl it through the doorglass.

Jagged shards tore at my arms and hips as I stepped through the opening and out onto a pavilion. I shook bits of glass from my sleeves as I hurried down the steps, looking this way and that for a path leading away from the manor.

"Charmian." Dredmore sounded angry now.

No path appeared, but a formal garden formed neat beds of flowers around a dark spiral maze of rose hedges almost twice my height. I trampled innumerable posies, violets, and zinnias as I rushed into the maze.

There were no helpful gaslamps and no way to navigate through the fragrant darkness; the only way I knew I'd taken a wrong turn was when I ran into a thorny wall of canes, too densely packed to let me squeeze through them. I stopped to catch my breath, think, and listen.

"Stay where you are," I heard Dredmore say from some point in the maze to my right.

"Eat dirt," I called back.

"You're wounded," he said. "I can smell your blood."

"Leeches always can." I went left and nearly knocked over a pedestal bearing a marble bust of, who else, Lucien Dredmore.

The cold stone chilled my hands as I tried to lift and toss it, but it was too heavy to move. I settled for picking up a handful of the ornamental pebbles surrounding the base of the pedestal. They weren't large enough to inflict any serious damage, but with a good hard throw one might blacken his eye or knock out a tooth.

I couldn't see the tops of the rose hedges, so I had no idea if I was heading in the right direction. The tonners loved hedge mazes, as did Rina, who always regretted that living in the city had prevented her from planting one.

"Not one of those dull old branching mazes, either," she'd told me once. "I like these new island mazes. There are so many wrong turns and corner traps that you can send someone into them and not see them again for days."

Travallian Castle had been built by one of Lucien's ancestors at the turn of the last century; it would be safe to assume the maze was branching. That meant that there was only one path to the center, and one path out.

I emptied my reticule on the ground and used it to wrap my hand, then followed the hedge by touch to the next gap, which I ducked in. I kept my hand on the hedge as I followed it to the next dead end, and then around until I found another gap. The rose thorns snagged and tore at the fabric, but I kept going until the hedge became smooth black stone.

I stepped into the center of the maze and saw a gazebo by a small pool of water. The reflecting pool was being fed from a black-and-white stone fountain. As hot and tired as I was, I didn't go near the water but circled around it, looking for a place to hide. I had to go round four full-size marble statues of Lucien Dredmore. I stopped by the fifth to unwrap my scratched, painful hand.

The statue reached out and clamped its stone hand over my wrist, making me scream.

"Release," Dredmore said from the gap in the black stone wall, and the statue's fingers uncurled.

"Sweet Mary." I backed away from the thing and heard gears turning as the arm lowered. "What is that thing? A mechanized statue?"

"The property is protected by movement-triggered sentinels." He started toward me. "They're too heavy to knock over, invulnerable to injury, and utterly impossible to escape. Quite efficient in detaining uninvited, unsuspecting guests."

I backed away. "Well, then, since I wasn't invited, I should go." I darted to the gap opposite the one I'd used to find the center, only to come up against another of the mechanized statues standing in it. I dodged its stone hands and ran smack into Dredmore.

"Hello again." I offered a smile. "Lovely maze. What's the forfeit?"

"Come here." He dragged me over to the pool, holding my hand under the gaslight to examine it. "What were you thinking?"

"I've been thinking . . . run away, escape, call the authorities, have you arrested and charged with assault, see you imprisoned for several decades." I yanked my arm, but he wouldn't let go of me. "You know. The usual things."

He forced me to kneel down on the pool's narrow ledge and immersed my wounded hand in the icy water.

I yelped. "Damn you, Lucien, it's freezing."

"It will stop the bleeding." He tore his cravat from his throat and used it to blot my palm, examining it again before wrapping the neckcloth around it. "Walsh might have beaten you to death tonight."

I pretended interest. "For standing up for his wife? Does that generally merit a death sentence?"

"This has nothing to do with Lady Diana." Dredmore tied off the cravat. "Walsh is involved in some sort of conspiracy against the Crown. He's been seen with Talians, and they've not come here for the fishing."

"Talians? Then why are they here?" I demanded. When he didn't reply, I yanked my hand away. "All right. Why would he want me dead if I know nothing about this business of his?"

"You do know something. You simply don't know what it means to Walsh and his plans, and neither do I." He gave me a long look. "But he does."

Kneeling there as we were, him tending to my wounds, me wanting to pummel him, and the two of us exchanging confidences, felt a bit too romantic for my tastes. "I would like to go home now. I keep early hours and if I don't get my rest, I'm an absolute hag in the morning."

He lifted his head. "Don't run from me again, Charmian."

I didn't like what I saw in his eyes. "Oh, is this when you confess your deep and abiding affection for helpless, wounded females, and declare that you would never, ever do anything to hurt one?"

"No."

"Pity." I balled up my good fist and punched him in the face.

My knuckles crunched against his chin, which was apparently made of iron, and then the world turned sideways, and cool, soft grass filled my face. Dredmore straddled me, using his weight to keep me pinned under him as he hauled my arms up over my head and kneed my skirts to keep me from kicking.

"What are you doing?"

"We have several matters to settle, my sweet." He bunched his fist in the back of my bodice and pulled it out of my waister. "At the moment, this is the most pressing."

"Don't." I kept my tone calm as I lifted my face out of the grass. "If you do, I swear, you'll regret it for the rest of your life."

He lifted, rolling me over before he yanked at the front of my bodice and pulled it up over my head. "That would be nothing new, Charmian."

Once he had exposed my chemise, I waited for the ravishment to begin. Society held that seeing a female in her undergarments stimulated a male beyond any hope of self-control, and a woman who disrobed in the presence of a man—voluntarily or not—had only herself to blame for the inevitable inflammation of his passions. So even if I got away from him later and went to the police, they would tell me only that it was all my fault.

Instead, Dredmore lifted me up in a curious position, my skirts bunched around my waist, my bare legs draped over his. He used his fist to bring my hands down between us, and then tore open his shirt before inserting them and pressing them flat against his chest.

I felt the incredible heat of his skin, the hammering of his heart, and the hard bulges of his muscles beneath my palms. Touching a man in such an intimate fashion was not within my scope of experience. This was the work of strumpets, mistresses, and wives. Unmarried females were supposed to keep their hands to themselves.

I glanced up, and in that moment Dredmore looked more remote and aloof than I'd ever seen him. "What do you want from me?"

"Everything," he said.

But he wasn't going to take it, I knew that now, and the realization smashed through me, harder than a fist, more painful than finding my way through ten thousand mazes of thorns. He was not the monster I'd always hoped he'd be. He was only a man, and in his arms, I could be simply a woman.

If I chose to be.

I could face his wrath without flinching. He could beat me black-and-blue and I'd still taunt him. But this, this tenderness, this self-denial on my behalf, it infuriated me. I could not fight an enemy who would not attack. I would not give myself to a man whose downfall I had dreamed of causing and whose ruination I had dearly anticipated celebrating. I might as well offer myself from a street corner to anyone with two coins to rub together.

"It will end here and now," he murmured. "All you need say is no, and I will take you back to the house."

He was ravishing me by not ravishing me, the evil bastard. In that moment I had never hated him more. "You think you know me, Dredmore?"

"Not at all," he said politely. "But I can feel you, Charmian. Your loneliness. Your silent longing."

As he gathered me close, I closed my eyes and made my choice. "Goddamn you, Lucien."

"He already has," he murmured against my hair.

I tucked my face against his throat, opening my lips and using the flat of my tongue against his skin. He tasted salty and smoky, and stiffened when I dragged the edge of my teeth up to his jaw. There I followed the strong bone with my open mouth, turning my face into the silken locks of his black hair, letting them soothe my hot face. He bore it a few more moments before he worked his fingers into my hair and turned my mouth to his.

His breath blended with mine, and then we kissed, not with unsure pecks or tentative brushes of lips, but mouth to open mouth, capturing each other for the thrust and glide of tongues, the gasps of pleasure, the explosion of tastes. The raw intimacy of it astounded me, as did the way it stole the air right out of my lungs. That two people could do such a thing to each other and not have their chests collapse or their hearts explode seemed impossible.

I heard myself making the oddest sound, and then I went deaf to myself and the rest of the world as he slanted his head and took me deeper.

Things became rather frantic after that. I tore at his shirt, and he ripped my chemise apart, thrusting my bare breasts against the bruising plane of his chest. I rubbed myself shamelessly against him, eager to relieve the heavy aches and sharp tightness all over plaguing me. Like water on a lamp fire, I only caused it to spread.

His hands kept moving and adjusting me, a supreme annoyance until I felt more cloth tearing and the night air on my bare thighs. The shock and delight of it sent me up on my knees, my spine arching as his mouth attacked my breasts and he shoved his hands between my legs.

I felt the smooth bulb protruding from his fist the moment it touched the astonished, slick folds of my body; after a moment I understood he was positioning himself, and gazed down at him as I curled an arm around his neck.

"Lucien." I took in a quick breath as he pressed up, seating that heavy, full plum of flesh against me. "A certain confession is perhaps in order."

"So I feel." He already knew, but he didn't cast me away or shove through the thin membrane that kept him at bay. He held me suspended, watching my face. "I want it, Charmian."

Rina had educated me about the gift I was only supposed to give a husband. Among other things, the giving often caused discomfort and sometimes bleeding. She firmly believed a woman should see to it herself before taking her first lover and had often scolded me to do the same.

I hadn't, and now—perversely—I was glad. "Then have it."

Dredmore's entire body tightened as he laid me down in the grass and came up over me. At the same time, his body pressed into mine, and I felt a burning, tearing sensation.

Prepared as Rina had made me, I still bit into my lip to keep from yelping as he worked himself deeply inside a place Rina swore was made for just such a reason. I was beginning to have serious doubts. "Tell me this is the worst of it."

"Aye." He seemed to be in as much pain as I was. "Just . . . be . . . still."

Skewered as I was, I couldn't seem to do that. My insides clenched around him, and there was some quivering involved. My body wanted up and I wanted him out, and my hips rose under his.

He withdrew, leaving behind a hot, wet emptiness, but that was no good, either. I clutched at his waist, not knowing how to make it right, and then he filled me again with a force that was only slightly less painful than his initial foray.

"I don't think we're suited," I told him once I felt the full length of him throbbing within me. "But I did like the touching, very much. Could we do that—"

He cut me off with another of his open-mouthed, completely indecent kisses, which distracted me from the other things he did for a time. Only gradually did I become aware of his hands on my breasts and his shaft in my body, and how he was using them with steady, deliberate intent.

I wanted it to stop. The way he worked inside my body, dragging the heaviness of himself out before driving it back in again, created a new degree of discomfort, not as injurious but just as unbearable.

He kissed my eyelids. "Look at me, Charmian." When I did he moved faster, driving deeper. "You can feel it now."

I shook my head, pushing at him. "Leave off. I gave you what you wanted."

"So you did. Now this is what you will have in return." He propped himself up higher, spreading my legs wider so that the top of my sex lay open and exposed to the thrust of his. The knot of nerves there seemed to swell, and my body went liquid as the intolerable ache grew to a silent, wrenching agony.

He wouldn't stop, he was never going to stop, and then something caught me, a dark and furious engine of pleasure and pain. I couldn't fight or think or free myself, and suddenly I didn't want to. Some terrible, glorious beast came to life inside me, one that roared in my ears and laved my skin, and wrapped around me, a demon from hell torching me alive; an angel enfolding me with the softest, silkiest of wings.

Dredmore held me as I convulsed and murmured to me, words I didn't understand. His body became a merciless mech, hammering at me without stopping. Only when he went very still and said my name did I understand that his own beast was having at him.

I was convinced I couldn't move after that and felt grateful that he could as he turned on his side, his hand latched against my body to keep our parts meshed.

When he kissed my brow I actually stiffened, thinking there might be more and convinced it would be the end of me. But he only held me and stroked my hair back from my face.

He looked all over my face before he smiled. "Thank you, Charmian."

"My pleasure, Lucien."

CHAPTER THIRTEEN

"Is it always like that?" I asked him a little later as I let some strands of his hair sift through my fingers. "Or are you insanely talented in this area?"

His chest rumbled with a chuckle. "No, not insanely, and it is *never* like that."

"I beg to disagree." I snuggled closer to him. "If you'd done this the first time we'd met, I'd have liked you much more."

He thought about it for a minute. "There wasn't enough room in the coach."

"Lust at first sight?" I lifted my head. "On the Hill? For shame, Lucien."

"You weren't on the Hill. You were standing in the fruit market. It was a Tuesday morning." His expression grew as distant and detached as his tone. "Connell stopped to allow some goatherd to cross the street, I looked out, and there you were, haggling with an old woman over the price of peaches."

I didn't recall the day, but it sounded like me. "I haggle with everyone."

He didn't seem to hear me. "The sun was very bright that morning, so much so that I could see the motes of dust in the air, and the blemishes on every face. Except yours. Your hair seemed to soak up its radiance and pour it back out through your eyes and skin."

"You noticed me because I was glowing?" I didn't know how to feel about that. "Maybe you mistook me for a lamppost."

"I am a man of this world, Charmian. I know how relentless its indifference is. I solved all the mysteries of navigating through it long ago." He looked at me. "Or I thought I had, until that moment I first saw you."

"So you were after my peaches," I tried to joke.

"I wondered if you'd smell of them, or sunshine." He put his face in my hair and breathed in. "Tonight you're all over moonlight and roses."

"We're in a rose hedge maze," I reminded him, "under a full moon. What were you thinking anyway, spying on me like that? Surely you had better things to do."

He shook his head. "That day I thought of very little, except the manner with which I could persuade you to get into my coach so that I might take you away with me."

"You could have had Connell snatch me off the street." Then I remembered the time he had sent his driver after me, and reared up. "*That's* why you had him chase me down and gag me that day? So you could make off with me? You bastard."

"On that day I had every expectation of success," he said, "until Connell informed me that the rear wheel rim that he'd repaired with a mending spell that morning had for no apparent reason split in two."

A dim memory of hearing a sharp crack came back to me. "That's why you let me go."

"That was when I realized what you might be. What I discovered you are." He ran his hand along my arm from shoulder to elbow and back again in a smooth, soothing caress. "It was maddening to watch you and know I could do nothing. A hundred years ago I could have claimed you that day in the market."

He referred to the old practice of freeclaiming, something caused by the shortage of women among the original colonies. In those days, any man could take an unprotected or abandoned woman from wherever he found her and with or without her permission put her into his household, where she would be subject to his will until such time as she married. No decent man wanted to take a freeclaimed woman to wife, however, so the abducted women were helpless to escape their captors. Fortunately, after the Uprising the Crown had discovered men keeping as many as two dozen free-claimed women in their households. After hurriedly getting them married off, the authorities had promptly outlawed the polygamous practice.

"How romantic." That killed my mood as effectively as an ice bath, and I pushed his hand away.

He caught my arm again as I tried to rise, his touch less gentle. "You are not leaving."

"As you know, keeping women against their will is now illegal, Dredmore. So is slavery." I reached for the remains of my chemise, examined it, and then tossed it aside. "Where the devil is my bodice?"

"It's no longer safe for you in Rumsen." He fastened his trousers and stood, scanning the ground around us. "I can only protect you from Walsh here at Morehaven."

"I've done nothing wrong. Well, aside from the obvious." I shook down my skirts, straightened my waister, and spotted my bodice hanging from a lilac bush. "Walsh can't have me arrested for being criminally cheeky."

"He won't." Dredmore retrieved my bodice and held it out of reach. "He'll shut down your business, seize your property, and leave you penniless."

"You forgot ruining my name," I said as I grabbed at my bodice. "Come on, now, that's not fair. You're at least a foot taller than me."

"Everything Walsh said and did tonight was only for show. There is something seriously wrong with the man." Dredmore held out the bodice like a nurse dressing a child, and I let him help me into it. "He knows exactly why his wife is being assaulted, but he hasn't put a stop to it for reasons I can't fathom. But if you're liable to stumble onto the truth, that makes you a liability he cannot afford."

"I never stumble." I turned my back on him so I could fasten my own buttons. "I investigate. The lady deserves to know why she's being tormented like this, especially with Walsh threatening to divorce her."

"Men in Walsh's position do not take their wives to court." He picked up his cloak and wrapped it around me. "They arrange an unfortunate accident and, after an appropriate period of mourning, they remarry."

"She didn't choose to marry him." I saw his expression and lost my temper. "For God's sake, Lucien. Diana Walsh is barely out of the schoolroom. She's shallow and brainless, but she's still an innocent person. Her people are all up near Settle. There's no one else to look after her."

He started walking me toward the gap in the stone wall. "You can't help her, Charmian. She was doomed from the moment she knocked on your door."

"Why don't you kidnap her and bring her up here, then?" I strode ahead of him. "Walsh has her well trained. She's lovely. Maybe you could teach her to enjoy it."

"You're going in the wrong direction," he said, and waited until I came back to him. "Stay here with me, Charmian. It's the only way I can keep you alive."

Dredmore could be a deceptive, theatrical jackass, but he didn't fear anything. Now he looked afraid . . . for me.

I considered what I could do to protect myself. "We'll go to the police. The chief inspector is the grandson of an old friend of my family's."

"You no longer have family."

"I did once, but . . ." I peered at him. "Why, you nosy sod. You had me investigated."

"Several times," he said without a shred of remorse. "All my men discovered was that you are an orphan without money, people, or connections." His tone changed. "I assumed that it would make things simpler."

"You mean, you thought you could carry me off and no one would give a bloody damn." I was starting to hate him again, and as soon as we emerged from the maze, I turned on him. "All this talk of freeclaiming and kidnapping, as if I'm some prized cow instead of a person. How do you sleep at night?"

"I don't." He hauled me into his arms. "You're going to change that."

The kiss he gave me caused me to temporarily forget the various aches and pains afflicting me, and for a moment I allowed myself the luxury of imagining a life where I could have such kisses whenever I wanted them. Slipping into Dredmore's arms every night, spending long hours rousing each other's beasts and then falling asleep, boneless with exhaustion and saturated with contentment . . .

It would only cost me my independence, my heart, and every ounce of my self-respect.

"I did mention that I was leaving," I said as soon as I was permitted to breathe again.

"Someday we'll go to Paris, and I'll introduce you to more Raphaels," he told me. "But for now, you will remain here." He looked past me and nodded.

I glanced back and saw Connell and another brute coming down from the pavilion, both focused on me. Which meant— "You can't be serious. Not after what just happened between us. *Lucien.*"

"It's for your own good, my sweet." He handed me off to the men. To them, he said, "Lock her up."

PART 2

~

HIS LORDSHIP POSSESSED

Chapter Fourteen

Half an hour after giving myself to my worst enemy, and daftly imagining myself to be falling in love with him, I paced round the confines of the bedchamber in which he had imprisoned me. I knew for my foolishness I deserved nothing more than to spend my remaining days there, a wretched captive, an illegally freeclaimed woman, alternately forced to attend to satiating Lucien Dredmore's lusts and left to pine in solitude for the life I had so thoughtlessly thrown away. This was what women like Lady Walsh endured.

But I was not Diana Walsh, and I'd cut out my own heart before I allowed Lucien Dredmore to ever touch me again.

A thorough search of the chamber—which despite its sumptuous trappings was little more than a prison cell—turned up no exit or the means by which I might create one. The only entry had been locked in three places from the outside by his minion, Connell. Masonry had replaced the glass panes in the single window frame on the opposite wall, too. As I poked at the brick, I wondered how many other women had suffered this fate, and what had happened to them once Dredmore had tired of them.

"He probably buries them under the rose hedges," I

muttered, absently clutching at my pendant for comfort. "Please God, if you'll get me out of this I'll never glance at another man again. I swear it." I looked down at the dark stone and realized otherworldly intervention was right in my hand. "Bloody hell. Harry."

My eager fingers fumbled a bit with the clasp, but at last I released it and dropped the pendant on the floor, backing away from it quickly.

My grandfather's specter materialized instantly, and as soon as he looked round he shouted at me. "Do you know where you are? Do you know who he is? Have you lost your tiny mind?"

"I'm happy to see you, too," I said. "We'll catch up once I get out of here." When he didn't reply, I added, "You keep saying you're Harry Houdini, the world's greatest escape artist. Well, then here's your chance to prove it."

"Oh, shut up." He went to the window and poked at the brick. "After what you've done, it would serve you right if I left you here to rot."

"How do you know what I've done?"

"A guardian spirit knows everything. Watches everything, whether he wishes to or not." He eyed me. "Romping with that bastard in the dirt like some scullery wench. If I were your father, I'd give you the thrashing of your life."

He was right, but I refused to cringe. "I suppose you never lost your head in a moment of passion."

"Of course I did. If I hadn't sired your mother, you wouldn't be here." He searched along the baseboards before testing the door. "I was fortunate in my choice of wives. Bess forgave me my dalliance and took me back."

"But I'm not named Bess."

"No. You're named after my best mate's wife. I comforted her after his untimely death, rather more than I should have." He sighed and rubbed his eyes. "The result was your mother."

"You *did* have a forgiving wife." I sat on the bed. "Did this Charmian raise my mother, then?"

"She had to think of her family and her other children," he snapped. "She remained secluded in the country for her confinement, and even kept your mother for a time after her birth. Her family grew suspicious, however, so she sent Rachel to me as soon as she was old enough to travel."

It had never occurred to me that there would be someone else I hated as much as Dredmore, until Harry began haunting me. "How did you persuade my mother to name me after the adulteress who abandoned her?"

"I didn't, not directly. I merely ensured that Rachel heard the name in a dream just before your birth." Harry glanced at me, and his anger faded into weariness. "Don't judge your namesake so harshly, lass. Charmian never forgave herself for giving up our child. It broke her spirit as well as her heart. She died only a few years after sending your mother to me."

"I'll give her the benefit of the doubt," I said, "if you'll agree to overlook my lapse in judgment tonight."

"Pray you don't end up in the same condition as your grandmother." He eyed my belly before he turned round to inspect the rest of the room. "The door and window are impassible from the inside of the room. Even if you could get at the locks, there is nothing you can use to pick them." He turned about one last time, studying my prison. "It will have to be a possession, then."

"A what?"

"Stay here." He floated out through the door.

"Harry!" I went over and pounded on the door. "Come back here."

The door opened, but in came Connell, who slammed the door behind him. I shuffled back, unsure if I should try to dodge round him or kick him in the unmentionables.

"You've been ill," he told me as he walked right up to me and studied my face. "You believe you've been poisoned. There's blood coming from your lips."

"What are you talking about? There's no bloo—"

My head snapped as he slapped me, hard enough to make my ears hum.

"Now there is." Connell handed me the container of scented powder. "Toss this in the guard's face. It will blind and choke him long enough for you to get outside. Then lock him in."

I stared at him. "Connell, why are you helping me?"

"Charm, it's me, Harry." For a moment I saw the old man's face appear atop Connell's, like a half-transparent mask. "I've taken *possession* of this man's body." He glanced down at himself. "Which isn't all that bad." He stretched out an arm. "Very strappy fellow."

"Get out of there," I almost shrieked.

"If I dispossess him now, he'll regain his senses immediately and spoil your escape." Harry/Connell patted my cheek. "Now remember, give the guard a good dousing with that powder."

"You're possessing a guard, so why don't you simply walk me out of here?" I demanded.

"No time to explain that now," my grandfather said. "There's a guard in the front hall, and one repairing the door you smashed in the kitchen. Once you get out of here, go to the servants' stairs and take the tradesmen's entrance out."

"All right." I gingerly tested the bleeding cut on the inside of my lip before smearing the sides of my mouth with the blood to make it look more convincing. "Once I'm outside, then what?"

"You'll find three horses in the stables," he told me. "Saddle the black gelding with the white star on his nose. Ride through the pasturelands, and don't allow anyone to see or stop you."

I stirred the powder with a fingertip. "You're certain this will work?"

"I wasn't a hoodlum, you silly twit. I was Houdini." He gave me an awkward, one-armed hug. "And your lover will not remain in town forever, so you had best get going."

"*Former* lover." I dragged some hair over my eyes and went to stand by the door. "Did you become Houdini as a cover for the spying?"

"You mean you haven't worked it out yet?" Incredibly, he chuckled. "I possessed the body of a spy, Charm, and used him as my cover. Being a spy concealed the fact that I was, ah, Houdini."

"Why would you have to hide that?" I demanded. "From what I've read everyone adored him—you."

"Everyone but your parents, and that story will have

to keep for another time. Wait." He picked up my pendant from the floor and set it on a table near me. "Count to ten after I leave, put this on, and don't take it off unless you need me."

"Why?"

"Things have changed now that I'm . . . never mind." He opened the door and hurried out.

I slowly counted to ten before I put my pendant back on, drew a deep breath, and then bowed over, concealing the powder behind my arms. "Please . . . help me," I called out in a strangled, frightened voice. "I'm throwing up . . . blood. I think I've been . . . poisoned . . ."

I had to keep that up for several minutes until the brute who had brought me to the room from the garden stepped in and scowled at me.

"What's all this?" he demanded, peering at my face and then straightening. "Where did you—?"

I hurled the scented powder in his face, shoving him aside and darting past him through the door. As he coughed, I slammed the door shut and engaged the locks.

He began immediately swearing at me and hammering on the door's inside panel, but I didn't linger to hear his poor opinion of me. I ran down the hall to the servant's stairs then took them to the first floor, where I stood in the shadows until I saw the guard there rushing upstairs. Then I ran round the corner and fled to the deliveries door.

It refused to open at first, but then the knob gave way and I was outside. I scanned the grounds to look for other guards and saw the coast was clear.

Bunching up my skirts and running across the lawn

put me in view of the house, but I felt sure I had another minute or two before Powder-face and Dredmore's other hooligans came after me. I made it to the stables and darted inside, stopping long enough to listen for a moment and glance out. Lamplight flicked against the side windows of the house, descending from the second to the first floor.

I turned and dashed to the stalls, where five black horses were watching me with some interest.

"All right, which one of you has a white star?" I went to the center stalls, avoided a nip from a cranky-looking mare with a white stripe, and then found the gelding, a placid-eyed fellow who nuzzled my fingers looking for a treat.

"Saves you for the ladies, does he?" I glanced at the saddles hanging on the end wall before I took down a bridle from a post peg and unlatched the stall door. The gelding dipped his head as I bridled him, and only gave me a mild look of surprise when I tossed a blanket over his back.

"Sorry, no time for anything else," I told him, and climbed up the side of the stall to swing onto him. The only times I rode horseback were when I dressed as a native male, so I was used to sitting astride. For his part the gelding turned his head as if to inspect me. "For God's sake, just *pretend* I'm a man."

I guided him out of the stall and rode him to the double doors, where I reached up for the latch pull. Dredmore had installed a mechanized opener, the wheels of which whirred as four telescoping bars pushed open the big doors. Through them I saw the indistinct shapes of two men halfway between the stables and the house.

"Now let's make a run for it." I thumped my heels into the gelding's sides, and he trotted out with a sedate, fastidious trot. "I said *run*, my lad, not *mince*."

After two more insistent thumps, the gelding reluctantly stretched his legs and galloped across the lawn away from the manor and across the clearing that led to the cliffs.

I reined in the gelding when I reached a grove of cypress and took cover there to watch for Dredmore's men. When the horse became restless, I stroked his neck. "I know, George, first time you get a decent rider and now you have to wait. You don't mind if I call you George, do you? You look like a George."

George snorted and dropped his head to crop some grass.

I rode horseback often enough not to be sore, but one already tender portion of my anatomy made me acutely aware not only of how daft I'd been, but why women were rarely seen in public the day after their weddings.

"I'll wager *he* isn't suffering," I muttered to the gelding as I watched several men riding Dredmore's other horses gallop past. "I imagine he's swaggering about and bragging of his conquest and feeling quite the master of all he surveys. I should have set fire to that damned hovel of his before I escaped."

Once the posse had disappeared over the next hill, George and I came out of the cypress and went in the opposite direction, toward the first spread of pasturelands that surrounded the city. The gelding perked up as soon as we were in the clear, and I eased off the reins to let him have his head.

"Go on," I said as he went into that mincing trot again. "This is probably the only chance you'll ever have to really run."

George seemed to understand me and took off in a long, elegant lope that gradually increased in speed until we were fairly flying across the pastures. I glanced back now and then, but no one appeared behind us. Dredmore's men were too accustomed to dealing with ladies, I imagined.

I stopped the gelding twice: once to water him at a spring-fed trough in a cow pasture, and the second time just within sight of the city's streets. George had proven himself a worthy steed, so I abandoned my initial plan to turn him loose outside Rumsen and instead rode him through the back alleys to Halter's, a small stable near my flat that I often frequented.

A few minutes after I rang the service bell, John Halter came out of the barn in his shirtsleeves, his penders still hanging round his hips. "We don't open 'til dawn, so you can . . . sod me, Miss Kit? That you?"

"No, John, it's not me." I handed him the reins and dismounted. "It's just George here. Say hello to my mate John Halter, George."

The gelding blew out some air.

"Morning, George." John gave his neck a few gentle slaps. "So why is this big fellow getting me up out of bed before I've had m'tea?"

"Last night George wandered away from home and has since become lost," I said. "You can tell by the sadness in his eyes."

"Bugger looks right happy to me." The stablemaster frowned. "Where's George's home, then?"

"That would be Morehaven."

John swore softly.

"I've watered and rested him. He'll need a rub and some feed, and his master will pay you when he comes to collect him." I hesitated. "He'll likely have some questions, John."

"Then I'll let George answer what he can." John sighed. "You're not here, Miss Kit. Best you go on home."

CHAPTER FIFTEEN

From John Halter's I did go home, arriving at my door a few minutes before sunrise. I scowled at the row of wardlings nailed above the entry before I went inside and bolted the door behind me.

Glancing down, I saw how my night's adventures had reduced Bridget's beautiful gown to little more than a bundle of dirty rags. I stank of horse sweat and my own sweat, and something else.

Beneath it all, I smelled of Dredmore.

I was distracted from my dark thoughts by looking at my bare forearm. Dredmore's men hadn't found my pendant but had relieved me of all my other, borrowed jewels before locking me up; hopefully Bridget's husband could use his influence to get them back, because I could never afford to replace them. A suspicious little trickle between my legs made me crane my head round, and I saw spots of blood on the back of my skirt.

Reminders of more things that could never be taken back.

I ran to my bath, tearing off the gown before I grabbed my sponge and stepped into the tub. The cascade doused me in frigid water as I scrubbed myself all over, washing away the sweat and the blood, the dirt and the tears.

And Dredmore.

After ridding myself of all the unwanted reminders of the night before (as well as a layer or two of my skin) I dried my hair and dressed, ignoring the siren song of my sympathetic bed. I'd triumphed over a tragedy of my own manufacture; my life would go on. My monthlies had just finished, so chances were that I would not become pregnant. If anything I could be grateful to Dredmore for smashing the last of my romantic notions.

Men and romance, two notions I fully intended to avoid in the future like the rats and plague they were.

When I arrived at the Davies Building, Horace Eduwin Gremley the Fourth stood hovering just outside the main entry. He rushed over as soon as he saw me turn the corner.

"Mr. Gremley." I bobbed. "You're in early today. Making up some hours to allow for an early day on Friday?"

"No. Yes. Ah, Miss Kittredge." His eyes darted back before returning to gaze at me with a kind of wild distress. "I bear unhappy news this morning. Mr. Davies's solicitor paid an early call. About you."

"Indeed." I looked over his shoulder at the stone-faced doorman who was decidedly not watching us. "What about me?"

"You've been evicted," Fourth blurted out. "This very morning, I fear. The solicitor quite forcefully communicated Mr. Davies's desire that you not be permitted in the building by the doorman or any of the other tenants. Unfortunately he was not at all forthcoming as to why such a grossly undeserved action is being taken." He twisted his hands together. "I assured the man that you are the kindest and most considerate of tenants, but he refused to be swayed. I cannot fathom why Mr. Davies would do this to you."

I could. *Walsh, or Dredmore.*

I looked up at my office window. "Have they closed it up, or cleared it out?"

"Both. Mr. Docket told the solicitor that he would see to your belongings." Fourth grimaced. "As soon as he mentioned casting them into the incinerator, the solicitor happily agreed."

"You needn't worry," I told him. "Docket is a mate; he won't torch my things. If you would be so kind as to drop him a note through the tube and say that I'll arrange for a cart to come round tonight, after the building closes."

"Anything," he said, nodding. "Miss Kittredge, I cannot express how sorry I am about this. I will be writing a letter of protest to Mr. Davies as soon as I return to the office."

"You're very kind, Mr. Gremley." I patted his arm. "But under the circumstances, it would be wiser not to openly associate yourself with me."

His expression changed to one of unhappy understanding, and he offered me a sad smile. "You should know that your advice to me was brilliant. I was introduced to Maritza Skolnik by her father, who also obtained her consent to be my escort on Friday night."

Skolnik was no fool; within a fortnight he'd have Mr. Gremley engaged to his daughter. But as she was a lovely, gentle creature, I imagined Fourth could look forward to a very pleasant future. "I'm so glad. I wish you and the lady all the best, sir."

Fourth hesitated before bending and giving me an awkward peck on the cheek. "As I hope for you, Miss Kittredge." With his face still turning red, he hurried off.

Davies had always been a conservative man but genial landlord; he wouldn't have thrown me out unless he'd been given ample cause. *Walsh, or Dredmore.* Whichever man had made the complaint against me, I knew I would not be invited to renew my tenancy at this or any other of Davies's buildings.

I might have sought sanctuary with Rina or Bridget, both of whom had been completely justified in their advice to me, but I couldn't do it, not yet. Not until I found out which man was responsible.

I walked slowly back toward my flat, but had no interest in spending the day alone sulking. I also realized that there might be other reasons I was being hounded. What was Nolan Walsh hiding? Was it as Dredmore had hinted, that I'd inadvertently stumbled onto something that threatened Walsh more than the scandal of divorcing his young wife?

And then there was Dredmore. He was a man of the world, an important man not to be trifled with. Why had he pursued me, and seduced me, and imprisoned me? I was young, healthy, and attractive, but hardly anything beyond that. Rumsen was filled with women whose beauty made me seem a veritable troll by comparison. Hundreds of posh, nubile women Dredmore could take to wife with a snap of his fingers—professional, talented women he could purchase for the night or however long he wished to use them. Lucien was not only rich and mysterious, he was virile and handsome. Virtually any female within the city would be eager and happy to oblige him.

My stomach growled, so I changed direction and went to the fruit market, where the stands were just opening for the morning's business. There I walked along until I reached the old peach seller, who had just sliced open a red-gold beauty to release the delicious fragrance.

This was where Dredmore had claimed he had seen me the first time. Where he had . . . no, the most powerful deathmage in the country could not have looked across a market and fallen in love with me at first sight. One required a heart for such a thing to happen. But why would he wish me to believe he'd done so?

"Trying to tempt the browsers?" I said over the open crates.

"Always, miss, always." She handed me a slice. "North country golders, sweet as honey this year, they are."

I popped the fruit in my mouth and found it to be precisely as she claimed, as well as sun-warmed and remarkably juicy. "It's scrumptious."

She looked side to side before shoving a small paper sack in my hands. When I reached for my reticule, she shook her head. "A gift, dearie." She gave me a meaningful look. "I'll wager you could use a bit of sweetness today."

That put me on alert. "Why's that?"

She leaned over the crates. "Bunch of beaters came

round earlier, asking after a gel who looks a bit like you. They said she lives a goldstone round the corner." When I glanced round she added, "No one knew this gel, 'course, so they went off. I heard one of them say something daft about looking for her in some eagle's nest." She straightened and said in a louder voice, "Morning's a bit chilly, don't you think, miss? Best cover up until the air warms."

I drew my hood over my head. "I will, thank you."

If Inspector Doyle had sent beaters looking for me, it was either to bring me in on another phony charge or to give me protection. I wanted to believe it was the latter, and might have, if my eviction from the office hadn't taken place. Dredmore might have filed a charge against me as well, and he had a legitimate one: I'd stolen George. Although anyone with enough coin to afford one motored about in a carri, horses remained the primary means of transport round the city. No young blue ever made a circuit of the parks in a carri, and even merchants who could afford a fleet of carris still kept horses as a show of their wealth and status. Because of this, horse thieves remained universally reviled by all the citizens of Rumsen, and when convicted were regularly sentenced to be whipped in public to serve as a warning to others.

Dredmore would love to see me bound to a punishment post and lashed until I bled, I thought, my mood dark. *He'd probably volunteer to ply the whip—*

No, he wouldn't.

As much as I hated him and his spectacular arrogance, Lucien had employed his unsavory methods in an attempt to protect me. Whatever we had been to each other before last night, the man and I were no longer enemies. I didn't know what we might become, but our interlude in the maze had changed everything.

I took my bag of peaches to a little children's park three blocks north of the market. A few nannies were pushing prams along the walks, but the benches and sandboxes were empty. I sat down on a bench half-hidden from the street by a large red-and-white-striped glory bush and took out a peach.

"North country golders," Doyle said as he sat down beside me. "I hear they're as sweet as honey this year."

"That they are." I took the other peach from the sack and offered to him.

We sat and ate the fruit in silence. Doyle left me briefly to purchase two mugs of spiced tea from a cart. I warmed my hands against the sides of the hot porcelain before taking a sip.

"I came in to find a stack of complaints on my desk this morning," Doyle mentioned as we watched a fierce-looking nan bend over her pram to coo at her fussy charge. "Funny thing, they all bore your name. Busy night, Kit?"

I shrugged.

He blew some steam from his mug before tasting. "The commissioner would very much like to, what were his words . . . oh, yes. 'See that one dragged through the streets by her ankles.'"

I turned up my toes. "Not much to them. Knots had better be tight."

"I also received a very interesting communication

from Lord Dredmore." Doyle finished his tea with a few swallows. "It seems that someone trespassed onto his property last night and stole a black gelding from his stables."

I made my sigh heavy. "How terrible for him."

"This particular gelding was trained to be ridden only by a lady," Doyle said. "And yet no sidesaddle was found to be missing."

"You know, I think I heard someone mention rumor of a black horse this morning, too." I pretended to think. "Oh, yes. One was found at dawn standing outside Halter's stables. Lovely big black fellow, name of George." I glanced at him. "What a coincidence."

"I'll send a man over to collect George and pay Halter for his troubles." He regarded me directly. "Now that I've told you how dreadful my morning has been, you will tell me exactly what you were doing last night."

"Before being kidnapped and held against my will at Morehaven, or after?" I enjoyed the shock on his face. "You really should do some investigating now and then, Chief Inspector. I thought you Yardmen were trained for it."

"Why would Lord Dredmore abduct you?"

"He's a pompous, controlling ass; I'm difficult to scare off, and we're competing for the same job." I dropped my peach pit back into the bag.

Oh, and he believes that he's in love with me. I kept that thought in my head.

"Were there any witnesses to your abduction and captivity?" Doyle persisted.

"Who were not in the employ of Lucien Dredmore?

Ah, no, sorry. He's not that stupid." I saw the lines round his mouth deepen. "Just forget it, Tommy."

"I don't think I can do that just now." He put his hand over mine. "Did he hurt you, Kit?"

Beyond all hope of recovery, I was beginning to believe. "No. Dredmore could never do anything to me but make me laugh."

"That's not what I mean."

Here was my opportunity for some genuine revenge. Tom Doyle could take me to a physick, who would examine me and find the physical evidence of what Dredmore and I had done. Since I was unmarried and had never been charged with soliciting favors from gentlemen, I could claim ravishment and have Dredmore charged with assaulting me. Without witnesses it would be difficult to see him convicted, but filing the complaint along would be enough to destroy his reputation. He'd never again be invited to the governor's mansion to show off his grubby bag of tricks.

It will end here and now. The memory of Lucien's voice in the gardens at Morehaven echoed in my mind. *All you need say is no.*

"Nothing else happened between me and Dredmore last night that concerns the law," I told Doyle.

"Perhaps you'll change your mind after I tell you why I'm here." He finished his tea. "You're wanted at the magistrate's."

"Court?" I frowned. "Why, whatever for?"

He took my mug from me. "You'll be arraigned on charges of practicing magic in a residential area."

"Even if I did practice magic, which I don't, my

office is in the business district." When he said nothing, I added, "My landlord had me evicted from the building about an hour ago."

"The address cited in the warrant is for your flat, Kit." He rose and carried our mugs back to the cartlass, who tucked them in her wash bin before handing Doyle back fo'pence for the return of her crockery.

I went to the fountain to wash the peach juice from my fingers, and was drying them with my kerchief when Doyle joined me.

"Do you know a barrister?" he asked. When I shook my head, he sighed. "You'll need one. A good one."

"Can't afford so much as a bad one, Tom."

"Bloody hell, Kit," he snapped, startling a pair of passing nans. "Have you any idea of how much trouble you're in? These are serious charges. Violation of trade practice law carries a sentence of three to five years, hard labor. What the devil have you been up to on the Hill?"

"I tried to help someone." Before he could shout again, I added, "You needn't fuss at me, Inspector. I was warned; I knew something like this might happen."

"And you did it anyway."

"Some things are worth a bit of risk." I smiled up at him. "I don't suppose you'd pay attention to the flowers for the next few minutes."

"I wish I could, Kit, but my beaters are standing just over there, and they'd give chase." He held out his hand. "I'll speak for you at court."

"And say what? You know I'm a good lass because we played together as children? You'll get the sack." I turned round and held my wrists behind my back. "Do your job, Inspector."

A few moments later the cold steel cuffs of Doyle's shackles clamped over my wrists. "Charmian Constance Kittredge, you are charged with practicing magic in a prohibited area. Be advised that anything you say while in my custody can be entered into evidence and used against you. You are permitted representation before the magistrate. If you cannot afford such representation, an aid-solicitor will be summoned to counsel you and speak on your behalf. Do you understand what I have told you?"

The reasons, no, but the words, of course. "I do, sir."

"Right, then." He arranged my cloak so that it covered my manacles and then took my arm. "Let's go."

Chief Inspector Doyle spared me the humiliation of taking me to Rumsen Main first to be glassed and recorded. While I knew eventually I would have my image and personal information added to the vast number of criminal countenances and case files kept in the police archives, the reprieve gave me a bit of time to decide what next I would do.

My enemy—either Dredmore or Walsh—had thrown down the gauntlet by having me hauled before the magistrate. My choices were to fight, arrange bail and flee, or surrender myself to an unhappy fate.

I wasn't going to run away or give up, which meant I needed to arm myself.

Montford District, the building where the magistrate courts were housed, stood in the shadows of Montford

Central, the judgment courts. Both were named for Lord Montford, the Queen's Architect, whose building designs had been brought over along with Crown law after the Rebellion had been crushed. The only way I'd ever see the inside of Montford Central was if I killed someone, burned down a block of houses, or did something equally as dastardly; Montford District was reserved for civil and common criminal cases.

I suppose I should have admired all the grandeur of the soaring Doric columns and the heavy chiselwork above the archways, but the stodgy, Crown-nodding affectedness of the building's design ruined any appreciation I might have for the bloody place. So did being hauled to it as a prisoner.

Doyle brought me into the great hall, which had been hung with paintings depicting the Empire's triumph over the rebels and stone plaquettes inscribed with tiresome axioms about the nobility of justice.

"'The law of the Crown is a spring of life,'" I read one out loud as we passed it. "Do you think our forefathers would agree, Chief Inspector, seeing as it put most of them facedown in shallow, unmarked graves?"

"Be quiet," he warned as he steered me through a security checkpoint and down to an entry marked *Advocacy*.

Inside were two chairs, a table, and a balding solicitor in a shabby suit who barely glanced at us. "Morning. This the Murphy gel, or the Holmes boy?"

"Kittredge," Doyle told him.

"Damn it all. I told Scotty I didn't want that one before I left the office." The solicitor dug through his papers until he found a thick bundle of papers and scowled at me. "You know why you've been brought up before the magis, miss?"

"I've been wrongly charged with practicing magic in a residential area," I said, sounding as forlorn as possible. "And what is your name, sir?"

"Douglas Clark, at your service." He didn't bother to get up or bow. "You can leave her, Chief."

Doyle removed my manacles. "Keep your chin up."

"Always." I watched him go before I sat down beside my aid-solicitor. "I'm not lying, sir. The charges being brought against me are utter nonsense."

"They always are, dearie." He turned to me. "You're young, which will help, although you can't claim ignorance of the law. That always sets hissonor's wig on end. Someone coerce you to wave your wand in the wrong place? Your da, maybe?"

"I'm an orphan."

"That's too bad. Got a teller off last month for having a home seeing by blaming her brother for not paying their rent. And her without a proper license at all." Clark studied my face. "What sort of magic you practice?"

"None."

He shook his head. "Can't go in denying your business, miss. They wouldn't file charges without hard evidence."

"They have none. I've never practiced magic."

He turned back to the papers and scrabbled through them, his frown deepening with every page he turned. "No witnesses, no confiscations, no testimonies. That can't be right. Hang on, here it is." He pulled out a paper and held it up. "His lordship charges that the defendant bespelled her physical residence to protect the occupants and repel intruders."

"I did nothing of the kind," I assured him.

He nodded absently. "They've listed some enchanted objects that were found openly displayed on the exterior of your residence."

"Seven wardlings, nailed above my entry," I said. "Put there by a police warder, not me."

"The cops?" He glanced up, completely perplexed. "Why'd they want to ward your place, then?"

I detailed the attack on me by the snuffmages as well as my subsequent detainment and drugging at Rumsen Main. "I did not fashion or display the wardlings. There is no other magic item on the premises or in my possession." I almost reached for my pendant before I thought better of it. "Nor have I uttered a single spell."

"Hang on." He dug down to the very last page of the charge statement, and after reading it sat back in his chair. "The charges are being brought by Lord Nolan Walsh. Himself's one of them bankers downtown what's got more money than H.M. What in sweet Mary's name did you do to bring his wrath down on your head, gel?"

So Walsh, not Dredmore. An invisible burden lifted from my shoulders, not that I welcomed the tiny surge of relief that came with it. "I'm working for Lord Walsh's wife, Lady Diana. Someone inside his household has been—"

"No." Clark held up his hand. "Don't tell me any more. I can't have knowledge of that and stand for you." He studied the statement a second time. "This police warder, will she bear witness that she was the one who put up the protection at your home?"

"Yes, sir."

"And you've never read so much as a tea leaf in your kitchen?" When I shook my head, he gathered up his papers and stuffed them in his case. "This is how it will go, then. I'll refute the charges, have you repeat the statements you've made to me to the magis—and only about the coppers warding your place, if you please—and then we'll see just how much money the banker spent on this."

"Do you think he bribed officers of the court?"

"To bring you up on charges, probably several of them." Clark regarded me steadily. "But it's your lucky day, my lass. He didn't think to bribe *me*."

CHAPTER SIXTEEN

Clark and I were summoned before the bench a short time later. The wood-paneled courtroom was divided into two, and my aid-solicitor led me to a stand on the right in front of several rows of pews that were occupied here and there by several gentlemen, including Tom Doyle.

I nodded to Doyle but then saw the face of the young clerk sitting beside him. "Mr. Gremley?"

Clark hushed me and had me sit in one of the two chairs behind the stand while he took the other.

"Not a word out of you until I say so," he warned. "And not a peep about Walsh or working for the wife."

The bailiff entered, calling for everyone present to stand. "Attention, attention, the seventh court of Rumsen city is now come to order, the Honorable Jason Newton presiding."

A stout middle-aged man in an ancient white wig and dusty-looking blue robes trudged in and took the chair behind the magistrate's desk on the platform at the center back of the court. He looked at me for several moments before saying, "Be seated. Mr. Jones, you may present the first case."

The magistrate's clerk rose from his seat to the right of the bench and called out, "City of Rumsen versus Miss Charmian Constance Kittredge."

Clark urged me up on my feet again as the clerk handed the magistrate the warrant.

Magistrate Newton put on a pair of reading spectacles and reviewed the warrant. "Aid-solicitor Clark, Miss Kittredge appears to be charged with illegal practice of magic. How does she plead?"

"Not guilty, your honor," Clark said promptly.

"Barrister Fordun," Newton said to the prosecutor. "I dislike seeing unprotected young ladies in my courtroom. This had better be very good."

The man standing behind the opposite stand adjusted his new wig before standing, which gave Clark time to speak in his place.

"If it pleases the court and the Crown," Clark said quickly, "my client wishes to enter statements that will doubtless convince Your Honor to dismiss these charges."

"Oh, doubtless." Newton eyed me. "Well, young miss? What have you to say for yourself?"

I went to the stand and tried my best bewildered look on the magistrate. "Your Honor, I am being charged with practicing magic in my home, which is located in a residential area. I have never done so, and the evidence being brought forth to condemn me is police property."

"Naturally it is in their custody," Fordun said. "They confiscate any magic paraphernalia in such cases, so that it might be presented in evidence."

"No, sir," I said. "The wardlings that were found nailed above the entry to my flat are property that *belong* to the police, and were put there by a police warder. They are not mine, nor is their display my doing."

"Is this warder present?" Newton snapped.

"Her supervisor is, Your Honor," I heard Doyle say behind me. "I am Chief Inspector Thomas Doyle, assigned to Rumsen Main. After Miss Kittredge was the victim of an unprovoked and brutal attack, I sent our staff warder to search and secure the young lady's home, in the hope of preventing a second assault on her person."

The magistrate turned to Fordun. "What other evidence do you have to support these charges?"

"This woman's home has not yet been searched, Your Honor," Fordun said quickly. "I am convinced that when it is, we will find ample evidence of her crimes."

Newton sighed. "Inspector, you said your warder searched the young lady's home. Did she find anything unlawful?"

"No, Your Honor," Doyle said, "and she searched the premises quite thoroughly."

"It sounds to me as if someone is trying to use my court to attack this young lady again." The magistrate handed the warrants back to his clerk. "Miss Kittredge, have you at any time practiced magic in your home?"

"No, Your Honor—"

"I have a statement to the contrary given by a titled gentleman," the prosecutor said. "He was most emphatic about her criminal behavior."

"I suppose he personally witnessed her committing these crimes?" Newton asked with exaggerated patience.

"The gentleman in question is a pillar of the financial community, Your Honor," Fordun assured him. "His assurance of her character is certainly good enough for me."

The magistrate looked out. "Is there anyone else present who has knowledge of this young lady's character?"

"I do, Your Honor." That was Fourth, and he cleared his throat twice before continuing. "I have enjoyed the privilege of being acquainted with Miss Kittredge as a business associate for several years."

"Business? What's this?" Newton looked over the rim of his glasses. "She's a working gel?"

"Indeed she is, sir," Fourth said. "She keeps an office downtown in the Davies Building, where I am also employed. In all the years I have known her, Miss Kittredge has never once practiced any form of magic. She does not believe in it."

"I challenge this testimony," Fordun said at once.

"Mr. Jones, summon the court detector," Newton said.

I turned to Clark and whispered, "What's a detector?"

"Useless," he murmured back. "Coin holes, the lot of them, but old magis like Newton think they're infallible."

A few minutes later an elderly man in a plain dark green robe was led into the courtroom. Milky cataracts occluded his eyes, and he appeared to be completely dependent on the clerk guiding him up toward the bench, for when the clerk stopped, so did the detector.

"Magistrate," the old man said in a surprisingly strong voice. "How may I serve the court?"

Newton gestured for Fourth to join the old man, and the clerk guiding the detector turned him to face him.

"Hold out your hands, palms up," the clerk told Fourth. "Stand still and do not speak unless you are spoken to."

Fourth did as he was instructed, and the old man rested his fingers over both palms. "You are the witness whose testimony has been challenged."

Fourth swallowed. "I am, sir."

"Hmmm." The detector moved his fingertips over the palms under them. "Why are you here, young man?"

Fourth glanced at me. "To help a friend who has been unjustly persecuted, sir. That is all."

"Not all." His wrinkled brow furrowed. "Something..." He slowly turned his head toward me, although it was obvious from the vacancy of his eyes that he was stone-blind.

"Well?" the prosecutor demanded, his tone impatient. "Is the boy lying to protect this female?"

"No." The old man turned back toward Newton. "This young man speaks the truth, Magistrate. His testimony may be accepted as such."

Fordun seemed to explode. "I challenge the use of this detector, Your Honor. He is clearly unable to discern the falsehoods being presented by this boy. I demand to bring forth my own detector, who will refute his findings."

"That one," the detector said as he nodded at the prosecutor, "is your liar, Magistrate. I needn't touch him to ferret that out."

Newton sighed. "Sit down, Mr. Fordun."

"I am not on trial," Fordun snapped. His voice rose to a near-bellow as he addressed the magistrate. "Your Honor, I vigorously insist you—"

"In *my* court, sir, you insist on nothing," Newton shouted over him. "Now take your seat and stay your tongue, or I'll have you charged with contempt and hauled out of here in shackles."

Fortunately for Fordun, he appeared so furious as to be rendered speechless, and stalked back to his seat. The detector tugged at his guide until the clerk brought him over to me and Clark.

The old man held out his hand but didn't touch me. He seemed to be fanning me as if he were afraid I'd faint. "Remarkable. I can almost feel it."

"Feel what?" Clark wanted to know.

"Nothing that is lost is gone forever, my dear," the detector said to me, but not in a kindly or reassuring manner. He sounded so stern it almost seemed like a reprimand for some wrong I had done.

I felt puzzled, but he had supported Fourth, so I tried to be polite. "I will remember that, sir."

"Yes." His lips drew back from yellowed teeth in a pained grimace. "I think you will."

"If it pleases the court," Fordun said, and barely waited for Newton's nod before he continued, "I believe from the detector's address of this defendant that she has somehow tampered with his ability to carry out his duties. Indeed, she may have bespelled him as well as her aid-solicitor before being brought before Your Honor."

The detector chuckled and shook his head. "As she is, she can bespell no one and nothing."

"You were not asked to testify," Fordun flared.

"Thank you for your service, detector," Newton said, and gestured for the clerk to remove the old man. As soon as he left, the magistrate clasped his hands and regarded Fordun. "Barrister Fordun, in consideration of your previous service to the Crown, I will not issue an arrest warrant for you on charges of obstructing justice and accepting bribes. However, I do intend to file a lengthy and detailed complaint with your superiors. If you have accepted some sort of remuneration for these theatrics of yours today, I suggest you spend it at once, or hide it under your mattress evermore."

The prosecutor paled. "You cannot suspect me of wrongdoing, Your Honor. I am charged with enforcing Her Majesty's law."

"Then, sir, you have utterly failed the Crown today." Newton toyed with his gavel as he regarded me. "Miss Kittredge, I would very much like to hear precisely why you are really here in my court, but I daresay that once I know the reason it will cause an equal amount of havoc in my life."

"Doubtless it would, Your Honor," I agreed.

"Very well." He glared at Fordun. "I find that the Crown has not fulfilled its obligation of presenting proper evidence or any lawful substantiation of the charges against the defendant. The charges against Miss Kittredge are hereby vacated, and this case is dismissed."

He slammed his gavel down once.

"You can stay the holidays at the farm," Doyle said as he tucked the riding blanket over my skirts. "Mum wouldn't let you leave before Christmas, and the snow usually cuts off the roads up there until well into February anyway."

"I'm not going to your parents'," I told him for the third time. "I have to work—I have to find a new office—and my home is here in the city."

He didn't start the motor. "Lord Walsh will be out for blood now, Kit. He won't rest until he's driven you from Rumsen, and that might well be in a gravecart."

Snow was beginning to fall, so I pulled up my hood and tugged on my gloves. "If that happens, Chief Inspector, then I'm counting on you to send him to the gallows."

"Hang *you*, Kit." He thumped the dash with his fist. "You'd rather lose your life than give up this damned independence of yours?"

I saw a dark figure standing between the two court buildings. Not a flake of snow marred his long black hair, and not an ounce of pity softened his eyes. I thought he might approach us, but he simply stood there watching.

"If I can't live as I want," I countered, looking away from Dredmore to Doyle, "then why go on?"

A loud whine turned into a quick smash, and a large, jagged hole appeared in the glasshield in front of me. I glanced down to see gleaming shards covering the blanket over me, toward which Doyle pushed my head.

"Stay down—" He drew his pistol and leapt out of the carri, crouching down low.

Someone had shot at us. I heard another bullet ping off the radiator grill before Doyle fired in return and men began shouting.

I lifted my head just enough to see over the dash, and watched as Dredmore advanced on a red-cloaked figure taking cover behind a tree. He ignored the shots being fired at him as he brought up both hands and made a strange slashing gesture.

The tree fell over, its trunk sliced apart. A moment

later a wide spray of red splashed the snowy ground, and the head of the snuffmage rolled through the gruesome puddle.

Doyle jumped in and started up the motor. "Hold on, Kit."

He drove off toward the street at a reckless speed.

I stared back at Dredmore, who was standing over the dead assassin, and then focused on my hands, mainly to avoid seeing the drivers frantically diverting their horses and carris out of our path. "That was meant for me."

"Maybe so." Doyle gave me a quick glance. "Are you hurt?"

"No." Seeing Dredmore kill with just a gesture, however, was making my heart pound in my ears.

A few minutes later Doyle stopped the carri in front of my goldstone, but when I tried to climb out he caught my arm.

"Wait here," he said.

"And freeze? Why?" My eyelashes and hair were already icy, but then I saw the front entry to my flat standing open. "No."

Doyle snatched at me but I was too fast for him. I nearly fell as my boots slid on the icy slush covering the floorboards of my front hall, and I grabbed a wall hook as I spotted the broken glass and wilted flowers on the threshold of my front room.

"They might still be in here," Doyle told me as he caught up. "Go outside and wait like a good gel."

"Leave off, Tommy." I picked my way round the slush and went into my flat.

Whoever had broken into my home had not been instructed to take anything; every possession in the room had been systematically smashed, slashed or shredded. A plaster-dusted, twenty-pound hammer lay on the floor under the holes it had knocked through my paintings and walls. Cold wind washed my face as it blew in through the shattered windows, and had begun to freeze all the food that had been emptied out of my icebox and pantry.

More ice was forming from the puddle coming out of my bath; I looked in to see three small fountains of water gushing from the pipes that had been torn out of the walls. My sink and old bathtub had also made the acquaintance of the hammer, judging by the pieces they lay in.

At first I couldn't understand the torn, twisted mound of material heaped atop my commode, until I made out the pattern of my favorite red bodice. Every garment I owned had been emptied out of my armoire and dressers, torn apart, and shoved into the loo.

To my surprise, seeing the destruction of my wardrobe hurt most. I'd never been much of a fancy dresser, but because I'd left Middy with only the clothes on my back, it had taken me years to put together a decent, serviceable supply of skirts, bodices, and cloaks. Some I'd taken in trade for my services; others I had saved for months to afford. And there, dangling from beneath the pile, a torn strip of pink from the gown Rina had lent me, the gown I'd not had the chance to return.

My friends had dressed me in their finery; my foolishness had now cost two gowns, my virtue, my office, and my home. What did I have left?

"Kit?"

"The main shutoff valve for the pipes is out by the boiler," I told Doyle. My voice sounded flat and hollow, echoing in my own ears. "Or whatever is left of it."

"Kit." He put a hand under my elbow. "Come away now."

I pulled my arm away. "Go and shut off the water before the place floods out. Please, Inspector."

As soon as he left I went to my cashsafe to see if I did have anything left. The door had been badly dented, but it had not been opened; the locks had held. Quickly I used the combination to release them and clean out the safe, putting all the cash I had to my name in my reticule. Happily I'd never trusted banks, and kept only a small amount of funds in my business account, to which Walsh had likely already helped himself. Then I went upstairs to see what more he'd done.

Doyle stood waiting at the bottom of the stairs when I came back down. "Did they get at the rest?"

I nodded. "He must have sent in a whole gang. By the look of things they were well paid, too."

"I'll have my men question the neighbors," he assured me. "We'll find them, Kit."

"Don't bother." My heart felt like a stone in my chest. "If you would post a beater outside to watch the place, I'll have someone over before nightfall to board up the windows and doors." I walked out.

"Where are you going?" Before I could answer, he said, "Wherever it is, he'll find you."

I didn't look back at him. "Not this time, he won't."

〜

Wrecker met me on the street halfway to the Eagle's Nest; he removed his cap and held it between his hands but couldn't seem to get any words out.

"I've seen it," I told him. "I need someone to board up the place."

"Already on his way." He scuffled his heels round the snow a bit. "I'm real sorry, Miss Kit. No call to be doing such things to a lady like you. Carri's over here."

Wrecker drove me the rest of the way to Rina's house, where I found her wrapped in furs and pacing back and forth in the alley. As soon as she spotted us she ran to the carri and practically dragged me out of it.

"Bugger all, Kit. Someone said you'd nearly been shot outside court. I nearly worried myself into the vapors." She smothered me with her furry collar before holding me at arm's length. "Inside. Now."

I followed her inside, up the stairs and into her chambers, where she divested me of my cloak and used her fingers to loosen the icy tresses round my face.

"I've put a tray upstairs, madam," Almira said as she came out of the kitchen. "Miss Kit." She folded me into her arms and gave me a tight hug. "Go on with you."

Rina guided me upstairs to her chambers and forced me to drink a cup of tea so hot it scalded me into silence. Which was handy, as she had a great deal to get off her chest.

"Bleeding Walsh's going to pay for this, I swear on the cross." She threw her furs over a chair and kicked a tuffet across the room. "Having you tossed out your office, then taken into court like some two-pence alley-tart—and then, while you're ducking bullets, razing your place? It's too much, even for a nobheaded, tightassed son of a poxbox like him."

"No, it wasn't." For some reason I couldn't stop thinking about Dredmore, and how quickly he had killed the snuffmage outside court. Why had he come there? To see me convicted, and applaud as I was sent off to prison? Or to bribe someone to place me in his custody? Why had he bothered to defend me?

"Wrecker'll do him in a minute," Rina was still ranting. "No, I think he'll do him in hours and hours, while we have a bottle of wine and watch and make useful suggestions."

"Rina." I waited until she looked at me. "Wrecker will do *no* such thing."

"But after what old blueballs did to you—"

"No killing, no torture," I told her flatly. "The same goes for Dredmore. He saved my life." I set down the cup before rising and reaching for my cloak.

She positioned herself in front of the door. "You're not going back out there."

"I have to." Even if I had nowhere else to go. "If Walsh learns that I'm here, he'll come after you and your gels."

"Oh, please, God." Her smile was a dreadful thing to behold. "Let him."

"Let him do things to you that make my misfortunes look like a spring stroll down the prommy?" I shook my head.

"Then we'll call on Bridget's Charles. He'll squash

Walsh like a gnat." She went to her desk. "I'll have him come round and you can tell him—"

"Carina. Stop." I joined her at the desk and took the pen and foolscap out of her hands. "Just stop now. It's done. It can't be undone, none of it."

Tears filled her eyes. "Do you even know what you look like, Kit? You're as white as bone. There are marks on your wrists from the shackles and glass all over your bodice. You're shaking." She held out trembling hands. "God blind me. *I'm* shaking."

"We're angry, and hurt, and frightened." I touched her cheek. "But one thing we're not, the one thing we will never be, is daft. We need to take some time now to think and to plan." I put my reticule in her hands. "This is every pence I have left in the world. I need you to hold it safe for me."

"You're staying here."

"I can't risk—"

"Shut up. I needed a new gel—and so I hired one." She tucked a piece of my hair behind my ear. "Name of Connie. A bit dark and on the skinny side, but some gents like that."

I sighed. "Walsh knows my middle name."

"Then Rosie, or Lucy, or . . ." She stopped and suddenly smiled. "Prudence."

Chapter Seventeen

"If I like the looks of someone, can I give him a free one?" I asked my new employer, and then hissed as a hairpin dug into my scalp. "You're hurting!"

"You're not selling or bartering or giving anything to anyone under my roof," Rina told my reflection. She pinned the new switch in several more places. "You're a good gel, and you're going to stay that way."

I tucked my bottom lip under my top teeth to keep from correcting her.

"Don't do that; you'll scrape off the tint." She sprayed my switch with a light mist of her perfume and stepped back. "You make a pretty hothead."

I studied my reflection in Rina's vanity glass, turning my head this way and that. The elegant scarlet curls of the expensive hair switch should have made my tanned skin appear yellow, but instead they brought out the pinkish tones and gave me a rosy look.

"Bridget has freckles," I mentioned. "I always wanted freckles."

"You always wanted to be a man, a firebrigader, a pilot, and seven feet tall. Let us be grateful that heaven has remained stone-deaf to your prayers." She went to her working-hours armoire. "Take off everything, including your drawers."

I didn't mind the switch or the lip tint, but I couldn't imagine myself parading about in one of Rina's filmy business garms. "Couldn't I be Prudence the new scullery, or Prudence the apprentice cook?"

She began pushing hangers back and forth as she searched through a rainbow of cutout velvets, thin silks, and spangled nettings. "He'll be expecting that."

I got up and joined her. "But my posing as a working strumpet would be a complete stunner."

"You may stir up trouble on the Hill, poke your nose in the wrong corners, and have all the worst sort of friends"—she turned and held a bronze satin corset against my front before replacing it in the armoire—"but you're still a decent woman with a business and your own home. You're regarded as such by all who know you. Women like you would rather starve, go to prison, jump a cliff, or embrace a blade than give it up for money." An odd look came over her face. "No matter how desperate you lot become."

She was only repeating the words her father had hurled at her the one time she had tried to see him. I knew because I had taken her. "Rina."

The side of her mouth curled. "No worries. We'll need a nudie. Be right back." She hurried out.

I didn't know what a nudie was, so I went to refill my tea and sat down on the window seat. Fingers of icy air poked at me from where they crept under the sill, and I saw drifts piling up on the street below. The temperature was still dropping, which would keep trade light tonight.

It had been a bright and sunny day two years ago when I'd taken Rina on the shopping expedition. She'd hated the proper bodice and skirts I'd lent her for the excursion, and had refused to take off her hat and veil, even when we stopped for tea and cakes. I hadn't understood until after I made her come with me into the glove shop.

"You paid for tea, and you need a new pair for church," I'd argued as I dragged her in through the entry. "Besides, I can't afford anything grander than kid, so they'll be warm and serviceable."

"Aye." She looked at the proprietor, who was coming round from behind the counter to wait on us. "I'm certain that you'll find that here."

"Ladies." The shopkeep, a pleasant-faced older man with ruddy skin and a suggestion of native round the eyes, bowed politely. "May I be of service?"

"We'd like to see something in thin kid for my friend here," I told him as I ushered Rina over to the counter.

"I have all colors dyed, bleached, or natural," he said, holding out his hand to Rina. "If the lady would let me size her?"

"You needn't," Rina said, taking off her hat and veil and gazing at him with big eyes. "I'm a four slim, remember?"

Watching the change that came over the shopkeeper was like seeing a man turned to stone. "Carina."

"Hello, Da." She offered him a beautiful smile. "How's trade?"

Much bellowing had followed, all from the glove-maker, who had called his daughter nine kinds of a slut before I'd tried to intervene. Then he had told me exactly why he and his family had washed their hands of their strumpet daughter before kicking us out of the shop.

Once we were in the cab I hailed, I'd turned to Rina. "Why didn't you tell me that was your father's shop?"

"You wouldn't have gone in, and I wanted to see him," she'd said simply. "I haven't, you know. Not once since Medford broke our engagement. Last time I saw Da was when he'd tossed me out the house and bolted the doors. When I wouldn't leave the front stoop he had the servants summon a beater to drive me off."

That was the last of our shopping excursions, and although I hadn't known until it was too late, I'd always felt guilty over causing the ugly reunion. Now I'd reminded her of it again.

Rina returned with what appeared to be a pair of flesh-colored stockings sewn to the bottom of a thin corset-style bodice in matching fabric. "Here, this one should fit you."

My gaze went to the open crotch. "I can't wear that contraption."

"It's called a nudie, and it's to preserve your modesty, madam." She tossed the odd garment at me. "You wear it under your negli, and it keeps your naughty bits from showing through."

I held up the crotchless bit. "Not here, it doesn't."

"Oh, right. Sorry." She went to her dresser and began sorting through her lingerie. "The open crotch is for convenience; some gents can be too impatient to wait."

She produced something that looked to me like a thin nappy.

"You're going to diaper me?" I asked.

"They're called knickers," she explained as she brought the abbreviated garment to me. "All the rage across the pond." When she saw my face she held it up against her pelvis. "You see? You put them on just like drawers."

"So I'm to wear drawers without legs under stockings and a corset without a crotch and then a gown on top." I caught the knickers she tossed to me. "Couldn't I pretend to be a client? A fully dressed, male client?"

"That's a good idea," Rina admitted, "but I haven't any men's clothes small enough for you here. I'll send out for some tomorrow, but in the meantime you'll have to be patient, Prudence."

I gave her a narrow look. "You're enjoying this."

"Enormously." She went round me and began unfastening my waister. After a moment she added, "I didn't mean to go off on you before, love. That business with Da back then, that was all on me."

"I never stopped wishing I could do something about it." I pulled my bodice carefully over my head so as not to dislodge the switch. "Expose Medford's son for what he did, or at least make him tell your da the truth."

"No one would believe the word of a woman over a man's," Rina said, her tone firm. "If someone had, the rot bastard would've just had all his mates swear that I'd bedded them, too." She helped me step out of my skirts. "Let's talk about something happier, please. Like that clerk from your building who stood up for you in court. He sounds promising."

"Fourth?" I chuckled as I stripped out of my drawers and held up the knickers. "He's just a lad. Besides, I practically have him married off already. Do I put both feet through the holes here?"

"One in each." She held my elbow to keep me from

toppling over. "You've not lost your head over that tow-headed copper, I hope. He's pretty enough until you see all that disgusting truth and justice gleaming in his eyes."

"Inspector Doyle's a good sort." I hauled the knickers up until they covered my front and back bits. "He spoke up for me in court, you know. He didn't have to do that."

Rina held out the nudie. "Step into it. That's it." As I braced my hands against her shoulders, she pulled the flesh-colored garment up my legs and over the knickers. "Maybe he fancies you. He'll want marriage and a baby every year, you know. His sort always do."

"I am not having babies; Tom Doyle's or anyone else's." While Rina laced up the back, I pulled over my shoulders the short penders and buttoned them to the edge of the corset, which kept the flimsy, skintight contraption in place. "Marriage is also not in the cards."

"Cards can be shuffled, love." She came round to inspect the front. "Once this thing with Walsh goes away, you can move on, start over. Maybe go up to Settle."

"All it does there is rain." I plucked at the fabric clinging to my breasts. "This is too small."

"It's perfect. Stop fussing." She brought a sheer gown made of diagonal strips of black net and deep gray satin over from the armoire. "This one will do."

I refused to allow the colors to remind me of Dredmore. "Can't I wear something with a bit more cheer to it?"

"I've a lovely little pink thing," Rina said. "That and a switch with ribbons and tails, and you can play Daddy's Despair."

I shuddered. "I'll wear the black and gray."

"Coward." A knock sounded on the door, making Rina glance at her pin watch. "It's past time I got downstairs to manage the gels. Finish dressing and then go to the Amber Room on two. And unless you want to earn your keep the hard way, Kit, keep the damned door locked."

Draping myself in the black and gray gown didn't make me feel any less naked, but I didn't see anything showing through when I checked the full-length glass. Wearing the garments of a working strumpet had to be my most scandalous disguise yet, but after I made a few rounds of the room I began to appreciate the lightness of the nudie and the unrestricted movements I could make in the loose gown.

Comfortable as I was, it still required a fair amount of nerve to step out into the hall and make my way to the stairs. There I froze halfway to the second floor as a blond gel with an older gent passed by me.

"You've a decent fire built?" the man was asking her. "My feet are ice blocks."

"No worries, dearie." The strumpet dropped me a wink. "I'll have you thawed in no time."

The man hadn't even glanced at me, I realized, and I chuckled as I continued down. My costume was as good as a cloak of invisibility.

A few gels had already brought up their first clients of the night, judging by the noise coming from behind the closed entries I passed. I heard one shrill voice demanding to be spanked harder, and cringed as the gel in the room obliged, making him shriek all the louder.

"Hey, Birdie's been holding out on us," a sodden voice said behind me, and a damp hand turned me round to face three gents and the gels they'd hired. The one holding my arm grinned and stepped closer. "Oh, I do like gingers, I do. What's your name, ducks?"

"'At's Prudence." The busty blonde clinging to his arm tried to pull him back and gave me a hard look. "Her's been hired out for an all-nighter, 'aven't you, dearie?"

I nodded and tried to hurry off, but the blonde's gent wouldn't release me.

"Must be good," the drunk told his mates. To me he said, "Whatever he's paid, I'll double it." He tried to shove me into the blonde. "I want to see the two of you have a go at it."

"I don't entertain ladies," I said without thinking, which made all three men burst into laughter.

"Gel's got a sense of humor, too. Capital." The drunk cuffed my shoulder. "Tell you what, Pru. Since you're so shy, you can play the maid."

"No," a voice I had never wanted to hear again said. "She cannot."

I looked between the drunk and the blonde and saw the dark figure standing just beyond the group. He'd donned a heavier cloak and a mask that covered every feature above his mouth, but the voice was unmistakable.

I glanced at the blonde. If I went with her and her client, I'd have to perform an illegal sexual act with another woman for which the Church said I would be damned for all eternity. Or I could go to Dredmore.

I really had to think about it.

"Milord." I didn't smile or natter on about how happy I was to see him; I had a few shreds of pride left. I gestured in the direction of the Amber Room. "This way."

"Oh, don't go running off to do the dirty right away, ducks," the drunk said, and wheeled round to give Dredmore a foolish grin. "Come and have a drink with us first."

I waited for Dredmore to refuse the offer. Instead he came and put an arm round me.

"We'd be delighted," he told the drunk.

I felt no shame in playacting the strumpet. My garms may not have been to my personal taste, but I didn't consider myself superior to Rina or her gels. Had fate been only a fraction more unkind to me, I might have sold myself on the streets of Middy.

But to be marched along and obliged to behave like Dredmore's whore made me feel as if I'd poured several gallons of lamp oil over my head while standing next to a bonfire. It wouldn't take much of a spark to set me off.

Why had he come? Furthermore, how had he known that I'd be here?

You've been spending too much time in the company of strumpets.

I held my tongue until we reached the large party chamber the gents had rented for their revelries. I couldn't make myself cross the threshold, not until I felt Dredmore's hand at the small of my back.

"Afraid?" he murmured.

"Bored." I wondered how I might get rid of him in front of six witnesses. Perhaps when he lit one of his infernal cigars I would accidentally tip an oil lamp in his lap.

At first glance Rina's party room resembled a parlour, with settees and lamps and elegant drapes. Then I noticed how wide the settees were, and some baskets that contained unmarked bottles of golden liquid, lengths of satin ribbon, and, of all things—

"Peacock feathers?" One of the gents reeled over to a basket and plucked out a long plume. "Now, what can you do with one of these beauties, love?"

His strumpet, a leggy brunette who had thin lips beneath too much tint, whispered something in his ear, making him roar with laughter.

Dredmore steered me round the others to a settee by the crackling fire in the hearth. Rather than sit I leaned against one arm and held out my hands as if to warm them.

He hovered, not quite touching me but close enough to keep the others from hearing him. "You shouldn't have run from me."

"I didn't run." I turned my hands over and wriggled my fingers. "I rode."

He grunted. "I suppose I should be grateful that you left Velvet at a decent stable."

"Velvet." Of course, because he was black.

"I didn't name him." He came to stand beside me. "You could have killed yourself, riding alone in the dark."

I glanced up at him. "Disappointed?"

His mouth twisted. "I came to court today for you."

"I saw," I acknowledged. "Yet you never made it into the courtroom."

"I was waiting by the prisoner's gate," he said. "When they brought you out, I was going to take you from them. Then I had to deal with that snuffmage."

"For which I am grateful, Lucien." I had to say that much.

He regarded me for a long moment. "No, you're not."

"You two bickering already?" The drunk thrust a tumbler of gin into Dredmore's hand and then presented me with a much smaller measure in a finger glass. He lifted his own drink, sloshing a bit over the brim as he toasted me. "Here's to all the gels with ginger curls, be they east or west, they shag you best."

"To the compliments of discriminating, fine young gentlemen." I pretended to take a sip and watched Dredmore do the same.

"Come on, you two." The drunk gave me a playful push that almost knocked me over. "Have a sit and get acquainted."

To avoid another shove, I went and sat on the end of the settee farthest away from Dredmore. Naturally he followed and boxed me in by seating himself directly beside me.

"That's more like it." The drunk patted my head with a clumsy hand before stumbling back over to the blonde.

I felt Dredmore's arm snake along my shoulders as I watched the others cavorting. "Madam Eagle will not allow you to remove me from the premises."

"Ging doesn't seem to fancy you as much as me, mate," the drunk called out, and slapped the blonde on the hip. "This one's more than willing, if you want a swap."

"Oh, I fancy him, sir." Before Dredmore could accept the offer, I turned and linked my arms round his neck. "I just take a little while to warm up."

I swung a leg over his, straddling him much as he had done to me last night, which allowed me to hide the hand I slipped between our bodies. I slid my fingers between his legs, taking secure hold of his testicles before I put my lips next to his ear.

"Tell him you're pleased with me," I warned, "or I'll squeeze until your eyes pop out your ears."

The grip I had on him demanded immediate obedience, but Dredmore only turned his head to brush his mouth across mine.

Chapter Eighteen

I couldn't believe Dredmore was kissing me while I had my fist round his stones, and he took advantage of my shock by seizing my wrist and dragging my hand up so that I was gripping his shaft. When I jerked he held me fast and looked over my shoulder.

"Tonight I must hold on to my Prudence," he told the drunk. He looked into my eyes. "Whatever it costs me."

His play on words brought another round of laughter from the men, but I dug my nails into him.

"We should perhaps go to our room," I suggested through my teeth, "so that you can begin to pay for your pleasures."

"An excellent suggestion." He released my wrist, clamped his hands on my waist, and stood with me still on him. The unexpected movement forced me to cling to him as he strode out of the room and into the hall, where he did not put me down but continued on to the Amber Room.

"Don't you think you're carrying this a little too far?" I asked as he entered and kicked the door shut behind us. "I mean, I'm not a native. Your saving my life doesn't mean you now own me."

"Walsh has men out searching for you." He set me

down and went to the window to check the street. "If I could find you, so can they. We have to go, now."

"I am not—"

He came to me, seized my shoulders, and shook me hard. "For once in your life, you daft twit, listen to me. That snuffmage wasn't the only one sent after you. And what Walsh's men did to your flat is what they were told to do to *you*. When they learn that you're here—and they will—they'll come for you."

I wrenched out of his grip and folded my arms. "Let them. Rina has Wrecker."

"Walsh has twenty Wreckers out there tonight," Dredmore said. "They'll surround the place, put a few guards on the outside doors, and cut the kneecapper's throat. Then they'll look for you, Charmian, and they'll take their time. Especially with the women."

Bile rose in my throat, and I swallowed against it. "I'll call Rumsen Main and speak to Inspector Doyle. He'll send his men over to protect the house."

"His superiors won't permit it," he told me.

"I'll tell him what you told me—"

"Walsh owns the police commission; he'll already have warned them to stay out of his way." Dredmore sighed. "Even if your friend Doyle found a few survivors tomorrow, the commissioner would be more inclined to give Walsh a medal for cleaning up a disgrace to the city."

Almira came in carrying a tray with a bottle of champagne and a silver bowl piled high with strawberries. "We've trouble downstairs," she said as she thumped down the tray. "Two blokes with a warrant, wanting you, Kit. They say they're Yard but they look like fists for hire."

"So you should have no problem telling them I'm not here," I suggested.

"The warrant's for a search of the place," the cook told me, "and Rina's had to let them in." She glanced at Dredmore. "If you mean to fool them, milord, you two had best get busy."

He nodded, and once the cook departed he took my arm and tugged me over to the bed.

I resisted. "There's no need for that. We can play cards."

He straightened my wig. "Cards, in a brothel. Yes, that should be quite convincing."

"Oh, very well." I drew back the coverlet and sheets, rumpling them in the process. "I'm not taking off my clothes, and neither are you."

"Agreed." Dredmore turned me round and pushed me onto my back, reaching to pull up my skirts. "New lingerie?"

I glanced down and seized his wrists. "Borrowed, not mine." I heard a shriek from down the hall and cringed. "Take off your jacket."

Before he did Dredmore retrieved the champagne and strawberries and brought them to the bed.

"Don't bother with that," I urged when he uncorked the bottle with a loud pop. "Just come down here and kiss me."

"Men do not kiss harlots," he said as he straddled me and yanked at my bodice, tearing it open. "Not on the mouth, anyway."

I muffled my own shriek as he poured some champagne on my front. "Lucien." The cold, bubbly stuff felt shocking on my skin. "What are you—?"

As the door flung open he popped an overlarge strawberry in my mouth and put his to work on my champagne-soaked skin.

"Police," a rough voice called out, and I closed my eyes briefly.

Dredmore made a vague gesture I couldn't see, mesmerized as I was by the sight of his lips on my breast and the feel of his tongue as he licked some drops of champagne from one tight, reddened peak.

"We're here for a woman," the intruder added. "Name of Charmian Kittredge."

Dredmore raised his head an inch. "This one's called Ginger," he said as he stared down at me and used one hand to cover my now-rosy breast. "If you want her, you'll have to wait your turn. I'll be another hour."

A crude snicker answered him. "Not tonight, sir. Sorry to bother."

As soon as I heard the door slam I removed the strawberry, which I'd bitten in half, from my mouth. "Good." I chewed and swallowed, and then on impulse offered him the rest. "Your reward, sir."

Dredmore took a bite, watching me as he removed the remainder from my grasp and brought my hand to his mouth. One by one he sucked the traces of juice from my fingers, causing a terrible heat to gather inside me. I could also feel his muscles tightening under his garms, and the hard bulge of his shaft now pressing between my legs.

"We can't," I whispered. "This is a pretense, remember?"

"Is it?" His eyes gleamed as he lashed my palm with his tongue before he caught my mouth with his.

The taste of the strawberry sweetened the kiss, which was not at all sweet, but wet and deep and passionate, and seemed to last an hour. I was very glad I was not a harlot, I thought as I worked at the buttons of his shirt and opened it to bare his chest. They had no idea what they were missing.

"I like this lingerie," Dredmore mentioned as he tugged the knickers out of the way and found the open crotch with his hand.

"So do I." As his fingers breeched me I arched up, catching my breath when I felt my body receive him with a soft slickness that should have been embarrassing. "What if someone comes in?"

"I am a deathmage." He shifted over me, reaching down to open the front of his trousers. "I'll kill them."

"Lucien, you can't, ah." Words deserted me as he worked the swollen head of his penis past my folds. Nothing had ever felt so good, or so right, as the way he came into me. I found my voice somewhere. "You're determined, then? I cannot persuade you—"

"Charmian." He penetrated me with a single, forceful movement. "Be quiet and think of England."

As I relished the stretching sensation his shaft created inside me, his advice made me frown. "God, why?"

What followed was, like our first time together in his gardens, utterly astonishing to me. Dredmore moved in me with what should have been the most basic of motions, pressing deep, dragging out, and then forging back in. Magic was made from the delicious friction involved, perhaps, or the way my body responded, rather like a mad creature on its own. I could not keep my hands from him as the pleasure built between us, and the damp sounds of our coupling grew louder and faster and wetter.

Dredmore seemed equally undone; he bent his head to alternate between kissing my mouth and sucking at my breasts, while I scored his shoulders with my nails and pressed my lips to his chest. The room seemed to dim as the ache inside me swelled, tormented now by the hard thrusts of his shaft into me. I could feel the heat we stoked growing liquid and spreading out, melding us in our frantic movements.

I found I could not wait for him as I hurtled through the dark and shattered under him, my whole being consumed by the delight of it. Distantly I heard his voice, rough and shaking as he jerked atop me, and the luscious pulse of his seed jetting and flooding my clenching sheath.

I murmured some nonsense, holding him fast to me as we drifted together, bound by body and heart. Now I understood why women could not resist men; they were our physical completion.

Dredmore eventually withdrew from me, turning onto his side and gathering me against him. He seemed to take quite a long time studying my face. "What are you thinking?"

"If someone had come in," I answered truthfully, "I think *I* would have killed them. That and we should never play cards."

He nodded slowly and brushed some hair back from

my eyes. "I should like to spend the next week in this bed with you, but we must go."

I recalled the unfortunate aftermath of our first love-making and gave him a narrow look. "To where, exactly?"

"A place safer than this." He propped himself up on one elbow. "There is something I have to show you."

I glanced down. "I believe I have seen everything you have now."

"This you have not." He rose from the bed and offered me his hand. "Come."

I went to the armoire and found a reasonably decent dark blue gown with white braided trim, and after washing up at the basin in the corner I dressed in it. Dredmore came to button up the back for me and draped his cloak over my shoulders, pulling up the hood to conceal my head. "Stay behind me on the way out, and don't say a word to anyone."

"If you're thinking of imprisoning me again," I told him, "you'll lose more than a horse this time." Which made me think. "Someone will see us leave the house. Walsh will know you have me."

"Of course he will," Dredmore said as he led me to the door and opened it a gap to look through and check the hallway.

I frowned. "You *want* him to come after you for saving me."

"I want him to believe I did my job." He glanced back at me. "Last night he hired me to kill you."

"I see." His confession struck me hard, and left me feeling numb and daft, as if he'd already shoved a dagger between my ribs. "Why didn't you?"

"I was too busy making arrangements to get you out of the country." He saw my face and took my cold hands in his. "I intended to tell you when I returned this morning, only to find you'd escaped right back into Walsh's hands."

"You might have said something last night." But I'd barely given him a chance to tell me anything before my temper had gotten the best of me. "How much am I worth dead?"

"Twenty."

I felt a little miffed. "Surely I'm worth more than twenty pounds."

"You are. He gave me twenty thousand." He checked his watch. "Connell will have the coach out back by now. Come."

Still reeling from the thought that my death would be worth a small fortune to Nolan Walsh, I followed Dredmore out into the hall and down the back stairs. Almira intercepted us by the kitchen.

"You sneaking away without paying, milord?"

Dredmore placed enough coin in her hand to make the cook gasp aloud. "If anyone asks," he told her, "please tell them that you saw me leave with Miss Kittredge, and that she was fighting me."

"Miss Kit?" Almira peered round him. "You're not fighting this gent."

"Tell anyone who asks that I did." I pushed back the hood enough so that she could see my face. "And please, do tell Rina I'll be in touch when it's safe."

Dredmore hustled me out into the side alley, where Connell was waiting with the coach. I peered up at him, hoping to see a hint of Harry in his face, but the man ignored me. Dredmore retrieved a woolen blanket from the rear-facing seat, wrapping it about me before he scooped me up and placed me on his lap.

"I can sit over there," I told him.

"This is warmer." He glanced out through the side window before clamping an arm round my neck. "We're being watched. Struggle."

Out of reflex I did, and then I caught a glimpse of two nobbers trotting toward the coach. "Let go of me, you bastard," I cried out, loud enough for them to hear before the horses were slapped and the coach took off.

Dredmore released me as soon as we were out of view and called up, "Go to the blackstone, Connell. Stay to the alleys."

I slid off his lap as soon as he removed his arm, but stayed close to him. "You have a house in the city?"

"Several." He tucked in the blanket round me before leaning his head back and closing his eyes. A shaft of light from a gaslamp we passed briefly illuminated his weary features.

"You haven't slept."

"I imagined I'd find you in some gutter today," he said, his voice low. "With your throat cut and your blood draining into the sewers. It was not an image I found conducive to slumber."

"As if your beheading that snuffmage should give me sweet dreams?" I pulled the blanket up under my chin. "Maybe it would have been better all the way round if I'd ended up in the gaol."

"Better." He turned his head to regard me. "Walsh's

consortium controls most of the city, including the police and the courts. You'd have been found dead in your cell within an hour of your incarceration."

"Speaking of murder for hire, why would Walsh offer you twenty thousand, simply to kill a nobody like me?" My feet were freezing, so I tucked them up under me.

"He's frantic to see you dead, but I can't fathom why," Dredmore admitted. "It's gone beyond the truth behind the attacks on his wife. Something happened last night that made him terrified of you."

"What?" I thought back over the dinner. "I know I spoke out of turn a few times, but he mostly ignored me. The only time he became really agitated was when I challenged him."

"Lady Walsh is a pawn in a much larger game." He felt me shivering and pulled me closer, lifting one side of the blanket over him in order to share his body heat. "When you spoke of the wound paste, he reacted strangely. He stared at you for several moments."

I remembered that look. "As if he were seeing me for the first time. But that old trick isn't anything important. Other than it's being used to drive his wife mad."

"I think it's something else." He looked out as the coach came to a halt. "The snow is knee-deep. I'll have to carry you."

I pushed off the blanket. "Should I struggle again for the benefit of the neighbors?"

"I have no neighbors."

I saw why when he helped me out. "Dredmore, this is Feathersound."

"It is." He swung me up into his arms.

I linked my hands behind his neck. "The lord mayor allows you to make use of his private residence?"

"His *former* private residence." He carried me up the steps and through the door Connell had unlocked and held open. "He signed the deed over to me for services rendered."

"Does the governor know about this?" I frowned as I saw his driver lighting a candle to illuminate the dark hall. "No servants?"

"Officially the house has been closed for two years." He set me down and instructed Connell to light the fires before taking my hand. "Unofficially, it's haunted. Legally, it's mine."

Dredmore guided me into Feathersound's library, which appeared to be as large as my entire flat. Every wall had been fitted with shelves from floor to ceiling, save the center of one where space had been made for a massive cherrywood secretary. "You cheated the mayor out of his home by telling him it was haunted?"

"No. I saved his life from what he believed was the vengeful spirit of his former business partner." He went to the hearth and lit the kindling under a large stack of split seasoned oak. "The specter turned out to be the gifted and rather resourceful aide of the mayor's opponent, who had hoped to frighten away his competition before the election."

"But you didn't tell the mayor that," I guessed.

"After I assured His Honor that I had dispelled the spirit from the premises, I discreetly arranged for the mayor's opponent to withdraw from the election." He sat back on his heels and watched the flames catch. "Directly after that, he and his aide left Rumsen."

He hadn't killed them, as everyone had believed. "You blackmailed him."

"I persuaded him to relocate to a city in the east where he might enjoy more success in the political arena." He rose and brushed some melting snow from his shoulders before regarding me. "Why are you smiling at me like that?"

"You don't believe in magic any more than I do." And now I had proof of it. "You're an investigator like me. You only dress it up with spells and nonsense to hide your methods. So how did you disguise the blade you used on the snuffmage outside court? Was it some sort of trick, like the way you pretended to pop through the floors at Morehaven?"

"Come here, Charmian." He removed a dust drape from a cushiony lady's armchair by the fire and gestured for me to take a seat in it. When I did, he said, "I will answer your questions, but you must first do something for me."

My first, automatic response was to refuse, but Dredmore had just diverted Walsh's men from harming Rina and her gels, and had provided safe sanctuary for me. I owed him some cooperation, and we both knew it. "What do you want?"

"Take off your pendant and hand it to me."

The moment I did, I knew Harry would appear, but at least Dredmore wouldn't be able to see him. I reached up, unfastened the catch, and held out the chain to him.

The moment the pendant left my fingers, my grandfather's misty form appeared. He didn't say a word, but lunged at Dredmore, who quickly pocketed the pendant. As soon as he did, Harry turned semitransparent.

"Why on earth did you do that, you silly twit?" my grandfather shouted.

"Because I asked her to." Dredmore looked directly at Harry. "Hello, Ehrich."

"You know my grandfather?" I looked from Dredmore to Harry and back again. "Hang on. You can *see* him?"

"It's a trick, Charm." Harry solidified enough to cast a shadow on the faded but still colorful Turkish rug. "He's only making a pretense so he can use you. You must leave here at once."

"You'd rather send her out to die in the snow than tell her the truth?" Dredmore came to stand behind me, and I saw his angry expression reflected in the oval mirror above the mantel. "She's your own flesh and blood, old man. She deserves to know more than the bits and pieces that you've been feeding her."

"He seems to be able to see and hear you quite well," I advised my grandfather. The thought of how he had possessed Connell at Morehaven, and the prospect of him doing the same to Dredmore, made me gesture at a cluster of brass-studded bronze leather armchairs. "Why don't we all sit down and talk about this?"

"Sit down and talk. With him?" Harry uttered a bitter laugh. "You don't know what spawned him, or what his sort can do." He looked at Dredmore for the first time, and there was pure hatred in his eyes. "But I know, boy. I know exactly what you are."

"Have you told her what you've done?" Dredmore asked this with exquisite courtesy. "Why don't you explain that, Ehrich? Or are you leaving that for others to do, just as you did in France?"

"I know he was Houdini," I told Dredmore, and watched the white puff of my breath float from my lips. "Why is it so cold in here now?"

"That is his doing." He eyed my grandfather. "No more half-truths, Ehrich. Tell her who you were before you took possession of that Crown spy. Who you were when Harry White led his regiment into the Bréchéliant, and what you were when you came back out." He waited, but Harry said nothing, and the ticking of the great clock by the door seemed to grow very loud. "I see. She's good enough to torment, to use, to manipulate, but not worthy of the truth. Fortunately for you, Charmian is now under my protection."

"I beg your pardon." I stared at him. "Your *what*?"

"Your *what*?" Harry strode forward without looking, banged into an end table, and caught it before it toppled. When he took his hand from it he left an icy print of his palm and fingers. "Your father may have wanted recompense for being taken. Like the others, Jack deserved it. But his battle was never yours. You can bloody well do as you like, but you won't drag my granddaughter into it."

"She's in it to her ears." Dredmore was sneering now. "You had your chance to do right by her, Ehrich. More than a thousand of them, I should think. But you sacrificed her, and her mother, and her grandmother on the altar of Queen and country and your own pathetic schemes."

"So now you'll cut her throat?" Harry's eyes took on a strange purple glow. "I will end you first, boy."

The mention of murder made it high time for me to intervene. "Whatever quarrel you two have with each other, it's nothing to do with me. Lucien, I can look after myself, so stuff your protection. Harry, I'm not interested in carrying on whatever feud you have with Dredmore or his father." I remembered Hedger's strange reaction to learning that Harry was my grandfather. "Is there anyone who likes you?"

"His name isn't—" that was all my grandfather got out before Lucien stepped between us. His broad back kept me from seeing what he did, but his back muscles shifted, and then Harry abruptly vanished.

"What did you do?" I asked, shuffling back a few steps.

"I banished him back to the netherside." Dredmore turned to face me. "As long as you are with me, he cannot manifest or meddle with you."

"Harry's never meddled." When he would have come closer I went round behind the chair. "You, on the other hand, have inflicted an excessive amount of damage to my reputation, my person, and my life."

He didn't like that. "How have I harmed you, Charmian? By wanting you? By taking what you freely offered me? Or by trying to shield you from Walsh and dark forces that you cannot even begin to fathom?" He extended his arms in a helpless fashion. "Please, enlighten me as to which it was."

I did. "You abducted me and held me prisoner against my will. You raced about assassinating snuffmages, never mind that I might be blamed for the murders. Oh, and you also agreed to kill *me* for twenty thousand pounds."

"I took that fool's money to give to you," he shouted. "It was to help you settle into a new life—"

"After I left Toriana with you for some secluded lovers' nest overseas," I tacked on, "where I could nightly entertain you until you tired of me? I'd rather work for Rina."

"You might as well." He turned away. "I've tired of you already."

That stung, more than I cared to admit. "Problem solved, then."

I came round and sat in the armchair. "Before I'm forced to leave the country and flee for my life, perhaps you should tell me about this thing between you and Harry. Start with how you're able to see his specter, and exactly how you sent him off." I was particularly interested in the latter so that I might do the same if Harry became troublesome.

Dredmore went to the overly large secretary and opened the upper cabinet, sliding aside a panel. "He's not a specter. He's a manifesting spirit."

"There's a difference?" I frowned as he shifted and I saw the rows of switches that the panel had hidden. "What's that for?"

Dredmore put his thumb beneath one switch and glanced back at me. "You." He flipped the switch.

Two velvet-covered bars shot out from the ends of my chair's arms, bending at hidden joints and locking together at the ends. Before I could get to my feet, they retracted, shoving me back against the cushions. A smaller pair of bars swung out beneath my skirts and did the same, trapping my ankles in place. When I pushed at the bars locked across my waist, two cuffs popped out of them and snapped round my wrists.

"Don't bother struggling," Dredmore told me. "You haven't the strength."

I tried but I couldn't budge the chair's automatic manacles. I'd never heard of such mech, but Dredmore could afford things other mortals could only have nightmares about.

I looked up at him. "When you're finished," I said pleasantly, "you'd better plan to sleep with one eye open for the rest of your bleeding life."

"That I do already, Charmian." He turned his attention to the panel, and I heard doors being bolted and window latches fastening, and then a white-painted board descended from the ceiling.

I had nothing to do but wait and plot his slow, painful death, but still I jumped when the table beside me sprouted a complicated pile of gears, pulleys, and lenses.

"Is it a torture device?" I asked, wondering if he meant to feed my hands to it.

"It is called an illuminator. Let's hope it lives up to its name." He left the secretary, going round to all the lamps and turning them down until the room became shrouded in darkness. He pulled the chair to the other side of the table machine, and popped a matchit.

The bizarre rituals confused me, but the matchit didn't. Surely he wouldn't set me on fire, trapped as I was. "Lucien, perhaps I've been too harsh. You and I should talk more—"

"Do shut up, Charmian." He used the flame to light a small row of candles inserted in the back of the device. As soon as their wicks caught, he adjusted a row of small mirrors, and several shafts of light merged and formed a glowing circle on the hanging board.

"There is a difference between spirits and specters," Dredmore said as he placed a cylinder lined with tiny, silverblack-etched glasses in front of the rows of candles. "We didn't know what it was, not until after the war." He switched on the machine.

My eyes widened as a flickering picture appeared on the white board. In it tiny figures of soldiers marched across a field toward a forest, and they moved just as if I were standing there behind them, watching.

"The illuminator uses a zoopraxiscope to show many images in succession," I heard Dredmore say.

"Then it needs a shorter name." Angry as I was, I couldn't stop watching the moving pictures. "Who are they?"

"A regiment in the North country." Dredmore left the machine running, picked up a fire iron, and poked at the logs in the hearth, creating an updraft of orange and yellow sparks. "Your grandfather and my father were among them. They were friends once."

"Lucien, your father is titled," I said. "I know he's exempt from service. Think of a better lie."

"Lady Travallian was my mother, and her husband recognized me as his heir, but Jack, the man who sired me, was a commoner." Dredmore came to sit on the floor beside me. "He was also a tintest, attached to your grandfather's regiment."

Having such a large, dignified figure at my feet seemed ridiculous, especially when I couldn't kick him in the head, but it wasn't as if I could change seats. "Is that why Lord Travallian disowned you and left the title to his nephew? Because you're a bastard in truth?"

"No." He curled a hand round my calf. "After I discovered that Jack was my father, and what he could do, I told my mother's husband to disown me, and I cut all ties to my family."

The rub of his thumb against the bare back of my knee made me grit my teeth. It also made my shoulders turn to pudding. "How noble of you."

"Before I reached my majority, Jack came to see me. He told me how he and my mother had met, and why she married Travallian. He explained what had happened to him during the war." He glanced up at me. "My father was a Lost Timer. So was your grandfather."

CHAPTER NINETEEN

For all his obsession with sciences and mech, my father had dearly loved history. Each night, when he came to tuck me in, he'd tell me a story about strange people and their forgotten worlds, as if they were faeriestales. He particularly loved the mysterious and unexplained, like how the Nile people had built such enormous pyramids, or why four hundred Norders had vanished overnight from their first Torian settlement.

Da had mentioned the Lost Timers to me once, too, and now I searched my memory until I recalled something of what he had said. "That was what they called those soldiers who went missing in Britanny during the war. They got lost in some forest and weren't seen for months."

"That is how it began." Little prisms, cast off by the glass cylinder as it turned, slid down Dredmore's face and chest. "Ordinarily the regiment's tintest remained behind the lines to protect their equipment, so my father wasn't even supposed to be with them. The depth and breadth of the Bréchéliant made it impossible for Jack to capture the fighting from a safe distance, and he was obliged to follow the regiment into the forest. He thought he would be safe if he stayed in the trees." His voice went hollow. "He didn't know what was waiting for him . . . for all of them."

A deep suspicion began to gather inside me as I looked at the moving picture again. It had started over from the beginning and was showing the men crossing the field. "Is this your father's work, then?" I asked, nodding toward the board.

"The original ambrotints were his. I had copies made smaller to fit the device." He glanced at it and then got up to change out the glass cylinder, replacing it with another.

This time, the moving picture showed the soldiers creeping through the trees, sometimes looking back as if they sensed we were following them.

"Jack told me that from the moment he crossed over into the forest, he felt as if something was watching them," Dredmore said. "When it grew dark, he began packing up his tinter to wait to shoot until he had morning light, but then there was light. Strange light that came out of nowhere."

Strange indeed. On the board I watched bizarre glowing streaks darting behind the trees, and while the silverblack on the glass ambrotints rendered all of the light gray, the faster the streaks moved, the brighter they seemed to flash.

"Lampflies," I murmured to myself as the soldiers came upon a dense grove of old oaks and more lights began filling the moving picture. "A swarm might look like that."

"I thought the same," Dredmore said, "until Jack told me the frost a month before the battle had already killed off all the insects."

I felt impatient. "Then what were they? More specters? Leg-sprouting candles? Dancing Yuletide trees?"

The moving picture stopped as Dredmore changed cylinders again. New images appeared that showed the soldiers taking firing positions behind the oaks' immense trunks.

"Your grandfather assumed, not entirely incorrectly, that the lights were torches being waved by the Talian forces. As you see, he ordered his men to take up defensive positions in an old oak grove. He had no way of knowing that the lieutenant leading the enemy troops toward the grove from the other side thought the English were doing the exact same thing, and had put his men in identical positions. Which is all they wanted."

The moving picture started again from the beginning, showing the soldiers following the lights and then taking cover from them. Dredmore said nothing until I prompted, "They?"

"The trees." He switched off the machine and blew out the candles. "They took them."

"The *trees* took them." I was right; he was mad.

"They seized every soldier on both sides of that grove. They pulled their bodies into their trunks. They swallowed them whole." Dredmore went to the mantel, bracing one arm against the carved, polished wood to look down into the merrily crackling flames. "The men had to become part of the trees so that the Aramanthan trapped inside could possess them and escape."

And for this he had trussed me to an armchair? He couldn't be drunk; he'd barely touched the gin at Rina's. Harry's sudden appearance certainly hadn't frightened him out of his wits. No, whatever had addled his brain must be more serious than grumpy ghosts and the blue ruin. "Lucien, I'm sure your father saw some terrible things during the war, but really. Man-eating trees?"

"The oaks had been bespelled long ago. No," he added when I looked away, and came to loom over me. "You will listen to me this time."

"Very well." I was annoyed, but he was an unbalanced deathmage, and if regaining my freedom and preserving my ability to breathe meant catering to his insanity, then I'd make a decent show of it. I glanced up. "I'm listening. Tell me the rest of this faeriestale."

"Faeries didn't build the Bréchéliant," he said. "It was the haven of the Druuds, the old high priests who protected humanity. A thousand years ago, they saved the world by putting an end to a civil war being fought by the Aramanthan. They combined their powers to lure all of the warring immortals and their minions into the forest, where they bound their spirits to enchanted stones and cast their bodies into the oaks. They then warded the forest itself to prevent anyone from entering it."

"Using magic that, oh, didn't work." I controlled an impulse to begin tapping my slipper by nudging the edge of the Turkish rug with one toe. "How awful for them."

"The spells didn't fail." He walked over to an antique standing globe displayed beside the heavy tapestry window curtains, and with a nudge of his thumb set the little sphere to spinning. "The world changed. Over the centuries, weather, floods, and earthquakes created new paths round the old wards into the Bréchéliant. The soldiers on both sides simply stumbled onto them."

I again marveled at how magic always seemed to evaporate at the most convenient moments. "Tragic."

Dredmore stopped the globe. "Time had changed the immortal prisoners of the grove as well. Nothing remained of their bodies except dust. Their immortal spirits endured, however, trapped as they were in stones used by the Druuds to imprison them. By that time they had learned what they needed to escape." He came to me, and absently tucked a stray piece of my hair behind my ear. "Can you guess what it was?"

"A woodman's ax?" I guessed. "Lightning? Termites?"

"Hosts, Charmian." He popped a matchit and lit the lamp nearest my chair. The frosted glass diffused the flame into a soft amber glow that gilded every edge in the room. "Living bodies that could house and transport their spirits."

"So when the soldiers came, these imprisoned spirits dragged them into the trees so they might use them like carris." Did he even realize how ridiculous he sounded? "Is this when the white rabbit makes an appearance and leads them and a little gel into a garden of talking flowers?"

Instead of growing angry again, he smiled a little. "I said almost the very same thing to Jack. He told me that at first none of the soldiers who came out of the forest truly believed what had happened to them. It seemed like nothing but a long, bad dream, until they discovered exactly how much time had passed, and how greatly they had been changed."

Dredmore setting me on fire suddenly didn't seem as bad as before, and once I convinced him to release me from the chair I'd have to make a run for it. The window latches were the heavy, solid sort that were inclined to stick; it would have to be the door. "I suppose their feet had been turned into roots, their arms into branches, and their hair into bird's nests."

"The men found they could move objects, start fires, even see into the future," he said, and touched a center spot on his brow. "From here, simply by thinking it."

"Mind power." I sighed. "Of course it would be that. Couldn't exactly walk about with roots for feet, could they? Imagine the dirt they'd track everywhere. And the cobbler's bills."

"You agreed to listen," he reminded me. "Some of the spirits—indeed, most of them—wanted to atone for the great damage they had inflicted on the mortal world during the mage war. They guided the soldiers they had taken to take up their normal lives again, and to use their mind powers discreetly and wisely. They formed a secret association so they might help and govern each other. The less benign spirits were not so benevolent, and wanted to kill the spirits of the men they had possessed so the bodies would be theirs alone. To avoid another war, the two groups agreed to go their separate ways."

"After which they all lived blissfully ever onward," I guessed, eyeing the high shine of the waxed cherrywood flooring. When I ran for it, I'd have to be careful to keep to the rugs or my slippers would have me skidding straight into a collection of botany books.

"The group of men who hosted the benevolent spirits went back to England and called themselves the Tillers," he told me. "The others withdrew to Talia, and became known as the Reapers. Little is known about the Reapers except some rumors. It's said that they still desire to settle old scores."

It was incredible how much detail he'd worked into his delusion . . . or perhaps there was nothing wrong with his mind, and he'd employed this complicated farce in hopes of bringing me under his sway. I began to suspect the latter. "So which was it? Harry became a Tiller, and your father a Reaper? Is that why you despise each other so much?"

"Jack was a Tiller," he said softly. "Harry's spirit never did choose a side."

I decided I'd indulged him long enough. "I must say, that was an excellent story, Lucien. Quite imaginative, having the moving pictures to add such a dramatic feel. You could perform this show daily in the park. I think you'd really clean up."

"What you are disregarding is that the Tillers and the Reapers did go back to live normal lives," he said. "They became men of business, politics, and importance. They all succeeded beyond anyone's expectations. And they married and had families, because they never suspected hosting the Aramanthan spirits would change their physical bodies. Not until they realized that their offspring were not like other children."

My nose itched and I couldn't scratch it, and it was driving me insane. Just as he was. "Please, Lucien, stop. Just stop now. It was a good joke, a very good joke, but you're taking it too far. It isn't funny anymore."

"The Tillers managed to hide what they were, but their children were born with abilities not so easily disguised." His voice dropped low, as if he were confiding in me. "Some superstitious fools began calling their progeny names. Shade-born. Demonites."

I went still. *Hellchild.*

"Some of the children had ordinary gifts, but others proved to be even more powerful than their sires." He went to the panel to flip some switches and the cuffs round my wrists parted, and then the bars folded themselves away. "Your mother not only rejected her powers, Charmian, but I believe that she and your father used the nightstone to assure that you would never know yours." He came over to take my cold hands in his. "Thanks to them, you've remained ignorant of the fact that you are spiritborn, and possess incredible—"

"Enough." I pushed him away from me and got to my feet, wincing as my muscles went pins and needles. "My parents are dead. I don't have any power—mind, magic, or otherwise. I am an ordinary person, just like you. I don't even want to know what a nightstone is."

"You are not like anyone." He also stood. "You are a spell-breaker, Charmian. Perhaps the most powerful in existence. Magic cannot work in your presence because your own instantly unravels it."

"Brilliant." I clapped my hands. "You've managed to invest me with the one power that explains why magic never works. Oh, in my presence, of course," I added. "Once I leave the room, however, then it's business as usual. Wardlings and potions. Enchantments. I'd like to leave now."

"I can prove it."

I whirled round. "How? By not performing magic in front of me—again? Yes, that should convince me. Go ahead." I gestured. "Fail to conjure something."

"There is only one power that can overcome yours, Charmian," he said softly. "Happily, it is mine."

I didn't like the look in his eyes. "Yet somehow you've never thought to use it on me."

"I did try, but your parents made sure no magic could ever touch you." He took out my pendant and dangled it. "This is a nightstone, one of the last in existence. It was used by the old Druuds to imprison the mages in the Bréchéliant. Your parents somehow mechanized it to shield your spirit in a similar manner. From what I have gathered by observation, it releases your power while holding you oblivious to both it and the forces within the netherside."

"So that's the reason magic doesn't work near me?" I nodded. "I wonder what my da's pocket watch does."

"Allow me to demonstrate." He curled his fingers over my pendant, opened them, and it was gone. "Now you are unshielded."

"Let me guess." I folded my arms. "You can turn me into a great fat frog. Or, if my mind power is now working, you can't."

His eyes glittered as he came to me and dropped a small blue stone down the front of my bodice. As I tried to slap him, he said, "Take off the cloak."

I looked down at my hand, which on its own had stopped and joined my other fingers to untie the strings under my chin. "This is ridicu—" I stopped when I realized I wanted to take off the cloak, more than anything in the world. "What is this? What are you doing?"

"I've told you, spell-breaker." He smiled. "You're mine."

I pushed the cloak from my shoulders and straightened the dark blue gown I'd borrowed from Rina's.

Oddly, this gave me a distinct glow of pleasure. "Why does that feel better?"

"You want to please me," he said. "In another moment you'll do anything I ask."

"Yes." Something began pulsing deep inside me, as if I'd grown a second heart. "Of course I will. Should I take off the rest of my clothes?"

"My father became host to the immortals' greatest enchanter," Dredmore said as he went round me and encircled me from behind with his arms. "An Aramanthan who could bend anyone, even the most powerful spell-breaker, to his will. That was the gift Jack passed along when he sired me."

"This is why Harry wanted me to leave you." Poor Harry, he was a fool. "He knew you'd try this." Not that I was especially worried, not with this delicious contentment glowing inside me. "How long does it last?"

"If I choose," he whispered against my ear, "for the remainder of your days."

Delight sparkled inside me as I imagined it. "Yes, please, Lucien. I'd like that. I like you." *No, that wasn't right.* "I love you."

"So you do, as long as I will it." The air pressed in against me, and then I was turning to put my arms round his neck. "But this is not real love, Charmian. This is enchantment. Enslavement."

"Nonsense. You know how much I fancy you. There will never be anyone else for me." I beamed at him. "Lucien, all I've ever wanted to do is make you happy."

"You've never wanted anything of the kind." He kissed my brow before he plunged his hand down the front of my dress, removing the stone he'd dropped there. "And I'm sorry I've done this, but I had to show you."

A heartbeat later my mind and body became my own again, and I drooped, as limp as an underdone crispie.

"Once I release you from the enchantment, there is a period of weakness. It will pass in a few moments." He carried me over to the chair and sat down with me. "The longer I bespell you, the greater the weakness. With each hour that passes, more of you surrenders to my control, until I command the very beat of your heart. Then I can never release you, or you will die."

"I can't believe it." I didn't try to fight him off or argue; I was too stunned. "I really wanted . . . I would have happily . . ." I stopped and stared at him. "And you can do this to anyone, whenever you wish, just by thinking it and popping a stone down their dress?"

"Anyone like us." His mouth curled at one corner. "To my everlasting regret, the power I inherited from Jack doesn't work on ordinary mortals. Only the spirit-born."

"Bloody hell." I rested my cheek against his shoulder. "How do you live with something like this?"

"I avoid the temptation to use it." He stroked my cheek. "When I first encountered you at that merchant's house I knew you were like me; I sensed it at once—but my power had no effect on you. I tried everything, even planting spell stones in your garments, but nothing worked. I believed it to be a miracle."

"You've actually tried to do this before to me?" I sat up and remembered all the odd times I'd found blue pebbles in my pockets. "How could you?"

"I wanted you."

"You want to be beaten senseless." I pushed away his hand. "Is there anyone more powerful than you? Do they hire out?"

"We all have our weaknesses." His expression became shuttered. "You needn't worry. I'd never use my power on you unless you were in danger."

"That's what you say now. Next week you might decide to have me shine your boots with my tongue." I grimaced. "Not that I mean to suggest you do." Something occurred to me, and I sat straight up. "That night in the maze, you didn't use your mind magic on me, did you?" I hadn't seen any blue stone then, but it might have fallen out of my pocket while I'd ridden back to the city on George.

He ran his thumb along my jawline. "You were wearing the pendant, remember? It's always protected you."

I glanced about. "Where *is* my pendant?"

"You'll have it back, in time." He turned my face toward his. "Charmian. You can't keep wearing it. Your parents meant well, but nightstone is very dangerous and unpredictable. The manner in which they've mechanized it blinds you to the netherside. If the mechanism were to fail at the wrong moment—"

I wasn't convinced I wanted to see the real world anymore, much less the netherside of specters and mages and only sweet Mary knew what else. "Perhaps it's better that I not know such things."

"You can't hide forever from what you are, love." He sounded weary now. "No more than I could."

I tucked my head against his neck, my eyes drooping.

"Lucien." I yawned. "Why am I falling asleep on your lap?"

"You've had a long day." He sounded peevish now, as if talking were too much effort.

The air seemed to be turning pink, and very hot, and with all my strength I pushed myself off him. My limbs turned to noodles and I landed heavily on the floor.

"Charm." He tried to reach out to me, but his hand fell against the cushions. "Fire."

I gritted my teeth and began crawling toward it, the pink smoke coming from the logs making my eyes burn, but halfway to the hearth I couldn't feel my legs anymore. Nor could I turn over to see who had come into the room and was walking toward us.

A hard boot kicked me over onto my back, and I looked up to see Montrose Walsh standing over me, a noz over his mouth.

"Poor Cousin Kit," he said through the mask. "You and your lover might be impervious to magic, but you're still obliged to breathe, now, aren't you?"

CHAPTER TWENTY

The next hour came to me in blurry flashes as I drifted in and out of consciousness. I glimpsed Dredmore's body being dragged past me and dropped onto the dirty boards of a cart, and snow falling into my eyes. The cold roused me even as it chilled my limbs; the flashes grew closer together until they merged into a veil of snowy lace above my head. By the time my wits were restored they had moved us to another place and put me on a bed. Beside me Dredmore lay unmoving, but I shifted my arm to press against his side, and felt his ribs expanding and contracting.

Lucien still breathed. They hadn't killed him.

Men's voices spoke in low, ugly tones all about us; I could hear Lord Walsh, his diseased son, and someone with a faint Talian accent. They were arguing over something. Montrose spoke insistently, his father responded harshly, and the Talian seemed to be trying to placate both of them.

The voices came closer, and I played dead. Through my lashes I could see Lord Walsh taking polished stones from a pouch, which he rolled in his hand like coins he was reluctant to part with, until he held them out and a black-gloved hand chose one. More words were spoken, none of which I understood, and the glove lowered a white stone to Dredmore's face.

I felt a movement of air over me, terrible and cold, which rushed at Dredmore. When I saw a wide, red streak of light shoot past my face, and felt Dredmore's body jerk, I almost screamed. Although I held my tongue I must have moved, for someone grabbed my hair and lifted my head, giving it a shake.

"She's come to," Montrose said, and my head dropped onto the pillow again. "Can I have her, Dad?"

"No." That was the Talian. "He took great trouble to protect her. She must know something of value to us."

"I'll get it out of her," Montrose offered. "Come on, Dad. I did everything you asked. I haven't had a fighter in ages."

"Shut up, Monty." Walsh came to stand over me, his cologne filling my nostrils, and then he slapped me, hard. Through the ringing in my ears I heard him say, "Enough stage play, Miss Kittredge."

I surged up and drove my elbow into his diaphragm. As Walsh doubled over, I shoved him aside and ran. A short man with oily dark hair and a very sharp-looking dagger pointed at my belly brought me to a stop.

"Dredmore," I said, never taking my eyes off the blade, "now would be a very good time to demonstrate your deathmage magic."

"I would be delighted, Charmian," Dredmore's voice rasped, "if you would first remove this boulder from my brow."

"Can't get to you just now." I regarded the oily-headed one. "I don't suppose you'd oblige him."

"No, miss," he told me in a Talian-accented voice, and glanced down. "Master?"

"Kill the stupid bitch, Celestino," Walsh groaned from the floor.

"We will let her choose." The Talian gestured, and Montrose appeared with a length of rope. "I can do as his lordship wishes, miss, and cut your throat. Or you can sit down and hold out your wrists. How will it be?"

I backed up against the bed. "Screaming and running away not an option? How disappointing." As the villains converged on me, I jumped up on the bed, tumbling backward across Dredmore's form and in the process knocking away the small white stone they had placed in the center of his forehead. Montrose uttered some vile words, while the Talian dove at the bed. Dredmore came out of his paralyzed state, grabbed me, and dragged me from the bed, thrusting me behind him as he assessed the two men.

"I thought magic didn't work near me," I whispered as I glanced over his shoulder.

"They're not using it on you," he muttered back. "And I have no power against Aramanthan-charmed icestone."

"You couldn't have mentioned this earlier?" We were cornered, and the Talian and Montrose were coming round the bed after us. I thought of what the diseased little sod wanted to do to me and shuddered. "I'd like to be killed first, if you wouldn't mind."

"No one has to die," Celestino said to Dredmore. "Zarath will see to it that you live for a very long time, my lord."

Dredmore's hand nearly crushed mine before he spoke to the Talian. "I will give you what you want, as soon as you release Miss Kittredge."

Montrose giggled. "That'll be a snow day in Hades."

"She's nothing but a stupid, nameless skirt," Dredmore continued, making me want to kick him in a few sensitive places. "You don't need her."

"True, but you seem to care for her, my lord." Celestino flipped his dagger over his hand in a flashy, useless show of dexterity. "Cooperate with us, and I will spare her life." He smirked. "Perhaps Zarath will choose to make her your body servant."

Dredmore turned his back on them and grabbed me by the arms, kissing me hard on the mouth before hauling me through an adjoining door, slamming it shut in the Talian's face.

I glanced round us but saw no other door or window to provide an avenue of escape. "Lucien, we cannot stay in here forever." Indeed, the men on the other side of the door were hammering on it.

"I know. I am about to be possessed by one of the Aramanthan, Charmian," he said as he braced his shoulders against the door panel. "A Reaper warlord, who means to eat my spirit in order to own my body and use my power for his own purposes. I am too weakened by the drugs to fight him off, and he can control mortals the way I control the spiritborn. With my power added to his, no one will be able to resist him, not even you."

I saw the door shudder in its frame as someone on the other side bashed against it. "Lucien—"

"Shut up. When they are finished, it will be on you to put an end to it." His grip turned bruising. "This thing will occupy my flesh, but my spirit will go where it can never touch me. I understand now. I will be where Harry has been, all this time. Now swear to me that you will kill it. Kill my body." As I remained silent, he shouted it again. "Swear to me."

"Lucien." I saw the terror in his eyes, and it shocked me into agreement. "I will. I swear it." And then, because I simply couldn't help myself, I said, "I love you."

The door gave way, thrusting Dredmore against me. I held him as long as I could, my throat too tight now to speak.

"So touching." Montrose looped the rope round Dredmore's neck, dragging him back out of the way, and forced him to his knees. I started after them, but the Talian got hold of me again and marched me toward the door.

The knife at my throat kept me from struggling. "I'd like to stay, if you don't mind."

"We cannot have you in the room," he told me. "Nothing can interfere when the warlord takes possession."

"What warlord?"

"Zarath, like we said." He grinned exactly as a child let loose in an unsupervised sweets shop would. "Do not worry. Soon you will come to know him very well."

He guided me into the next room, the furnishings of which were oddly arranged in a half circle facing the wall. I saw an unframed oval of glass, through which I saw into the room where Dredmore was being held by the Walshes. I vaguely recalled seeing a mirror of the same shape on the other side.

"You trust them so much you have to watch them in secret?" I asked as the Talian shoved me down in one of the chairs.

"Be quiet." He moved to stand behind me and placed the knife under my chin.

I heard Lord Walsh's voice, and glanced down to see where it came from: a small grate at the base of the wall.

"—my intent from the beginning," Walsh was saying. "Your assaults on Lady Walsh have been entertaining, but I cannot fathom why you settled on her as a method of getting to me."

"I never touched your wife, you daft prick." Dredmore gritted his teeth as Montrose tightened the rope round his neck. "The Tillers will know what you've done. The moment he begins casting, they'll come for you. My only regret is that I will not be here to watch your carcass being dragged from the river."

"My dear Dredmore." Walsh's face stretched into a broad smile. "The wardlings that hang about almost every neck and door in the city have hearts of dreamstone. I know because our Talian friends forged them. The Tillers won't even know we're here."

I didn't know what dreamstone was, nor did I think Dredmore could be duped by anyone, but from the look on his face Walsh had done the very thing.

"I take it you lot are Reapers?" I asked the Talian.

"For a stupid skirt, you know much." Celestino didn't sound as if he approved.

"Women in this country have always been vastly underrated." My throat tightened as Walsh took a gleaming red stone from a white velvet pouch. "Lord Dredmore is insanely wealthy, you know. If I could convince you to intervene on his behalf, I can guarantee he would see to it that you would never have to dirty your hands again with this sort of nonsense."

"Oh, miss." He chuckled. "For this, Zarath will make me king of my country."

I saw Walsh drop the stone in Dredmore's hand before he took the pistol from his son.

I reached out to touch the surface of the two-way glass. "Lucien."

As if he'd heard, Dredmore turned his head to look directly at me, put the stone in his mouth, and swallowed. At the exact same moment, Lord Walsh placed the pistol at his own temple and pulled the trigger.

Someone screamed—me, I think—and I gripped the knife at my throat with my fingers and wrenched it out of the Talian's hand. The blade cut deep into my fingers as I ran out and into the room where Lord Walsh's body lay on the floor, and his son gagged as he swiped at his father's brains, which were all over the front of his fancy jacket as well as the wall behind him.

I switched the bloody blade to my left hand, ready to use it as I stepped between the men and Dredmore. I stepped back until I could reach him. "Lucien, we're leaving." I reached out and grabbed his sleeve, but he didn't move. *"Lucien."*

This time the red streaks of light came out of Lord Walsh's body, first from his slack lips, and then in a burst out of the hole in his head. They flew past me, surrounding Dredmore, who had doubled over, choking and heaving. The red lights swirled, closing in on him until his entire body glowed. At last he stopped fighting it and slowly stood, and the lights were sucked into the darkness of his eyes, dwindling until they were two tiny red glints.

"Dredmore." I told myself it had been a trick, one of his ridiculous illusions. "Say something."

He said nothing, but held up one hand and turned it over, as if he'd never seen it before. Then he smiled, his face changing into something beautiful and terrible, his eyes taking on a horrid red glow. I didn't even resist as the Talian took the knife from my hand and forced me down on my knees.

"*Ecco, sovrano mio,*" Celestino babbled as he dropped down beside me. "*Sia benedetto il compagno oscuro.*"

Dredmore looked round the room, and then spoke a single word. "*Rieccomi.*"

His voice rang out, clear as church bells, and the wrongness of it set my skin to crawling. But the man had just been forced to swallow a rock; couldn't have been easy on his throat.

I was sure I could keep telling myself lies like that for as long as was necessary.

"*Dove sono capitato?*" Definitely not Dredmore's voice, yet it came from Dredmore's mouth.

"*Il continente Victoriana, sovrano. La Cittá di Rumsen.*"

"If he doesn't speak English," Montrose grumbled, "how are the rest of us supposed to understand him?"

"*Chiudi il culo,*" the Talian said, smacking the younger man in the back of the head.

Dredmore spared Monty a glance. "Who do you think gave you your tongue, boy?" He took a step, looked down at his legs, and then pressed a hand to his chest and arm. "Strong. Young. You chose well, *umano.*"

"My wife knew this body would please you, Master. Especially after you were forced to wait so long in . . ."

The Talian gestured vaguely at Nolan Walsh's corpse. "Our ships will be arriving at dawn with your army. We will meet them at the docks, and once you have marshaled them, we can move against the city."

"Dad never said anything about blowing his brains out," Montrose muttered. "And I still don't see how one man can control armies and cities just by thinking it."

"I am not a man." The thing in Dredmore's body eyed me. "I am Zarath, warlord of the Aramanthan Scourge." He ran the tip of his tongue from one side of his mouth to the other.

That decided it for me. The thing had admitted what it was, and Dredmore would never lick his lips in such a repulsive fashion.

Celestino cleared his throat. "My lord, forgive the boy for speaking out of turn. Young Lord Walsh is much beloved by my wife, who in return for the sacrifice of his father's flesh humbly asks that you heal him."

"So I will. Later." Dredmore ignored Montrose altogether as he reached down to take hold of my chin and lift my face. It was like being touched by a corpse. "And this flesh? It too serves me?"

Montrose snickered. "Not bloody likely."

"Do you even know whose body you've stolen?" I asked Zarath. "Lucien Dredmore is a deathmage, and Grand Master of the dark arts. He can slice a man in half with one blow." I shoved a finger into his chest. "Get out of him, this minute, or he will see to it that you suffer a long and ugly death."

No one said anything, and then Celestino began laughing. "Oh, miss," the Talian wheezed between guffaws. "The Aramanthan do not die as we do. They have lived for thousands of years here in our world as well as the netherside."

Zarath peered down at me. "The spirit of this body, this Dredmore. He was your lover."

"Is," I insisted. "He *is*."

"His spirit has fled from his flesh, woman. Even if it were somehow to return, it could not take this body from me." His black eyes took on a scarlet sheen. "What your lover is, is dead."

I could hardly hear him for the roaring in my ears, and then I heard nothing at all.

"Kit."

Big, gentle hands cradled my face, brushed back my hair, and checked my pulse. I knew that touch as well as the voice, but I didn't want to deal with Inspector Doyle just now. No, what I wanted was a nice room at Morehaven where I might sleep for a thousand years. That way I wouldn't have to think about magic, which I knew now to be real, spirit stones, or the man I loved being possessed—his soul eaten—by an immortal monster. I had to face it: Dredmore was dead, and I might as well be.

"Should I send for a whitecart, then, 'Spector?" someone asked.

"No," I answered for Doyle, my voice a rasping ruin. "I'm not injured." I struggled upright and looked past the man holding me. Tommy's beaters were searching through the wreck of an expensive-looking hotel room and coming up with nothing. I lay on the floor beside the bed, my arms and legs tightly bound with curtain cord. It was not the room where Lord Walsh had killed himself, either, for there were no brains on the wall.

"The concierge called the station," Doyle told me. "Everyone on this floor heard a woman screaming for help." He held up a bit of torn cloth, and his angry expression grew especially fierce. "You chewed through this."

Small wonder my throat felt lined with cotton: it actually was. "I missed my dinner bucket."

One of the beaters chuckled and earned a glare from the chief inspector.

"How can you joke about it? No, hold still." Doyle took out a pocketknife and sheared through the cords binding my wrists together before he chafed my hands to restore the blood flow. "Who did this to you, Kit?"

I could tell him the entire sorry tale, most of which I still didn't believe, and go quietly after. Not all the asylums in Rumsen were horrid. Wherever they sent me for treatment, Doyle would bribe one of the loon herders to look after me.

"Don't you tell him the truth." Harry materialized behind the inspector, and his mostly transparent eyes fixed on mine. "Say you hit your head, and that you can't recall. *Now*, gel."

"I can't recall." I looked at the glitter of white and blue stones scattered about the bed on the floor. "I hit my head."

"Lucien Dredmore paid for this room," Doyle said. "He told the concierge that you were newlyweds before he carried you up here."

"Agree with him," Harry said.

I nodded. "Yes, he did."

One of the beaters made a scoffing sound, which he quickly turned into a fake cough as he moved to search the corner farthest from his boss.

Against his trouser seams Doyle's fingers knotted into fists. "Dredmore was also seen abducting you earlier from a brothel called the Eagle's Nest."

"That was a ruse, to protect Carina and her gels from Walsh's men." I watched Harry throw up his hands in disgust and felt a dismal satisfaction. "I want to go home, Inspector."

"You don't have a home. Your property and monies have been seized by the Crown." Doyle studied my face. "You've the clothes on your back, Kit. Now do you want to tell me what the bloody hell happened here?"

The door to the adjoining suite opened, and Lord Lucien Dredmore swept into the room. His cloak swirled with imperial elegance, and the points of his snowy neckcloth stood in stiff relief against his dark skin. In his eyes I saw a dreadful shadowy presence, as if the evil demon inside him were looking out of them like windows.

"I can tell you," the thing pretending to be Dredmore said as he strode forward, his gleaming boots thumping on the floor as the beaters scattered from his path.

"Lord Dredmore." Doyle's features took on a decidedly bland cast as he inclined his head just enough to suit courtesy. "You witnessed something?"

"Yes." He lifted his hand and pointed at my face. "This woman murdered Lord Walsh."

In the five seconds of astounded silence that followed, I noticed that Harry had vanished again, Dredmore had acquired a faint Talian accent, and Doyle appeared ready to commit murder himself. Then, without devoting much thought to it, I relieved the inspector of his blade and launched myself at Dredmore, only to be hauled back by a strong arm.

"Kit." Doyle wrestled the knife from my hand before he shoved me away. "Have you gone mad?"

"That is *not* Lucien Dredmore. Before Walsh killed himself, he forced the spirit of an evil warlord into Dredmore's body." I told Doyle the rest of it as quickly as I could, and added, "He calls him Zarath. He and the Talians have come to take over Toriana and go to war with the Crown. He'll use Lucien's power to do it."

Dredmore smiled. "Such an entertaining tale. You should have become a novel writer instead of murdering fine gentlemen."

Now I would have no trouble at all killing him. "Give me back that blade, Tommy."

"You see?" The thing wearing Dredmore's body cupped his fingers and snatched at the air. "She is on the rampage."

"Give us the room," Doyle said to the beaters, who hastily filed out.

"You must take her at once to prison," Dredmore told him, "before she kills again."

"Is that right." Doyle glanced at me. "I imagine I will, milord, but first I'd like you to answer two questions."

"Of course," the monster said. "Anything."

Doyle watched him. "If Miss Kittredge murdered Lord Walsh, then how did she end up bound and helpless in this room?"

"Obviously she arranged to be found so," the monster replied. "It would make anyone believe her innocent of the crime she has committed."

"You *put* me here after you killed Walsh and Lucien, you evil ass." I tried to dodge round Doyle again, but he caught me and held me fast.

"Right. Just one final question, then, milord," Doyle said. "What's Miss Kittredge's given name?"

Dredmore's eyes blinked. "I don't understand what you say."

"You've known her for several years," the inspector said. "You've paid to have her investigated, harassed, and even snatched from the street a time or two, or so I've been told. Tell me her given name."

"He doesn't know." My smile turned acid. "Because he's not Dredmore."

The thing lunged at Tommy, punching him in the gut and then the face, so fast his movements became blurred. The inspector flew across the room, hit the wall, and slid to the floor.

I braced myself for the same, but before it could touch me, Harry materialized between us. In his hand he held a pale stone that gave off beams of light. "Never even think it, spirit-eater. This child carries my blood."

Zarath reared back, lifting his hands to block the light, and cursed viciously in Talian as he backed away.

"That's right," Harry said, following after him. "Get out."

I went to Doyle, who lay groaning and hugging his middle, and checked him over. Blood streamed from his nose, and I found a huge knot on the back of his head, but otherwise he was all right.

Suddenly the door to the room slammed shut and one of the beaters came in. "He'll be fine," he told me as he pocketed the pale stone. He was the beater who had snickered at me, but he wasn't laughing now. "I've sent the other coppers downstairs to clear the hall. Now, you're to leave Rumsen, this very minute. Get as far from the city as you can manage before dawn."

I eyed him. "I thought you were arresting me."

"Oh, for the love of Victoria—it's me, Harry, Charm." The beater knelt down and looked over Doyle's bloodied features. "Blind me, this is Arthur's grandson. Fancy him becoming a Yardman. Ah, well." He tried to pull me away from him. "You've little time left before the sun rises. I'll help you procure—"

I slapped the beater's broad cheek. "Why didn't you come to help us? Why didn't you stop them from hurting Lucien?"

"I couldn't." He winced and probed the reddening side of his face. "Did you have to smack me so hard?" When I curled my fingers into a fist, he said quickly, "I couldn't stop them or help them. I'm not part of this war. I can't be."

"Oh, so you're a coward as well as a traitor." I turned my back on him. "Why didn't you say so?"

Light blasted me from behind, and when I squinted over my shoulder I saw the beater floating six inches above the carpet and glowing like a cop-shaped sun. At the same time everything in the room began to blow about as if in a high wind.

"You dare insult me," Harry said, his voice booming so loudly the windows rattled. "With the power I command, I could banish you to the netherside with a single thought."

"Is this how you generally behave toward family?" I sniffed. "And you wonder why my mother wanted no part of you."

The light vanished, and the beater's feet dropped down on the floor. "My apologies," Harry said meekly. "My temper sometimes gets the better of me."

Doyle stirred, groaning a little.

"Help me with him," I said.

"I can't be a part of this conflict," he said as he moved to the door. "Good-bye, Charm." Out he went.

"*Harry.*" I rose to go after him, only to be yanked back down by a strong hand. "Doyle, let go of me. He's getting away."

"Yes, and you're not." With another groan he shoved himself upright and staggered to his feet, still gripping my wrist with an iron hand. He bellowed out two names, and a pair of his beaters rushed into the room. Neither of them appeared to be possessed by my grandfather.

"Lord Travallian has just assaulted me to escape custody. He's not right in the head. Find him and bring him back to the station." Doyle held up a hand. "Be discreet."

The beaters touched the brims of their helmets before they trotted out.

"Brilliant." I wanted to slap him. "I told you, that thing is not Dredmore."

"Right, it's an ancient magical being that possessed his body, and if we don't stop him, he's going to start a war." He prodded the back of his head and winced.

"How does he mean to do that again? Toss a few pebbles at the whole of the militia?"

"More like a thousand or so Talians," I snapped. "He can command entire armies with his mind, and he has Dredmore's powers now as well. For God's sake, Tommy, stop rolling your eyes at me like that. He's an immortal warlord, I tell you."

He shook his head. "You've been drugged and knocked about, Kit. If Dredmore had told you he was the Queen, you'd have believed him."

I told him how wrong he was as he hustled me from the room, down the stairs, and out the hotel. I repeated the entire story as he pushed me into his carri and told his driver to take us to a street in the better part of the working-class quarter. I didn't begin begging until we arrived at a narrow greystone sandwiched between a carriwright and a pottery.

Doyle dragged me out of the carri, issued some terse instructions to his driver, and led me up the steps to the front door of the greystone. As I promised to prove everything to him if he would simply go with me to the docks, he pushed me inside and bolted the door behind us.

I paused for breath and took in my surroundings. Instead of a foyer or a hall leading to several flats, we stood in a tidy front room arranged with comfortable-looking walnut and leather furnishings. Someone had banked a fire in the broad-based riverstone hearth, beside which sat a little cart loaded with a filled BrewsMaid, neatly wrapped finger sandwiches, and a cloth-covered mound of tiny jam cakes.

"Sit down." He prodded me toward an armchair

before turning on the brewer. "Not on your life," he added without looking at me. "You'll not make it as far as the steps outside."

I stopped inching toward the door. "Why did you bring me here?"

"I can't take you back to the Main. They'll toss you in a cell and lose the latchkey." He took off his jacket and carefully rolled up his sleeves before he used the basin to wash his hands. "The Crown's seized everything of yours, so Walsh's men will be watching your friends."

"Walsh can't watch everyone." I occupied the settee closest to the door. "I have friends in other places."

"You're staying here." He filled a plate with sandwiches before he brought it to me. "Until I sort this out, you're under house arrest."

CHAPTER TWENTY-ONE

I didn't want Doyle's food or protection, but my stomach chose that moment to gurgle loudly, and I needed to rest and think. I accepted the plate he offered with all the ladylike grace I could manage before I attacked its contents.

"Dredmore couldn't keep me locked up," I mentioned between bites of some rather marvelous salt-cured ham. "What makes you think you can?"

"Dredmore's an arrogant ass." He went back to the cart and returned with a steaming mug of rich, fragrant country black. "I'm your friend, and this isn't a prison cell." He offered me the tea. "It's my home."

"So I'm under *your* house arrest. I see." I put the plate on my lap so I could warm my hands on the outsides of the mug. "Do you mean to shackle me to something immovable? Perhaps that secretary in the corner there. Looks too heavy for me to budge."

He chuckled. "No doubt you'd find a way, even if you had to drag it out of here after you."

He may have fumbled things back at the hotel and brought me here against my will, but Doyle did care. He was also a decent man who would be made to pay dearly for becoming involved in this. Especially after I . . . My thoughts turned the food I'd wolfed down into an unpleasant lump in my belly. "You don't want any part of this, Inspector. If they find out you've sheltered me, they'll take everything. Your shield, your money and property. Maybe even your life."

"I'm an officer of the law, Kit, and until I've sorted this out, you're in my custody." He nodded toward the mug. "Now be a good gel and drink your tea."

I pretended to take a sip. Because it was so strong and bitter, country black was regarded as more of a man's drink. Customarily served as a morning brew, it roused sluggards from their beds and sent them off braced to build another bit of the Empire. Not at all the sort of thing to be serving to a lady at night, unless of course one had other motives.

I reached into my pocket, springing the back latch on Da's pocket watch that opened the back of the case, and removed one of the dippers before I pretended to check the time. Then, as Doyle fixed his own mug, I checked the tea.

Fortunately for me Tom's crockery was all plain heavy white china, the sort a bachelor who hated female frippery bought for himself. When he came to sit beside me on the settee, he placed his own mug next to mine.

"The sandwiches were scrumptious; you should give up being a cop and cater picnics and hen parties instead." I handed him the empty plate. "Could I have two more of those ham sandwiches? They're absolutely delicious."

As soon as his back was turned I took care of the present problem, and smiled when he brought me the food.

"Lovely, thank you." I settled back and let my eyelids

droop a little. "Tell me something, Doyle. Why haven't you found yourself a wife yet?"

"I don't know," he said, testing the tea before taking a swallow. "Mum says I'm too particular. Da says it's the job."

I used my hand to cover a yawn. "What do *you* say?"

He gave me the oddest look. "Could be that I was waiting for you."

"For twenty-odd years? My, you've patience." I uttered a sleepy chuckle as I pillowed my head against my arm and the backrest. With Tommy Doyle it would be courtship, then engagement, then marriage and a house full of little ones. I would never give up what little freedom I had left for that, but still I felt as if I'd been given a tremendous compliment. "Well, whether that's true or not, I think your grandda would have approved."

"He said we were meant for each other, but then he adored you almost as much as I did." He hunched his shoulders and gulped his tea. "I'm going to send you to my folks' place in the morning."

I watched him through half-closed eyes.

"You'll stay on the farm until I sort this out." He put down the empty mug and turned toward me, and put his hand over mine. "Then we'll see if Grandfather was right about us."

On impulse, I leaned forward and brushed my lips across his mouth. He stiffened, and then reached for me, only to look down at the hands that fell against his thighs. "Kit . . . you . . ."

"I switched the mugs," I confirmed, catching him as he began to topple forward. "It was the country black that gave it away. It's the only tea strong enough to mask the taste of sleeping powder." I eased him back against the cushions. "That's why you didn't bother to shackle me to the furniture. You didn't think you'd have to."

"Don't . . . go," he said, slurring the words. "He'll . . ."

"I'm sure you're right." I got up and retrieved the crazy patch from the armchair and draped it over him. "But I made a promise to the man, and it's one I have to keep." I waited until his head slumped over before I helped myself to several things, including the heavy trench and long brim I found hanging on his coatrack. "Good-bye, Tommy."

As soon as I slipped out of Doyle's back door, the raw slap of air against my face reminded me that I couldn't chase after Dredmore on foot. I needed transportation that would conceal as well as convey me.

A quick peek inside the window of the carriwright's shop revealed about a dozen wagons, carts, and carris, all in various stages of disrepair. The lock on the back door would be simple to pick, but the carris would make too much racket, and I had no horse to draw the others. They would be watching anyone approaching the docks, too.

As I stepped back, my foot shuffled over the lip of an access hatch. The old sewer lines on the Hill and in the smarter quarters of the city had been sealed off or filled in, but here in the working quarter they hadn't bothered. Hedger had once told me that before the city's incinerators had been installed, all the old sewer lines had emptied out directly into the sea.

I hadn't forgotten the old tunneler's last warning, though: *Ye're to go now, and ye're not to come back down here, do ye understand? Never again.* I glanced up at the sky. Dawn would arrive in another hour, and so would the invasion. "Harry? Harry, where are you? I need you."

My grandfather's almost-transparent form appeared before me. "Ready to leave, then?"

"I'm going belowground," I told him. "You're coming along."

"You can't hide from it down there," Harry snapped. "Nor can I help—"

"Oh, shut up, Harry." I crouched down and with some difficulty released the old hatch. "I'm not asking for your help. All you need do is come with me."

I climbed down the ladder and made my way through the malodorous confines of the old sewer, but as soon as I emerged into the tube junction Harry took on more substance and moved ahead to block my path.

"You're as daft as you are stubborn," he told me. "Zarath is not Dredmore. He's not even a man. He hasn't the slightest regard for mortals. He'll crush you, Charmian, with no more than a pebble and a few words. Or he'll do things to you to make you wish you were dead."

Hearing him use my given name only made me think of Lucien and want to throttle my grandfather. "Mr. Hedgeworth," I called out as loud as I dared. "I know the rounds have you in this section of the tunnels now. If you're watching us, please, come out."

The old tunneler emerged from behind a cluster of tubes. He'd wrapped his stooped body in layers of thick meshing and held a pair of wicked-looking cudgels in his hands. "Get out of me tunnels"—he pointed one of the clubs at Harry—"and take that thing with ye."

I glanced at Harry. "How can he see you?"

"Long story," my grandfather mumbled back.

"I'm sorry, Mr. Hedgeworth, but we can't. I am in desperate need of your help. My grandfather also wishes to make amends for whatever caused this rift between the two of you." I turned to Harry. "You go first."

My grandfather made an exasperated sound. "For God's sake, Archibald. Put down those things." As the old man eyed me, he added, "Obviously I've not possessed her. Nor has any other."

"Not yet," Hedger agreed. "With what she can do, won't be long. Without that ginny bauble hanging about her neck she glows like a right black beacon. Soon as they come for the citizens they'll take her, too." He jabbed one of the cudgels toward me. "And that's why ye'll go topside, Miss Kit, this very moment, or I'll finish ye meself."

"You see? It's hopeless. You've no option but to leave Rumsen and save yourself." Harry's tone grew wheedling. "You're the last of my mortal bloodline, Charm. I can't lose you."

"You never had me, Harry." To the old tunneler, I said, "Mr. Hedgeworth, you may do exactly as you wish to me. From the sound of things, bashing in my skull will probably be a kindness."

Hedger's arm tightened, and for a moment I thought he really would strike me. With great reluctance he lowered the club and scowled. "If ye were a lad, I'd not hesitate, ye know."

I kept my expression respectful. "Thank you, sir."

Hedger jabbed his other cudgel at Harry. "If she's

truly the last, then ye tell her everything. All of it, ye hear me?"

"He'll tell me later," I assured him. "For now, I must hurry. Can you tell me if any of the old sewer lines to the docks remain open?"

"Aye." He pointed across to a moss-covered hatch. "That one runs about three mile. Comes up into the alley behind the old fish tinnery." As I started for it, he added, "Hang on, Miss Kit," and bent down to open his kipbag.

"I'll go on ahead and check the line. Wait here." Harry floated through the closed hatch and vanished.

"Spineless sod." The old tunneler rummaged through his bag for a moment before he produced what looked like a large, rusty nail, which he tossed to me.

I caught it and turned it over in my hands. "I can't really use this, Mr. Hedgeworth."

"'Tis an iron rail tie. Only thing what gets rid of Harry's sort, permanent-like." He tapped the left side of his chest. "Plant it in the heart, straight through. As the body dies, the iron traps 'em inside it. They're dragged off with the departed spirit, and can't ever come back."

The blunt end of the rusty spike suggested that the only place I'd be planting it would be the ground, but to avoid more arguments I nodded. "I appreciate the advice." On impulse I walked to him and kissed his whiskery cheek. "I'll be all right, you know."

He looked over my shoulder at the hatch before he muttered, "Ye'd be all right shed of him, Miss Kit. Harry's naught but trouble and tragedy awaiting ye."

"He's my family." There, I'd said it. Out loud I'd claimed Harry as my kin. It didn't feel as terrible as I'd thought it might. "Why are you so angry with him, Mr. Hedgeworth?"

He shuffled his feet. "Ye won't like knowing."

"I don't like *not* knowing," I said.

Hedger heaved out a long breath. "Me family were miners in Cornwall, cross the pond. Every man I knew and called mate worked down in the shafts." He shifted on his feet as he scowled, but his expression appeared more pained than angry. "One shift we hit a gas pocket, the tunnel blows, and we're trapped, fifty of us. Air goes thin, and we know we're done for, so we make our peace with it."

"Fifty of you." I felt horrified. "But surely you were rescued?"

"We were too deep, Miss Kit. Weren't nothing could be done for us." The corners of his mouth turned down. "All the others had blacked out, and I were a blink from it when I saw a bit of pretty speckled stone, all the colors of the rainbow, and picked it up for luck. Soon as it's in me hand, Harry shows up. Like some angel to save us." He started to say something, paused, and then shook his head.

"You don't have to tell me any more, Mr. Hedgeworth," I hurried to assure him. "I shouldn't have asked."

"No. I can tell ye. I have to, I think." He looked down at his battered waders. "Harry led me out some back tunnel none of us knew were there. He'd been digging himself, ye see. But as soon as I'm topside, everything goes black again. Harry, he were in spirit form. Took me body over so he could use me to do sommat his spy business for him."

I winced. "But he did save your lives."

"Aye. One. *Me* life." He spat on the ground. "While he was riding me about like a carri, the rest of me brothers and mates choked to death in that hole. Forty-nine men, Miss Kit. After, when I was shed of him and came to, I went back to me village. Seen all me brothers' wives in black, all the other widows, and then everyone crowded round, wanting to know how I got out. How I could leave 'em behind. When I told 'em about Harry and what he did, they thought I'd gone mad. Tried to send me to the loony bin, afore I nipped out of there, signed on a cargo ship, and came here. So yeah, Harry saved me life. It just cost me home, me family, me mates, everything in the world I cared for."

I knew exactly how that felt. "I'm so sorry, Mr. Hedgeworth."

"Ah, weren't none of yer doing, lass." He looked a little embarrassed now. "I shouldna've scared ye with me clubs. Ye're a good gel. Only make the old bugger mind ye, not the other way round."

"I'll do my best." I took out my father's pocket watch. "Harry's been gone almost ten minutes."

Hedger made a rude sound. "Ye still think he's coming back for ye?"

I couldn't afford to wait and find out. Since I couldn't drift through the hatch like Harry, I asked Hedger to help me pry it open.

Just as I stepped inside, he touched my shoulder. "He'll never tell ye anything unless ye force it out of him, Miss Kit. If naught else, make him tell ye his name. His true name, what he was born with, afore all the others."

I frowned, but before I could ask him what he meant the old tunneler scurried off, disappearing behind the snarl of tubes.

I turned and started down the old line. The rounded walls remained coated with a layer of dried, caked-on mold, and the lingering stench was equally alluring. But there was enough room for me to walk upright, and I didn't encounter any living vermin along the way.

I knew I was getting close to the tinnery when I picked up the scents of old fish, brackish water, damp rope, and tar. Although Rumsen's fish market had relocated to the north side of the docks, where the fish merchants had built their new canning factories, the old tinnery was still used by anyone who needed inside space to work, mostly hull menders, trap builders, and net makers.

When I came to the end of the line I encountered the rotting wood of the planks nailed over the sea outlet, and carefully climbed up the rickety ladder to the top-side hatch. I emerged in an empty alley just behind the tinnery, and stopped only to brush from my head and shoulders the snow that I'd dislodged coming up.

Harry's form took shape beside me, but almost immediately he moved several feet away. "Archibald gave you iron."

"A nice, big rail spike." I patted my pocket. "Can I try it out on you, see if it works like he said it would?"

"There's a more pressing matter." He pointed out to sea. "The Reaper ships are beginning to appear on the horizon. Once their army is in place, all Zarath will have to do is cast a spell, wake the dreamstone, and take whatever he likes."

"Dreamstone, icestone, spirit stone," I taunted. "Why can't you mages do anything without these bloody rocks?"

"They're all that's left of Aramantha," Harry told me. "The rest of it the ocean swallowed long ago, after the first mage war. That is how old and powerful we are, Charm. You can't fight my sort or kill them. You can never defeat them. Get away from here while you still can."

I looked at the cluster of vessels coming in with the tide. They were large military galleons flying Talian colors. "If I kill Dredmore before Zarath's army arrives, and I keep Zarath from possessing any other body, what happens then?"

"Without a physical form to channel and project his power, Zarath will be unable to use it. None of the other mages in his service have his gift for marshalling armies. If the men choose to fight, they'll have to battle like ordinary men." Harry glared at me. "These immortals aren't fools. You'll never get close enough. Even if you could kill Dredmore, Zarath will jump from him to the next warm body." As a flicker of daylight came over the horizon, he began to fade. "For all that is holy, Charm, please. When the fighting begins I have to retreat to the netherside."

"Why?" When he didn't answer I stamped my foot. "Harry, you can't be neutral anymore. You have to choose a side."

He shook his head. "Run, gel. Run for your life."

I had no burning desire to be Rumsen's savior. Since I'd come here, the city had shown no particular affection for me. Nor did I want to kill Dredmore, who despite being an arrogant ass had cared for me in his own fashion. I even understood why Harry didn't wish to get involved; this business between the Reapers and the Tillers was none of mine.

But there were the women of the city, the women who were so often treated like so many nameless cattle, who would not know to run away. Carina, and Bridget, the cartlass round the corner from my building, they had no one to defend them. Even Lady Diana Walsh, snob that she was, would be left helpless before Zarath—and from what I had seen in his bloody eyes, the women would be made to suffer unthinkable horrors.

I waited until my grandfather had almost faded from sight before I said, "I'm staying, Harry, and I'm fighting."

"So like my Connie," he replied, but he was still shaking his head when he vanished.

Once Harry had gone my courage wanted to accompany him. To keep from changing my mind I crept along the back of the tinnery and peeked round the corner at the docks, which stood empty. Zarath and his men had either not arrived, or had taken refuge in one of the cargo houses to wait for the ships.

As I put together a plan, the wind off the sea made Tommy's coat flap. I cinched it tight and pulled the long brim down before I darted across to one of the scale shacks where fish were brought to be weighed. I opened the door to the stench of death, and the sight of a woman's mangled corpse.

"I'll be." Something batted the long brim from my

head. "If it isn't Dredmore's little tart." A hard hand spun me round, and Montrose leered at me. "Nipped away from the beaters? You should have stayed in jail."

"Cousin Monty. How delightful to see you again." I looked round for Zarath and the others, but Walsh's son appeared to be alone. "Where are your Talian mates, then?"

"Waiting in the cargo house with the master." He gestured toward the largest of them. "Zarath sent me to see if you'd crawled out the rubbish yet. Don't know how he knew you'd show yourself, but he did."

My heart sank a little. "How could he know I was here?"

"Felt you like an itch he couldn't scratch. Seems the spirit-eater fancies the taste of cheap trollop. Meant to come back to the hotel to collect you for him once we'd finished some business." He smirked as he nodded at the dead woman. "Likes to play with them a bit first. Not especially careful, either."

"But I'd much rather be your plaything, Monty." I sidled up to him. "You wanted your da to give me to you, didn't you?"

"Yeah." He reached down and pinched my buttock through my skirts. "So you fancy it with me, then?"

"Oh, I would, if you still had something to use. Too bad all you can do now is talk. And drip." I rammed my knee into his groin, delighting in the shrill squeak he uttered as he sank to the deck. I shoved him inside the scale shack atop the dead woman, mentally apologizing to her spirit as I did for the indignity. Even with his stones bruised Montrose could come after me when he recovered, which I didn't need, so I used Hedger's spike to jam the door latch.

I wouldn't need the spike for my plan to work; all I needed was to get close enough to Zarath while making him believe he'd already enchanted and enslaved me. I didn't expect it would be difficult. Spirit that he was, the warlord was still a male, and he had been *very* interested in my body. Finally I could make useful the ridiculous ways in which men regarded my sex.

I straightened my skirts and smoothed my hair before I hurried to the cargo house. I made no effort to be stealthy or silent as I hurried inside, putting on my best loon face as I looked about. "Lucien? Lucien, where are you?"

Celestino showed himself first, and held a pistol that he pointed at my chest. "Do not take another step, miss."

"Where is Lucien?" I demanded, striding toward him as if I didn't see the gun. "I have escaped those who tried to keep us apart, milord." I raised my voice and called out his name several times, wringing my hands as I did. "Please, Lucien, I need to see you so desperately."

Dredmore stepped out of the shadows, his head tilted back as he surveyed me.

"How did you evade the authorities?" Celestino demanded.

"Lucien." I ran to Zarath as if he were a great pile of prezzies on Christmas morn and threw myself at him. "Thank heavens you're safe."

The warlord held me at arm's length. "The last time you saw me, you called me a monster."

"I *didn't* understand, Lucien. That awful inspector

person had me *terribly* confused." I smiled up at him. "I've been *so* lost and frightened. Finding you is *such* a relief."

He didn't look convinced. "So happy you tried to put a blade in me."

"I was wrong to do that, and I don't know why I did. I've been in such a muddle—or at least I was, until I found this." I ducked my head, searching through my pocket until I produced the blue stone Dredmore had used to bespell me, and hoped Zarath wouldn't be able to do the same. Holding it made me want to weep, and to add to the effect I let the tears well up into my eyes. "As soon as I picked up the stone everything became clear again."

His eyebrows rose. "The stone made you think clearly."

"Oh, yes." I pressed myself against him. "It made me remember what was important. You, Lucien. I would do anything for you. Anything at all. It's just as you've always said. I belong to you. I love you." I ran my fingertips along the front seams of his jacket. "Please, let me show you how much."

"Show me." His black eyes glowed red, and he latched on to my wrist. "Yes. I would enjoy a show."

"My lord," Celestino said, "this is a charade. The only reason this female came here is to harm you."

"Perhaps she did. It matters not." Dredmore lifted my chin to study my face. "Did the old one not tell you, woman? Your power cannot drive me out. I am tethered by the spirit stone."

The damn stone they'd made Lucien swallow; I'd forgotten about it. "I don't understand your magic, Lucien. I never have, and don't need to. I only want to be with you."

Behind my simper I thought frantically. There was one more thing I could do, and I wasn't even sure it would work. But it was that or have relations with this thing, and I'd stab myself in the heart before I did that willingly or otherwise.

Dredmore dragged me back to the cargo master's office, where he closed the door in Celestino's face. "Take off those rags. From this day forth, when you are with me you will wear nothing but your skin."

CHAPTER TWENTY-TWO

"Nothing would make me happier," I cooed as I reached behind me. "I'll never again have to launder anything but our bed linens. Unless you hire a laundress for us. That would give me more time to attend to your every want and need, you know."

Undoing my buttons also gave me time to tear open the packet I had tucked in the back band of my waister. I filled my hand with the powder, closing my fingers over it as I shrugged out of my bodice and let it fall to the floor.

"You are taking too long." His gaze dropped. "Undress faster."

"The buttons are so small and slippery, and the excitement is making me all thumbs. Could you help with the rest?" I presented my back to him. "Pretty, pretty please?"

I felt him approach, but instead of unfastening my waister he grabbed a fistful of my hair and used it to drag me back against him. "I will fill your belly with my seed," he muttered against my ear. "Again and again, until you swell like a ripe, fat date."

Cloaked as he was in Dredmore's body, I should have felt some small comfort. Over the last few days I had become embarrassingly fond of Lucien's touch. Yet even the brush of this impostor's breath on my skin nauseated me. I didn't bother to suppress my shudder, knowing that

Zarath's ego would have him assuming I was shivering with delight or some other such nonsense.

"I can hardly wait to see myself become so, ah, figgish." Of course if I turned and vomited all over his chest, he might begin to doubt the veracity of my ardor. "I have something for you, too."

He jerked me round. "I need nothing from you but silent obedience, woman."

Emphasis on *silent*, naturally. "Of course you don't. But this is something that you *wanted* from me that should keep me quiet for a time. You remember, you wanted me to . . ." I let my voice trail off as I brushed my knuckles lightly over the front of his trousers and artfully puckered my lips. "Now close your eyes, my love." When he didn't, I pouted. "Lucien, please. I can't do it if you're staring at me like that. I'm a good gel."

He smirked a little before his eyelids dropped.

I held my breath and flung the powder in my hand directly into his face. With my clean hand covering my nose and mouth I scurried backward until my shoulders slammed into a wall.

Dredmore coughed and choked, swatting at the cloud about his head. "What is the meaning of this?"

"I forgot to mention, I borrowed some sleeping powder from that awful inspector." I watched him stumble. "Which means you're going to have a nice, long nap."

He fell to his knees, and tears rolled down his cheeks from his reddening eyes.

"Followed by a very massive headache," I added, feeling quite satisfied to see him slump forward into a limp mound.

My suspicions proved correct; Zarath might eat spirits, control armies, and command an invasion, but Dredmore's drugged body was as good as a gaol cell. I took the dagger he carried and looked down at his still form. Trapped as he was, I could kill Zarath now. Cut him open, reach into his belly, rip out the stone, and it would be finished.

Lucien could rest in peace.

Lucien.

I crouched down beside him, pulling his shirt free of his trousers to bare his flat, hard belly. I lifted the blade—

Which decided to fall out of my hand. I couldn't do this to Lucien. I'd held his body in my arms; I'd covered great stretches of it with my kisses. Stabbing him in the heart would be like doing it to myself. Somehow I found my cheek pressed against his skin, and tears rolling over the bridge of my nose to plop down and slide into his navel.

Behaving like a silly female cost me as soon as I took in my first shuddering, sobbing breath, and a lungful of sleeping powder along with it. In one corner of my heart I knew I'd done it on purpose. The sad truth of it was that I couldn't stop Zarath because I didn't really care anymore. Now that Lucien was dead, the world no longer held anything of interest for me. I reached for my pendant, for the comfort it gave me whenever I touched it, and then I went still.

The pendant. Lucien had never given it back to me.

I staggered to the door and fumbled with the knob until it opened. Outside the office Celestino came at me, and in a dreamy haze I saw the blade fly from my hand

and bury itself in his shoulder. I wandered past the writhing, shrieking mound of him on the floor, and shuffled my way down a long row of large crates. One stood open, half-filled with straw, and it looked so comfortable that I chose it as my hiding place.

I had enough sense to pile the straw atop me and pull the slatted lid back in place before I closed my eyes and surrendered to a sleep from which I might never awake.

I dreamed of the maze at Morehaven, where I walked through the hedges looking for my pendant and my lover. I had the notion that Lucien had hidden it somewhere there, as I could feel it, like him, very near to me. Yet no matter where I looked neither he nor the pendant were to be found.

I gave up the search when I reached the center of the maze, where his mechanized statues lay in pieces round the reflecting pool. Sitting down in the exact spot where I had given him my virtue, I thought of all that had happened since I'd come to Rumsen.

It should have taken some time for my life to parade before my eyes, but it had gone so quickly. I'd only lived a handful of years, years I'd spent as quickly and recklessly as my lost childhood. Now that I faced the end, I could only imagine how disappointed in me my mother would have been. I had survived losing her and my father, my home, and nearly all that I had owned in the world. I'd tried to spit in the eye of fate by helping others, and perhaps I had, but in the end I had nothing left to show for it.

I might have another chance when the powder wore

off. If I survived Zarath and the Reaper invasion, I might flee Rumsen and start over somewhere else, but I would do it alone.

All at once I understood how wrong I had been to spare Zarath.

"Lucien," I said out loud. "I'm sorry that I couldn't . . . If I have another chance, I'll try again."

The reflecting pool began to bubble, and from it a column of water rose and shaped itself into Dredmore's form.

"You were fated to be the end of me, to release me," the man made of water said. "I saw it over and over in my dreams. Now that you have defied the portents, I am neither alive nor dead."

Even in spirit form he was annoying. "I did say I was sorry."

He sloshed over to the side of the pool and sat down on the edge. "If you hadn't been so damnably stubborn, Charmian, I might have prevented this and saved us both."

"If I'd been a docile, obedient gel, you'd have never looked twice at me," I told him, ignoring the way his face was dripping onto my shoulder. "So here we are. I'm a failure and you're a fountain. The city is about to fall to the Reapers. Everyone I care about will die." I glanced at him. "Why are you still here? Zarath said you'd gone over to the netherside."

"I have not gone, not yet, but it is a struggle to keep myself . . . intact." He glanced at his broken mechs before he reached out as if to touch my face. "As I am I cannot be with you in this world or the next. Nor can I escape my prison. I would bear it for you if I could." He drew back his shimmering hand. "But you must release me."

I nodded. "Tell me what to do."

"That can wait. Come here." Dredmore offered me his hand and drew me down into the pool, where he melted away into the water. I lay back, floating on the surface, and the soft coolness sank into me, permeating every corner of my mind and spirit with all that had been Lucien. I saw his life, how dark and cold it had been. His mind power to charm had appalled his parents, who had sent him away to spend his entire childhood at the strictest of schools. Upon gaining his degree, Dredmore had been given a small fortune by his mother, on the condition that he leave England and never return.

Making the crossing had been a wretched ordeal for Lucien. He feared the sea, for it was his only weakness. It prevented him from using his mind power, but worse, it terrified him. He couldn't even swim.

Once in Toriana, a spiteful relation had made public his illegitimacy and the name of his commoner father, rendering Lucien an instant outcast among the blues. He might have used his gift to make a place for himself among the ton through his ability to charm, but instead he walled himself up in Morehaven to learn all he could about the dark arts. For ten years no one but his servants had even acknowledged his existence.

Becoming a deathmage had gained him the entry into society that his unfortunate birth had denied him, and his grateful clients had certainly made him rich, but behind his practiced cynicism Dredmore remained a lonely, wretched pariah. Until the day Connell had driven him through the market and a shaft of sunlight had illuminated the face of a common gel buying peaches. And in that moment, the torrents of passion and longing had flooded Lucien Dredmore's cold heart, bringing with them the first hope he'd ever known.

It seemed ironic that for all his magic he had been made powerless against me, thanks to my pendant.

The pendant.

Something Harry had said the first time he'd appeared echoed through my thoughts: *After twenty years of waiting and watching, I'm here. I'm free.* And the curious thing Hedger had spat at him: *Without that ginny bauble hanging about her neck she glows like a right black beacon.*

If Dredmore were to be believed, I was a spellbreaker. Which meant magic had no power over me, nor could it be used in my presence. It explained why Rina's teller had been powerless to read for me. The snuffmages' balls had been rendered useless the moment they came near me. I'd kept Liv from strangling, not by slapping her, but by touching her. By sitting on the bench next to Bridget's Charles, I'd broken the no-love spell placed on him in France by his mother.

Could it be that simple?

Without that ginny bauble—

Dredmore had been wrong. My parents hadn't created the pendant to protect me against magic. If I were a spell-breaker, I'd never need that sort of protection.

—ginny bauble—

Something hurt my face, hitting me so hard my teeth chattered.

"You're not dead," I heard a hard voice say. "Do you

hear me, Kit? Open your eyes this minute, or I swear I'll *kill* you."

I opened one eyelid to see Carina standing over my crate with a lantern. Her hair fell in a tangle about her dirty, bruised face, and blood trickled from a nasty cut across the swollen bridge of her nose. She wore some sort of rough, ragged cloak covered with filth and soot.

As she raised her hand to wallop me again I raised an arm to shield myself. "Stop hitting me, will you?"

"Mother of Christ, you deserve a proper thrashing. And you will get one, the moment we're out of this mess." The ferocious anger on her face twisted into grim satisfaction as she put aside the lantern, shoved her hands under my arms, and hauled me out of the crate. "Wrecker's outside with a cart. Come on."

The air smelled hot and smoky, and made me cough as Rina dragged me through the darkness. "What's on fire?"

"Anything that isn't warded," she snapped. "So shake your ass."

As we emerged from the cargo house, I saw three things I couldn't quite comprehend: Wrecker dressed in soot-stained yellow; a gravecart filled with dead harlots; and the Hill on fire.

"No time to gawk." Rina jerked my arm as she marched to the back of the cart. "We'll be lucky to make it out of the city alive."

I stared at the corpses of a dozen battered gels. All of them I recognized from the Eagle's Nest. At the top of the pile lay Almira, her apron spattered with blood round a gaping black gash in her abdomen.

I shook my head. "We have to go to the police. We have to tell them—"

"The coppers are busy with the blues," Rina said as she climbed up and wedged herself in a corner before offering me her hand. When I didn't take it, she swore. "Kit, I swear, I'll tie you to the back and drag you by the rope—"

"She's scared," Almira said, lifting her head a little to glare at me. "We're not dead, you goose. It's a ruse—tar and tomato juice—and it itches like sin."

"Least you're on top, old woman," a younger voice complained. "Ouch, Jude, that's my tit. Get your knee off."

I climbed up and curled into the corner opposite Rina. "Why are they pretending to be dead?"

"Bunch of Talians locked us up in the Nest before they set fire to it," she said flatly. "We got out through the old sewers, but if they see any of us I've no doubt they'll try again. Little bastards are nothing if not determined."

So Rina and the gels had been fleeing for their lives . . . and had ended up at the docks. "How did you know where to find me, and why did you bother to look?"

"An old tunneler met us in the sewer. Said you were in trouble and directed me to the cargo house. I almost didn't come, you know." Rina turned her head toward Wrecker. "Take the road that runs through the teller's quarter. They've not burned anything there."

Setting fire to the great houses on the Hill would have diverted the militia and the police there to do whatever they could; the ton represented Rumsen's wealthiest and most powerful families. That had left the rest of the city vulnerable. I could even understand why the Reapers had tried to incinerate Rina and her gels; they probably thought I had gone there to seek haven.

But why set the other fires? Why burn the unwarded?

When I asked Rina that, she made a bitter sound. "Sorry to say they've not stopped to have tea and chat about it. Too occupied with torching houses and slaughtering innocents, I expect."

"They've gone after anyone what don't have them wardlings, Miss Kit," Wrecker said over his shoulder. "They're checking every door and neck."

"You're sure that they're sparing anyone with wardlings?" When he nodded, I felt my stomach clench. Dredmore had been shocked by something Walsh had said about the popular talismans. Something about dreamstone. I looked over at Rina. "We have to stop. I need to find a charm maker."

"I'm sure you do, and for some very good reason," my best friend said in a murderously pleasant tone, "but we're not stopping. Not for you, or wardlings, or even Herself if she suddenly appears and steps in front of the cart. George can be King."

"Then push me off in the teller's quarter." Before Rina could reply I reached for her hand and gripped it. Her fingers felt like ice, and I realized how hard she was trying not to tremble. "Carina, when we first met, when you left my house and went back on the stroll, do you know why I didn't try to come after you?"

"Sod you, Kit." She dug her fingernails into my palm. "It's not the same thing."

"After everything that had been taken from you, you deserved the right to make your own choices and live your own life, no matter what I thought of it." I kissed her cheek and whispered, "Time to pay me back, my gel."

"The Talians want you dead, don't they?" When I nodded, she swore viciously. "Wrecker, find an alley behind the tellers' shops. And give Kit two of your blades."

I swallowed against the lump in my throat and smiled my thanks as the big man held two of his best knives over his shoulder. "Where are you going from here?"

"Settle, maybe, if we can make it that far before it snows or the Talians catch up. We'll stop at the lumber camps for provisions, see if we can pick up some trade." She reached into her pocket and took out a small, bulging reticule, which she thrust in my hands. "There's enough here to buy yourself a young horse or an old carri. Take it," she added when I tried to give it back to her. "It's the chance to change your mind and get the bloody hell out."

The cart stopped, and before I climbed down I tucked away the blades, reached over, and wrapped my arms round Rina. "I'll see you again someday, you know."

She gave me a tight, trembling hug in return. "Not if I see you first, you daft twit."

CHAPTER TWENTY-THREE

Once the cart had gone I moved to the end of the alley to check the streets, which appeared empty, and the shopfronts, all of which were dark. Lamplight flickered in some of the windows on the second and third floors, and I noted which of the charm makers was closest to me before retreating back into the alleyway.

Pulling down the fire escape ladders would have alerted anyone within three blocks to my presence, but fortunately most of them had already been lowered. The tellers might have been spared by the Reapers, but none of them seemed to be assuming they were safe.

I climbed up to the second floor over the charm maker's shop, and leaned over to look through the grimy window into the flat inside. One candle stub burned on the opposite side of the room, and I made out the vague silhouette of an old man wrapped in a blanket.

I tested the window, found it to be locked, and had to tap on it several times before the old man came over and opened it a few inches. "Evening."

Frightened, angry eyes glared out at me. "What do you want, gel?"

I thought of how to put it. "Can you tell me what happens when a particular stone is charmed?"

"Get stuffed." The window slammed shut.

"Wait, sir." I reached in my pocket for Rina's gift and tapped it against the window. "I can pay you."

The window remained shut for another minute, then rose just enough for me to squeeze through. "Well? Come on, then, before you're seen."

I wriggled through the gap and made a quick if undignified entrance. The flat inside smelled of paper and cabbage, and had almost no furnishings. Great circles of wardlings had been nailed to every wall.

"Thank you, sir." As soon as I had my feet under me I bobbed a curtsey for good measure. "I am truly sorry to disturb you on such a night."

"My name's Jasper, not sir, and you're about as sorry as the cat what got caught with the canary feathers." He retreated back to his chair by the banked fire and swaddled himself again with his blanket. "Give me ten in silver. No, twenty."

I had enough coin in the reticule to pay him a hundred times that, but dutifully counted out twenty and handed him the stack.

He checked each piece with his teeth before they disappeared under the blanket along with most of his face. "All right," he said, his voice muffled. "Which stone is it you want to charm?"

Since there were no other chairs in the flat, I went to stand by the mantel. "Dreamstone."

His head poked up. "You climb up into my flat to ask me about a faeriestale? Have you gone off?"

"So you *have* heard of it." As he scowled at me I lifted my hands. "Please, sir—Mr. Jasper," I corrected myself. "I have to know what happens when it's charmed."

"Can't be charmed since *there's no such stone*."

"Then how could you know of it? You must have heard something from someone," I wheedled.

"Years ago some miners told tales about it. Said it were found in some pisshole in Cornwall. They only wanted to scare folk." Jasper saw my expression and sighed. "Way the story went, some mage had been digging up half of Cornwall looking for it. Only it were the miners what found it first. The mage brought down a tunnel on their heads, stole it from them, used it to put them to sleep, and left them to die. Only one came out alive, and his people said the mage had used the stone on him."

The story was too similar to Hedger's for me to doubt it. "So charmed dreamstone makes people go to sleep?"

"Their minds, aye. Their bodies stay awake and do whatever the mage what bespelled them wills. That's why they are also called the possession stones." He made a rude gesture. "Only there weren't no mage, no miners, and sure as Satan no bloody dreamstone."

I glanced at the wardlings he'd nailed to the walls. "If a stone like it were real, Mr. Jasper, would it have to be carried or worn by the person it controls?"

"Why would it, once it was 'spelled? Stones give off power like the sun gives heat. All people'd have to do is stand close enough to be caught in the radiance." He glared. "Don't you know nothing about magic, gel?"

"Until a few days ago, I didn't believe in it." I tried to smile, but if what I suspected was true, in a few hours all of Rumsen would belong to the Reapers. "Is there any defense against a stone that could do that?"

" 'Course there isn't. Why would there be ? It don't exist."

"The mage in the miners' story," I coaxed, "how was he defeated?"

"Like all the evildoers, by being killed in a body what was outside after dawn." He chuffed out a breath. "Nothing made of darkness can stand the light of day."

Did that mean my grandfather was evil? Dredmore, now, he could be crowned Prince of Darkness and no one would even question it, least of all me. But as annoying as Harry had been since he'd come into my life, he'd never behaved in any particularly evil manner.

Except to Hedger, who hated him. And Dredmore, who despised him. And my mother, who had made me promise to wear for the rest of my life the pendant she'd made to keep me from seeing him . . .

Confused and angry now, I strode over to the wall of wardlings.

"What are you—hey, you quit that." He got up and tried to stop me from removing one of his talismans. "Is that why you really crawled in here? To steal my only protection from me? I'm calling for a beater."

"You'd best shout loudly, then. They're all up on the Hill." I brushed his hands away and wrenched the wardling from the wall, throwing it as hard as I could to the floor. Silver-white light exploded across the room as it shattered into three pieces.

While the light faded and the old charm maker squawked, I picked up one of the pieces and examined it. The outside of the wardling, which appeared to be silver, had cracked like cheap porcelain. Beneath the faux metal coating lay a dirty, speckled gray stone disk.

"Gimme that." The old man brought over his candle, and as soon as the light from the flame touched the stone the speckles glinted with all the colors of the rainbow.

The flashing colors made me feel light-headed. "What was the light?"

"Dispelled its power, you did," he muttered, snatching the piece from me and turning it this way and that. "Shattering charmed stone always do."

"So this is dreamstone." What was it doing inside the wardling?

"These wardlings were struck from pure silver, they said," the old man griped. "Charged me double for 'em."

"Evidently they lied." I picked up the other pieces. "Where did you buy them?"

"There's a cargo house down by the dock that deals in stone and metals." He brought the broken wardling over to the lit candle and studied it again. "Quarry masters have been bringing 'em in by the shipload for months. Can't keep 'em stocked. Demand was so high they had to start importing 'em from Talia." He looked up at me. "That's all being sold now: Talian-made wardlings."

Walsh had said something about the Talians forging them, but I'd assumed he meant forged as in hammering them out of metal. I was dealing with another counterfeiting operation, like the one that had robbed Rina's poor old gent Wiggins of his bacco boxes, only on a much grander scale. "But everyone still believes they're from the queensland."

His shoulders hunched. "We knew, but silver's silver. Don't matter if it's English or Talian."

Unless someone was planning to invade a country. "If every wardling in the city has dreamstone inside it then why haven't the stones affected the people?"

"Because it's always been thought stuff and nonsense. Stones always work their charms, unless . . ." He fell silent, dropping the broken piece and shuffling back from it. "No. Couldn't be. They'd never put so many unspelled stones in one place. Who'd be mad enough to do that?"

I went after him and grabbed his arms to keep him from crumpling to the floor. "Why aren't they working, Mr. Jasper?" When he didn't speak, I shook him. "Tell me."

"A stone don't work its charm if it's raw. Never been spelled," he added, his eyes wide and his voice going hoarse. "Raw stone soaks up power a hundred times quicker, too. Longer it's left unspelled, the more power it takes."

"From what?"

"Anything what lives: people, animals, plants. That's why all stone's spelled for the first time in the quarries, before it's shipped. To keep us safe." His face screwed up and he clutched at his chest. "I can't take any more of this," he wheezed. "My heart's no good."

"Calm down." I helped him over to his chair and tucked his blanket round him. "If the stones in the wardlings were never spelled, then they've been absorbing power for months."

He closed his eyes. "Aye. Go away."

"One more question, Mr. Jasper, and I will." I bent

down so I could see his face. "What happens if a mage tries to spell all these raw dreamstones now?"

He opened one eye to give me a hopeless look. "He's only got to spell one, gel. Raw stones stay connected to each other, like they are under the ground before they're mined. That and all the power they've soaked up will cause the spell to spread on its own. There'll be nowhere to hide from them then."

I didn't want to leave him like this, but I had to find Zarath before he cast the spell. "I'll ask one of your neighbors to take you to the hospital."

"Don't bother. I'm the only one what has a carri." He sounded more peevish than worried. "I'd rather spend my last hours here, in my place."

I felt horrible. "Is your heart really that weak?"

"Not my heart, gel. The stones." He made a fretful sound. "With that kind of power, as soon as the spell's worked, we'll all go into the dreams. Every man, woman, and child in the city. No one will ever wake up from them. Not ever again."

It seemed I was going back to the docks sooner than I'd planned. I persuaded the charm maker to let me borrow his transport, which he stored in the merchant's carrihouse on the corner. Mr. Jasper gave me his keyfob, which he said the doorman would demand to see before letting me in.

"I'll return it as soon as I can," I promised.

"'Twon't matter to me if you do," he muttered, staring into the hearth's embers. "We're finished, all of us."

I wasn't giving up, so I hurried down to the corner and presented the keyfob to the lad working the door.

He looked me over, his cheeks pinking as he did. "You're not Mr. Jasper."

"How astute of you to notice," I praised him. "I'm Mr. Jasper's daughter, Constance Payne."

He frowned. "You're Old Jasper's kid? But he weren't never married."

"Much to my mother's everlasting sorrow, my father abandoned her after one night of love." I sighed. "After enduring decades of needling guilt, he came to regret his cruelty and searched high and low for me until we were reunited. Now here I am, to run his every errand and make golden his final years. For which tonight I need his carri. Where is it?"

"In the back. Stall thirteen." Reluctantly he handed back the keyfob. "You shouldn't be out driving by yourself, miss. There's a bad lot of furriners running about hurting people and setting fires. Burnt the Hill, they did."

"Thank you for the concern, but I'll manage." I walked back to stalls, found the one numbered thirteen, and surveyed Mr. Jasper's transport. Of course it was as old and cantankerous-looking as its owner, but as soon as I punched the ignition and cranked the motor it wheezed and chugged to life. As I wasn't used to driving, I took my time easing it out of the stall, then drove to the front, where the doorman opened the gate. Since it had no glasshield I had to squint against the smoke pouring out of the old coal burner into my face.

The lad held up his hand for me to brake, and once I had he handed me some gogs for my eyes. "You take care, miss," he yelled over the sound of the old motor.

I wanted to climb out and hug him, but settled for strapping on the eyewear and giving a fond wave.

The carri puttered along steadily as I drove it to the Silken Dream. From Bridget's storefront I could see the houses on the Hill still burning out of control, and the long line of carris and heavily laden carts clogging up the roads down. If anyone survived this night, it would likely be the rich, as they had all the cops dancing attendance on them.

I knew Bridget kept a spare keylace in one of the lilac-filled planters flanking the front door, which I used to let myself in. The dresses on the forms in the front were all ball gowns, which would be impossible to put on without a maid, so I went to the back storeroom. There hung a selection of day and evening frocks on long racks, and I searched through them looking for something simple I could pull over my head.

"Thieving bitch. Get your filthy hands off my clothes."

I whirled round to see Bridget standing behind me, a pistol in her fist. "Bridget, it's me." I pulled up the gogs to show her my face.

"Kit?" She lifted the lantern in her other hand and peered, and then lowered the gun. "What in nine hells are you doing here?"

"I needed something to wear." I gestured at my stained, torn skirts. "Something a bit cleaner."

She set down the lantern. "Rumsen's been attacked, there are Talians out there torching the ton and slitting the throats of disbelievers, and not a cop to be had away from the Hill." Her voice climbed to a piercing octave. "And you've come to borrow a *dress*?"

I nodded. "If you wouldn't mind lending me another one that will end up fit only for a ragbag."

"Blind me." Bridget flung her hand about. "Take whatever you want. I don't care. Take it all."

"Only need one, but thanks." I pulled a pretty light green silk from one of the hangers. "Why are you still here in the city?"

"Charlie got wind of this yesterday," she said as she came over to help me. "I told him to take the kids and go south. We've a place down in Zhuma, on the coast, where they can wait it out. They'll be safe there."

I knew her husband to be an extremely practical man who would naturally protect his family first. "He wouldn't leave you behind."

"He thinks me and my parents are following him by train. Lift your arms." As I did, she pulled my skirts over my head and tossed them aside. Wrecker's knives, which I had forgotten, fell to the floor. Gingerly she retrieved them. "Why are you carrying kneecapper blades?"

"Because a cannon's a bit too bulky." I watched her set them on a pin table. "Why aren't you and your parents on a train now?"

"You know Da; he won't leave the mill to burn, not with all the goods still on the looms. Mum won't leave him, so I had to stay to look after them. I only chanced coming to the shop to see if any of the gels were using it as a hidey-hole." She stripped off my petticoats. "God, you reek. Don't you ever bathe?"

"Not of late." I wriggled as the first fresh petticoat went over my head, and withstood another atop that before I protested. "That's enough. Any more and I won't be able to run."

"These are silk, not cotton. You can fly in them." Bridget eased the dress over my head and worked it down, straightening the full skirt and adjusting the sewn-in waister. "I'm going to the mill when I leave here, and that's where I'll stay until it's finished. You should come with me, love. Mum and Da have laid in enough supplies to last us to Doomsday, and Charlie left five of the stablemen behind as my guards. They're proper bruisers, all of them."

I shook my head. "When you get to the mill, take down all the wardlings your Da has about the place." I picked up a thin hairpin from a dressing table and tucked it inside my mouth. "Then toss them in the gin."

"What?" She stopped buttoning me up. "That'll mash 'em to pieces."

"Exactly." I told her what Mr. Jasper had said, and added, "You don't have to believe it. Just do it for me. Please."

"No, I believe you." She backed away from me and pulled out the pistol. "What I'd like to know is, how did a stupid little twit like you find out?"

My heart almost stopped. "You're not funny."

"I'm not jesting." She didn't take her eyes off me as she called out, "She's ready to go now, boys."

It didn't seem real until two of Walsh's footmen came in. Even then I didn't want to believe it. "You can't be part of this, Bridge. Not you."

"Why not me? You still think I'm a loomgel at heart? I haven't been, Kit, not for years." Her face changed

325

as she put on one of her haughty Madam looks. "I am Madam Duluc, wife to one of the richest men in Toriana and France. Why should I care about the likes of you?"

She was acting. She had to be. "You've always been my friend."

"Wait," Bridget said to the men as they started toward me. "She'll try to run, this one. Get some rope." She handed one of the blades Wrecker had given me to the other brute. "Put this in my carri. I want it as a souvenir."

Once the brutes had left and we were alone, I expected Bridget to lower the pistol and tell me it was all a farce. She didn't.

"You're not really going to do this," I assured her. "You can't hand me over to them like I'm nothing to you. I was your friend long before you met Charlie." When she said nothing, I felt my heart clench. "Sweet Mary, Bridget Sullivan. Were you ever mine?"

A mask of real anger settled over her face. "I never met anyone as bloody mule-headed as you, Kit. Told you to stay away from the Hill, didn't I? But no. You had to go nosing round Walsh and his business. You did this to yourself, dearie." She strode to me, grabbing me by the hair and jerking me close. In a murmur, she said, "They took Charlie and the kids, and they're holding them on a ship somewhere. Said I'd only get them back alive if I did this. Sorry, love." In a louder voice she said, "And I'm done with you." She slipped her hand into a seam on the side of my skirt that shouldn't have been open. I understood why it was when I felt the second of Wrecker's blades being tucked in my garter. "If you know what's good for you, you'll shut up now, and when they take you to the master, give him exactly what he deserves."

I had to put on a show for Walsh's men when they returned, so I struggled and called out to her, begging for her to save me while wanting her to do no such thing at all.

Bridget pretended to be indifferent, although just as they dragged me off she looked sick.

Outside the shop the men used the rope to bind my wrists and ankles, so there was no getting to Wrecker's blade after they tossed me in the back of their carri. I fell over on my side and stayed there, enduring the jolting as I thought through every possible course of action.

Obviously Zarath wouldn't be fooled by renewed protestations of my love this time round. I'd count myself a lucky gel to get a word out before he took retribution. As long as I was bound I couldn't use Wrecker's knife to defend myself. Anyway, the blade was steel, and would do nothing to hurt the Aramanthan. If I was smart I'd plant it in my own heart as soon as I got a hand free. Zarath couldn't hurt a corpse.

But the Reapers intended to turn everyone in Rumsen into walking corpses, and I couldn't allow that, not if there was something I could do to stop them. I'd also promised Dredmore that I would set his spirit free.

I smelled the docks a few seconds before the carri screeched to a stop. I closed my eyes and went limp, keeping up the pretense of a faint until one of them tossed me over his shoulder. From that vantage point I saw (upside down and in snatches, of course) that they were delivering me to a big clipper with black sails and a pitch-covered hull. Up the gangway we went, and I caught a few glimpses of a group of men in bankers' suits before I was dumped on the deck before them.

"Untie her; she's not going anywhere. This *is* the one who attacked the master?" one of the suits asked as the rope was removed from my wrists and ankles.

"Aye. Caught her at the gowner's."

Through the slits of my eyes I watched the two footmen retreat before I concentrated on being nothing more than a pile of laundry.

"Very good. I wasn't anxious to cut the throat of such a valuable pawn as Duluc," the suit said, his chilly voice closer now. He nudged me over with a careless prod of his shoe. "I know this tart. She hires herself out to dispel magic." His tone hardened. "Bringing her here was foolish. Even on the Hill she has a reputation for being most effective."

"She has but a few pathetic tricks," a new but very familiar voice replied. "None of them will stop us or save her now." Celestino. So he had survived my stabbing.

I could only cringe on the inside and pray that Zarath would make an appearance before his underling repaid me in kind.

"I know what happened when the master returned to us," the suit said. "If she is so harmless, then why would Lucien Dredmore surrender his body to protect her?"

"Walsh said the fool was in love with her."

I dared lifted one eyelid, just enough to see the Talian, his hair hanging in oily rings over his forehead, his arm bound up in a sling tied over his blood-blotched jacket. He walked to me and as he crouched down I closed my eye again. "Why is she like this? Did you beat her into unconsciousness?"

"No, sir," the footman said. "She fainted."

"They are so delicate, the ladies of this country." Celestino stood up. "But this one, she is more like the cockroach. You must crush her under your heel slowly, like a tick."

Guessing what he meant to do, I bit the inside of my lip, but the boot that slammed into my belly kicked a cry of pain up through my teeth.

"That would be for stabbing me," the Talian mentioned as he drew back his boot. "And this"—he kicked me in the back—"is for the master."

Knowing there would be more of the same or worse, I curled over and made pitiful noises, crawling a bit while I measured the distance between my body and the edge of the deck. There was railing to contend with, but not a great height of it.

"Zarath wanted her alive, did he not?" one of the suits inquired.

"So he will have her," Celestino said. "A few broken bones will not make any difference to him."

When his boot struck my ribs, I turned onto my side, tucking my arms against me and wailing as if he'd cracked something. The fourth time he came at me I let the impact roll me over—and kept rolling until I collided with the railing.

I was up and over the side before anyone could react, and plummeted down the side of the ship like a stone. Before I fell between the hull and the dock into the murky water I reached out, catching a mooring rope with my hands. Splinters of oakum stabbed into my palms, and grabbing on in midfall nearly wrenched my arms out of their sockets, but I didn't let go. Once I stopped bobbing I swung my legs out and back, out and back until I had enough momentum to make the leap to the dock.

I collapsed on the boards as soon as I landed, and for a moment I wasn't sure I could rise again. Then I heard fast, heavy thuds and the gangway bouncing and struggled to my feet.

I hiked up my skirts and ran from the ship to the way station, where I glanced back. Celestino and his men had reached the bottom of the gangway, but they weren't chasing me. They were just standing there, watching.

Slowly I turned round to see Dredmore walking toward me with an unhurried pace. He wore a new set of powder-free clothing, over which he had put on Lucien's greatcoat, and carried a strange black club covered with scarlet symbols.

"Oh, hello, Lucien." I had nowhere to run, and too many reasons to stay. "Did you have a nice nap? Sorry about the headache. A little chamomile soother will work wonders on that. Shall I go fetch some for you from a cart?"

"I knew you would return." He didn't try to club me over the head or grab me, but put his knuckles under my chin to tip up my face. "Mortal love makes you this foolish. But even if you could dispossess me, woman, the spirit of your man will not return to this body."

"I know." And I was a fool for thinking I could do this.

Someone groaned, and I heard the door of the way

station rattle. "You out there. I can't get out. Help me."

"I see." Zarath ignored Montrose Walsh's squealing as he stroked my cheek with his fingertips. "You came to prevent me from casting the spell. That will not happen. You may watch instead. In a few moments, you and every mortal in this city will belong to me."

I turned my face away. "Not if I break the spell first."

"It is not one spell, foolish child. It is thousands upon thousands. Once it is released, not even I could stop it." The scarlet symbols on the black club began to glow. "But I shall use it to send you into a waking dream, where you will know every time I take my pleasure of your pain and your flesh, where you can do nothing but feel it."

"How delightful." I shuffled back and reached behind me for the way station's door latch, and from it removed the iron rail tie I'd used to keep Montrose imprisoned inside. "I can't fathom why everyone finds you so utterly repulsive," I mentioned as I pocketed the spike. "I mean, other than the way you talk, behave, think, and smell, you're quite the catch, aren't you?"

He grabbed hold of my bodice, tearing it as he jerked me close. "Open your mouth."

"Go back to hell." I spat in his face.

He took hold of my throat with one hand and cut off my air, and no matter how I clawed at him, kept strangling me. Shadows loomed before my eyes, inviting me to throw myself into them. Looking into death was such a terrible relief that I gasped.

Zarath's hand clapped over my mouth at the same time he released my neck, and the need to breathe overcame everything. I didn't realize he had shoved a stone into my mouth until it slid to the back of my tongue and went down my throat. It burned my insides as it went down, and I fought to stop it, coughing and retching violently. Nothing came out, and then I felt it in my stomach, hot and cold, an unbearable weight.

Zarath put his mouth next to my ear. "Do you feel her? That is my queen, Anamorg. She is inside you now, and she will keep you from breaking any spell. I have only to release her from the stone, and your body will be hers. Then Anamorg will devour your spirit, and you will be nothing."

"Not a very pretty name, is it? Anamorg." I rasped out the words as I reached in my pocket for the rail tie. "Sounds to me like a disease of the bottom."

His expression tightened with outrage. "For that I will make you know agony as you could not imagine."

"Sorry, but it's my turn now." I threw myself against him, knocking him down on his back. I had only a moment to straddle him, raise the iron spike I'd taken from the door handle of the way station, and strike.

I thought I might hesitate, staring down at Dredmore's face, knowing what I was about to do. Yet my hand never wavered or faltered, and I plunged the spike deep into his chest, thrusting it down with all my strength.

Zarath heaved me off, clutching the end of the spike as he convulsed. He rolled onto his side, curling over before he lurched onto all fours. His head came up and he roared out his pain and fury until the sound died and a bloody froth bubbled from his lips. I backed away into Montrose, who stood gaping at the sight.

"What have you done?" he yelped.

Zarath staggered onto his feet, pulling at the spike as obscenely wet sounds poured out along with the blood from his mouth.

"I killed a monster." I couldn't bear to see him die, but I couldn't look away until I was sure he had. "And I saved a man."

The Aramanthan reeled toward the ship, but he strayed too close to the edge of the dock, where he fell into the water with a tremendous splash.

Celestino, who had run toward us, stopped in his tracks. His eyes rolled back in his head, and he collapsed like a rag doll. I saw the other men by the gangplank do the same, and then Montrose fell in front of me, face-first into the dock.

I knelt on the edge of the pier, shoving my fingers deep into my mouth so that I might cast up the stone, but it wouldn't come out of me. The sensation of burning and freezing faded, leaving me with only the feeling of a rock in my belly. Anamorg, queen of the Reapers, waiting to awake inside me.

"Miss Kittredge."

I turned my head and saw Inspector Doyle standing a few feet away. "Oh, hello, Tommy." Two beaters flanked him, and each held their nightsticks ready. "Filthy day, isn't it? All this smoke is plaguing my eyes something awful."

CHAPTER TWENTY-FOUR

As I sat in Questioning at Rumsen Main Station I idly wished for a dagger. They'd taken Wrecker's from me, but I didn't especially need a kneecapper's blade. Any dagger, even a penknife, would suffice for the last bit of killing I had to do.

I caught a whiff of piss as I imagined it. A quick slash across the carotid. Lots of blood—lots of mess—but they were used to tidying up death here. I knew no one would shout for help or call for the whitecart. If anything, they'd have their tea hour down at the pub and share a few good-riddance pints.

They might still at that. I had one sleeve left intact. When they tossed me in my cell, I'd be alone.

For now I'd have to endure this. Sitting shackled to a chair for hours wasn't comfortable, but it was a nice break from the hell I'd been through over the past two weeks.

Questioning, for all its hideous rep, wasn't as bad as all that. Dust coated the gaslight chimneys, all of which were blackened on the inside from long use. Yellowed wanted posts and faded ambrotype tints hung on point from a warped cork-backed board, on which someone had pasted a headline from *The Queen's Voice*: *Your Colonial Taxes at Work*. It hadn't taken that long for Her Majesty to decide to appropriate all unprocessed colonial gold for Herself, or men would still be out panning the rivers.

Grimy footprints and skid marks from rubber-soled shoes made odd trails across the cheap pine floor planks. Old pipe and cigar smoke had shriveled an orange-clove pomander hanging from the window bars to the size of a walnut.

I wasn't in any better shape. I needed a bath, a drink, and my head examined. Whatever they did to me, though, I wasn't explaining what had happened at the docks. I wasn't even sure I understood it. All I could feel was the awful weight inside me, like some hidden rot just waiting for the right moment to bloom.

Chief Inspector Tom Doyle came in and closed the door behind him. He didn't come at me but walked to one end of the room, and then the other.

I watched him back and forth it. Working three straight shifts hadn't wrinkled his jacket or trousers, and damp comb marks streaked his short hair. It didn't surprise me that he'd taken the time to wash up and shave. He'd spent ten years in H.M.'s Fleet, and now had a bit of that all-hands-on-deck look about him. Now I was the enemy, and naturally he had to evaluate my threat potential before he issued any orders. I wondered if he'd ever dreamt we'd come to this.

Doyle finally tired of pacing, yanked out the chair on the other side of the table, and dropped in it. Gave me that cool, flint-edged stare he'd inherited from his Grandda, and said: "Why did you do it, Kit?"

I gave him my full statement in four words. "I didn't kill him." Of course I had, but admitting it wouldn't gain me much chance to finish the work. For that I'd need a nice, quiet, isolated cell in lockup. "Is that what this is about, then? You've got the wrong—"

"They'll send you to the gallows." Beneath his rage was something more I hadn't expected to see: regret.

"I doubt it. They hardly ever hang women." A cramp in my right shoulder made me adjust the drape of my arms round the back of the chair. The five-link chain between my shackles jingled. "You've no body, no credible witnesses. How could I have done him, what with me being such a young, helpless female and all?"

"I've better." He bent to one side, took something from his case, and placed it on the table between us. A small, flat square, carefully swaddled in soft black cloth. He didn't have to unwrap it to show me what it was.

I stared at it, fascinated. "You've glass."

"Aye, I've glass." He braced his hands on the table and leaned over it. "Why did you kill him?"

It had to be a trick, the glass blank, the threat empty. Unless— "Show it to me."

Tom unwrapped the cloth to expose the plate inside.

Silverblack mottled the slick surface with splotches and lines. They formed the reverse image of a long dock, a tall woman, and the possessed lover she was straddling. This tint showed the finer details. The tears in her bodice. The blood on her mouth. The iron spike she was just about to thrust into the monster's chest.

Damn me, he had it all on glass. "That's not what it looks like."

He picked up the ambrotype showing me killing Lucien Dredmore. "This is *not* you shoving a rail tie through the man's chest, then." Hot blue eyes shifted to the remains of my bodice. "And I suppose that's not Dredmore's blood all over your tits."

"No." Well, most of it wasn't his blood.

"You've a homicidal twin sister tucked away somewhere?"

"Sorry." I grimaced. "Only child."

Tom checked his pocket watch. "After you didn't kill Dredmore, did someone else kick him over the side of the dock and send him for a bathe?"

"I don't recall." I wished I could explain, but he'd never believe it. "Tommy—"

"Inspector Doyle to the likes of you."

"Inspector Doyle." So much for the tender bud of that relationship. "I did not stab Lucien Dredmore in the heart or pitch his ass in the bay. I may have wanted to—I may have even dreamt about it now and then—but I am innocent of these charges being filed against me."

"You're lying."

I smelled piss again and glanced down. No wonder the floor and the seat felt tacky; the chap they'd brought in before me had disgraced himself. Maybe the Yard hadn't cleaned it up very well in order to break down the resistance of subsequent suspects. The stench was certainly working wonders on me.

"Kit."

"Can't you see what's happening here?" No, he couldn't, that much was obvious. "Think about it, Tommy. I hate the bleeding bastard. Everyone knows that. They wanted him and me out of the way. One stone, two birds. So they arranged to make it look like I killed him, and we're both done for. Oldest trick in the book."

"So you're being framed for Dredmore's murder."

I kept a straight face. "Yes."

"There's just one problem with that."

"What?"

"I'm the one who took this, and the others." He shoved the glass across the table at me. "I was there at the docks the entire time, Kit. I watched you kill him. I arrested you at the scene." His blond brows formed a vee over his bright blue eyes. "And I will testify."

So he would, because that was the sort of man he was. If things had gone differently, Tommy and I might have been mates. Another thing to regret, but not enough to keep me from hanging myself. It didn't matter. My life had ended hours ago when Zarath had shoved that spirit stone down my throat.

I had to finish this.

"I'll say that we've slept together," I said. "My barrister will use it to destroy your credibility—"

Pain exploded across my face and my head snapped to one side as his swinging hand connected with my cheek. I spat some blood-streaked saliva on the floor and rolled the bottom of my jaw.

"Very good, Inspector. Go on, hit me again. Use your fist this time. I deserve it, lying bitch that I am." If I were very lucky, I might be able to goad him into breaking my neck.

"So you can use the bruises to discredit me?" He shook his head. "What happened, Kit? What did he do to you? How in God's name did he drive you to murder? You were lovers."

I laughed. "I'd rather bed a jackal."

Doyle took something from his pocket and tossed it down in front of me. The last time I'd seen the old chain, Dredmore had made it vanish. Now, looking at it and the crystal-encrusted stone pendant hanging from it, I could hardly take in enough air to form words. "Where did you get this?"

"We recovered it," he snapped. "We also have the murder weapon, which was recovered from the docks. It'll be tested. They'll find his blood on it."

My hand shook as I scraped my fingers against the table, catching the chain and using it to tug the night-stone to me. As soon as I covered it with my palm, I felt something like tiny gears inside turning a notch. Before Zarath had possessed him Lucien had said he would be where Harry had been . . . and then I knew. I knew it all.

"Where's the body?" Without thinking I tried to stand, only to be jerked back as my shackles cut into my wrists. "Where is it?"

"Down at the docks in a skip net," he said. "Awaiting transport to the morgue. And why the devil do you care?"

The pendant changed everything. "I want a vicar."

Outrage flagged his cheekbones red. "You don't get—"

"I'll confess," I said quickly. "To all of it. Everything. In my own hand, if you like. *After* I speak to my vicar."

He stared. "You've never been Church."

I ran my tongue along the seam where my cheek met my gum line. "Remorse has converted me. It's a miracle. Now, the vicar, if you please."

Fury left Doyle speechless, and he stalked out. As

soon as the door slammed I hooked the hairpin nestled next to my bottom gum with my tongue and caught it between my teeth. I turned my face as far as I could to the left and spat it carefully over my shoulder. It fell neatly into my cupped hands. I took a moment to work my wrist until it felt looser, stretched out the chain between the cuffs, and went to work.

The air vent was too small, and I'd never make it to the end of the corridor outside. That left the window, and the lock on the inside grid. Once I'd opened it I shoved it up, catching by reflex the old pomander as it fell. I left it on the table along with my shackles for Doyle.

The pendant I took with me.

CHAPTER TWENTY-FIVE

Escaping Rumsen Main in the middle of being questioned by Inspector Doyle proved almost comically simple; perhaps Tommy thought someone who had essentially just confessed to murdering the most important mage in the province incapable of such a feat.

As I jumped from the window to the alley, I hoped his anger and outrage over what he thought he'd seen at the docks would keep him from returning to the questioning room for at least another half hour. I needed to put some distance between me and all the beaters Tommy would be sending out to hunt for me. Once again on foot, I made haste down the alleyways.

I wrapped the broken chain of my pendant round my fist. I'd cherished it as a gift from my parents, and worn it practically every day of my life, but now it felt like an iron ball. As soon as this was over I'd find a nice big furnace to toss it in. And then there was the stone in my belly, waiting like some slumbering, poisonous snake. Somehow I had to get that out of me before something woke up Zarath's queen and she had my spirit for tea.

I halted at the corner of the next street, forced to wait on a long row of hog carts coming down from the smoldering remains of the mansions on the Hill. Someone had piled costly furnishings, paintings, and other trappings of wealth in the back of the carts, right on top of the old, filthy straw. Even what didn't end up stained with the former occupants' waste and fluids would definitely absorb the distinctive stench.

Servants would have set fire to their masters' possessions before permitting them to be hauled away in pig carts.

I caught up to one of the tired-looking nobbers providing escort for the carts. Soot blackened the end of his nose, his eyebrows were gone, and patches of burnt flesh showed through the rags he'd tied round both hands.

"Evening," I said as I stretched my legs to pace him. "Are you lads back from the Hill? Were you able to save anything from Walsh's Folly?"

He spared me a tired glance. "Piss off."

"I'm Lady Diana's cousin and companion, actually." I tried to pitch my voice to sound half-snobby, half-forlorn. "Her husband got himself killed last night. I've just come from the morgue, and now I've got to break the news to her."

"Tha'so?" He looked a bit uncomfortable now. "Pitiful, this night's business. Bloody Talians."

"Where are you taking all this?" I gestured to the cart.

"Some bigwig said move what we could down to the cargo houses." A glimmer of sour humor came over his features. "Wouldn't give us naught for hauling, 'course, so we had to make do."

Evidently the nobbers had loaded the ton's treasures deliberately into pig carts—and everyone said they had no sense of humor. I let him hear a little of my chuckle before I turned it into a polite cough. "That's where I'm headed. Milady and her maids were taken down to the docks for their safety. Can't find a cabbie to save my life, though." I tugged at my bloodstained bodice. "I'd walk, but I've already been attacked once by some bloke covered in blood. Be all right if I walk with you, then?"

He looked doubtful. "With this pong, you'd want to?"

I shrugged and let my voice quaver a little. "Better than going on alone."

"Aye." He tugged on the lead rein, stopping the horses before offering me a hand. "But you'll ride this time, lass. Like a proper lady."

"Thank you." I smiled and let him help me up onto the empty driver's seat. Once he whistled the tired horses shuffled back into motion, and we were off.

As I suspected, the smell drove everyone away from the carts, even the beaters who came trotting from the direction of Rumsen Main. I hoped as long as I kept my head down and didn't do anything to draw attention to myself I'd be as good as invisible.

Through the snarls of my hair I noted the brigadiers who were putting out fires by pumping seawater from tanker carts into the household tubes. If the owners survived the night, they'd be returning to a wet, scorched mess, but at least the stone shells of their homes would still stand. I hoped my own place would still be intact, and then I recalled that it wasn't mine anymore. A laugh escaped me as I realized that I was not only a fugitive murderess but also a vagrant.

The cart creaked to a stop at the back of a loading dock, and the nobber helped me down from the seat.

"They're keeping the gentry over there, with their boats," he told me, nodding in the direction of the yacht yards. "I'd walk you over, but I've to unload all this scram first."

I started to thank him, and then did one better by giving him a deep, respectful curtsey. "I will always remember your kindness, dear sir."

"Aw, now. Weren't nothing." He looked pleased and embarrassed. "Get on with you, then."

I started toward the yacht yard, but as soon as my escort went to hitch the horses I turned and hurried toward the docks. I could see the militia standing guard on the deck of the Talian ship, and counted among the prisoners shackled to the mast Montrose Walsh as well as Celestino. On the dock below stood a beater next to a row of bodies covered by blood- and soot-stained tarps; on the very end was one soaked with wide patches of brackish water.

This thing will occupy my flesh, Dredmore murmured from my last memory of him, *but my spirit will go where it can never touch me. I understand now. I will be where Harry has been, all this time.*

Zarath hadn't won. Not yet.

The beater bristled as I approached him. "You can't be here, miss. Crime scene, this is."

"Inspector Thomas Doyle sent me," I lied. "I am—I was—in the employ of Lord Dredmore. I've come down from Morehaven to identify his remains."

"What now?" The beater looked confused. "I thought he were already tagged."

"I've been asked to confirm it's him." I walked past him, moving down the line of tarps. I glanced back. "Which one, please?"

The beater took a step after me, stopped, and then waved an arm. "On the very end. Mind you don't touch him."

I got to the tarp and dropped down beside it, gripping the pendant tightly as I uncovered Dredmore's head. Death had leached the cruel beauty from his features; they resembled a waxen mask cast in a too-smooth mold. When I lay my hand on his brow it felt like icy, damp stone.

"I said not to touch!" the beater called to me.

"Sorry!" I removed the pendant from my pocket, carefully draping the chain round his neck before I stood and stepped back. "All right, Lucien. The spell is over. I'm releasing you."

While I waited for Dredmore's spirit to return to his body, I wondered how he had fathomed the secret of my pendant. The mystery had come together for me only while Doyle had been questioning me, and even now I wasn't sure I'd worked it out exactly right. My doubts loomed as Dredmore's body remained still and lifeless.

"Don't you do this to me, Lucien," I muttered, reaching down to smack his face. "Not after all I've gone through this night. You're a deathmage, damn you. Surely you can overcome it—you must try. For me, please."

A shadow fell over Dredmore's body, one that was shaped like Inspector Doyle. "Step away from the corpse."

"He's not a corpse."

"Kit."

I turned my head. "I lied to you, Tommy. I didn't

kill Dredmore. He wasn't in his body, you see, because he put his spirit inside my pendant. Give him a minute and he'll come back."

"That's enough of that." He took hold of my arm. "Come away now."

"But he will wake up. He has to." My throat went tight as I considered the now very real possibility that I had been wrong about my parents, the pendant, everything. "I worked it out, I know I did." Was there some sort of spell I was supposed to cast? Surely not. I'd break it the moment the words left my lips.

"My fault she got over here, sir." The beater joined Doyle and glared at me. "Told me you sent her."

I looked up at the sky. "Lucien? I've made a mess of this. I need you to tell me what to do. How do I fix this?"

"Charm." Tommy grabbed me by the arms and shook me until my teeth chattered. "Stop it. You can't do anything more for him."

"Damn you." The moment he stopped I shoved him away. "You swore you wouldn't do this."

"I'm not—"

"Tommy Doyle calls me Kit, Harry." I pushed him a second time as I advanced on him. "Only *you* call me Charm. Tell me how to bring Lucien back. *Tell me.*"

"You're not Aramanthan, and neither is he. There is no coming back for mortals."

He dodged my quick fist, teetered on the edge of the pier, and dropped into the water with a huge splash.

I leaned over to see that he bobbed to the surface, and ducked the white mist that rose from the water before I tossed a rope down to a very confused-looking Doyle. "Grab hold of this, Inspector."

The beater came after me, his trunch held ready to pound my head in, but the white mist descended between us and reformed into Harry. That was enough for the beater, who spun round smartly and ran the other way, shouting for help.

"You can't defy fate, gel." Harry blocked my path back to Dredmore. "Killing him is what you were meant to do. What you were born to do. Even he knew it."

"Then why did he say I had to release him?" I demanded.

"Death is his release." Something like pity glimmered in his eyes. "You'll find another chap someday, Charm. One who will treat you as you deserve."

Since he was of no use to me, I forced myself to think. Mr. Jasper had said shattering the dreamstone dispelled its power . . . "What if I break the stone? Will that free him?"

"It's nightstone, my dear," he said. "You can't."

But I was a spell-breaker, and the stone was spelled, and suddenly Harry wouldn't look me in the eye.

"You're a terrible liar, old man."

I knelt down and pulled the pendant from Dredmore's neck. The only hard object I had was my father's pocket watch, and once I wedged the stone against the dock boards I pulled it out.

"No." Harry sounded genuinely frightened and swiped at me, but his hand passed through my arm. "Charm, if you smash it you'll be torn to pieces—"

"Then I'll go and be with him." I brought down the

pocket watch as hard as I could, smashing it into the stone. The watch's crystal shattered, and a piece banged into my chin, cutting me.

Harry let out a long breath. "Thank the Gods."

Blood dripped from my face onto the nightstone as I lifted the ruined watch a second time. "Goddamn you, Lucien, come out of there."

"Charm."

The second time I hit the nightstone I felt it crack. Purple-black light poured across my face, freezing my skin and blinding me. I fell back, feeling as if the dock had begun spinning like a top, and rubbed at my eyes until they cleared.

"You are the most stubborn, idiotic, mule-headed mortal female it has ever been my misfortune to know," I heard Harry say as the sky blurred and the Talian ship began to turn transparent.

"What? Wait." I looked over at Dredmore's body, but it and the tarp were gone. "Harry? Where is Lucien? What have I done?"

"Made your father happy at last, I expect." He sat down beside me, as solid as I was, and put an arm round my shoulders. "Close your eyes now or you'll get very dizzy."

I couldn't even blink; the world had gone mad. Night turned to day as the sun rose in the west and climbed backward through the sky. The tide rushed in and out. Great clouds of black smoke funneled down into the city, dwindling to thin streams before disappearing altogether. Cargo handlers working faster than could be followed dragged crates out to load them on ships that raised anchors and sails and moved against the wind out to sea.

"I don't believe it." I thought my eyes might pop out of their sockets. "Everything is going in reverse." I raised a hand to cover my gaping mouth, only to see it growing as transparent as Harry. "Am I dying?"

"No, my dear. You've worked the only magic you can. Your father's science." My grandfather made a rude sound. "That wasn't a pocket watch. It was another of his blasted mechs."

I glanced down at the ruins of the watch. "What did it do before I smashed it?"

"Doesn't matter now; you've bonded his mech and her magic with your blood, and the watch's power has been released." His voice grew distant. "I'm afraid you've turned time on its head, Charm."

I tried to stand, but my legs wouldn't work. "When will it stop?"

He was only a faint outline in the air now. "When you've returned to the beginning of it all, of course. Assuming you survive the journey."

Harry vanished, and then, so did I.

"Charmian."

I floated through the darkness, seeking the voice calling my name. Only after some time did I realize it came from inside me, and was enough like my own for me to believe I'd spoken.

Until it came again, and scolded me. "I did not raise you to be ignorant, or a coward, and you have conducted yourself as a clever and resourceful woman. Since we were parted, you have made me and your father very proud of you."

I lifted my head and searched for a Harry-like presence, but no spirit appeared. "Mum?"

"I don't trifle with the passages between worlds as my father does," my mother said. "I am quite content here. Or I was, until this moment."

It had to be my mother; no one else could make me feel such guilt. "But you're dead."

"There is the death of the body, which comes to every person in the mortal world," my mother said primly. "It cannot be stopped or avoided; it must be accepted as inevitable. But that which animates us, that which is the essence of us; that never truly dies." A comforting warmth welled up inside me, as if I were being hugged all over. "This is not your time to leave this world, my dear. Or his."

"But he's dead, too." I should know, I'd murdered him. "Mum, I don't think I can go on without him."

"You won't have to now, Charmian." Something tugged at me, pushing me through the darkness. "You must return now, and put things to rights. When you wake, you will know what is to be done."

I felt the warmth receding. "Don't leave me, Mum."

In my mind she whispered, *We'll be reunited someday, my darling. When it's your time, your father and I will be waiting for you.*

As my eyes cleared so did the darkness, and I found myself looking across my desk at Lady Diana Walsh.

CHAPTER TWENTY-SIX

"Are you unwell, Miss Kittredge?" Lady Diana asked, taking a lacy handkerchief from her reticule and touching it to the dark circles under her pretty eyes. "Is that why you refuse to help me?"

"I'm not sick, milady." The burning sensation in my stomach had vanished. So had all my aches and pains and the soot blackening my skin. My mind began to reel as I glanced down at the little calendar I kept on my desk and saw the date. The date that was a fortnight past. The day I'd met Lady Diana Walsh for the first time.

Time. Harry had said something about it. It took a moment before I remembered what it was.

You've turned time on its head.

"The attacks on your person are not the result of a spell, nor are the words cut into your flesh actual wounds," I told Lady Diana. "You are the victim of cruelty and contempt, not magic."

"How could you—?" She stopped and rose to her feet. "I should have known better than to come here. Good day, Miss Kittredge."

"Proof. Of course, you'll want that before you believe me." I took a flask from my drawer, went round the desk, seized one of her wrists, and pulled off the glove. "Here, hold still." As I poured the brandy over her hand she uttered a shrill sound that I ignored as I picked at the edge of the letter *S* in SLUT, lifting the dried wound paste just enough to peel it off. "You see? Just as I said. The brandy acts as a solvent, but don't yank at it too hard, or it will still tear your skin."

Lady Walsh stopped protesting and stared. "How in the world . . . ?" She went to work and in a few seconds had carefully peeled all the paste off her unmarked flesh. Her wide eyes shifted to my face. "You knew how this was done to me? Without ever meeting me? Who—?"

"I'm afraid this time I do have an urgent appointment across town," I told her as I reached for my walking cloak. "Perhaps we could meet later, at your home?"

"You are not invited to my home. Nor can you tell me such things and then walk out." Her voice grew shrill. "I must know who did this to me."

"In a few hours, you will. Or we'll all be dead. I'm not quite sure how it will go." Once I fastened my cloak I grabbed my keylace from the wall hook. "Oh, and you should know that the only reason your husband married you was to get another heir. Your stepson is diseased and barren. Good day, milady."

I ran past her footman for the stairs, praying that my assumptions about my own circumstances were just as correct. Puzzling that out made me forget about Fourth, who intercepted me on the stairs halfway to the first floor landing.

"Good morning, Mr. Gremley." Hoping to squeeze past him I moved to one side, but he did the same. "I do beg your pardon, but I'm in something of a hurry."

The clerk bent from the waist in one of his overdone bows. "Miss Kittredge, I'd hoped to—"

"—run into me today," I finished for him. "I regret to say that I cannot be your escort to the opening of the opera on Thursday next, excuse me, Friday next, as I will be away on business. Mr. Skolnik's unmarried daughter, Maritza, will make a fine substitute. She speaks no English, so your dear mother will be unable to grill her."

By this point Fourth's nonexistent chin had dropped to his reedy chest. "Miss Kittredge, you have anticipated my every thought. How in heaven's name—?"

"It's magic. I was wrong. It does exist." I patted his shoulder. "Must fly. Do enjoy the opera."

He didn't try to stop me as I darted round him and made it to the basement access door on the first-floor landing.

"Docket." My voice couldn't be heard above the clanking and hammering, but as soon as I spotted the bottom half of him sticking out from a familiar cabinet I didn't bother to shout again. I did rap my knuckles on the side of the HangItAll to get his attention.

"What the devil is it now?" Docket emerged, his face shiny with sweat and patches of black grease. "Oh, Kit, fabulous. I'm just putting the finishing touches on—"

"—the HangItAll. Problem is that the boiler steam will soak all the garments you put in it, so best you call it the WashItAll." I paused to catch my breath. "Docket, I need to borrow your carri for a few hours."

"WashItAll. That might work." As he looked at me, his grin turned upside down. "Sorry, my dear, but the carri's done for. Took it apart last week to repair the boiler." He squinted at me. "What's the matter? You look white as a wedding frock."

Without a carri I'd never get there. "I have to go." Wouldn't be the first time I'd stolen one. I hurried outside and looked down both sides of the street. No carris in sight, and the trolley wouldn't reach the corner stop for half an hour. I felt so desperate I even thought of the tubes, but even if I could survive the pressure of being shot through one, I'd never fit inside.

I sat down on the curb to prop my head against my fists. I would not wail or weep or otherwise make a fool of myself. I would think of a way.

The clop of hooves came toward me, growing slower until they stopped. I raised my head to see a big black horse looming over me. He had been bridled but not saddled, and his sides were sweaty, as if he'd been on a long run.

"George, what are you doing here?" The horse dropped his head to nudge my shoulder, and I automatically caught his reins. "You can't be here. You weren't here that day. This day. We haven't met."

He snorted and tugged, pulling me to my feet. I had to hike up my skirts to mount him, which bared my legs almost to the knee as I rode down the street. Decent men stared, decent women turned away, but a few clerks and cartlasses laughed and waved me on.

I guided George across the city, out to the farmlands, and down the long road to my destination. The black iron gates were closed, of course, but George leapt over them, as quick and nimble as a hare.

I reined him into a respectable trot—dashing up to the great ugly place would only alarm the hooligans guarding it—but took him straight to the front of the house. Connell appeared before I could dismount, but as soon as he saw my face he turned and hurried back into the main house.

"Well, we're here, George," I said as I dropped to my feet. "One of us has to go in there."

The big black horse eyed me before he turned and trotted off toward the stables.

"Coward." I shook out my skirts and took a deep breath, letting it out slowly as I walked up to use the knocker. But the door was already opening, the man inside stepping out.

"Charmian." Lucien Dredmore, resplendent in his usual silver and onyx, surveyed me from toe to crown and back again. "Am I to understand my man correctly? You've stolen one of my horses?"

"No, sir." He was alive. "I am returning it." He was himself again. "It ran away and came to my building in the city and I have to sit down now." I was going to cast up my accounts, all over his boots.

The marble step felt so cold it was like perching on a block of ice. That was why I was shaking so badly. I felt a strong hand at the back of my head, an arm under my knees, and then he was lifting and carrying me through his dark dungeon of a house to a softer spot, a chaise lounge by a sunlit window. I heard him call for brandy, and then he was putting the rim of a glass to my lips.

"Drink." When I didn't, he took hold of the end of my nose and pinched it shut.

I drank, and coughed, and felt the fire in my throat spread through my insides as it settled to an agreeable warmth.

He made me take another swallow and then he watched me until the shaking stopped. "Should I call for the smelling salts, Charmian, or is that the end of it?"

"I don't know," I admitted. "I've never been in shock before now. I'm so sorry."

"You are apologizing. To me." He put his hand to my brow. "You've no fever. Were you thrown from my horse?"

"George would never unseat me," I said, and took a deep breath. "This morning I was tossed back through time. I'm here because of that. Because I've seen the future, and I need your help to change it."

"You *have* hit your head on something." Lucien glanced over at Connell. "Send for the physick at once."

"Wait, please." I considered what to tell him. I'd killed the man, or rather his body; he deserved to know at least that much. But he had no memory of the wonderful or terrible things that had happened to us—or hadn't yet done them, now that I'd thrown us all back in time—so he would think me terribly addled, or even perhaps gone mad.

Unless I offered him evidence to the contrary. "No one knows about your life before you came to Toriana, do they? You've never confided it to anyone. Certainly not me."

"What are you about now, Charmian?" he asked, his voice going soft and lethal.

"You were five when your parents sent you away

to school. They didn't tell you that you would be kept there, that you wouldn't go home for holiday like the other boys." I looked round at his things. "You've always had the best that could be provided. They paid for you to have a private room, the finest tutors, the most expensive garments. But there were no letters, Dredmore. No birthday cards. No visits. Nothing. They wouldn't even permit your nanny or valet to write to you."

His eyes took on a dangerous glitter. "Who told you this?"

"You did, or more precisely, you will." And I proceeded to tell him the rest. I spared him no detail, and when I named the exact sum his mother had offered him to leave England forever, he turned his head and stared into the fireplace.

It wasn't anger or wounded pride. He was ashamed of what they had done to him. Perhaps because they had felt no shame in doing it.

Once I had finished, I picked up the glass of brandy I disliked so intensely and took a large swallow. After another round of coughing, I handed the remainder to him. "In fourteen days there will be an invasion of Rumsen. Talian Reapers will come here with an army, led by the agents of an Aramanthan warlord called Zarath. They plan to use the dreamstone they've hidden all over the city inside phony wardlings to turn our people into puppets."

He drained the rest of the brandy. "I don't know how you found out about my boyhood, but dreamstone and time travel are myths. The Tillers would never permit the Reapers to set foot on Toriana soil." He regarded me carefully. "You haven't been trifling with poppy dust, have you?"

"The Reapers have already infiltrated the Tillers," I assured him. "They're controlling Lord Walsh."

"Nolan Walsh, the banker?" When I nodded, he made a dismissive gesture. "The man is nothing but a pompous ass."

"Takes one to know one, does it?" I asked sweetly. Before he could reply, I added, "In a little over a week, that pompous ass will capture you and me at Feathersound. Yes, I know you own it. To save my life, you'll swallow a spirit stone, Walsh will kill himself, and your body will be possessed by Zarath. The warlord needs your mind power to remove the final obstacles and set off the dreamstones."

He stared at me. "You've never in your life believed in magic."

"That reminds me." I smiled. "Your current suspicions about me are correct. I am a spell-breaker, Lucien. That's why your magic has no effect on me." I didn't have to tell him that his spiritborn gift of enchantment worked extremely well; that little detail could remain between me and the future Dredmore.

He came to me and jerked me to my feet. "If what you say isn't some bizarre fancy you've dreamed up to confound me, and by some impossibly wild chance you have returned from the future, then why didn't you stop the Reapers while you were there?"

"I did." I rested my hand against his chest. "Just before Zarath cast his spell over the city, I drove an iron spike through his heart and killed him." I looked up at him and let him see everything I felt. "Which was, coincidentally, your heart."

"You *killed* me."

I nodded. "Before you surrendered your body to Zarath, you made me promise that I would. I didn't enjoy it as much as I expected. Really a lot of blood."

His hands fell away. "Now I do believe you."

"Excellent." I turned my head. "Bring the carriage round, Connell." I saw the surprise on the servant's face before I said, "Your master and I are going to call on Lord and Lady Walsh."

Dredmore said very little as we rode to the Hill. I pulled up the shade so I could see the mansions glittering in the sunlight once again. While I would never care for the ton's lofty community, seeing it burnt to the ground had not been an improvement.

"Do you mean to expose Walsh in front of his family?" Dredmore asked.

"Not at all." As the carriage stopped, I reached up and felt for my pendant. "We will speak to him privately."

He frowned. "If he is under Reaper control, he will deny every charge, and then use his influence to destroy my credibility and your life."

"Not this time." I reached out and patted the back of his hand. When he seized my wrist, I didn't pull away. "We've arrived. Don't change your mind now."

He held on to me. "You haven't told me everything about the future, have you?"

"What, and spoil the surprise?" I smiled as Connell opened the door. "Where would be the fun in that?"

The Walshes' forbidding old butler came directly to answer the door, doubtless astonished by the prospect of anyone calling at such an unseemly, early hour.

"Lord Dredmore and Miss Kittredge to see Lord Walsh," I told the old winge before he could open his mouth. "On quite urgent business."

The butler reared back, the skin surrounding his nose drawing up as he ignored me and addressed Dredmore. "The master is not receiving, milord."

Dredmore brushed past him. "He will see me now."

"It's a terribly private family matter," I told the outraged butler as I followed suit. "We'll wait for him in his study."

It took Lord Walsh less than three minutes to stalk into the room and slam the doors behind him. There was egg yolk on his chin and he still wore his morning jacket and what looked like fur-lined bed slippers. "Lucien. Good God, man, what is the meaning of this?"

"Your wife came to see me this morning, Lord Walsh." I waited for him to lower himself to notice me. "She believes your deceased first wife has cast a spell on her. But as it turns out, you're the one who has been bespelled."

The first tinge of purple bloomed in his florid cheeks. "How dare you—"

"With very little trepidation, actually." I closed the distance between us and lifted my skirts. "But I do apologize in advance for my actions."

I kicked him in the groin with as much force as I could muster, and stepped back as he shrieked and dropped to the carpet. He didn't vomit, however, which annoyed me. "I see you're going to be difficult. Lucien, please hold his head for a moment."

Dredmore came up from behind and clapped his hands over Walsh's ears.

"Thank you." I grabbed the man's chin and inserted two of my fingers into his mouth, pushing them back as far as I could until he gagged. "Watch your boots." I sidestepped the spew of Walsh's breakfast, waiting until he coughed out a gleaming red stone. Using a kerchief to pick it up, I wrapped it carefully before passing it to Dredmore. "Don't swallow this."

"I've no desire to." He pocketed the bundle.

Lord Walsh finished vomiting shortly thereafter and, once Lucien had helped him to his feet, began to make his own apologies. "I say. Terribly sorry. Must have eaten something that was . . ." He trailed off as he looked at both of us with visible bewilderment. "Do I know you?"

"Dad? What the devil?" A bleary-eyed Montrose burst into the room, tottering a little as he rushed to his father's side.

"You can come in, too, Miss Walsh," I told the woman hovering outside the door. "This concerns you as well."

The timid Miranda tiptoed in, her hands worrying at the edges of her lace fichu while she surveyed the messy scene. "It seems my father is ill," she said, her voice wavering. "You should perhaps leave so that we might attend to him."

"There's nothing wrong with Lord Walsh anymore," I assured her. "I helped him get the spirit stone you shoved down his throat out of his belly."

"He will suffer some gaps in his memory," Dredmore added, "but they should not be permanent."

As Miranda shrank back, I eyed the mess on the floor. "You'll probably want to have the carpet cleaned right away. When egg yolk dries it's as hard to comb out as plaster on cashmere." Dredmore got to the door before Miranda and closed it. "Thank you, Lucien."

He leaned back against the door. "My pleasure, Charmian."

Miranda skittered away from him, going to stand behind a wingbacked chair. "Monty, call for the nobbers. Hurry."

"Dredmore is a deathmage, Monty. I wouldn't twitch an eyelash." I went to Miranda, and dragged her over to face the still-wheezing Nolan Walsh. "It's time to tell your father exactly what you and your husband have been up to."

"My husband is dead," she protested, at the same moment Lord Walsh said, "My daughter is a widow."

"On the contrary, her husband is still alive and hiding somewhere in the city," I told him. "He's probably too young to be a Lost Timer, but I expect his Talian father was."

Miranda gaped at me. "My dear Lestin died in battle."

"Your husband faked his death to get out of the militia, come to Toriana, and—with your help—begin the groundwork for the Reaper invasion." I nodded at Nolan Walsh. "While he didn't have any powers for Zarath to use, I imagine your father's wealth, power, and influence proved quite useful, once the Aramanthan took control of his mind and body."

Lord Walsh looked horrified. "Miranda, what have you done?"

A transformation not unlike that of an Aramanthan possession came over Walsh's shy daughter. "You think money can buy anything, Father? We live every day under Her Majesty's grinding boot heel. The Reapers are coming to save us. They will muster our forces, crush the Empire, and end the occupation. Toriana will finally be free."

"Is that what they told you?" Dredmore sounded scathing. "The Reapers have no motive to fight for our liberation. Their sole interest in Toriana is to occupy it, and use its citizens and resources to ignite another mage war. Had your plan been successful, Miss Walsh, they would have burned their way across our country, and installed their *own* tyrants as our rulers."

"All Torians would have been bespelled and turned into mindless, thoughtless slaves," I put in. "Rather like you."

"You know nothing about our plans." She struggled viciously against my hold. "You think you can stop them? It's too late. The ships are almost here."

"They're still a fortnight from shore," I corrected her. "By the time they arrive I expect the coastal fleet will be waiting to greet them." I glanced at Dredmore. "You can arrange a proper reception, can't you, milord?"

His upper lip curled. "Indeed."

Miranda screamed something wholly unladylike as she hooked her fingers into claws and lunged for my eyes.

I put an end to that nonsense by slapping her. "You might have pulled it off, had you left your stepmother alone. But you hated her for taking your mother's place, and you feared she might discover that Lord Walsh had been possessed. It wouldn't have mattered if she had, you know." I looked up to see Lady Diana standing in the doorway. "No one would have believed her."

"My father should never have married that sniveling bitch." Hatred contorted Miranda's half-red face. "Always pretending to be so kind and sweet and loving. All she was interested in was his fortune."

"My family was." Lady Diana joined us. "I married so I wouldn't end an old maid." She looked at her husband. "Nolan, I expect you have business to attend to in town. If you would send for our physick before you leave, I would greatly appreciate it. Montrose, please escort your sister to her room and sit with her until the whitecart arrives."

"You can't put me in hospital," Miranda shouted.

"Of course not," Diana soothed. "There's a lovely little place called Havenwood, not far from my father's country estate near Settle. Some of the best families in Rumsen have sent their troubled relations there to recuperate."

Miranda grabbed her brother's jacket. "Monty, you have to help me. Please. They're going to ruin everything."

"We'll talk about it upstairs." Montrose guided her out of the room.

Lord Walsh gave Dredmore a desperate look. "My lord, if you would be so kind as to accompany me, and provide some explanation to our mutual friends and associates . . ."

"It would be my pleasure. Lady Walsh." Lucien inclined his head that way, and then came to me. "Miss Kittredge." He raised my hand to his lips and kissed it like a perfect gentleman. Then he nipped one of my knuckles. "I will be calling on you later."

"Meet me down at the docks instead," I murmured back.

Once the men left the room, Lady Diana rang for the housekeeper, who summoned maids to remove the carpet and apply citrus oil to the floor to remove any lingering stains and odors. The butler himself delivered a tea cart generously piled with a beautiful cream tea.

"With Lord Walsh's compliments, Miss Kittredge." He bowed to me as if I were royalty before he addressed Diana. "Milady, when the physick arrives, do you wish to speak with him?"

"Not at all," Diana said. "Inform Dr. Elgis that he is to remove Miss Miranda and have her immediately and securely transported to Havenwood for whatever treatment she requires. You might mention that Lord Walsh expects her stay to be of some duration."

"Yes, milady." The butler bowed his way out of the study.

"What about the husband in hiding?" I asked.

"Lestin?" Diana picked up the teapot. "Without Miranda to supply him with his needs, I expect he will show his face here quite soon. We have footmen to deal with that. Sugar?"

"No, thank you. Such an unusual name, Lestin." I thought for a moment. "An abbreviated form of Celestino, isn't it?"

"I believe it is." She filled two cups and handed one to me. "You might have warned me of your intentions this morning, Miss Kittredge."

I took a sip. "It is possible I could have convinced you that Miranda was responsible for the attacks on your person," I agreed. "But the fact that she arranged for her father to be possessed to assist in an invasion of the city?" I set down my cup. "That you had to hear from her own lips."

"I expect you are right." She left her own tea untouched. "Lord Walsh and I are exceedingly grateful for the discreet manner in which you have acted on our behalf."

I gave her the answer to the question she wasn't asking. "I've worked before for other families on the Hill, milady. I know how things are done here." When she reached for her reticule, I shook my head. "This morning I refused to provide you with my services, so no payment is necessary."

The tight lines round the corners of her mouth smoothed away. "Is there nothing I can do for you?"

"At times my work requires me to make inquiries. I am always discreet, of course, but as an ordinary cit I am denied access to certain circles." I sipped my tea before I added, "Under such circumstances, I would be most appreciative if I could rely upon your counsel and assistance."

"Were he to discover such an arrangement, my husband would absolutely forbid it." She smiled. "I will have to see to it that he never does. Would you care for a crumpet?"

CHAPTER TWENTY-SEVEN

Lady Diana did not provide me with her carriage when I left her home—that would have overstepped the limits of ton gratitude—but she instructed the butler to summon a cab and have it take me wherever I wished.

"Where to, miss?" the driver asked as he helped me inside.

Somewhere in the city Dredmore and Walsh were no doubt astonishing the Tillers with news of the Reapers' planned invasion. Even if I could find the secret meeting place of the spiritborn, as a female I would likely not be permitted entrance.

Not that I cared to be privy to Tiller secrets. I had my own to sort out.

"Drive to the docks," I told the man. "But don't rush. I'm in no hurry."

He touched his cap before he closed the door.

As the cab headed down from the Hill, I reached up and curled my fingers over my pendant. I felt the movement of the gears inside, assuring me that it still functioned as my parents had intended. The chain snapped as I jerked it from my neck and tossed it onto the back-facing seat.

My grandfather appeared in the next instant, his

white hair neatly slicked back, his old-fashioned suit exquisitely pressed. "I'm not going to hurt you, lass. In fact, if you'll give a moment to explain, I may be of some considerable assistance to—"

"Save the speech, Harry," I said, cutting him off. "Traveling back through time didn't rob me of my memories."

He hid his dismay by becoming chatty. "Well, then, you've time enough to stop the invasion. You should start with Walsh and his daughter, but steer clear of that wretched Dredmore. Perhaps that Inspector Doyle fellow can be recruited to assist you. He seems a clear-headed chap. Why are you scowling like that? I like Arthur's boy. Young Thomas has great potential."

"You know very well that I've already been to see Nolan Walsh, and that Miranda has dealt with. You were there with me, old man." I leaned forward. "As you've been with me every day and night since I was a little gel."

"All right, then." He sat back and folded his arms. "I've watched over you. You're my granddaughter, Charm. No crime in that, is there?"

"You're lying to me again, Harry," I said with great patience. "You never had a choice in the matter."

"Whatever you think, Charm." He lifted the edge of the window shade and pretended to admire the scenery. "I say, are we near that fruit market? I smell peaches."

"Hedger gave it away when he called my pendant 'a ginny bauble,'" I said. "Certainly there are ladies among the ton who wear tiny flasks fashioned to look like bracelets and watches and pendants, and I presumed he mistook it for something like those. But I misheard him. It's his accent; it's almost as bad as Wrecker's."

"I just now realized, I've never seen your office." Harry gave me an inveigling look. "We should take a ride over that way. I've time enough for a tour."

"Hedger didn't say *ginny bauble*, did he?" I waited, but my grandfather only stared at the floor of the carriage. "He said *genie bottle*."

Harry made a halfhearted attempt to continue the ruse. "Don't be foolish, gel. There is no such thing."

"My parents did make the pendant to contain a spirit, but it wasn't mine." I watched his face. "They used it to capture and imprison the spirit of the Aramanthan they feared most. They used it on you, Harry."

My grandfather opened his mouth, closed it, and hung his head.

"That's how you knew everything that has happened to me," I continued. "You've been hanging about my neck all this time, unable to escape the nightstone."

"I did try, quite often, those first ten years." He sat back. "I might have overcome your mother's magic, or your father's science, but the two together were beyond me. And then there was you and your devilish gift."

"Every time you tried to cast a spell to release yourself, my power broke it." I moved over and sat beside him. "Why, Harry? Why would Mum and Da do such a terrible thing to you?"

"I'm to blame for it, not them." He shriveled down against the seat. "It was when I came to live in Toriana. I fear I was a little too eager to see Rachel. I hadn't, you know, not since she was an infant. Without thinking I called on her, and, well, she took the news that I was her father, an Aramanthan, and a spy for the Crown rather poorly."

I nodded. "Did she reject you?"

"She told me to get out and never darken their doorstep again." He made a face. "Then, when I wouldn't leave, your father tried to shoot me."

"Go on."

"I made several more attempts to speak to your mother. I even sent her the nightstone pendant as proof of my affection, but she still refused to see me." He rasped a hand over his cheek. "I couldn't accept the idea that my own daughter would reject me, Charm. I didn't consider how much a stranger I was to her. And then there was you, my only grandchild." Harry spread his hands. "Since Rachel wanted nothing to do with me, I began visiting you in your nursery at night. I hardly thought it would upset anyone."

"Until Mum caught you at it," I guessed.

"It terrified her to see me there, standing by your little bed," he admitted. "She ordered me from the house and forbid me from having any more contact with her or you. I'm afraid by then I'd grown very fond of you, and I lost my temper with her. I told Rachel that if I wished to see you that I would, any time I wished, and there was nothing she or your father could do to stop me."

I closed my eyes for a moment. "Oh, Harry."

"Christopher, your father, already hated me because I couldn't be explained by his science. When Rachel went to him and repeated my threats . . ." He made a helpless gesture. "I'd say that was when they decided to do something about me."

I didn't understand how such a powerful being could be so foolish. "Why didn't you just leave us alone?"

"I didn't mean to frighten your mother, so I intended to leave off, but I got into a spot of trouble while I was carrying out my duties for the Crown." He ran a finger across his neck. "My host body was murdered."

"The police came to our house that night to give Mum the news," I recalled. "She and Da left me with the maid so they could go to the morgue and identify you."

He nodded. "I was there in spirit, of course, waiting for nightfall so I could move on to another body. As soon as I saw Rachel come into the room with your father, I presumed she had forgiven me." He heaved a sigh. "I didn't realize how much they had meddled with the nightstone until the spell your mother cast dragged me into its confines. Once there, I discovered I had no means of communicating with you, Rachel, or anyone in the outside world."

"And they knew my power would keep you trapped in it." I felt more regret than anger now. "They made me your warden without ever telling me."

"They thought it the right thing to do, I'm sure," he chided. "Rachel had learned a little about the Aramanthan from Arthur Doyle. She must have known that once my host body died I would need another."

I nodded. "So by putting you in the pendant, and having me keep you there all this time, they assured that you would never possess another mortal."

"They saw to it that I would never possess *you*, gel," he corrected. "That was your mother's greatest fear."

I hadn't thought of that. "Did you ever *want* to possess me?"

"Take on the body of a young, impulsive female with no money, no connections, and no prospects in a ridiculously primitive, utterly repressed society under imperial occupation?" He shuddered. "I'd sooner inhabit a stray pup. At least I'd eat better."

"Then you won't mind if I pop you back into the genie bottle?" I asked sweetly as I reached for my pendant.

He looked hurt. "You wouldn't. Not after all we've been through these past two weeks. That haven't happened yet." He made a disgusted sound. "This is why I hate time travel. Everything you say about time is wrong and right."

"I suppose I could be persuaded to allow you your freedom." I sat back and thought for a moment. "I have three conditions."

"I'm not a genie," he reminded me. "I can't grant you three wishes, turn you into a princess, or any of that nonsense."

"You can give me your word that you will not possess anyone permanently," I said.

"Oh, not to worry." He waved his hand. "I've grown accustomed to living in spirit form."

"Promise me."

He looked up at the ceiling of the cab as he pressed his hand over his heart. "On my honor, I promise not to possess any host body permanently." He winked at me. "Temporary's more fun anyhow."

"Second," I continued, "you go into business with me as my partner."

"Business? Work?" He recoiled. "What for?"

"Because you have nothing better to do," I reminded him. "If you get bored, you can teach me everything you know about magic and mind powers."

"You'll never live long enough for that." He saw my face and sighed. "All right, I'll be your business partner." He squinted at me. "What's the third condition?"

"Tell me your name, Harry." As he started to reply, I raised a hand. "Your true name, the one you were born to."

"You'll not believe me." When I said nothing, he muttered something vile under his breath. "I haven't used that for ages, Charm. Hundreds of ages."

"Then back in the pendant you go." I saw the panic in his eyes and added, "If you want me to trust you, Grandfather, then I deserve equal consideration. Tell me your name."

And so he did.

When the cab reached the docks I was alone again. To avoid being trapped again in the nightstone, Harry had to put some distance between us before I touched the pendant.

"He'll never change, you know," he said before he left me. "Dredmore will always be a cold, selfish, dark-hearted bastard."

"Yes." I felt an odd quietude settle over me. "I expect he will."

I was not surprised to find Lucien Dredmore standing in the exact same spot as I'd left him in the future, at the very end of the pier. It was like George suddenly appearing outside my office building; as if time had rearranged a few things to fill some gaps no one could see.

I stopped beside him to look out at the cold, dark ocean. The wind brought with it a cutting edge, promising snow. "Did you have any trouble dealing with the Tillers?"

"Hardly. They know my reputation." He took the kerchief-wrapped stone out of his greatcoat and regarded it. "I have some knowledge of the warlord Zarath, and how many armies he commanded during the Aramanthan wars. His power to control had almost no limits. He is one of the greatest mages of all time."

"He was." I took the kerchief from him and heaved it into the waves. It sank out of sight. "Now he's just another rock sitting on the bottom of the bay."

He blinked. "That won't kill him, Charmian."

"He's immortal," I said, nodding. "Nothing can. But no one else saw, so only you and I know he's there." I glanced up at his stern face. "I've no reason to dive in after a rock, and you can't swim. Isn't that nearly as good as dead?"

A rusty sound came from his throat, and it took a moment before I recognized it as a chuckle. "Yes, I believe it is." He faced me. "Are you ready to tell me about the future?"

I wasn't going to enjoy this as much as chucking that Aramanthan jackass in the drink, I thought, wrapping my arms round my waist. "What do you want to know?"

He took off his greatcoat and draped it over my shoulders. "Why did I confide the most private details of my personal history to you?"

"I can't say." I tried not to breathe in the delicious scent he'd left on the wool. "You weren't yourself at the time."

Dredmore pulled up the collar so it shielded my ears against the wind. "What made you stop despising me?"

"I met him." I nodded toward the water. "By comparison, you are a saint."

Dredmore tipped up my chin with his hand so I had to look into his eyes. "Why did you save my life, Charmian?"

"You're not dead," I countered. "Do you want me to promise not to do it again?"

"I want to know"—he bent his head and touched his lips to mine—"why you're not slapping me, or threatening to push me off a cliff, stab me in the heart, or lock me in my carriage and set it alight. Why you looked so terrified when I came out of Morehaven this morning, and then in the next moment, so relieved. I want to know what changed things between us, Charmian, and how."

I had to tell him something, but the future that we'd shared no longer existed. It didn't matter what we'd done; all that mattered was what we would do now . . . and then I knew exactly what to say.

"I had a dream, a few days from now," I lied. "I was buying peaches at the market, and I stumbled over a curb and twisted my ankle. You helped me up and offered to take me home. After that we became great friends." I felt him go very still. "That never happened, of course, but when I woke from the dream, all I could think was how much I wished it had. That you and I had become friends instead of enemies." I smiled. "It was all downhill from there."

He didn't say anything for a long time, and then he nodded slowly. "We could try to be friends."

"We could."

"Then as a friend I should tell you, that was a terrible lie," he added. "Someday I will make you tell me the truth."

I lifted my brows. "Is that what friends do?" I saw how he was staring at the spot in the water where I'd thrown the stone. "He's gone, Lucien. Forget about him."

"I wish I could, but Zarath was not the only warlord among the Aramanthan." Dredmore's voice grew as icy as the breeze. "There are many more out there. They are waiting, and watching, and plotting their return to power."

Something rose up in me, something that almost felt like icy burning of the spirit stone Zarath had forced me to swallow. "Do you expect me to burst into tears and clutch at you and wail about how powerless we are against them? Because we're not. I've seen how we are, and we are . . . formidable."

"We are mortal," he corrected.

"Oh, very well." I tossed up my hands. "I don't think I can cry, but if you like I could swoon. I'm actually getting rather good at faking that."

"You're not afraid of what's coming."

"Among other things, milord, I am a spell-breaker, and a time traveler." I turned my gaze to the sea. "Let them come."

Chapter Twenty-eight

"Disenchanted & Co.," the sign painter read out loud from my office window. "That's a right strange name for this sort of business."

His young apprentice began mixing up some paint in a small can. "Sort of a pun, isn't it, miss?"

"Sort of." I handed the painter the shilling we'd agreed on for the job along with a slip of paper. "There's the name of my new partner. Make sure you mind the spelling."

"Whatever you say, miss." He read the note. "Now this one's mum must have known he'd go into the magic trade."

As he and his apprentice went to work, I retreated into my office to sort out the mail. On top of the pile I'd taken from the tube lay a thin gray envelope sealed with silver wax that bore the impression of a spike-wielding fist.

I sat down behind my desk and used my letter dagger to slice off the seal and remove a single sheet of thin silver vellum folded in thirds.

The paper exuded a faint scent of ripe peaches, which made me smile a little. Who would have guessed the most powerful deathmage in all of Toriana had such an infatuation with fruit?

Charmian,

*Come to dinner tonight and you may
have some.*

Dredmore

P.S. Please.

Two of my former clients had sent referrals, one for a haunted carri, and the other to remove some wardlings that had become wedged in a door frame. Rumsen Main must have missed those; upon learning from an anonymous source that nearly all of the talismans in the city were counterfeits containing a very dangerous raw stone, the cops had been very busy confiscating and smashing them.

I penned a message to the desk sergeant at Rumsen Main, attached the referral to it, and got up to send it by tube, only to stop as the sign painter's apprentice opened the door.

"Gent to see you, miss." He stepped aside as the gent strode in.

Fair-haired and average-sized, Thomas Doyle wore his plainclothesman's long trench and low-brim. Past his shoulder I saw a beater in dark blue hovering in the hallway.

The inspector doffed his hat, revealing the tough, wind-weathered features and sun-faded blue eyes of a former navyman. "Forgive the intrusion, madam—"

"It's miss, To—ah, sir." Barely remembering that to him this would be our first meeting, I sat down behind my desk. "And you are?"

"Inspector Thomas Doyle, Rumsen Station. I'm here to speak to Mr. Kittredge," he told me. "If he's stepped out, I can wait."

"You'll wait for a very long time, then, as there is no Mr. Kittredge. I am the proprietor." I held out my hand. "Miss Kittredge."

He gave me a firm but gentle handshake as he inspected my features. "Surely not Charmian Kittredge of Middleway?"

"Guilty as charged." I pretended to study him back. "Would you be related to the Middleway Doyles?"

"I am. I believe we played together as children, at my grandfather Arthur's home."

I smiled. "I believe we did."

He paid closer attention to my face. "I haven't seen you in years, not since you were a gel, but still you look . . . familiar."

"I haven't changed all that much. Mostly taller." I folded my hands in front of me. "Now how can I help the Yard, Inspector?"

"We received a report of some fake wardlings needing collection, but my men are having some trouble removing them. Our staff warder, Mary Harris, recommended Kittredge of Disenchanted & Co." He glanced over at the door. "But I see you've a partner now as well."

I smiled a little. "Yes, he's just joined the firm. Unfortunately he works nights, so you'll have to settle for me, if that's acceptable."

"Of course." He seemed a little embarrassed. "We'd appreciate any help you can give."

"Let me get my cloak and keys." I stood up and went to the rack.

On our way out, I inspected the sign painter's progress:

HARRY MERLI

"Very nice lettering."

"We'll have it done before you get back, miss." He nodded toward the glass. "Then you and Mr. Merlin will be in business."

Acknowledgments

The only name on the cover of a book is the author's, and sometimes I wish I could change that. It took nearly four years to make this novel happen, and while I've rarely worked as long or as hard to get something into print, with this one I never fought alone. Since I can't give everyone who had my back a byline, I'll offer them instead my gratitude:

Tim Kim and all the wonderful folks at National Novel Writing Month and the Office of Letters and Light, who provided me with motivation for writing this story, and followed up that with unstinting support and enthusiasm. What you do for writers and kids all over the globe is nothing short of miraculous.

The readers of *Paperback Writer*, who cheered me on while I was working on the first draft, and all of my readers out there who have followed this journey with enthusiasm and encouragement. You are a constant joy and true blessing in my writing life.

New York Times bestselling authors Gail Carriger and Larissa Ione, whose generosity and kind words kept me going even when things fell apart completely. Ladies, I will never forget that.

New York Times bestselling author Darlene Ryan,

who has been there for me in so many ways that it would take another three pages to list them all. Dust bunnies will never be safe again, and Bubba, you rock.

I wouldn't be able to write anything without the support of my guy or our kids, but for this book they went above and beyond, and for four long years never once complained. I love you, and you are my heart.

The art department, copyediting, and production teams at Pocket Books, who collectively have done magical things for this novel. I know how lucky I am to have you, and I hope you all know how grateful I am, too.

There's one more person whose name should be on the cover of this book, and I saved him for last because if I could I'd put it there in fifty-point font right now. For believing in me and this story, for fighting for it (twice), for restoring my faith in the creative partnership between publishers and authors, for being so damn good at what he does, and for giving me this marvelous opportunity to bring *Disenchanted & Co.* into our world, I'd like to thank my editor, Adam Wilson.

Torian Glossary

abstainers: religious agnostics

across the pond: When in Toriana, a reference to
   Great Britain or Europe; when in Great Britain or
   Europe a reference to Toriana ("pond" being the
   Atlantic Ocean)

aid-solicitor: legal representative provided by the
   Crown to defendants who can't afford to hire a
   barrister

ambrotype: photography that uses chemicals
   (silverblack) to etch images on glass plate
   negatives

annum: year

apothecary: pharmacy

Aramantha: the island homeland of the Aramanthan,
   destroyed by mysterious forces that caused it to
   break up and sink beneath the sea

Aramanthans: a race of superhuman magic
   practitioners who ruled the world before the rise
   of mankind

bacco: tobacco

barrister: attorney

bathboy: a male attendant/masseur who works at public baths for women

beater: a uniformed police officer who patrols the streets, usually on foot

believer: someone who believes in magic

belowground: beneath street level

binding: a stone or other object that can contain psychic energy until its release is triggered by touch or proximity

black: very strong, thrice-brewed tea

blackpot: a coal-fueled boiler

blacks: formal suit worn by high-class male servants

bloodbane: one of the highly toxic magic poisons used in snuffballs

blower: a chamber that uses air leached from the city's tubes to dry wet items

blue ruin: gin

blues: people of aristocratic birth

bookmaker: printer

braves: warrior class of native Torian people

BrewsMaid: an automatic tea maker

bronze, bronzen: a theatrical cosmetic that temporarily darkens the skin

brown: Talian currency

bruiser: a large or physically intimidating man; thug

bucks: clothing made of buckskin

bum: ass

calendula: an herbal tincture used as a topical disinfectant

care kit: first-aid kit

carri: steam-driven carriage

carriwright: maker of steam-driven carriages

cartlass: a girl or woman who sells food and/or beverages from a portable cart on the street

cashsafe: a hidden, locking recess in a private home where money and other valuables are kept

catchall: an extending/grasping device with a pinchers at one end

Church: the Torianglican Church, the only religion recognized and approved by the Crown; the Church of England

clearstone: quartz

clopboard: building siding made of planks recovered from abandoned horse barns

coal burner: engine that runs on coal

coddles: cod cut into chunks

coin: money

collar: vicar

commoner: an ordinary, untitled individual; someone of low birth

conciliator: mediator

cosh: bludgeon

crispie: potato chip

croke: croquet

Crown, the: the English monarchy as well as its authority over Toriana

crowswalk: a viewing deck that encircles the upper portion of a building

dear: costly

deathmage: magical practitioner licensed to kill

deb: debutante

detector: a magic practitioner (generally employed by the court) who uses touch to discern truthfulness

digger: miner

dink: a small or short man

dipper: strip of treated paper that changes color when exposed to poison or drugs

drawers: underwear

drips: syphilis

Druuds: mortal magic practitioners who captured and imprisoned the Aramanthans to end the mage wars

ducklings: children

echo: device used to detect hidden objects

elshy: hellchild

entitlement: inheritance of title and property

exormage: exorcist who nullifies curses and rids people and places of demon infestation

faeriestale: fantasy story told to children

fete teller: the humblest of fortune-tellers who set up tents at village fetes to do many readings for very little money

fichu: a shoulder wrap, usually made of lace

firebrigader: firefighter

fishncrisp: a shop that sells fish fillets fried together with potatoes cut in various shapes

flat: apartment

flathouse: a building that has been divided up into flats

Fleers: remnant members of the American rebel forces who fled west after losing the war to England

flystick: a clear glass rod containing live lightning bugs, used like a flashlight or lantern

foundling: abandoned orphan

freeclaiming: a social practice caused by the shortage of women among the original colonies, which allowed men to kidnap and hold captive unprotected or abandoned women

freedman: ex-convict

fry bread: bread fried in bacon drippings

furrin, furriners: slang for *foreign, foreigners*

garms: garments

gaslamp: exterior lighting powered by natural gas

gel: girl (common, casual, generally used to refer to females of the merchant class)

get the sack: be fired

gildstone: marble

ginger: woman with red hair

glass: common term for ambrotype glass plate negative

glassed: photographed

glasshield: windshield

glassies, glassines: protective, preservative glass coatings applied to documents

glasslung: terminal respiratory disease caused by inhaling sparkglass; suffered by painters and construction workers

gogs: protective eyewear

goldstone: building made of blocks of pyrite-flecked granite

gone off: suffered a mental breakdown

gowners: dressmakers who specialize in creating gowns for wealthy society women

gravecart: hearse

Great Uprising, the: Toriana's name for the failed revolutionary war against England

Great War, the: Toriana's version of WWI

hatch drop: manhole access to underground tunnels

hellchild: a child believed to be demon-possessed and therefore impervious to magic

Herself: slang term for the queen of England

hidey-holes: small, concealed places in houses for people to hide in or use to spy on someone

Hill, the: an area of Rumsen where most of the wealthy and titled reside

H.M.: abbreviation for Her Majesty

hothead: woman with red hair

illuminator: a device that works like a primitive film projector

Independence: freedom from English rule

johnnies: men who hire prostitutes

keroseel: a combination of seal, whale, or fish oil and kerosene

keyfob: a chain-and-loop key ring, carried by men

keylace: a ribbon key ring, worn around a woman's wrist

kipbag: mesh tote

kneecappers: criminal enforcers who use clubs to shatter the knees of their victims

knickers: underwear

lampflies: fireflies

lass: girl (affectionate, proper)

lav: lavatory

loo: toilet

loomgel: a girl or woman who works in a menial position at a textile factory

loomworks: textile factory

loon: a mentally disturbed person

TORIAN GLOSSARY

loon herder: an orderly at an asylum

loonhouse: asylum for the mentally disturbed

Lost Timers: brigades of English and Italian soldiers who became lost in the Bréchéliant forest and were there possessed by Aramanthan spirits

lungfever: slang for influenza

mage: magic practitioner

magis, magistrate: judge

maiden night: the first time a virginal woman has sex with her husband; term often used for betting purposes by men who want to break an engagement

mariners: sailors

matchit: a disposable, one-use lighter

mate: friend

mech: a mechanic; anything mechanical

mechworks: mechanical rooms

mercantile: a shop selling some variety of merchandise

Middleway: industrial Torian city located on the Great Lakes; also called Middy

mixpot: mixing bowl

mole: city underground worker

nappy: diaper, women's panties

navyman: a current or former member of H.M.'s naval forces

necktwister: assassin

negli: negligee

netherside: the spirit world, invisible to ordinary mortals; the source of magic power

new industry: the beginning of the industrial age in Toriana

New Parliament: governing body of Torian officials who petition the Crown and enforce the Queen's legislation; the Torian version of Congress

nightstone: a semiprecious mineral used to contain the spirits of long-dead mages and Aramanthan wizards

Nihon: Japan, Japanese

nits: head lice

nobber: private security guard hired by Hill residents to patrol their streets and keep out any undesirables

Norders: people from the North of England

nozzer: nose; a face mask used with a portable oxygen tank

nudie: a flesh-colored garment worn to give the illusion of nudity under a semitransparent gown or overgarment

Occupancy, the: a period of thirty years after the Rebellion failed during which Toriana was occupied by English troops and governed by martial law

on the stroll: working on the streets (said of prostitutes)

pain powder: a mild opiate or analgesic

partymage: a magic practitioner who uses his power to entertain

pasturelands: farm lands

penders: suspenders

physick: doctor

piesafe: kitchen cabinet where food is stored

piper: plumber

pong: stink

portents: predictions or signs of future events

portints: portraits made from ambrotype photographs that are hand-painted to colorize

posh, posher: wealthy aristocrat

poxbox: diseased prostitute

prayerhouse: the Fleers' religious gathering places

privy: restroom

prodder: iron fireplace poker

prommy: the promenade in the city's central park used by horseback riders and carris

pyre: crematorium

queensland, the: England

Queen's Voice, The: the Crown's official newspaper

questioning: police interrogation at New Scotland Yard

rasher: strip of bacon

red joy, ruddy joy: opium

redcoats: English militia

redstone: brick

reticule: purse

rondella: an automated carousel-type apparatus

rounder: a rubber carri tire

rub: massage

Rumsen: major city on the west coast of Toriana, roughly equivalent to San Francisco in the United States

satchel: tote bag carried by women

scrabbler: a person who makes a living by scavenging

scram: salvage

seeing: an act by a fortune-teller of predicting a client's future

seeking: an act by a fortune-teller of finding someone or something

Settle: Seattle

shaman: a native Torian holy man

shopkeep: shop proprietor

short sheet: a hastily printed, illegal daily list of horse races and other events for the purpose of placing bets

silverblack: chemicals used to etch photographed images on ambrotype plates

skip: boat

Skirmish, the: a recent, brief naval conflict between England and Spain

slaterow: a row house with slate shingles

snuff: kill

snuffballs: hollow glass spheres filled with magically enhanced poisons like bloodbane that kill on contact, used like grenades

snuffmages: mage assassins who generally work in teams of two

Son, the: Jesus Christ

soother: chamomile herbal infusion, usually added to tea, to relax, relieve stress, and help with insomnia

Southern Church: a Baptist version of Church of England, begun in the southern provinces of Toriana, tolerated by traditionalists

sparkglass: a substance made of various minerals such as mica, galena, and silica that have been ground to a fine dust and mixed with exterior paint in order to create sparkle

spellcraft: the methods and materials used by magic practitioners to cast spells

squawks: slur for native Torian females

stones: testicles

streaky: a carri's copper sideboards from which the black paint is wearing off or has been stripped off to simulate wear

strumpet: prostitute

sweet Mary: Mary, mother of Jesus

sweets: candy

switch: wig

Talia, Talian: The Torian universe's version of Italy, Italians

tealass: a girl or woman who sells hot tea and cakes in a café or from a street cart

teller: fortune-teller

tenner: ten-pound note

Tillers: a secret society comprising important political, business, and social figures

timepiece: watch

tinnery: a factory where fresh fish and other perishables are processed and canned in tin containers

tint: a paper-copy image printed from an ambrotype glass plate; makeup used to redden cheeks and lips

tinter: device used to imprint images on ambrotype glass plates

tintest: a professional ambrotype plate developer and tint maker

to let: available for rent

tonners: members of high society

Toriana: short name for Provincial Union of Victoriana, the alternate-history name for the United States

tosser: a drunk

trade: business

trolling: looking for work

trunch: a wooden baton carried by beaters

tubes: a system of pneumatic pipes that deliver goods and food across the city

tunneler: an underground city worker who polices

the subsurface tunnels and keeps the city's tube in operation

understair: belowground level of building; cellar or basement

unjammer: a mechanical snakelike device used to unblock tubes

uptoppers: above street level

vicar: priest of the Torianglican Church

waders: thigh-high protective rubber boots

waister: a wide cummerbund-type belt made of fabric that females wear around their waists to cover the joining of skirts and bodices

warders: magic practitioners who create protective charms and spells to protect people, possessions, and property

wardling: an object used as a protective charm

warren: a tunneler's assigned work area

watershed: raincoat

Welshires: people from Wales

whitecart: horse-drawn conveyance used to transport the wounded to hospital or the mentally disturbed to asylum

wichcart: a street cart that sells sandwiches

willowbark: herbal remedy for headaches and hangovers (equivalent to aspirin)

winge: slang for an older, grouchy person

Yard, the: short name for New Scotland Yard

zoopraxiscope: a device that uses images on glass disks as the first form of stop-motion projection

Connect with the Author

Since 2000, Lynn Viehl has published fifty novels in nine genres, including her *New York Times* bestselling Darkyn series, the StarDoc science fiction series (as S. L. Viehl), and the Tales from Grace Chapel Inn series (as Rebecca Kelly). Ranked as one of the top-one-hundred female, top-fifty book, and top-ten science fiction author bloggers on the Internet, Ms. Viehl hosts *Paperback Writer*, a popular industry weblog she has updated daily since 2004 with free market info, working advice, and online resources for all writers.

VISIT HER ONLINE

At her blog, *Paperback Writer*: http://pbackwriter .blogspot.com/

At the *Disenchanted & Co.* blog: http://toriana.blog spot.com